OUT OF PLACE

Diane Lefer

Fomite
Burlington, VT

Print ISBN-13: 978-1-95323604-3
E-book ISBN-13: 978-1-953236-05-0
Library of Congress Control Number: 2021931427
Fomite
58 Peru Street
Burlington, VT 05401
www.fomitepress.com

7/16/2021

In memory of
FRANÇOIS CAMOIN
whose voice I'll always hear

Yes, my name is Rennie Mulcahy and I don't know why I'm here.

I'm quite sure Emine isn't a terrorist and I do not hesitate to say so, though how can anyone ever be sure? The reasons I liked her to begin with, the reasons I'm loyal to her now, could of course be interpreted differently, as evidence she was up to no good. You suspect she was after something. Passwords, files. The inside track on budget allocations. Or you might see she simply recognized that I was—as she was—lonely. Emine became my friend.

She commented, yes, on the decadence of the West, but so did I.

I liked to think it was my cleverness that appealed to her, not my access. What's my point? If you want to believe that a nice Jewish girl from Istanbul is married to a nice Muslim boy, that a well-educated doctor who loves his wife would leave her in order to schlep around India with some deprived, diseased nomads, that India has such a powerful animal rights movement that the government is confiscating the dancing bears, that the only place in the world to buy a brown bear cub to replace the one that's been confiscated is in Peshawar—if you want to believe all that, what is there to stop you? My point is, Emine's husband Oğuz has done nothing, absolutely nothing wrong if you want to believe all that. And I do.

At least that's how I imagine her in federal lockup.

I want to keep my intrusions to a minimum, but please indulge me as I provide a short orientation to the compilation of materials now in your hands.

In late summer 2001, inspired by the work of Physicians for Social Responsibility-Los Angeles, I began researching toxic waste sites in Southern California. Then came 9/11. Suddenly I no longer had access to the scientists I'd been interviewing—most of them foreign-born. Some canceled appointments, some no longer wished to be quoted. Security clearances were revoked, often along with visas. Some of these people were simply gone.

I often wondered what had become of them but did no follow-up—until the WikiLeaks document dump: hundreds of thousands of pages of classified documents, internal memos, transcripts, emails. Many Americans still focus on what was revealed about war crimes in Afghanistan and Iraq and on emails affecting the 2016 election. What got my interest instead was the possibility of learning about free, scientific inquiry in the aftermath of 9/11. Most of all, I hoped to learn how our counterintelligence programs determined the fate of specific, individual human beings like those I had tried to interview. Easier said than done, given the bewildering wealth of information because data isn't knowledge and knowledge isn't wisdom, and we have more data than ever. No wonder we couldn't "connect the dots".

I cherrypicked—another term we had to learn—data by zeroing in on the Desert Haven Institute in the Mojave Desert, a place I chose—fortuitously, as it turned out—only because it was close enough to home that I could familiarize myself with the terrain. The

FBI cherrypicked when it came to Emine Albaz, one of the scientists engaged in research there. And you, reader, as an objective observer, what would you have done differently? What would you make of the dots that came to their attention?

Dr. Albaz

- abused her security clearance regarding US nuclear technology and test sites;
- attempted to breach security at the Naval Weapons Center China Lake;
- was married to Oğuz Demir, jihadi captured on the Afghan-Pakistan border;
- provided research and test results to Martin (AKA Mardan) Keller, an ecoterrorist conspirator with ties to Iran.

As you read, you'll find more dots: money transfers to the Iranian sister-in-law, irregular use of neurotoxins, mail delivered in biohazard packaging, coded communications with Uzbekistan and Kosovo, and many other data points. That is the damning story They chose to tell about her.

My imaginative reconstruction is also based on fact but the interpretation is mine. Any gaffes, cultural and scientific, come from ignorance, not disrespect. And yes, what you read now—the picture that emerges from dots and fragments and the way I've chosen to assemble the files—reflects my own values. In the process, I sometimes surprised myself: I became quite fond (at least in imagination) of Emine's FBI pursuers, Dawit Tesfaye and Daniel Chen. And when I began this project, I had no idea I would learn that the accident that left me in my current condition was an act of terrorism. While I don't claim wisdom, in this, at least, I did gain knowledge.

My gratitude goes to the anonymous source. You can no doubt find my own identity through a simple Web search, but at least for now I too prefer to remain anonymous. I would also like to acknowledge the Fairfax branch of the Los Angeles Public Library where I did my internet research in my wheelchair, at the computer reserved for my use at the end of the row, the left side of my face close by the wall so that other library patrons need not see it

File #1:

The Desert Haven Institute

The Middle of Nowhere Is Someone's Somewhere

In America, without regard to race, religion, creed, or socioeconomic class and whatever your walk of life, it's possible to find yourself with substance abuse issues, so why not Carson Yampolsky? It is quite unnecessary to look for reasons.

Safe place? You think there's a safe place? Why else had he buried himself in Desert Haven, away from temptation? But boredom, that's the killer, it drives you straight to where you swore you wouldn't go. Which on a personal private I-know-I'm-fucking-myself level was bad enough. And now here he was, trying to welcome Dr. Tang when the man didn't speak a word of English. His own fault. He surrounded himself with H-1B visas thinking they were his cover. If he seemed odd to them, well, they seemed odd to him. If his behavior was erratic, let them think that was how Americans behave.

Whatever.

Carsky motioned Dr. Tang into his office and left the door open. Anyone passing could hear Carsky singing, sort of: dut dut duh DUT duh DUT duh DA...

Anyone could see the back of the glossy black head seated with him and more or less make out the man's heavily accented response: "Nutcracker, Tchaikovsky." And then: DUM da DUM da dum dum dum dum DUM…

"Mozart!" said Carsky. *Carson Yampolsky* had been a great moniker when he left the east coast for LA, for a glorious career in the music business, but here it was simply ridiculous. He preferred his nickname. Maria Castillo called him *The Director*—with respect, or sarcasm? He never could tell what they—any of them, thought of him. It's lonely being the boss. They never invited him to the dinners they cooked for each other. What else was there to do in Desert Haven? A poor excuse for a city laid out on the arid surface of the earth. It got built but never took root. The Institute got its start when the investors acquired a defunct strip mall, then converted the almost empty structure to offices and labs, including the biocontainment unit which, being windowless, was mistaken at least once for a gay bar, hate graffiti sprayed on the wall.

He was too hip for Desert Haven. Carsky was the kind of guy who was always allowed inside the velvet ropes, but out here he'd turned into a redneck with an 18-year-old girlfriend. These days he went bowling, for godsake, and enjoyed it. He bounced around the desert on an All-Terrain Vehicle. If he didn't make a career move and get out of Desert Haven soon, he wouldn't just be sleeping with Tara, he'd end up married to her.

In the meantime, at work, he was an administrator without a high-level security clearance, which is another kind of velvet rope. And faced with Dr. Tang, he was feeling desperate, and as Emine Albaz passed the door, he gestured to her.

"DAH dum, da da DA," he said.

Dr. Tang smiled and said, "Debussy."

"We speak music," Carsky said. "He doesn't speak English and where the hell is Petey Koh when I need him? "

"At a conference," said Emine. "Till Wednesday."

"Dr. Tang," she said. She half-bowed her head, held out her hand and he shook it, almost gratefully.

Carsky drummed fingers on his desk. Dum diddle di dum diddle di dum dum dum

Dr. Tang tapped back: Dum diddle di dum diddle di diddle di diddle di

"Bolero?" said Emine.

Carsky liked her. It was the way her eyes lit up when she saw the poster in his office.

"Flowstone drapery!" she'd said. "Near here, there are caves?"

And he laughed but with some embarrassment because Flowstone Drapery was the name of a band he'd managed. It had never occurred to him that the words meant anything. They could just as easily have called themselves Veal Fuselage. And he liked Emine because she began chatting about geology as though he shared her knowledge and she said nothing in any way to humiliate him.

The bands he had tried to promote were nothing like Ravel. And cocaine was not his downfall. For a while what he loved was crystal, was tina, so you use a little at a party or when you're dancing, that doesn't make you an addict, but still, it was meth that drove him down, composing scores for uh *those* kind of films, sent him into rehab and back to school to study arts administration, which is how he learned a bit of the classical repertoire, and the arts now being treated like any other business though some malcontents grumbled about "market failure" making nonprofits necessary, he still believed if your product is worth having, people will pay and pay and pay and if they don't or won't, fuck 'em, and so his training was entirely transferable.

The scientists had a reason to be at Desert Haven, not many places where they could pursue their research, but directors didn't stay at DHI long. The pay wasn't high enough to make up for the boredom and isolation. What administrator would choose this life? He did. When JB Singh offered the position, he said yes. His thinking not much different from the families that left LA and moved to the Antelope Valley and beyond to get their kids away from drugs and gangs and found you can find what you want to find and even what you don't want anywhere.

So he had his faults. But they should be damn glad to have Carson Yampolsky.

"May I?" Rennie had a way of appearing out of nowhere. All right, from down the hall. But such a large girl. In LA, he'd developed a taste for aspiring models and accomplished drug addicts. Those memories, along with Rennie's loose clothing made her seem even larger, a blimp—that really wasn't fair to her—with wild red Irish hair, her skin, freckled milk, she was like a big ginger cat happy enough to stay safe indoors away from the sun and like a cat she could—despite her size—dart room to room, or appear without warning, underfoot.

She pulled a chair up to his computer. It warmed up immediately and she typed in her code. "He wouldn't have a visa unless...he probably reads English."

Dr. Tang, I am Rennie Mulcahy. On behalf of the Director, it is my pleasure to welcome you to the Institute.

Welcome, Carsky thought, to the end of the earth.

Rennie scooted the chair aside so Dr. Tang could read the screen and turned to her boss. "When Petey Koh gets back, don't ask him to translate. Korean," she said. "Born in Chicago." (Wrong, Rennie. He's from Queens, NY.)

Dr. Tang stood before the computer and read her message.

We are very international. You will like working here. The whole idea is to save lives. Your seismological research will be of the greatest value. Now, if you'd like, I shall show you your office.

Thank you, he typed. *Maps? Yucca Mountain?*

"Thank you," said Carsky. "Get him settled."

It was that easy.

"da da da DUM," said Dr. Tang.

"Beethoven," said the Director.

"da DA da," sang Emine.

"Leonard Bernstein," said Maria Castillo, passing by in the hall.

Rennie, Observed

So who is Rennie Mulcahy? We still need to know though we watch her day and night. We see her when she does the things civilized people do in private: picking our nose, scratching wherever we itch. Let's see if she can repress every normal instinct. Let's see if she can become better than she's ever been.

She used to watch her lizard. *The* lizard, though she brought it home, she had no right to call it *hers,* though that was exactly what her heart desired. She could do what she wanted with it: turn it over and study its white belly, take its little hand and spread the little fingers and feel the suction of its little pads. Or, from the other side of the room, simply stare at it for as long as she wished as it stayed motionless on the wall. It didn't seem disturbed by her gaze, unlike Rorion, her ex, startled, staring back: *Why are you looking at me!?*

We watch when she masturbates. Rennie has no sheet to shield herself with. (We don't want her to hang herself.) Sometimes she smiles in the direction she thinks is ours, defiant, shameless.

When we turn the temperature low, she hides her hands between her thighs to keep them warm.

But one problem still remains: she still has to shit.

There are ways, of course, to shit in public with dignity.

How is it done?

Never rush.

Avoid the graceless dropping of the pants. Begin by slowly removing such clothing as is necessary. Fold it neatly. Lay it gently in a dry corner of the cell. (This is not possible for Rennie given the regulation jumpsuit and the chain around her right ankle.)

It is still possible to move slowly. Each snap of the jumpsuit, without haste, as if each one worthy of a moment's meditation. Pull the suit down as if luxuriating in the feel of fabric brushing skin. Visualize a cat stretching its body. Lift the left leg free. Raise it the way a dancer would. Bend and as you rise, your right leg still clothed, gently lift fabric from the floor. Cradle it in your arms. Only now do you approach the seatless seat. Walk with the chain pulled just taut enough. Just far enough above the concrete floor to make no sound. Lower yourself, head held high, eyes focused on something beyond, or rather unfocused. Do not grunt. Do not sigh. Reach for the toilet paper with the delicacy you would use to touch the petals of a flower.

After cleaning yourself, do not look at the paper to confirm you are now clean. Do not look in the bowl to check for blood. Stay a moment seated there as if to prove your perfect comfort and ease.

The Dutiful Daughter

Why was she in Desert Haven?

It was an oasis. Southern California the way it used to be. White. Goodbye to Panorama City, where the GM plant was bound to close and where the all-white plan had, in her mother's words, "turned, like spoilt milk." The fault of the government, the fault of that new law that brought the Mexicans with their loud parties and loud domestic disputes, loud cars, and loud dogs.

The Mulcahys were among the first—and later, the only—to buy into the luxury condo development in the desert. Most of the units sold to investors who then couldn't unload them and tried to rent, cheap. The swimming pool and spa in the prospectus never materialized. The palm trees remained untended with their untrimmed pubic thatch. The community room stayed locked because there was no community.

Rennie had dropped out of Cal State Northridge to earn tuition money. Three years later she was still sharing with four roommates, still working as waitstaff at a diner where they didn't expect you to look like a model or be an aspiring anything. Then her father had his stroke. "I could use some help with him," her mother said. "You're not doing anything with your life anyway."

So goodbye to the San Fernando Valley. She joined her parents in Desert Haven, a dutiful daughter, not an accomplice to white flight.

Her parents were old enough to be her grandparents, not unusual these days, but still uncommon when Rennie was born. She became their daughter through a private adoption, probably from a family her father had known in his previous life as a priest. (At 40, he became radicalized and lost his faith, took a job on the line at the GM plant to organize the workers, lost his second—Marxist—faith, married the foreman's widowed sister, and began to worry too much about property values. You could call him consistently extreme.)

Rennie avoided any mention of him. She resented the way people always wanted to hear more, as though her father's life was the only interesting thing about her.

After he was discharged from the hospital and after a brief stint (all Medicare would pay for) in a rehab facility, Rennie and her mother cared for him at home. "Look what we do for him," Mrs. Mulcahy said. "But a woman needs to plan. A woman has to take care of herself." Though she had no real premonition of the disease that would claim her, Rennie's mother started paying for long-term care insurance.

One of the few good decisions that woman ever made, thought Rennie.

After her father died, she tried to keep her mother at home in the condo, but every time Rennie went out, the crazy old woman would strip off her clothes. Unscrewing locks or breaking windows, she'd make her escape, wandering the empty streets naked, risking sunburn and heat stroke more than scandal, there being no neighbors to scandalize. So now, on Sundays, Rennie drove to the SunDay Home—the Sunny Day Rest and Care Center—on the outskirts of California City, past the Russian olive trees and up to the front of the building with its towering palms and around to the parking lot where the absence of shade meant the steering wheel would burn her hands after a visit unless she ran the air conditioner for a few minutes before trying to drive.

Inside, she walked through the closed atrium with the grand piano that to her knowledge was never played, and down the glass-walled corridors that allowed you to enjoy the sight of gardens and fountains without exposing yourself to the heat. Nurses and aides walked along, their footsteps silent on rubber soles. Their voices chattered and when they passed her, they always said Hello. It was a relief that Carsky's girlfriend, Tara, rarely worked weekends. It always felt awkward to greet her. Family members pushed family members in wheelchairs. No one would really want to be here, Rennie thought, while at the same time, at almost full occupancy, the SunDay Home struck her as a livelier, more cheerful place than her condo.

Every week, Rennie brought a bouquet of supermarket flowers, never roses, never anything with thorns. Magaly was with her mother when she walked into the room. She gave Rennie a big smile. "I just love your Mom," she said. I hope that's true, thought Rennie. Not for her mother's sake but for Magaly's. The woman was at least her mother's age and still on her feet all day, lifting patients, working. "Mrs. M.," Magaly said, "your beautiful daughter is here."

Mrs. M. said something, as usual, unintelligible. As usual, Rennie patted her hand, nodded and said, "Yes, Mom. You're right. Of course, you're right."

The room was small, uncluttered, and shared. Mrs. Mulcahy's roommate was in something just a step above a vegetative state.

Residents in that condition were usually matched with the Alzheimic who might not be bothered or even notice. No one visited the roommate. Her breathing provided a background sound that could soon be ignored, like an air conditioning unit or a refrigerator's hum. Residents were allowed few personal items, to make the rooms easier to clean or, perhaps, the fewer the possessions, the fewer the staff could steal or be accused of stealing. Rennie couldn't imagine anyone accusing Magaly, who genuinely seemed to like crazy old people.

"She's talking about Bob Hope again," said Magaly. "When they were married."

Rennie didn't know which was harder to take, the fabricated memories or her mother's other mode of gushing an incomprehensible flow of syllables out of which Rennie could sometimes make out *iris, daisy, sunflower, daffodil.* The names of flowers had not been forgotten.

"Answer the door," said her mother. Clearly, for once.

"There's no one at the door," said Rennie.

Her mother shouted, "Don't keep him waiting!"

Rennie in Love, More or Less

For a while, Rennie had everything she wanted and needed: a job, and Rorion, his name pronounced *Whore-ee-oh* because in Brazil, which is where he was from, the R at the start of a word is pronounced H. Bet you didn't know that it's *Hee-o* de Janeiro. When he first came to the US, he didn't understand why people laughed or got embarrassed. He translated his name, turned it to *Orion.* The mythological hunter. That's the story Rennie was taught as a kid, connecting the dots in the sky. Fascinated by Rorion, she became interested in the stars. In California's Central Valley, in American Indian lore, she learned the constellation tells the narrative of the God of the Fleas. Working with scientists, she appreciated that astronomers see in the stars what most people can't understand, and many of us see a lot of points of light and no story at all. Regardless, at DHI they were uncomfortable having a myth or a belt of stars walking around the office. Rennie started to call him Rory.

She was in awe of him and their relationship—a man like that interested in an undereducated nobody—though she also understood that in Desert Haven it's not like he had a lot to choose from. It was reassuring to know he wasn't after her for papers. He was already a naturalized citizen in spite of one false step at his interview, a story Rennie liked to tell. "They asked, *Have you ever advocated the over-throw of the United States government by violence or by force?* and Rory said, *Is that multiple choice?*" The bureaucrat wasn't so bad, merely warned him, *You'll find humor won't get you far here,* not realizing that Rorion was never anything but literal. What counted in his favor was that he waved off the simple questions they asked and began to recite the Constitution verbatim.

Brilliant as he was, at most labs where he'd worked, Rorion didn't work out. He'd look at data and patterns would just pop out at him, instantly, and he'd pronounce *Answers! Truth!* but he couldn't explain where his results came from. Then someone would have to spend months doing the painstaking analysis to see if he was right. He always was, but his gift—his shortcut to the solution—would end up consuming more time than working the problem from the start by conventional means.

It was Carsky who made her see it. "Rennie, babe, he's on the spectrum."

Many people think the autistic can't bear to be touched. But Rory was starved for affection. Touch, touch, he always had to be touching Rennie, even at work. Sex? It was good but infrequent. Instead he held onto her, not so much as an infant clings to its mother, but with the desperation of a mother holding onto a dying child.

When he left DHI for an opportunity in Austin, he asked Rennie to go with him.

She could have said she couldn't leave her mother. Instead, "Are you kidding? They string up environmentalists in the Lone Star State."

He didn't know she was an environmentalist. (Neither did she. And she couldn't quite say why she refused him.)

They had been so compatible that Rennie was convinced she wasn't normal either. I'm actually very much like someone with Asperger's, she thought, except that I'm not smart.

She Was Lonely Until Emine Arrived

Rennie convinced her to lease one of the empty luxury units, modern, clean, and cheap.

She loved Emine, the way she giggled, her finger twirling through her long hair, all the while believing if she, Rennie, had ever achieved Emine's stature—by which she did not mean body size, *you could fit two of her inside me*—she wouldn't have been caught dead being girly. In Emine's case, all could be excused as culture, the way a woman, even one with a Ph.D., had to behave in the Islamic world while at the same time it occurred to Rennie that a female in a burqa was a very serious matter. No way could such a woman look flighty and trivial. Not that Turkish women wore burqas, as far as she knew. It was like being chosen by Rorion. It was the glory of living in a place as god-forsaken as Desert Haven. It allowed a glorified secretary to have an eminent woman of science as a best friend. Nobel Prize material, she liked to think, hoping this was not an exaggeration.

They kept each other company. Rennie changed her Sunday visits to her mother to very early in the morning so that she and Emine could head to the airport in Mojave for the champagne brunch, taking turns as designated driver. Rennie cooked dinner for two on Fridays and Emine cooked on Saturdays.

She hadn't meant to get so attached. When she refused to go to Texas with Rorion she thought she was through with love. With human love. It was in the days after he left that one day she saw a lizard doing its little lizard pushups on a rock. Without thinking, she reached out fast enough to catch it. It was the most miraculous thing she'd ever seen. It had fingers and toes, little eyes that looked at her, a mouth. A pulse. She held it in one hand and with the other spread the little fingers to look at them closely and then with the same hand she left the little fingers alone and stroked that smooth lizard skin. She was falling in love with life itself.

She decided there was no miracle in people. She could look at a baby and only see something that would grow up to be very much like herself and Rennie did not consider herself special. But to see and feel life coursing through the body of a creature that would never, could never, be like her—that was a miracle. And the heart that had closed down and armored itself during the last weeks when she felt stuck, imprisoned, desperate to escape from Rory, suddenly exploded open.

She carried the lizard home. Until Emine, that was enough: to watch it scoop up ants from the kitchen floor with its miracle tongue.

Enter the Serpent

When Maria Castillo arrived, she rented a one-bedroom apartment two units down from Emine. She'd never had a room to herself before. Living with others, she sometimes thought she would die of loneliness. Alone in the field, in a tent or under the sky, the ache transformed into a welcome, sometimes joyful, solitude. She stopped expecting companionship from human beings. In time she became fascinated with snakes.

Everyone teased her. *Penis envy?* Or *You must be cold-blooded too.* Then she studied with Dr. Sergio, Checo, and loved him, and wondered how she had ever lived without this and then there was nothing to protect her from her hunger. He loved her, must have, but he was preoccupied—research and teaching and university politics and government politics and so many other matters. She was not his priority. She had never been anyone's priority. For a while, finding her had been the cartel's priority. Was it still? She wondered if they had forgotten about her. Maybe she didn't really matter—even to her enemies. While Checo, poor Checo...

Why not something soft and furry? Or warm-blooded at least? Cold-blooded creatures weren't at the mercy of the weather. Whatever the environment, she thought, they fit it.

Except in the field, she'd always felt out of place. In her parents' home, dark, no bulbs in the overhead fixtures *because electricity costs money!*, the dark wooden furniture with the striped orange cushions, every possible surface covered with vases and baskets of artificial flowers, including the top of the broken TV, the useless screen draped with her mother's embroidery. The pictures on the wall: family portraits, one in which her grandmother's face had been scratched out. ("She did it herself," Maria's mother insisted. "She didn't like how she looked."); Maria's graduation picture; her parents' wedding portrait; a photo of the Pope; a crucifix carved on a twisted piece of wood and mounted in a frame with an embroidered backing, praying hands and the word *Perdón*. Everything meticulously clean with her mother's obsessive housekeeping but all the frames always hanging crooked as though an earthquake had always just struck. The constant stream of country cousins come to the city to go to school or look for work or earn enough money to make the trip north so that though Maria was an only child, she was always sharing her room and often her bed with two or three poor relations. Why did they eat off an oil cloth-covered table, from speckled enamel bowls when there were the boxes and baskets full of middle-class things: linens and the good plates and glasses, stored high up in the closets, never taken out, only saved, too good for use? As a child she had decided she would never live that way. Not that she decided she would have good things and use them. She decided she would never *have* things. Except for hats. In the mercado or when passing store windows, she would grip her father's hand with excitement: *That! I want that!*

What she and Checo had in common besides science: they weren't ashamed of where they came from even though their parents' world was not their own. And so he was not embarrassed for her to see the culture in which he was raised: all those glass-fronted cabinets displaying roses in glass globes, the brass bust of Chopin, bunnies made of cotton, collectible dolls. The Baker's chocolate stored amid the vinyl records. Paintings of flowers and cats and angels and Guadalupe in a golden frame; (all hanging straight!). On the dining table, always, the two-tiered lazy Susan holding bunches of grapes made of glass. The baby Jesus doll in a manger lying on the blankets Sergio's mother crocheted for him and wearing the little hand-crocheted swaddling clothes. Of course she couldn't sleep with Sergio in his parents' home; they put her in the guest room with cartons piled to the ceiling and the old sewing machine.

In California, she kept her place impersonal and austere, with fewer possessions than Rennie's mother. The sun glared off the bare white walls. The topo map of the Sierra Tarahumara remained rolled up in the closet. She hadn't brought a single photograph with her. If she closed her eyes, she could see Checo as clear as life, and so Maria preferred to keep her eyes open. She was in California for a new life, the dead are dead, but she was still the little girl who stood proudly for the Mexican national anthem. At the sight of the flag, the eagle devouring the serpent, she'd choke up, not from patriotism but a shiver of pity, *pobrecita, the poor little snake.*

Rennie arrived at Emine's for dinner and Maria Castillo was already there. The bottle of wine was already open. Emine and the Mexican had started without her.

On Sunday, Rennie visited her mother in the home and said, "Guess what? The neighborhood turned."

How the Other Half Lives

Carsky lived in a flat-roofed 2-bedroom 1-bath ranch so ugly you would think he was punishing himself. On one side, a vacant lot;

on the other, only the foundation left of what had been a house; just around the corner, the former strip mall that had morphed into DHI. Carsky chose the place so he could walk to work. He transformed the garage into a recording studio his friends could use when they visited from LA. He bought himself a Range Rover which seemed the proper accoutrement for desert living and parked it beneath an open tin-roofed canopy so the truck maintained a constant coating of dust. During the winter, he was startled by a loud grinding sound, the heavy rain drilling against tin, like a garbage disposal or, as Maria would later claim, the sound of male elephant seals ready to mate. Condensation formed and dripped from the underside of the canopy and left the vehicle spotted all rainy season with soot. What did it matter? He never drove it.

Petey Koh and his wife lived west of the air force base in Rosamond where she always had a headache. Juniper had thought they were headed to Seattle.

"Too rainy," he'd said.

It never rained in the high desert except when it did and then roads washed out and sometimes, after, Petey would get all excited at the half-assed rainbow you might see over the barren scrub. When it didn't rain, the Santa Ana winds messed up Juniper's sinuses. Headaches.

Yes, he admitted, he'd dragged her to the end of the earth, but still there were things she could have done to keep busy. In his free time, Petey was a volunteer at the Exotic Feline Breeding Center, cleaning the cages of ocelots and servals and margays and others the names of which she heard and quickly forgot.

"You should join me," he said.

To spend the weekend faced with what amounted to several big litter boxes?

If she made any effort at having a life, she was afraid they would stay. If she lay around in the dark bedroom or else on the living room sofa paging through magazines, complaining or else too depressed to complain, sooner or later, he'd have to call Microsoft back and say yes. For some reason, her dear husband thought working for Bill Gates was like turning your soul over to Charles Manson or else joining an organization as huge and wealthy and demanding as the Mormon Church. Instead he solved IT problems at DHI and designed computer simulations the scientists didn't even know they wanted or needed till he showed them—all for a pittance.

It wasn't that she considered money so important. It was that he thought *not* considering money important was, well, important. Which was, she had to admit, one of the reasons that she loved him.

Dr. Tang paid by the month at the Best Western in California City which he liked because it adjoined the golf course where he mostly spent his weekends. California City was near enough to Desert Haven that he could use his bicycle to commute. He arrived each morning with temperatures already in triple digits, parked his bike in the breakroom, placed two empty bottles of Gatorade in the recycling bin, sat down at his desk and turned on the computer with a satisfied grunt. Carsky watched him. They will take over the earth, he thought.

Dinner for Three

Rennie spent hours at home reading about Turkey on the internet. Military coup, political prisoners, torture. Now that she had to compete with Maria, she would impress Emine with serious conversation.

"The Armenian Genocide!" she said. "What about the Kurds?"

"The situation is complicated, and precarious," Emine admitted. "But you understand, we are moving forward. We need to be Europeans. Many of us believe the best way to progress is to keep faith with Turkish goodness. If we talk constantly of the bad, shame will only make people resist change. Change comes through love."

"You criticize America," Rennie said.

"What happens here affects everyone," said Emine. "And I don't think Americans feel shame."

"The United States can take it," said Maria.

Actually what Rennie heard was *Jew-nighty Esstays*. Her mind usually filtered out accents and grammatical lapses except for the malapropisms that amused her. But Maria wasn't wanted. It was only right that she sound ignorant.

"Guns, weapons, drugs," said Maria. "And who buy the drugs? Where you think the guns in my country come from?"

"So why are you here?" Rennie said.

Maria didn't answer. If Rennie's words were meant to offend, Maria didn't take offense at them. She and Emine were together, laughing at the table, writing and correcting each other's words while leaving it to Rennie to keep the rice from burning at the bottom of the pot, the chicken from going dry in the oven.

When Rennie had first learned Emine was Jewish, she looked up Yiddish phrases online and discovered how many she already knew from sitcoms. But mazel tov, Rennie. Wrong again. *Wrong-again Rennie*—what her father used to call her. And Emine's family spoke Ladino or what in Turkey they call Judeo-Spanish or rather Judeo-Espanyol.

So Emine was saying, "We don't have the tilde. See, we write *espanyol*."

She said *we*, though very few of her generation knew the ancient tongue but Emine had always loved languages.

"That would be helpful in email," Maria said. "Write clearly without having accent marks. No chance of wishing someone a prosperous new anus. Próspero año—or ano— nuevo."

"We use k instead of qu—like Latino rappers!" and "The closest we have to a sh sound is probably ll—as in *castellano*—but it's more like zh than sh" and "We do have to use an accent mark—but it's a Turkish one, you don't have it: *şalom*, she wrote, and her husband's name: *Oğuz*. "We don't make the *h* sound for *j*," she said. "We write *dj*. I don't know if it has more in common with Portuguese and French but it might be from the Arabic."

You could still say *Arabic* then without the momentary catch in the throat, the unavoidable discomfort.

Emine talked about the secular tradition of Turkey.

"And the military repression?" Rennie interrupted.

"I was just a kid when the violence started," Emine said. She hadn't really understood what was happening though she could hear gunfire. What she remembered was how frightened her parents seemed, how they didn't allow her to leave the apartment, not even for school. "The Army keeps us safe," she said.

Maria thought she showed too much trust. But what Emine saw was the beloved country where she was born, Jewish, and Oğuz, Muslim, neither one of them observant. Belief in democracy and social justice more important than belief in God. "Like

America," she said and Rennie thought that showed she hadn't been here long.

As for Maria Castillo, she told how in church one day the priest asked the children *Where do you feel God's love? Where do you feel His peace?* Some placed their hands on their hearts, some stuck out the tongues that had received the wafer. Maria lifted a leg and touched the sole of her foot, the part of her body that connected to the earth.

No, Maria. I asked where God's love gives you a feeling of grace and peace.

She obediently placed her hand over her heart and stopped believing. What kind of church could tell her where and how God entered her?

"I used to make fun of the Catholic Church," Maria said, "in order to retain my faith in God." In time she lost it anyway.

"My father," Rennie began, but Emine was still talking to Maria.

"Oroso," she said.

"Horoso? asked Maria.

There they went, linguistic expertise, enjoying each other's conversation, excluding Rennie.

"Same root no doubt as the French *heureux*," Emine said. "It doesn't mean horrible. It means happy."

I am not happy about this, thought Rennie. How could Emine just invite her without warning me? An intruder.

"A herpetologist," Emine said later. "Someone who appreciates them as much as you do."

Rennie forced a smile. "Reptiles," she said. "You mean snakes."

A Poison Can Be a Medicine

Maria Castillo had a special love for rattlers. The Red Diamond rattlesnake, a regular pacifist, would back off rather than strike; the Santa Catalina Island rattler was evolving to lose its rattles, it would strike without warning. She got a kick out of the hocico de puerco, pig's snout rattler, its black diamonds outlined in almost fluorescent green and its head which seemed to her not a pig's head but rather marked with the eyes of a Luna moth. She loved the rattlesnakes of her country, Mexico, even though she loved her native earth even more and it was because of the snakes she'd had to leave.

Desert Haven, though, was OK: natural habitat to the Mojave rattlesnake, the most venomous in the United States. From her collecting trips she brought back four species and assured Carsky the room would be kept locked at all times and each glass cage would have a lock on the perforated steel lid.

She wanted to map the rattlesnake genome, she told Emine and Rennie. Compare pacifist rattlers to the most aggressive. Were they hardwired, or did something in the environment affect enzymes, hormones?

"Talk about dual use," said Emine. "You'll find the key to turn a violent person peaceful—but it could also be used to turn a pacifist into a killer."

"They already figured out how to do that," said Rennie. "It's called basic training."

"She's right, of course," said Maria. "For humans, *not* killing is the default. Thou shalt not kill. Law and theology just put it in writing. It was already in our biology." And sometimes, something made that biology go haywire, she thought.

But when she told Carsky what she would need, he leaned back in his swivel chair, the list she'd prepared for him fluttering between his fingers. "Thermal cycler," he read. "Electrophoresis chamber. Erlenmeyers. Agarose. blah blah blah. Why can't you be like everyone else and use a computer?" Then he leaned forward, elbows on the desk in a posture that struck Maria as simian. "When I was encouraged to offer you a lab," he said, "no one said anything about snakes." He crumpled up the list. "You haven't generated any income."

"Director," she said. She had the idea he liked being called Director. "I can't generate anything without equipment. The genome," she said. "No one else in the world is even trying."

Carsky shook his head. "We don't want journal articles. We want something we can patent."

It was clear she'd get nowhere telling him the most significant discoveries happen by chance, just because someone was curious. Because of an anomaly. Because someone was troubled by something she couldn't explain.

"There's something we can sell," she said. "I can milk the snakes for venom." This was exactly what she hadn't wanted to do. She intended to milk each rattler for enough to use for her own research but on a regular basis, a commercial basis? Too dangerous. You probably wouldn't die, but you were sure to lose at least a finger. Maria looked at her hands. She didn't play piano or guitar. Typing would be difficult but. You make sacrifices. "There's a market for venom and anti-venom serums," she said. Of course she would need a freeze-drying system. He wasn't going to like that. "About six thousand dollars."

"Oh, please," said Carsky. "How many people in the US die of snakebite each year. Five. At the most. Forget it. What company will produce meds for five people?"

"Twenty thousand documented deaths around the world," she said. "The real number probably closer to 100,000."

"Third World problem. We're not in business here to save the world."

The subtext, she understood: Do you want to save your job?

"A poison can be a medicine," she said. "Derivatives from venom can cure—or at least treat—there's a good chance of it, heart disease, cancer."

At *cancer*, she had his interest. "How soon?"

"Hard to say. It's longterm. And difficult to make much progress without the genome."

"Longterm," he said. "I report back to our investors once a year."

Investors, shareholders, all this gringo bullshit, she thought. How to make him see, excite him with, possibility. If she only had her thorny-headed worms again, searching them for anti-infectives.

"Director, what does a snake lack?"

"Funding," he said.

"Arms and legs. It's all about high performance muscles in the spine. Imagine what this could lead to for treating spinal injuries in humans." She was making it up as she went along. "Devastating spinal injuries," she added.

"You're telling me to use my imagination?" he said. "You're telling me science is more an art than a science."

"Affirmative," she said.

"I like you, Maria," he said, "but you have to start pulling your weight. And," he said, "I don't like those snakes."

When You Milk a Snake

You can't wear gloves. You need bare hands in order to grip and feel what you're doing. Maria loved her snakes but there's no real love, she thought, without respect. They were used to her handling them but only because they were used to getting a tasty rat in the feeding bin every time she lifted them out of their homes. Now she held the snake close to her body, gripped the head and pressed it to the plastic film stretched over the funnel. The snake struck, fangs through film. This was a dangerous moment, when you might startle and let go. Maria wouldn't be startled but she had to repress the sense of marvel that made her weak with joy. The snake, doing what it was born to do. The babies were the most dangerous. They would pour the poison into you, holding nothing back. Adults, like this one, kept some venom in reserve and now Maria pressed the venom glands, taking everything the snake had. The tail and body writhed against her in protest. What happened between them, she thought, was intimate and violent and she thought for a moment of her grandmother, the women of her grandmother's generation, those sheltered and inno-cent ignorant girls who went to their new husbands with no idea of what a man might want. What are you doing to me? the snake might ask. She was the one with the power, the control, and for the time being, ten fingers.

Informational Pathways

"Carsky's pushing me," Maria said. "I need help with the quantitative proteomics study. Fast."

Petey Koh smiled and nodded which is what he did when he didn't really understand what she was talking about though he did understand about Carsky.

"First off," he said, "you need to understand that biology isn't about zoology anymore. It's information science. Informational pathways, and that's changed computer science, too. Primitive programming? Was binary. But the chromosome uses a 4-letter alphabet. We can't think or model in a linear way. It's all 3-D shapes of the proteins. How they fold up into molecular life-machines."

She smiled back at him. His tech talk had lost her.

"Can I tell you the specific problem?" she said. "I can't do anything useful with the venom without isolating the peptides and sequencing the genome. It could take years."

"Speed up the sequencing with a program I'll give you if you share it. Take amino acid chains and fold them to the most stable configuration. It will speed up your research to have more hands and eyes on the problem. The more the merrier."

He was right. She had too small a sample. Four snakes, one of each species, and no way of accounting for variation. "The results end up ambiguous. I need collaborators." Specifically collaborators working with *C. scutulatus scutulatus*. In Sonora.

Emine sat beside her. It was Emine who'd urged her to trust Petey Koh.

"The thing is," said Maria. "I can't let anyone in Mexico know where to find me."

"Woman of mystery," he said, and laughed.

"How does she stay mysterious?" said Emine.

"We give you an identity," he told Maria. "For whatever reason you find it necessary." He paused and when she said nothing, "You know, usually, in Witness Protection, you're not allowed to do the same sort of work as before."

"I'm not protected," she said.

"We route your messages and data via false IP addresses," he said. "Proxy servers in Uzbekistan, Armenia. They'll never figure out where you are."

"But I have to write to them," she said. "In English, or what? It's not like I can write them in Armenian."

"Write in bad Spanish," Petey said.

"No," said Emine. "Ladino. And not just proxy servers. We'll route the material to my computer. Even if they are able to track it, they won't find you. They'll come up with me."

Though why, it soon occurred to Dawit Tesfaye at the FBI, would researchers in Uzbekistan be working with the most toxic snake venom found in the US? Aerosolize it? And why would Emine help them?

Mountain People

Rennie resented Maria but promised her they would come up with funding. She herself would bring in cash running simple paternity tests and tox screens. "Not to worry. I'll take care of it." If she spoke with self-importance, so what? She had to be important to someone.

"You're good people," said Maria.

She often said "Mountain people are good people." It had a familiar ring to Rennie. From where? *Heidi*?

In the sierra, if you ran into difficulties, Maria said, someone would help. Humble campesinos would invite you to share their food.

They would give you a place to stay, a petate on the ground or, if they had a bed, they'd offer it to you and then they'd roll out the sleeping mat for themselves. You never had to camp out though she preferred to, a tent surrounded by containers full of snakes, a snake or two inside the shelter with her. She felt entirely safe.

Mountain people were friendly but respectful, she said, not like in the city where you couldn't walk down the street by yourself without men calling out to you. And on the coast! You'd think that coastal people would be the most open-minded, from all the contact they had to have with strangers. Maybe the more you know of strangers, the less you trust them.

What about desert people? Rennie wondered.

Maria felt peace in the soles of her feet, where she grounded herself walking on her native earth, on the narrow trails marked with lime, over the rocks, through the forests of oak and pine where the leaves gave their scent to the mulchy earth she stepped on, over the stones beneath her feet whenever she traded her boots for plastic sandals to wade through streams, dragonflies skittering over the water and butterflies all aflutter around her head.

When Maria went to the sierra, she went alone with only her snake tongs and hooks, her collecting bag and Rubbermaid containers. Dr. Sergio disapproved but she wouldn't listen. Go to bed with someone and he thinks he owns you. Or else he worries about you which in practice amounts to the same thing. She never felt in danger and she'd found that if she waited for another researcher to accompany her, she'd wait forever. What did she need of a companion or bodyguard? Mountain women are strong. Walking through the barrancas, hours from the nearest road, you'd find pretty girls, entirely unschooled, who rode horses and threw knives and handled cattle alongside the men. And as for Maria, everyone knew her, by reputation, at least. The snake girl in boots, jeans and leather snake gloves and the Panama hat.

Víbora, culebra, serpiente. All the words for snake were feminine.

The Rarámuri were nervous around her—of course, a girl carrying chachamuri, rattlesnake. And Maria had receding gums that left the long roots of her teeth exposed, the way they'd look jutting out of the fleshless jaw of a skull. Imagine, a beautiful woman whose face evokes death, walking alone in the mountains with a bag of rattlesnakes in a basket. It's a wonder they didn't fall on their knees and worship her. They would spit, not on her or at her, but to the side, a superstition, to protect themselves from venom. Except for those who sold handcrafts to tourists, weren't they shy around everyone?

"We used to be people who looked after each other. Now we've learned from you," she said, meaning not Emine or Rennie, but the United States—"Looking out for Number One, every man for himself, but without the gringo's self-restraint."

Now, North Americans were taking over Mexico, she said, with their factories and condos and beach homes, while Mexicans were forced by poverty to leave. And by violence, though she kept that to herself. No one would ever want to leave this land unless forced. To travel, yes, of course, to know other places and other ways, but not the way the little towns were being emptied, so many people torn from their roots. "We are supposed to be proud that the richest man in the world is one of us." She often thought that someday she'd head up to the sierra and there would be no people at all. Only snakes. The people all gone, with all their goodness.

"I never guessed I was the one who would have to be gone," she said. "I miss mi tierra. I miss my people."

The tears began and she fled to the bathroom.

"You do know why she's here?" Emine said to Rennie.

"You invited her," Rennie said.

"No," Emine said. "I mean *here*."

Señorita Cascabel

It began when she crossed paths with the men with the AK-47's, or so she says, though truth be told, Maria can tell *Crotalus willardi* from *Crotalus lepidus* but not one semi-automatic weapon from another.

She held out the basket "Look," she said, "I've got rattlesnakes. Culebra cascabel. Chachamuri. Sayahuki."

As though they felt her fear, the snakes began to vibrate their tails. Clickety-clickety-clack clack clack faster, louder, till the clicks became a single sound like the chirring of cicadas.

One of the men startled and jumped back. One pointed his weapon at the bag.

She smiled. "They don't frighten me. I collect them."

One of the men laughed. "They call me El Tigre. At your service."

She said, "They call me Cascabel."

After that, whenever they saw her, the men invited her to sit by their fire and share what they had: beans and tortillas, tins of sardines, pots of very hot, very sweet coffee. Like everyone else, she'd heard stories: victims with their heads cut off, people skinned alive, tongues cut out and other organs stuffed into the empty mouths and if it was true—and she didn't entirely believe any of it—that had to be Colombians, not these men who were simple campesinos simply trying to survive. She smiled and drank the very sweet coffee they gave her. When they handed her the satellite phone and El Chato himself said he wanted to meet her, what choice did she have? She let the men march her down through the canyon, pine forests left behind, to an almost hidden valley where the helicopter waited.

Brainjacking

When you come from a barely middleclass home—her father a railroad worker and proud member of the Ferrocarrilleros Union till the national railways were privatized with union leader consent; her mother who cooked and filled lunch pails to bring in some extra pesos—and your lodgings during college was a rented room where three determined girls shared a bed so that now, working toward a doctorate, it's luxury to have your own bed—except for those nights you share with your mentor, Doctor Sergio, when this is your background, taking off in a helicopter, landing by the coast then traveling by motorboat through the lagoons to where a Jeep is waiting for the last lap of the journey to a cartel boss's hacienda—clearly it's all so unreal, you might have to suspend judgment altogether.

Maria did judge herself but only for a moment. About this invitation, she didn't really have a choice. She didn't have to like or approve of El Chato to be his guest. Integrity was a luxury. Didn't the university host receptions for politicians and military men who were every bit as corrupt and deadly?

The waiting Jeep, the armed men. She had seen this scene in the movies, on TV. She carried her snake container before her. No one else dared touch it.

Bandanas over faces, surely against the dust rather than to hide their identities. But still, she reassured herself, when they cover their faces, they're less likely to kill you.

Maybe you've seen the movies too: the dirt road, guides with their pistols, the armed men facing out, their rifles aimed at the wall of trees and vines, the high guarded gate, cattle grazing in grass so high and lush they seem to float. Ancient cedars offer shade at one bank of a lake where herons and ibis stand, where black birds and parrots skim over the water and someone flies by screaming happily on jet skis. Orchards of flowering fruit trees, pickers on ladders, acres of roses. Another gate, and beyond it a domed church with two towers. Then the walls of the house and when did we start topping our walls with razor wire instead of broken bottles? she wondered. The clear bits of glass and shards of green and brown at least had some aesthetic appeal. As she said once to Emine and Rennie, "What was negative about our culture is still negative but now without the culture."

She entered the courtyard. The fragrance of roses had been too strong. Now she felt cleansed by the scent of sweet thyme.

He opened the door himself. "Señorita Cascabel."

He didn't invite her into the house but tapped the container and laughed, then led her along the corredor to a patio where a small green parrot squawked on a low branch of the lemon tree. Bougain-villea spilled over the white wall and they sat by the fountain (water spouting from the penis of the statuary little boy) and servants brought ceviche and sangría and minced shark on totopos.

"Tell me what you do with them," he said.

He wore dark glasses no more sinister than those worn by anyone protecting himself from the sun. What shocked her most was how ordinary he seemed. Mass murderer? He had the friendly, open brown face that the campesino shows to express an eagerness to cooperate or to please. She hoped he didn't plan to use her snakes as weapons.

"I'm looking for thorny-headed worms," she said. "It's a parasite with hooks on the proboscis."

"They said you studied snakes," he said.

"I do." Keeping the talk academic made her feel safe. "The snake serves as the paratenic host. *Paratenic* means being the intermediary in the life-cycle."

"Ah, the middleman," he said, "like me."

"In the end," she said, "the parasite needs to find a home in a warm-blooded creature. So the snake has to end up in the belly of something else, like a jaguar, a wild boar, a badger, or a skunk."

"If it's a patriotic Mexican snake," he said, "it will be eaten by an eagle."

"What I'm curious about," she said (aside from El Chato himself), "and what hasn't been studied is whether the worm affects the snake's behavior to make it more vulnerable to predators."

"I would be curious about that, too," he said.

"We know what happens when the worm infects marine invertebrates," she told El Chato. "The little crustaceans—when they're not infected—they protect themselves by hiding from the light. Then the ducks that want to eat them can't get them."

"Poor little ducks," he said.

"But the worm causes the release of a chemical in the brain that makes the creatures want to mate. Even if they sense danger, desire drives them up up up to the light."

"If you find that chemical," he said, "let's hope they make it illegal. One more market opportunity."

"We call it brainjacking," she said. He understood the English word *jacking*; she had to translate *brain*, which is not to imply his was inadequate.

"Would you mind killing one of them?" he asked. "To see if there's a worm inside? Would you mind that very much?"

A Traumatized Child

El Chato brought his son to live with him because Alex's mother back in Los Angeles was a whore.

"She is not," the boy told Maria later. "She's an idiot," preferring to raise her child in poverty than have him exposed to his drug-dealing assassin of a father back in Mexico.

"I would have sent child support," El Chato told Maria, "but it's a delicate matter. Money can be traced." He forgot about this excuse when he heard his ex was pregnant—by some Salvadoreño without papers, for godsakes! He immediately dispatched a courier with a first-class air ticket to retrieve his own son.

Alex had wavy light brown hair and big light brown eyes and he would have been an extremely attractive child if his shoulders hadn't been pulled up almost to his ears and his movements stiff. His big eyes alternated between staring into space and rapid blinking. She thought, this child has been traumatized.

"What kind of education is there in the United States?" said

El Chato. "Ten years old and he can hardly read and write. Not in English, not in Spanish. Cut up the snake. Make him curious. Get him interested in something for the love of God."

Alex had a private tutor. "Security concerns. I can't allow him to leave the estate. I can't allow him to see other children." But Luisa wasn't working out. El Chato had found her after she led a protest against the impending privatization of the school where she taught. She was arrested, tortured, raped, then thrown out of a moving car. "I thought, Perfect! A teacher who needs to go into hiding, a boy who needs a teacher."

But Luisa, one arm hanging limply, unable to walk without pain, spent the school day asking Alex about California. She refused to believe people there could be poor.

"My mother works all the time," he said. "People work so hard there, I never see her."

"I'll stay home and take care of you," Luisa said.

He told her about mold and rats and not having enough to eat and she said, "Take me there with you. Take me with you, please."

When Maria met him, the boy sat staring into space, frozen, making her think of the story about the burro and free will. The burro is positioned exactly in the middle of two identical bales of hay. Unable to choose one over the other, it starves. She thought Alex was frozen between two lives, but while either choice would have saved the burro, neither choice Alex could make was any good. And how much free will did the kid have now that his father had brought him here?

Afternoons, he took his son riding and taught him to shoot.

"I stand over a watermelon," Alex told Maria, "and then I put the gun against it." He swallowed and blinked before adding, "And shoot." She believed he was terrified that one day he'd be told to put the gun against a human being's head.

El Chato came to watch the lesson. "Stay back," she warned and she put on leather snake gloves with the long turned-back cuff, protection as high as her elbow. She took the top off the Rubbermaid. The sack inside moved. With the snake hook she loosened the tie and reached in.

"Alex," she said, "I'm reaching for him about 1/3 of the way down from his head. Stand back. I've got to get him—or her—on the ground quickly because he'll struggle if he's up in the air."

One smooth motion and the snake was out of the tub and pinned. She let one of the gardeners decapitate it with a machete. The boy flinched and the snake writhed headless a moment after death and when it was still, he asked if he could keep the rattles. She nodded and the gardener chopped off the tail and presented the trophy to Alex.

Maria laid the rattler out on the table. Off with the snake gloves and on with the tight latex. "We make a mid-ventral incision, to expose the organs so we can examine them." She opened the body. "See, it has all the things we have, and more." She pointed out the heart and lungs. "And here, see, this one is male. And here, like a long accordion, it's the small intestine." She sliced and slowly pulled out the worm.

"Did he eat that?" asked the boy.

"He swallowed the eggs, and the worms grew inside him."

"Like in the bellies of the poor," said El Chato.

Maria ignored him—"See how they attached themselves to the intestine wall"—but the boy's voice shook. "Do I have worms?"

"I wouldn't allow it," said El Chato and he asked "Is the snake meat safe to eat?"

She didn't know. "This worm has pulled its hooks in," she said, "but look at this one here."

Alex ventured close again.

"Alex, how many rows of hooks do you see?"

"Six."

"Can you describe them? I mean are they curved? Up or down? Short straight points?"

"You're a good teacher," said El Chato.

He leaned over the body of the snake and the boy and his father smiled at each other when their heads touched.

Maria Castillo Was Never a Hostage

She was El Chato's guest.

He needed protection from his enemies, not from the authorities. He had friends and people on his payroll in the army, the police, the governor's office, the state's attorney. But Dr. Sergio was worried when she didn't return from the sierra and he had friends too in the media and the DEA and he saw to it that the abduction of a brilliant and beautiful young scientist caused outrage. He was interviewed on TV. Maria's face was all over the news.

You sleep with a man and it all goes to hell, is what Maria thought later.

"You've never been here," said El Chato. "OK? And now you're gone."

Jeep to boat to helicopter to Jeep and she was left, wearing her Panama hat but without her hook, her container, her gloves, her surviving snakes at an intersection in Tepic. But her "rescue" hadn't happened soon enough. El Chato was killed in the raid. It was all over the news. American officials offered congratulations. It was an example of binational cooperation. No one mentioned the army general on the payroll of a rival cartel. No reliable body count was reported. Alex? Luisa? Maria didn't know.

"You need to leave the country now," Dr. Sergio told her.

"Why?" she said. "I'm the snake girl, not a sapo"—sapo, being a toad and a snitch.

"The organization will want revenge." He'd already contacted a friend in the States about a visa and a post-doc in microbiology.

Until Sergio was gunned down, she refused to go.

She took the post-doctoral fellowship and then ended up at DHI.

She lost her lover. She lost her country. She missed her home. She missed her snakes.

Maria del Rosario Saavedra Castillo who in Mexico went by Rosario Saavedra C.—Chayo to her friends—became plain Maria Castillo, to make her name easier for the gringos to get right and make it harder for the cartel to find her.

Rennie

Something on the food cart must be broken. I hear it coming long before it's here, a clickety-clack. A card in the spokes of a bike. Someone's teeth chattering. The rattlesnake in Maria's bag, clickety-clacking, clacking, clacking faster and faster till it works itself into a loud humming threat.

File #2:

Every Landscape Is a Crime Scene

A Deal with the Devil

Some Christians—the ones from whom Christianity has to be redeemed—read the imminence of the End Times in the Book of Revelation. Brent Fassen taught instead how to read evidence in the God-given world.

"The highway crews used Agent Orange to control the foliage along these roads. The workers were first to suffer. Then the dead growth was burned and the poison traveled through the air. Cancer. Women miscarried. So did wildlife. See these woods? Littered with the little bodies of deformed and dying fawns."

He could feel his rage flow from his hands into the steering wheel. But now, he was in charge. For the duration of the ride, these kids belonged to him.

They left Olympia, Washington in the morning, the five who'd gathered round him after his talk in the Student Union at Evergreen State. Now he'd spirited them away from the campus, the old growth trees, the trickle of water into the beds of moss, the walkways and the gray wood, the professors you called by first name and who smiled indulgently when you served them dinner at the pub where you worked part-time, they would listen to you talk about what you were reading and thinking and doing while their food grew cold, even though your words were coming out as fast as you could make them, everything about being a student there was perfect except that it wasn't the real world and Brent Fassen had made Marty face that. Marty was the best prospect, a boy who'd read too much—or maybe just enough—Nietzsche. Rather than sequester himself away in a place where he for the first time maybe felt happy and safe, Brent had made him understand he had a responsibility. To Do Something. Today, an Action, south, at Oregon State.

This was in the prelapsarian—pre-9/11 world—when there was evil enough to contend with. "When we worship Science, we sacrifice children on its altar. Research institutes...." He said the words and sneered. "What do they research? Better lives? Hell, no! More efficient means of mass murder."

Oregon State had made a deal with the devil: Monsanto. The criminal corporation was ruining farmers around the world, driving some to suicide. Monsanto disseminated Terminator seeds that spread their cancer to neighboring farms, rendering healthy seeds sterile. Monsanto, its tentacles everywhere like the Mafia, with toxic pesticides, genetically engineered bacteria...and now, offering morally compromised wheat to the agricultural sciences program. If OSU collaborated with Monsanto, the university was colluding in damage to Wheat, the Staff of Life.

Not that Evergreen—much as his passengers claimed to love the place—was blameless. At schools like Evergreen State, students learned that *patriarchy* was a dirty word. "But what has the end of patriarchy meant?" he asked them, looking back over the seat so the couple holding hands in the way back could hear. "Men no longer know their role in society. They no longer know they are responsible for the world God gave into our keeping. What do we see instead?" From the rearview mirror, Brent saw that Marty had eyes fixed on him. "All the irresponsible and destructive acts of men." You want to know how irresponsible I've been, he thought. Just ask my ex-wife. Either of them. "How far should a man go to protect his family? A man should give his life! and now, men don't even feed their children."

It was unjust to call Brent a deadbeat dad. He had given up everything. He'd had no money to pay child support, living in his car—at that time, a 15-year-old Honda Civic, and OK, he claimed four kids as dependents on his income tax though he denied paternity of one but that was a tax protest. Why should he support Big Oil and the military-industrial complex if he was unable to support his own children? And yes, the check-kiting got a little out of hand. Plus the environmental fundraising the feds misconstrued as mail fraud. Now he belonged to the FBI. It was self-preservation.

Inside the SUV with dark windows—along with posters, epoxy, and healthy snacks—Lionel, who apparently fit somewhere on the ever-expanding autism spectrum, was in the front passenger seat beside him fidgeting, holding the seatbelt away from his body, drumming his fingers on the glove box. Brent wanted to hit him though he should have been gratified at how the big overgrown boy echoed him, muttering rapidly under his breath about responsibility, stewardship. "Over-educated technocrats," said Lionel, "devising planetary colonies away from Mother Earth. Stop them, stop them." A nuisance but one that might prove useful. Directly behind him, Lori kept her hand on Marty's thigh. Brent couldn't see what Clint and Meredith were doing on the seat behind them until a crinkle told him they had opened up at least one of the Power bars. He wasn't sure his words could reach them in the way back. No matter. Clint was Marty's roommate and had just come along for the ride. Spring fever.

Then they were back in the new 21st century driving a freeway like any other, well maybe not like LA with multiple lanes and industry and sound walls on either side. The Pacific Northwest still had enough land to spare for a green buffer running alongside the highway and beyond it the trees.

"You drive a Fascist truck," said Lionel. As insensitive as any Asperger's genius could be.

"Operational," said Brent.

Three hours, four at most, to Corvallis.

The girl kept her hand on Marty.

Bringing Sex into the Discourse

There were the Oregon cottages placed on the crime scene, so small it was doubtful there was more than one bedroom, so either Oregon couples were childless or how did they find enough privacy to fuck? The roofs peaked to slant off the rain. If you made a bedroom in the attic, each time you sat up, you'd hit your head. But people went on living.

Brent had been accused of making war on women but that was utterly false. He waged a war to death against unmanly, unmanned dangerous men. The girlfriend, Lori, look what she was doing to the boy, he had to be stirring, bulging, how long would he be plagued by the erection, the swelling balls. The action would take an hour or two, then another four or five—they'd probably stop for something to eat, Marty was probably counting the hours till they could be alone and he could fuck her.

Brent caught Marty's eye in the mirror and smiled, then spoke in what he thought of as his preacher's voice, though he was not and did not pretend to be a preacher. "Let's assume for the sake of argument that all of you in the car are heterosexual—which I don't mean to set up as a privileged lifestyle. A true Christian knows better than to condemn sodomy." He was making them uncomfortable—which was very much the point. "I was your age once. I know you spend most of your time thinking about sex, and we might as well acknowledge it. If we bring sex into the discourse, we can entwine your fantasy lives with the work we need to do. Now, if a man—a male human being— were to kneel before you and take your erect member in his mouth and perform a skilled act of fellatio or, blow job, if you will—it would feel good. The act would be sexual without being in the least erotic."

Brent once had a quiet voice, soft as a caress. Acting lessons had taught him to modulate, to switch effortlessly to something more authoritative and sonorous. No, not sonorous, not booming. He'd describe it, rather, as resonant. His natural voice—which was now as calculated and artificial as the voice he'd learned—served best for seduction.

"Erotic! that's a mysterious and subterranean affinity, an inde-scribable, unalterable compulsion in which the object of desire awakens the magnets embedded not just in the genitals but head, heart, and soul." He took his hands off the steering wheel to raise them, open, in wonder. "The object of desire—not just the object, the *objective* is specific. It's desiring to experience pleasure through the

51

agency of a particular other. The erotic is sublimely personal, a part of identity. And what I'm asking of you—each one of you, is to feel an erotic connection—irresistible—to all of Nature and to our Mother, planet earth."

"Mother Earth," said Lionel. "That's incest."

A swath of meadow, trees. "Look! An industrial park," Brent said. "Words that should not go together."

"Appropriate, actually," said Lionel. "Etymologically, a park equals an enclosure for wild beasts. Not to protect them. To have them ready for the nobles to hunt. Then it became a paddock for sheep."

"The exploitation of the animal kingdom," said Brent.

"It evolved to a fenced area for military vehicles."

"Of course," said Brent. "The meaning remains stable. About killing and war and now it infects every aspect of civilian life. We *have* to have cars. We *need* space to park."

"Fascist truck," Lionel muttered under his breath.

"Tactical choice," muttered Brent.

A First Step

They parked the Fascist truck. It was easy enough to blend in on the campus. Clint's girlfriend Meredith, native Oregonian, even had a Beavers windbreaker.

They didn't tape the posters on brick but used epoxy on metal and glass. You have to do damage. Each poster featured a skull and crossbones. They split up, each taking one of the paths that radiated out like the spokes of a wheel, past the bell tower and out to the brick building with its rounded addition at one end like a rotunda slapped by a major donor in the wrong place. He thought the fanciful angles of the business school suggested creative accounting.

MONSANTO + OSU = CRIMES AGAINST THE PLANET
Gifts from Monsanto

37 million pounds of toxic
chemicals
(and counting)
in YOUR air land water
and underneath YOUR feet.

"We say *the planet* rather than the earth to be sure it's understood we're including oceans and rivers and skies."

"So is that it?" Marty asked. "A dozen posters is an *action*?"

"A first step," Brent said.

They'd studied the department head's photo on the website and when they spotted him, a clutch of papers in one hand, umbrella in the other, they followed him to faculty parking.

He unlocked a subcompact.

"Awesome!" said Lionel. "That's an Insight. Hybrid technology. Seventy miles per gallon highway and—"

"A two-seater," said Brent. "I couldn't very well fit all of you into one of those."

The professor removed a briefcase, put the papers inside, locked up the car and walked away.

"You want action?" said Brent.

Marty and Lori walked hand in hand to the car. They embraced as he leaned her back against the door. Brent could hear the scratch as Marty keyed the paint. Lionel kicked in a taillight. From the sound, he was actually wearing metal-toed boots. He could be a pain in the ass, but worth it.

I'm not a sociopath, Brent thought, not like, say, Dick Cheney. Manipulation made him sick to his stomach. I have a conscience, he thought, I feel guilt, but God wants us to use the talents He gave us.

"Good work. Now let's get out of here," said Brent.

Next Step, Memorial Day Weekend, 2001

From Highway 395, the Sierras look barren, granite sliced by a serrated knife, but the trail led to the campsite in a cleared flat area amid the pines. Brent Fassen packed in on foot, very ecological. Better yet, the campground with meeting hall had once been a church retreat; the ACLU hadn't known about or bothered with the cross still hanging in the refectory. He put away the pounds of beans, lentils, fresh carrots and onions, cans in the kitchen, bags and produce in the bear-proof locker. More food would be coming with the others. A cabin for Brent; the bunkhouse for the boys, eight of them, more than he planned to use, but the chosen would be impressed with themselves when they saw how few made the cut.

For now, all he had to do was wait.

He'd recruited at the most obvious places: Evergreen, Reed, UC Santa Cruz. Berkeley for old times' sake, the place had become so conservative. Starr King. Prescott. He didn't bother with his own institutions—not the ones where he'd earned degrees or the ones where he'd been exploited and had so unhappily taught. The sniping from other faculty, the students who nodded off in class after a night of partying and fucking—though to be fair, it was a public college and most of the students had to work, often nights, and the undocumented kids being paid under the table were paid less and often working not one job but two or three.

The best stroke of luck was Joseph, the ag student from OSU, they'd met while pasting up the posters. African American. A very earnest Christian who told Brent his people had wrongly equated freedom with leaving the land. His people would go on hurting till they reclaimed their relationship with the earth, redeemed their heritage as farmers from the bloody past of slavery and exploitation. Wheat farming meant reclaiming an agricultural identity without historical baggage.

"How perceptive. You're so right," Brent told him though he knew losing baggage wasn't quite so easy.

Waiting gave him the jitters.

He often told people he'd spent a month protesting atop a redwood which wasn't strictly true, but it was the sort of thing people liked to hear about Brent Fassen and if they really wanted the truth, they could have done a quick internet search. What he had done was to rent himself four weeks atop a fire tower, every bit as high and difficult and lonely as a redwood if you were a man who needed attention, who always needed to move, to pace, to mark out territory. Up there, only a small platform, up there so little room for an insomniac tempted by the open space and by gravity. There over the edge—this was the test of whether he loved his body, loved life. Or it might have been a test of his courage. Up there he could see for miles, see the approach of danger before danger had even made up its mind to approach.

Somewhere in the forest someone was grilling meat, far enough away Brent couldn't see the source, only smell the smell that triggered desire.

Sexual/erotic, he thought. And he thought he was most comfortable with his body when he could think of it as someone else or even something else. The days when he jerked off atop the fire tower, he didn't picture any human being, male or female, he felt one with the sky, the horizon, the resin pooling from the bark of the trees, the smell surrounding and exciting him, blissfully pungent as incense, as cunt.

Sometimes he masturbated when he felt sick to his stomach, a way of distracting himself, replacing one physical sensation with another.

He paced. He taped the maps and charts to the refectory wall. The topo map of the Eastern Sierras with the whorls he called fingerprints of the earth. Photographs of deformed Vietnamese children, of Colombian peasants standing amid brown fields, dead withered corn. Maps of Monsanto locations in California, Washington State, Arizona, the headquarters in St. Louis, more specifically, in Creve Coeur. Perfect name that, Creve Coeur: Monsanto puts a knife in our heart.

When they arrived, he would ask them to be seduced by a tree. Hanged men ejaculate when they die, he would tell them, and from their emission the mandrake is said to grow. He would have them masturbate among the pines. *What will be born from your seed?*

What was it they used to say? A man will fuck a hole in the earth.

A man will masturbate to stop thought, to empty himself, to be emptied, which meant to know himself as he really was: empty. It was ugly to face that truth but there was a vast relief in facing it.

That's what he did while he waited.

Then he paced. Waiting.

A Fairy Nice Boy

That's what they used to call him. He had been the teacher's pet. Always pleasant, always smiling. Helpful to others. You would think by now he could have put it behind him, the mocking voices rolling at him from all parts of the room.

Only he wasn't. Not a fairy and not nice.

He pretended not to hear. That didn't make him nice.

They shoved him in the hallways.

Oh, so sorry.

He didn't dare say *So you like touching me, don't you?*

He hadn't asked to be born this way, hair the color of honey, hazel eyes that could go from amber to a brilliant green, that could change gradually or suddenly. He realized early on that people could be trapped by his gaze and dizzied by it. He couldn't seem to walk like other boys did, who stepped on the earth ready to break things. He moved like a cat. And he liked girls—always had. Too much.

Learn to fight. His father punching him. *Use your fists!* and he could tell his father wasn't trying to teach him. He just liked using him as a punching bag.

He tried plucking out his eyelashes. It wasn't his fault they were so long. *What are you doing?* said his mother but in school he told people they'd fallen out because of a mysterious disease that might well prove fatal.

Oooh, it's catching! keep away!

Pretty boy, his father said, the fucking brute.

The only male person who was kind to him was Mr. Slayton. The spaghetti-cooker. The only one—relying no doubt on gaydar—who didn't think Brent was gay. *They're jealous of you*, Slayer said. *You have many more friends than they do.* Slayer understood some things and not others. Brent was popular. Popularity was not the same as having friends. Girls chased him, the ones who were skittish about sex. They all wanted to go out with him—a safe date—and then they'd freak when they found out what he wanted.

Slayer had kept him out of trouble so many times. He probably wouldn't be doing any of this now if Slayer weren't dead.

When people don't see who you really are, you learn to play roles. He couldn't fight so he learned to charm, to judge his audience and adapt. He could do it, he did it well, but it still made him angry.

Had he been bullied? Only if taunting counted as bullying. Except for his father.

He did have that crooked nose. He'd invented so many stories:

Drunk, he'd tried to look in a jewelry store window when he was planning to propose to his first wife and slam, his face hit hard against the glass.

Or: Age 25, he did it on purpose, went into a bar and picked a fight to get his nose broken, to earn the rugged face he thought he deserved, that he thought would protect him. But in truth he'd always fought with words and charm, not fists or weapons.

Never ever ever let them know who you really are. Keep them off balance. Then they don't have a stable position from which to attack.

The truth was his father's fist.

In the hospital, a tube through his nose and down his throat, Brent was visited. Jesus sitting by the bed as it levitated, touching his hand where the IV pinched and it immediately ceased to hurt, Jesus saying *I love you,* man to man, without anything gay about it. Your lies should always have a grain of truth. Whatever was false in what he said, he was truly a believer. Jesus: gentle, mild, and manly. He was Jesus and Judas and all of the above.

Good Fathers

The Prescott group arrived first, three of them, yammering on with a mile-by-mile account, crossing into California at Needles, and blah blah blah.

Then Lionel and Joseph. Accompanied by Lori. Had Marty invited her? She wasn't expected and where the hell would she sleep? They let everyone know they were virtuous and had carpooled as far as the trailhead. Lionel, less virtuous than the others, had no backpack and carried nothing.

Lionel, Lori, and Joseph. It sounded almost theological or in the nature of an expletive.

"Where's Marty?" Brent asked.

"He went to see his mother," said Lori. "He'll be here."

Under other circumstances, he might find her amusing, the way she kept correcting her posture. She hunched. Then she'd catch herself, shoulders back, chin up, like an alert, well trained dog.

The boys from UC Santa Cruz had shaved heads, piercings, and tattoos. They had been in Peru during spring break. In the jungle they'd done ayahuasca and received many visions including those that told them to join Brent and his mission. They hadn't known their mission would mean getting stuck listening to Lionel.

"All those years I didn't know what was wrong with me," he said. "Having a diagnosis is awesome. And an online community."

"A support group," said one of the pierced boys.

"No no no! An affinity-based association designed to resemble a self-selected family."

Where was Marty? A boy so unsure of himself, he was sure to be the brave one.

After the event at Evergreen, Marty had quoted Nietzsche and Brent had quoted back: *When one has not had a good father, one must create one.*

Marty would have to turn to Brent. Brent had turned to Mr. Slayton. He'd gone to his apartment one night bleeding and in pain. *No more pretty boy.* His father had broken his nose. He didn't want to go to the hospital. He didn't want anyone to know. He didn't want his father arrested.

Slayer gave him pain pills and an ice pack.

"Are you going to report my father?" Brent asked.

"The law says I have to."

In spite of everything, maybe his father loved him, the child with the broken lip, swollen to look even redder, fuller. He wasn't weak when his father beat him. He took it; he was strong. When his father beat his mother, he just stood there, queasy, like at school. "I don't want—"

Mr. Slayton's mouth twisted. Then he said, "I'll do what you want me to do." He put his arms around Brent and held him while he cried. That was the only time Slayer ever touched him.

It was Slayer who gave him Nietzsche to read, and that led to his dissertation about Nature in Nietzsche and Christianity and that was also the Nietzsche he didn't share with Marty: humans were unnatural in their drive for truth. He spent years teaching philosophy, an overworked, underpaid adjunct, bored to death with undergraduates and administration politics, convinced that academia was the assassin of thought. All those years he spent writing the damn thing to get his Ph.D., he couldn't work on it without thinking of Slayer. He'd cut off contact, ashamed that his surrogate father was a fag, and then ashamed of being ashamed, but he slogged through—through the dissertation, through two marriages, three (or four?) kids, two divorces. He was Mr. Nice Guy all right, not fairy but failure till one day his dissertation was rediscovered and published becoming—who knows how these things happen?—a cult classic for the ecopsychology movement. He gave up anything he couldn't carry on his back—like a turtle, he said—and took his message on the road.

Gay men were loyal. When he was arrested, he hadn't seen Slayer in years, but phoned him at once. Mr. Slayton paid for a lawyer. A good one. Arrested again in 1998, Brent phoned and the number was disconnected. That time he was on his own.

Hypotheticals

If there'd been a least-carbon-footprint competition, Marty would have won. He'd biked 15 miles to Mojave where he took the intercity bus to Ridgecrest, then the CREST bus up 395. He biked from the highway to the trail head at which point he was hot, exhausted, sweaty, and brown with dust. His legs trembled so bad he dismounted and walked, leaning on the bike for support. The bike fell amid the pine needles and he collapsed beside it. Lori rushed to him with a canteen.

"Ugh, you need a shower," she said, but the way she plucked at his padded shorts and jersey suggested his smell didn't turn her off at all.

"Rules for the weekend," said Brent. He went over the need for secrecy and security culture. "No public displays of affection. Those of you who came as a couple, forget about it. Same cabin—that's unavoidable. But we've only got eight beds. Marty, you're on the floor." He said. "I'm not negative about sex. But there's a time and a place."

Lionel lifted his shaggy head. "Where?" he said. "And when? Is it on the schedule?"

He lowered his head again when people laughed.

Before eating, they joined hands and said grace. White Christians and one black one. Joseph, like Lori, hunched inside his clothes, maybe trying to look smaller and harmless. Brent thought of the photographs he'd studied so carefully when he was a boy: Muhammed Ali—such sculpted magnificence, and Sugar Ray Leonard—those velvet eyes. Beautiful men, both of them, and no one could accuse them of being unmanly. While he was trapped forever, merely pretty, and white and here now with his sad little crew. If they couldn't save the planet, maybe they could at least throw out a lifeline to one poor sinner, Brent.

In the morning they prayed outdoors in the cold, waiting for the dawn. If they hadn't been Christians, Brent thought, they could have claimed responsibility for making the sun rise.

He cooked pancakes and cowboy coffee and during the morning discernment circle, he asked how many of them believed humankind superior to other animals and whether their beliefs had any impact on their responsibility to the planet. He didn't listen to the answers.

They hiked. Over lunch, Brent lectured on the history of civil disobedience and then they discussed nonviolent actions they could take to disrupt Monsanto activities and create public awareness. Brent taped two long sheets of paper on the refectory wall. He invited people to write on one what they imagined most Americans thought of Monsanto and on the other what Americans thought of protesters. He stared at what they wrote without reading it. Then they formed another circle to discuss how those impressions might be changed. And so on. He wondered if the members of his group were as bored by all this as he was.

At night, he said, "No PowerPoint. No flickering images or pixels. I want you to hold these in your hands." He passed around photos of Vietnamese children. "I want the reality to pass through your skin and enter you. Deformities. Dying children. I want you to feel their moans move through your fingertips. I want these crimes to be real to you."

"Wasn't that Dow Chemical, not Monsanto?" said Lionel.

"Yes, of course," Brent said. "But we don't have photographs for Monsanto which, incidentally, uses a formula for Agent Orange which is dirtier and carries even more dioxin than the poison that did the damage you're looking at. They had a way to eliminate the dioxin but it would have cost a few pennies so they didn't."

They talked about hunger strikes. They talked about letters to the editor. They talked about the disappearance of honey bees, poison sprayed over the fields and farms and national parks of Colombia, genetically modified seeds spreading like a cancer. They talked about street theatre and demonstrations. About workers laboring in virtual slavery. The Texas

City disaster. The war criminal CEO who said, *We may not have been as open as we should have been.*

They went outside to look up at the moon, a pocked bit of bone in the sky.

Day Two was war games. Hypothetical, of course. "This isn't paintball. It's more serious than that. Your challenge is to draw up battle plans. Tactics, strategy. Maximum impact, minimum risk."

Lionel led the workshop on how to make your internet searches untraceable.

"Let's imagine a team of terrorists, bringing the pigeons home to roost," said Brent.

"Malcolm said *chickens*," said Lionel.

"Thank you, Lionel, for the correction. The point is, we can use Monsanto's product to bring Monsanto to its knees."

"We're nonviolent," said one of the Santa Cruz boys.

"I said hypothetical," said Brent. "It's about learning to strategize. OK?"

"Yeah, sure, OK."

"Monsanto has corporate offices all over California. Research farms and centers, distribution centers for farm supplies."

"Why not strike all over the country?" said Lori.

Right on, he thought. But sooner or later, women always saw through him. No way he was going to use her.

The Chosen

The marrow buzzed inside his shoulder. No pain, just an effervescence that wouldn't let him sleep. Then his whole body, bubbling, till he found himself rising from the bed. He could float, not buoyant, not a balloon, but rather a corpse rising from the river lifted by its own gas. He felt such self-disgust when he wasn't moving moving moving. He fizzed his way through his cabin door and out to the bunkhouse.

The trees were black. The sky above was also black but lighter like charcoal smudged by a finger. The moon was hidden. The stars, cracked ice.

He heard a sound, probably wind. Flap, the flapping of the wings of predators in the night. We confine the dead inside receptacles closed tight and then bury them under all the weight of the earth to fight back against the buoyancy of death. Keep the dead from rising. Which is why people fear bombs, he thought, all that dying matter blown high to where it wants to be—in the air. Blown to bits, exactly what the living body craves. Only the mind resists. Western civilization degrades the wisdom of the body, telling us to listen only to the soul and to the brain. The dictatorial brain. Why don't you just mind your fucking mind?

In the bunkhouse, the air was noxious. Intentionally so. He'd fed them beans so that when they stepped out into Nature, the pristine pine air would be scented with the odor of sanctity. Side benefit: might turn Lori off about Marty.

He tapped the chosen awake. Marty, Joseph, then Lionel. Finger to his lips *Shhhh*, and then he beckoned.

He wished he had a mask. A stocking over his face. A scrim to erase identity so that he could tell himself if they agreed to do what he asked, they would have been moved not by his influence but by the need for action, the power of the unadorned words. It wasn't entrapment. They wanted it.

In the refectory, he turned on the light. "The three of you understand this isn't hypothetical anymore."

"Can I get my glasses?" asked Lionel. He left without waiting for permission.

Marty said, "He's a security risk."

"He'll be fine," said Brent.

They waited for Lionel. Brent sat and held onto the tabletop, kept himself from pacing.

When he had all three of them seated, "First," he said, "a commitment to secrecy. If you can't commit, go back to bed. Now."

The boys stayed.

"What else are you committed to?" he asked. "How far are you willing to go?"

"I want to go beyond Monsanto," said Joseph. "We have to stop the destruction."

"Monsanto is just a start," said Brent. "And by 'go' you mean—?"

Joseph said, "By any means necessary."

"You do what you have to do," said Marty.

For a moment, Brent felt sorry for them. Facing the most fateful decision of their sheltered lives, they fell back on other people's words. "Lionel?"

"I'm thinking. I'm thinking," he said.

"And?"

"You're my friends," he said. "My best friends. It's wrong to betray a friend."

"Monsanto is a leading manufacturer and distributor of ANFO," Brent said. "That's ammonium nitrate—porous prilled ammonium nitrate—with 6% fuel oil."

"That's what you use to make meth," Lionel said.

"Or a fertilizer bomb," said Brent. "Or an IED. A weapon of choice for terrorists. Joseph, you're at the ag school. You can acquire some without raising suspicion."

He moved to the map on the wall. "St. Louis, Missouri. More specifically, Creve Coeur, home to Monsanto's new CEO, Hendrik Verfaillie. So. This isn't a game. This is something that has to be done by committed warriors for the earth who can be trusted to carry out the mission."

"It sounds illegal," said Lionel.

"Duh," said Marty and laughed.

"We are part of Nature, and Nature is amoral," Brent said. "If we are going to defend the environment of which we are a living, breathing and at the moment a thoroughly destructive part, how dare we impose human morality on our actions?"

"You sound like the Unabomber," Lionel said.

"The Unabomber was not *strategic*."

They sat so quietly they could hear the wind, the refrigerator's hum, each other's breath. They could each hear a beating heart and pulsing blood, so insistent, whether each other's, or their own.

"OK," said Brent. "This was just...you're all with the program, right? Now to each according to his ability. Lionel, set up the secure communications system. Joseph, at least 500 pounds, not all at once. You'll let us know when you've got it. Then we'll meet again."

"What are we going to do with it?" asked Marty.

"Car bombs for the facilities. At night," said Brent. "No one will get hurt."

"And Verfaillie?" asked Marty.

"It will be harder to get close to him," Brent said. "I think, Marty, the best approach will be on a bike."

"You're saying he should die," said Marty.

"He and men like him are threatening our lives. The existence of all living things," said Brent. "It's justifiable. It's self-defense."

"I don't know," said Marty. "That's not—"

Brent placed his hand on the boy's shoulder. "Nothing is engraved in stone," he said. "Nothing is decided yet. Except that we're going to move forward."

How easy it was to reel them in. He had them now—conspiracy, and he would have to turn them in. For a moment he felt sorry for them and for himself, for the betrayal. But the moment passed. Let them plead entrapment, he thought.

They joined hands and prayed.

Rennie

It was days before they said I could call my lawyer. What lawyer? How many innocent people have a criminal defense attorney on speed-dial? When, they said, OK, you can make a phone call, the only person I could think of calling was Emine and she's the suspect. "In the wind," they said. Amazing. People actually say that.

File #3:

Some People Still Write Letters (correspondence removed from DHI by the FBI)

December 20, 2000

Dear Dr. Albaz,

My name is Alula Wright (you can call me "Lu") and I was referred to you by Rennie Mulcahy because of our shared concern with radiation dangers.

Several years ago, my body swelled up like a balloon. Being half-Chamorro, I tend to be large, but this was ridiculous. After several doctors told me "Diet and Exercise!", I was at last diagnosed with lymphoma and after debilitating treatments (including a bone marrow transplant that almost killed me) I was pronounced cured. (Of course they didn't use that word.)

Dr. Albaz, I don't think it makes me a loose thread on the lunatic fringe that I believe my illness is connected to the chunk of uranium ore that sat on the coffee table in our New Mexico living room the whole time I was growing up. (In New Mexico my mother was usually mistaken for Navajo and in time she decided at last to "pass." I tell you this only because if you google my name you may find some inaccurate accounts of a controversy and how I applied for a minority scholarship and was exposed for not actually being Navajo. I was/AM a minority. Chamorro! Or Pacific Islander, per the census. I identified myself as a colonized person of color not as a Native American! I was accused without just cause and I don't want you to come across slurs on my character and reach the unjust conclusion that I am untrustworthy and mendacious.)

It is a fact that throughout my childhood I handled the uranium ore, I played with it. A Geiger counter was my toy.

I hope you'll agree it was not an extreme reaction that after my near-death experience I purchased a cabin in the Siuslaw National Forest in an area that has been off-limits to toxic spray for decades and which is also 100% cell-tower-free. I eat produce from my own organic garden. I feel my system is already compromised and see no point in unnecessary exposures.

If you don't mind my taking up so much of your valuable time, a little more background might be helpful to your understanding. My father witnessed atomic tests. He was part of the advance US team on Christmas Island and he's the one who ordered the drop of hundreds of cotton blouses to cover up the Native women before the arrival of the Brits. He himself had a hankering for Native women or, one of them, as he later married my mother after they met on Guam. He became a mining engineer. Hence, New Mexico and the chunk of ore.

Dr. Albaz, my mother died of hypertension in 1990 and I miss her still. Dad couldn't bear to stay in the home they'd shared and retired then to Bend here in Oregon. In fact it was his bone marrow I received and I stay at his place during treatment because the commute to my isolated homestead would be impossible. As you can imagine, I can't really discuss any of my concerns with him. He's in fine health for a 90-year-old man. But you are a scientist and can tell me if I'm right in assuming radioactivity will surely have more of a deleterious effect on a child still growing than on a grown man. Dad still says, "How can radiation be harmful? Radiation kills tumors, it doesn't cause them" and indeed this is where I now find myself.

Earlier this month a brain tumor was diagnosed and surgically excised on December 14. Unlike the weeks when I was symptomatic (headaches, seizures, falling, trouble finding words, which I at first put down to anxiety over the election results), I now find myself entirely lucid (unlike, one might suggest without being considered aberrant, the Supreme Court) but my doctors who do not this time even suggest or imply the word "cure" are rather insistent that I undergo Whole Brain Radiotherapy. With WBRT, I probably have another 2-3 years. I understand you are a scientist, not a medical doctor, so I am not asking your advice. Rather, my desire is that with the time remaining me I can make some small contribution to science. The Whole Brain Radiation, so they tell me, may interfere with my ability to use words and communicate so I write you on the eve of this event thinking I might be worth studying. While I can still communicate clearly, this is to say I am soon at your disposal. That sounds rather harsh! What I mean is, I must remain here in Bend with Dad during the two weeks of treatment after which you are more than welcome to visit me at my Five Rivers cabin where a bed awaits you and I do have a delightful woodstove and indoor plumbing. (I hope you are dog-friendly. I could not live without Monty! Also, meals will be vegetarian. I am still large: much pasta and bread. Hope you are not on gluten-free.)

Please respond to the Five Rivers address below as I do not want my father to know of this! Sincerely,
Alula Wright
P.S. Kind regards to Ms. Mulcahy.

*   *   *   *

December 20, 2001

Dear Dr. Almaz or Albaz, I guess right now I'm not sure but you know I mean you, with all due respect.

On this, the anniversary of my surgery, I am still among the living and it occurs to me that if an "angel" should wish to contribute funds to my independent research, I am still a few hundred short when it comes to the purchase of strontium, polonium (the soil recovered from Hanford does not appear to be sufficiently toxic) and thallium — though maybe you have access to these elements

and could provide? I thought I could obtain the cesium gratis, but the hospital waste closet was locked each time I checked. I have exhausted my savings and have obtained only 5 microcuries of cesium-137 and two ea. 1-microcurie cobalt-60.
Sincerely,
"Lu"

*   *   *   *

[undated]
Dear Dr. Albaz,
In my last letter, I neglected to mention that I plan to undertake research that may be of interest to you. Have you heard of mycoremediation?
all best,
"Lu"

*   *   *   *

Dear Ms. Wright,
You sound like a strong and brave woman. As you noted, I am not a medical doctor and while mycoremediation is indeed a field worthy of investigation, my training is as a hydrogeologist so it falls well outside my area of expertise. I do wish you all the best and continued health.
Sincerely,
Emine Albaz, Ph.D.

*   *   *   *

March 2, 2002
Dear Emine,

Hydro means water so perhaps you will be
interested in neurotoxin. Even though they boiled
the water. Which is hydro, isn't it, unless that
is hydrogen. The whole family died. Late snow
killed power lines and pumps then out of work.
On the radio the skin of one kills 25,000 mice (if I
put the comma in the right place) I'm writing you
in the morning when I am the most clear. It was a
ROUGH SKIN NEWT! in the water from the creek.
"Lu"

*　　*　　*　　*

April 3, 2003
Dear Emine,

What do you think of Closterium
moniliferum? I understand it can sequester
Strontium 90 which sounds like a talent indeed!
There is, in fact, an algae-choked pond on my Five
Rivers property but the question is: Is my green
pond algae in fact C.M.? Would you know it if you
saw it?
My invitation remains open.
Your friend,
Alula

*　　*　　*　　*

2003. in the Merry Month of May
Dearest Emine,

I hope this isn't inappropriate, but I want you to know I found pictures of you on the internet. You are beautiful. Though you've never come and we've never met, because of you, in these my last days, I live with Beauty and very much in love.

with all my heart,

Lu

File #4:

Borderlines

Rennie, Questioned

Once a day, the door opens. All day Rennie hears doors open and close until it's her turn. The chain comes off, the shackles go on. She walks like someone with advanced Parkinson's. She walks like a Chinese woman of another century with bound feet and she stumbles on purpose, to brush up against the guard. Human touch. She walks outside to the dogtrot, the narrow cage where she can stand and feel fresh air and if the weather is good, a touch of sun.

Chinese, we think, and we ask her about Dr. Tang.

She answers willingly. Always does but with digressions. To distract us or to revel in the attention? The only human contact she experiences is during interrogation.

"Two years ago, when I turned thirty, I went for the first time to a therapist. Why doesn't anyone love me? I asked and true to stereotype, she answered, Why do you think?

"I said, Because I'm a woman.

"But then Rorion loved me," she tells us. "And I learned, it's not really what I wanted after all. And guess what? I love my life as it is."

We think she's lying. "Or rather, what it was, when I was free. I wanted to live forever. You know more women die at the hands of an intimate partner than from car accidents and cancer combined."

"You seem to have many foreign friends."

She laughs. "This country doesn't educate its scientists. We have to import them."

We note a certain cynicism about the American Dream.

"Tang," we say.

"He went back to China, saying—I think, given his limited English—that he had better facilities there and full support of the government without having to scrounge—not the word he used—around for grants. First he invested in some San Gabriel Valley real estate, just in case, is what I think he said, because in China, you never know what comes next."

"Did he have access to classified information?"

She shrugs. "Maybe. Maybe not. He said what China needed, what he was carrying back, was how to use imagination. Creative problem-solving. He said education there is all rote. He's a genius there for scoring well on tests. He said American education is now like Chinese. He said, Too bad for you.

"But Emine," she says. "You can't possibly believe she's done anything wrong. Even if her husband...even if Oğuz..."

"Ohz? What did you say?"

"Her husband. Oğuz. Rhymes with rose."

Which is how we realized we'd been pronouncing it wrong. When our agents went to DHI and were met with denials—oggus? august? we don't know him—it's possible they weren't fucking with us after all.

"Even if," we prompted.

"Even if she said..."

"She said?"

"Over there she said he changed."

We said, *"Tell us about Dr. Oğuz Demir."*

A Special Meaning

Out of place. You could say that's true of almost everyone, everywhere, at least sometimes. But when applied to a Muslim traveling, working, studying, visiting friends, attending a wedding, offering charity, or doing any number of perfectly ordinary things, if he's doing it in a Muslim country not his own, the label is a license to abduct, detain, torture, interrogate or make a person disappear, in the name of US national security and the War on Terror.

Oğuz offered his medical services free of charge to people in great need in India, then a proudly secular country though, of course, then as now, predominantly Hindu. He should have been safe. And he could not have been happier.

The people he'd come to serve were not only Muslim but tribal and casteless and therefore as low on the untouchable ladder as it was possible to go. Being secular himself, the fact that their religious observance seemed closer to pagan than Islamic was a plus as was the fact that they spoke Hindi/Urdu no more than he did. Back home, people told him he would get to use his English in India, that everyone spoke it. It pleased him to think that once back in Istanbul, he would smile and say, "Rubbish," which seemed to be the only word of English, always said with indignation, that was known by the people who knew any at all which the tribals did not. And if he managed to learn their language? He would devote himself to mastering a tongue spoken by a handful of lice-ridden illiterates, a tribe on the path to extinction, a worthless endeavor. Perfect. You ask no thanks for zakat. You offer your charity in full humility and what could be more humiliating than this? Doctoring the most wretched people he'd ever seen, knowing full well that his medical bag of tricks would save no lives, and the tribals would go on being fucked whether he traveled with them or not. They were nomads. Outsiders scorned them, called them *Khānābādōsh*, and that's what he called them, though unsure if it was pejorative. Some people, he thought, move on to seek a better life. Some just move on. Like these. Though sometimes of course they are *chased* on by villagers throwing stones when they camp near streams and watercourses and the fields where their goats want to graze.

The day he arrived in India, the immigration official had flicked roaches off the papers in front of him in a gesture so unconscious and casual, Oğuz had been startled, but he adjusted quickly. Now he has outdone his pious brother in every way. Ethics and morality come from our humanity, not from God, is what Oğuz would tell him. It will be a pleasure to see Ahmet again, assuming, thought Oğuz, I don't die first of dysentery, cholera, dengue, or being bitten, mauled or rolled over upon by Seemah, the dancing bear that sleeps in the tent beside him, her canine teeth removed but the rest of her dentition intact, her front claws cut out while her sharp hind claws mean she is still well-armed.

Look at these people: after Partition when their kinsmen went to Pakistan, though Muslim, they'd remained in India, shrewdly realizing that Hindus celebrate more holidays and that meant more opportunities to earn. And so Oğuz trudged hundreds of miles on foot along with his chosen people with their tents and their animals. His feet blistered and bled, then grew hard.

Where there was water, there were crops, but they also crossed miles of scrub land and desert where the trees hardly had the strength to put out leaves so it was easy to spot peacocks and peahens on the bare branches. During the hour or two when you could look up without being blinded by the sun, he saw falcons plunge and pierce the sky. Life was hard for his people but just as hard, he thought, for the villagers they saw scratching a living from the land.

Considering everything, the nomads were remarkably healthy. His own digestive system was in a state of constant cramping revolt. Not theirs.

The donkeys were loaded with whatever the people couldn't carry on their backs. Whenever they approached a village, the goats were hitched to carts and in each cart rode a monkey or a dog. Drums beating, pipes wailing, the nomads announced their arrival. It was the best season of the year for them, in the villages the harvest just done, the sheaves of wheat, the sorghum and maize and sesame brought in and the villagers at home, enjoying a brief rest. They came out of their huts to be entertained. The dogs and monkeys jumped out of the carts and put on mock fights with much barking and shrieking and baring of teeth but nothing thrilled the crowds like Seemah.

By the time Oğuz met her, she was old, her fur was matted, bald in spots, her belly almost as light in color as a glass of Turkish beer. She wore more jewelry than any of the nomads. Oğuz noted that when food was scarce and the children and the monkeys had to go without, Seemah was fed first. No matter how bad things got, Seemah was petted and praised and fed.

He slept beside her in the tent and listened to her wheeze. The first few nights he couldn't sleep, alert to any hint she might roll over on him. Then he began to trust her.

Yes, she gave off a strong smell, but so did everyone in the tent. So did he. There was hardly enough water to make tea, certainly none to bathe in. The daily ablutions were often more symbolic than effective— two fingers dipped in a bowl, then pressed to the forehead. The worst nights were after Seemah had rolled around happily in refuse. The children picked through refuse looking for food, but they didn't roll in it.

He had hoped for the liberating shock to his system that exoticism provides. Yes, he knew even the word "exotic" was now offensive, but that's what he wanted: to be overwhelmed by difference. Instead, within days he took it all for granted. If the experience disappointed, he could be pleased at least with himself, finding nothing "exotic" in the dirt, the scratching, the rashes, the mouths with brown broken stumps that served more or less as teeth, the threadbare clothing held together with the salt of rank old sweat, the mangy dogs and bleating goats, angry monkeys, the smell, Allah preserve us, the smell, the parrot shitting contentedly on Baba's shoulder, Oğuz shitting till his guts are empty, the bear chained to a post during the day when not performing, sleeping in the tent like a big fat matriarch at night. In the tents, the closest thing to a bed was the single cot at the back on which a teapot, a radio and batteries, were laid as if at a shrine, while during the day, old women sat before it to guard the family's treasures. He was living among people. Ordinary and familiar. Something in the way Parveen held her head reminded him of his grandmother. Baba's blind eyes made him think of, and ache for, his sister-in-law Nasreen. And then, magically, like entertainers anywhere, they go into the village to perform and children squeal with joy and the bear dances and the monkeys ride on the backs of goats and then jump up on the shoulders of the young men and the musicians play and adults gather round captivated and Oğuz believes every sedentary villager wants to leave that sedentary life behind and live like the Khānābādōsh.

What do they need him for? The bear rolls over in the night and kicks and tears open the flesh on a man's leg and they staunch the blood and pack the wound with a mix of honey, turmeric, and cayenne and they heal without the use of the antibiotics they'll have to do without once Oğuz is gone. (They do argue, sometimes violently, about using or wasting food on injuries. And he mostly reserves the antibiotics for himself, he is constantly sick.) They could get betadine microbiocidal sprinkling powder in any Indian pharmacy, but they can't afford it. Maybe we in the West, he thought—he still insistently thought of Turkey as a European nation—we are too sanitary. We've weakened ourselves by separating ourselves from Nature, from the parasites and microbes we evolved with. We've declared war on germs instead of finding harmony. All sorts of ideas come to a person whose feet hurt. At home, squatting to relieve himself, there would be clean white tiles and from the tap a stream of crystal-clear water to clean his hand. Here, nothing but a barren field as he empties his bowels.

In the desert, his eyes are drawn again and again to the damp spots of ground, what Emine would call "seeps" but seeps are places where underground water surfaces and what Oğuz stares at are the places where animals including humans have unleashed their streams of urine. The black mud is what comes out of the behinds of water buffalo, glistening until it bakes and dries, and then the only glisten comes from the wings of flies, buzzing, lit by the sun.

Mother India! If he were ever going to believe in anything spiritual, he would believe it here where every beggar has the powers of a swami. By what merely human agency can you explain how skeletal men and women who haven't had a meal in days or a restful night's sleep walk tirelessly up and down high shaking construction-site ladders with loads of concrete on their heads—and this is not a concentration camp, it's ordinary daily life? Or how people drink unboiled water with turds floating in it, how the children play in sewage, how people plagued with infection and disease grow old and never seem to die?

He is ready and able to set broken bones, suture wounds but they'd rather do without. Misshapen limbs and scars are good for begging. He tries to teach about cleanliness and sanitation, but they live in a world without water. He treats eye infections in the children with antibiotic ointment but he'll leave and they will be infected again and again until their corneas scar.

When he sees spills, red and wet, he no longer tries to distinguish blood from paan-spittle from pomegranate crushed underfoot. A spill of red is just that: a red spill.

If he were the sort of man who speaks to Allah, he would pray for this: that he be granted the favor of being shown something, anything, he could offer.

The Man with the Bear

The day after he sees his first camels—at a distance, but still prickling him with excitement—they are ushered into an ambush. A village elder who looks like every other village elder—dirty turban, betel-stained mouth—leads them to a collection of thatched-roof mud huts. There's a giant white shade umbrella mounted much too high to do much good. No, it's a satellite dish, he realizes as they enter not a village but a military outpost. In the distance, the road and the scrub will run out and, he thinks, there will be sand and dunes all the way to Pakistan.

Seemah is grabbed by her rope. Monkeys shriek and scatter to the rooftops, goats bleat and cry, and the people are surrounded by men in uniforms.

The nomads have uniforms of their own for when they dress up and impersonate government officials and go into rural settlements and terrify people—not to defraud them, but as entertainment, to get them all worked up over some claimed infraction and then reveal themselves as itinerant actors. Villagers take pleasure in being frightened just as city people do at horror films. They laugh and reward the Khānābādōsh with coins and food. (The more convinced and frightened you've been, the more you are honor-bound to pay.) But the nomads' costumes do not include firearms and these men in uniform carry weapons. What Oğuz notices even more is that the soldiers are cleanshaven except for their neat moustaches. They must have soap and water and mirrors, he thinks. Most likely toilets, too, and he wonders if he'll have the chance to use one.

The soldiers use heavy sticks rather than their rifles to push and prod as though they value their weapons too much to bring them in contact with dirty bodies and rags. They enter a large hut, primitive on the outside but inside there are desks, phones, computers, a big screen. It's comfortably cool inside—not for our benefit, he thinks, but for the electronics. Baba ignores the rows of folding chairs and sits himself crosslegged on the ground. Not enough room for everyone to do the same, not with all the chairs that no one thinks to fold and stow and so people stand close together, body heat warming the air. And now they are faced with something worse than a military border patrol: social workers and animal welfare officers.

The woman handed out leaflets printed in many languages. People accepted them eagerly, good for sanitary use. Only Oğuz could read it: Bears are tortured. Claws pulled out. Red-hot needles piercing the nose so a dirty rope can be pulled through. Terrible pain. And then the beatings. (You might agree and yet argue: Why was it OK to castrate a water buffalo and train it to pull a plow? It was legal to ride a camel. Why? Why was it OK to kill and roast a goat?)

The woman thanked the post commander. She spoke the nomad's language first and then repeated herself in Hindi. "The bear will be cared for and allowed to rest and heal." The man with her translated into English.

Then the man spoke. "We tried to help you by peaceful means, but now we are run into the blank wall."

When he turned his back to the crowd and tapped at the computer keyboard, Oğuz took a seat. Whenever there was a presentation, PowerPoint or video, there were tech problems. Something was always incompatible with something else. Someone would fiddle with the equipment and then someone else and usually after 45 minutes they would give up and the presentation would resume without the visuals. But here, the big screen lit up immediately. Oğuz was impressed; the Khānābādōsh weren't. They'd seen it all before. The photos of the government housing and the clinic and the school and the videos of smiling now-sedentary former nomads repeating the words they'd been induced to repeat.

Baba wagged his finger. "In your cities, people live in the street. People live on top of rubbish heaps. In shelters made of cardboard. All you care is to make people stay put. In relief camps, people live in tents. We have good tents, but because we carry our house on shoulders, you persecute us."

A little boy elbowed his way to the front of the room and nudged the social workers aside. "Rubbish!" he said. Oğuz had never been able to tell the boy's age. From his size, he seemed no more than three, and he still had what looked like all his baby teeth, but he was more mature and independent than Oğuz himself had been at ten. Hussain had learned a lot while begging in internet cafes. He spoke some English and he had the respect of the adults. He worked at the keyboard. "Rathergood.com," he announced, and the people murmured happily, moved close, and gathered round to watch the cats.

They saw the cat that jumped into a box and closed the lid and then opened it again and leapt out carrying a prize. The cat up on its hind legs having a fist fight with a child. Two cats playing ping pong. Kittens playing guitars. They'd seen this before but never got tired of it, especially the man swinging the rope around his head, the cat leaping up to catch it and swinging with it, body flying like a banner. It was a trick but they hadn't yet figured out how it was done. Everyone knew you couldn't train a cat. If you could, they might not need so many monkeys.

While they watched the cats, the uniformed men outside led Seemah into the back of a truck and darted her and went after the monkeys and the people stopped watching the cats when the monkeys began shrieking and shitting. They ran outside in time to see four goats hanging by their hind legs, throats slit. The soldiers tried to herd the people into the trucks but they weren't authorized to dart them so in the end they let them be. The trucks drove off with Seemah and some monkeys while others remained on the rooftops, throwing shit at people, teeth bared. One of the soldiers aimed his rifle and shot. A monkey fell. A little girl was crying, her arms around a surviving goat, her face buried against its flank. The people cried out and Baba led them away.

Once the outpost was gone from sight, the old man sat in the dirt, the people around him. Oğuz listened without understanding until the boy Hussein squatted beside him. "He say, The Khānābādōsh is the man with the bear. I am no longer a man." Baba had already lost his son, his sight, most of his teeth. Now Seemah. "Why should food go down my gullet?" he said. "Now I am no one."

Dislocation

Oğuz stood on the upper deck enjoying the wind on his body, giddy with happiness. But where was Emine?

She wasn't back at the seats they'd claimed by the window. Hungry, maybe. Thirsty? Seeking out the cafe? He went down to the lower deck of the ferry. No Emine. He climbed the back stairs. The calm sea became troubled; the floor shifted beneath his feet. He grabbed at the wall like a drunken man and stumbled down to the toilets. Knocked on the doors. Emine! Emine!

There was another deck, lower still, one he hadn't known about. Down he went and down and down and down and when he woke in the tent, it took a moment for the agitation in his pulse to calm. Emine was in California, she wasn't lost, there was no reason to be anxious, she was meeting him in New Delhi soon, and he knew exactly where he was. He smelled at once the bear's rank odor and that one of the children had peed again, the urine evaporating instantly in the desert air, leaving only the smell. Baba snored loudly, Seemah the bear softly, Jamila's breath whistled through her nose and she groaned in her sleep, a sound that made him sad to think that even in her dreams the pains in her hardworked body never left her. The children's bodies seemed to hum.

Where had the dream taken him? The Sea of Marmara, or the Black Sea?

He was in India. He knew where he was and why. He knew she was coming to meet him. What more could a person ask?

Kerida, mi amor

New Delhi, airport terminal. The crowd circled, swirled, unfurled like smoke. Extended families, children asleep in piles of colorful fabric on the floor, adults with palms pressed together in greeting, devotees waiting for their guru with garlands of marigolds, circles of orange flowers that made Emine think of the sunflowers of Anatolia, the women bending in the fields, the rumps of their floral trousers in the air. Men and women bent to the ground touching the feet of the man in saffron. There, the official greeters with their signs in English and other scripts tried to stand their ground, but where was Oğuz? In the midst of the spiraling and twisting crowd, the businessmen with their laptops, their garment bags, she could pick out individuals, but could not yet see him anywhere while everything moved around her, a startled flock of sparrows, chirping and twittering, she thought, all around her a moving breathing double helix, life becoming what it was meant to be.

"Kerida!" His voice was all she recognized.

Every day for months she had missed him. These last weeks, her vacation days growing near and knowing she would be with him soon, Emine had allowed herself fantasies of their reunion, the restraint that would be forced on their passion and hunger in the airport, in the taxi, until they could be alone, but now, his arms around her, she held him tentatively. He was skeletal, his stomach grumbled against her body, the beard—and Oğuz had always been clean-shaven—didn't hide his sunken cheeks, the dried and broken skin on the lips he pressed to hers. She wanted to take him at once to a clinic, not to bed.

"Mi amor," she said. Then lost him to the airport bathroom.

In the taxi, they held hands. His fingers trembled and twitched.

She smelled cooking oil, charcoal, diesel, brick dust, all of it coating her skin and hair.

By the sides of the road, women carried loads of brick and stone on their heads. His new eyeglasses made Oğuz look even more unfamiliar, the frames heavy thick black on top, clear plastic on the bottom. The lenses scratched and pitted. She assumed from blowing sand. And were the lenses tinted? The whites of his eyes seemed yellow.

"Darling, you look...are you well?"

"Just some parasites," he said. "I've been in Delhi for days, got some pills."

At construction sites, slender wand-like poles pointed to the sky. Emine ticked off the city's architecture: British, Mughal, Modern India, Third World. Broad avenues and traffic circles suddenly impassable with crowds. A protest demonstration or was this normal? There was a man, almost naked, just rags over his privates, his bony shoulders, his ribs so defined you could count each bone, she feared this is what Oğuz would look like without his clothes. The man's hair and his beard long and black, black soot smeared over his body. His mouth bright red—must be, she thought, that betel nut they chew here. It can't—mustn't—be blood. In his right hand he carried a human skull. No one but Emine gave him a second glance. And then he was lost to sight as the driver honking and swerving took them around the rotary.

There's no shock of the strange when you expect the unfamiliar, she thought. The shock is when the person you know and love best in the world turns strange.

Green and yellow auto rickshaws waited at the railway station, lined up in the first orderly arrangement she'd seen in India.

Their hotel room was gloomy but nice enough that she was somewhat surprised they'd let someone who looked like Oğuz book it. She wanted to take care of him. She wondered if this was how men felt sometimes with women, that making love would be an act of violence, too much for a human being who seemed so fragile. So much for fantasy! And in this dreary room—so many tones of brown—maybe to hide the dirt? But everything seemed to be clean. Instead of the usual hotel decor, small framed photographs of a man and woman who would surely be well known to Indians.

He closed himself in the bathroom.

When he emerged: "It's a luxury. Months of squatting in a field." He waggled his head like an Indian. "Did they feed you on the plane?" her husband asked. "Would you like to get something to eat?"

"I'm tired more than hungry. And I'd love a shower." She expected he would join her.

"Go ahead," he said. "Enjoy."

"You look like a mullah." It wasn't what she'd meant to say.

He didn't understand at first. Then his fingers went to his beard. "In the field, nick yourself and get a nasty infection." He turned away from her and went back to the bathroom to shave.

She tried to follow but he closed the door.

It Seemed Perfectly Sane to Him

They sat side by side on the brown bedspread.

"Let's go home," she said.

"What do you mean?"

"To Istanbul."

"You feel guilty, coming here and not there, to see your family."

"That's not it," she said. "Let's not ever do this again. Living on different continents, living completely different lives."

"Yes, yes, of course," he said. "But we have to finish what we started."

Hectic flush, she thought, a phrase from the old novels she'd read when first learning English. The bright red spots on his now-clean though sunken cheeks, the fervor—fever—in his eyes. In those novels, the teacher explained, it was code for TB. She put her arms around him. To calm him, to cool him.

"The people I'm traveling with," he said. "They are extraordinary. Spectacular"—Extravagant words, not the sort of words the man she married would use. Oğuz, kerido, where is my Oğuz? "We think of wellbeing as health and wealth. That's our privilege. While to them, what they most fear losing is their culture. Their essential identity."

"So if your doctoring is not valued, you are free to go."

"Emine, kerida," he said, "these people have nothing and they have shared everything with me. I must repay them."

Then he told her, as though it were a perfectly sane idea, that he would go to Pakistan and acquire a bear cub and smuggle it back to India to replace confiscated Seemah.

The idea was mad, and she was crazy too to have imagined this would be a week of lovemaking and sightseeing. Sightseeing! She'd made a list: the Red Fort, Birla Mandir, Chandni Chowk, the Garden of the Five Senses, Jama Masjid. That's what she needed to think of now, think of that list, think of anything but what you are hearing and thinking now. And she thought of the man with the tambourine back home who waited outside for the school day to end. *Bam bam* and the bear would stand, holding onto a staff to keep himself upright.

"I'll meet up with them again," said Oğuz. "I know they'll be outside Talhan, for the festival at the mazaar of a Sufi saint."

How did he imagine he could cross the border? Two hostile nations.

"People used to cross all the time," he said. "They used to go through the Thar, the desert, but lately there have been...incidents. Then, of course, guards can be bribed. I won't even need to do that, not with a Turkish passport and visa, and the bear drugged asleep in a sack."

"They asked you to do this?" she said.

"No. Not at all."

"If those people have put you in this position—"

No. It was his own idea.

She thought of what Maria had told her of parasites that can brain-jack creatures, overriding their truest instincts. She should say that to

Oğuz, in a joking tone of course, that he'd been brainjacked. Rennie said mixed marriages were best. When men love their mothers, other woman never measure up. If they hate their mother, they resent their wives when they remind them of her. But a wife who doesn't look like Mom is freed of all those expectations. Her different race, religion, culture liberate both her and her man. It was true he spoke his love-words in Ladino, a language his mother didn't know and couldn't understand. So what did that mean now, when Emine felt more like a mother—wiser and more worried—than a wife? Like a mother she rocked him, held him to her breast.

Somewhere in the distance people were chanting, there were drums. In spite of herself, she kept straining to hear.

Oğuz sighed, then slept. She didn't.

The Two People

"You're probably right about the bear."

Probably, she noted, but said nothing. It was surely as far as he was willing to go.

"I'll go to Peshawar anyway," he said. "See what Ahmet is up to."

To show off how weak and ill you look, she thought. Beat him at the zakat competition.

"But let's not wait," he said. "Let's start a family. Now."

"Yes," she said. She took his face in her hands. He reached for her hands and moved them away.

He said, "There's someone—actually two people—I want you to meet."

And this was the reason—not economy—that Oğuz hadn't booked them into a better hotel. The Sheraton would never have let the "two people" past the door. Two young prostitutes barely out of their teens, if that, and there they stood, the four of them Amina, Rana, Emine, and Oğuz, in line at the hotel's breakfast buffet. The smell of frying eggs and the girls' pomade left Emine nauseated. The prostitutes chattered excitedly, filled their plates.

Here was one more cultural tradition any government would have the right—the obligation—to stop. *Six months of the year, Oğuz told her, their husbands stay in the village. Their tribe thinks it's impolite for unmarried girls to sell their bodies. Six months a year, the married women travel for their work.*

Slices of mango and orange. Omelets—masala and Western-style. Puffy breads. Oatmeal. French toast. Salted fish and seaweed as toppings for steamed rice.

"No. I don't want anything. Maybe just some tea."

Jewels in their noses once would have seemed exotic and were now customary in the US; bangles up and down the arms; eyes downcast, then flashing up, lined with kohl. Fabric over their heads—what was it called?—that kept slipping down off their hair.

Oğuz had taken them to a clinic. They were clean, he said, disease-free. And India a leader in reproductive technology.

They sat at a table, a perfectly ordinary table with a clean white tablecloth. Oğuz stirred his oatmeal. The girls ate using their right hands. They paid no attention to the conversation in a strange language.

They'll rent their wombs, not their vaginas. Nine months instead of six.

Emine poured tea, held the teacup hoping it could warm her hands.

If the timing isn't right, extend your stay. We pay them enough to get them started in a business, or school, in a different life. We finish with our obligations abroad, and return home with two babies.

She closed her eyes, placed her hands over her stomach. Any child of ours, she thought, will grow right here. But no words came. For the first time, she wondered if there would ever be such a child. Dupatta, she thought. That's what the long scarf is called, at least I think so. I have vocabulary, she thought, I have words, but something stopped them, no channel now between mind and mouth. Nothing came out.

The tea didn't help. Nothing helped. Something iced over between her hearing and her mind, the words entered her ears but slid and skidded and didn't always arrive in the right order or at all as he talked on and on, how the children should spend school vacations with the Khānābādōsh, could he possibly have said that, really?, how the Khānābādōsh stimulate their babies all the time for fear they might die of boredom, how little children of 4 or 5 years old walk miles and learn languages and go out to beg and any child who brings in money has a vote equal to that of any adult in the council, independent, intelligent, resourceful, self-reliant, our children can be—

Emine retreated deeper and deeper into the cold. As she headed for the elevator, whatever happened behind her would happen: the girls chattering and eating; Oğuz, the stranger, paying the bill.

She took a wrong turn. Instead of the elevator, she was at the entrance, the turbaned attendant nodding his head, opening the door, and there he was again, that man with the skull. She couldn't help herself. She started to cry.

"Memsahib?" The attendant.

And Oğuz was there, taking her arm, leading her back inside, the way she had led Nasreen across the street in Ankara. What was wrong with the Demir brothers, that Oğuz could have such ideas, that Ahmet could have left his blind wife and their child behind? She pulled free.

Still Her Husband

"I'm changing my ticket. I'm going back to California."

There he was before her, still her husband, his collarbone jutting out beneath the new thin cotton shirt that replaced the lice-ridden rags he'd thrown away to be ready for her.

"Please," he said. "I thought you would like the idea. We'll forget about it."

How does a person forget such a thing, she thought.

In her fantasies, they'd throbbed, electric, their bodies charged, he, exploding inside her, sending the reverberations through her with enough power to change the course of stars. Instead they were tentative and gentle. Only enough heat to let him melt, enough to dispel for a short while the coldness that filled her.

Just a Saint

She didn't change her ticket. In the morning they walked the girls over to the train station. Oğuz bought their tickets and gave them money. I'm sorry, thought Emine. I'm sorry for how you must live, but I can't change it for you.

There he was again, the almost naked man, his mouth red, the skull held in his right hand. "What is that man? Who is he?" she asked.

Oğuz spoke to the girls in their language. Amina answered.

Oğuz said, "She says he's just a saint."

What was alarming to her was, in this culture, normal. Emine said, "I see him everywhere."

Amina grabbed an end of her dupatta and covered her face. Then she reached to touch Emine's arm. Rana pulled her back and spoke to Oğuz.

"She asks has he been following you," he said.

A week lay ahead, seven days to act as though all was well.

"I'm sorry," she whispered. "I'm truly sorry about their lives." Oğuz slept peacefully beside her. She couldn't sleep. All the honking, honking in the street. She was so tired, her heart pounding, her ears clogged, so exhausted it seemed strange she was still alive. This must account for her bad attitude, her confusion. "You are a good man," she said. "You are my love."

Why did the words come so easily when he was not awake to hear them?

His glasses all scratched by the sand. No wonder the poor man couldn't see straight.

He was the better person, always had been. Oğuz became a doctor to relieve suffering. While she—she had gone to America the way he had gone to India, with something to prove. In her case, environmental remediation, save the planet, help humankind, when really, all she cared about was water and rock. She had to show him she could put her private fascination to social use while he was showing Ahmet the most noble jihad. The jihad of war and terror was the lowest kind, easily given to corruption. Ahmet's was the higher jihad of spirituality and service to God. For Oğuz, it was clear that God, should he exist, needed nothing from us. He believed the most noble jihad is to sacrifice oneself to serve men and women in need.

Look at the consequences of your selfish sacrifice, she thought. I can hardly recognize you, my darling saint.

We'll be all right, she thought. The only life that makes sense to me is with you. Not the life that was expected of me in Istanbul.

Tell your cousin how talented she is! Her cousins were beautiful but that was all they had to do: look beautiful, get married, give birth, and then: *Praise her watercolors. Tell her they are marvelous, otherwise she'll be so sad.* Emine had escaped this life. *Ask your aunt to play the piano. Tia, what a delight to hear you play!* Clunk clunk. And then her mother's favorite treat, teatime at the Hilton entertained by that same dreadful string quartet, Alas, poor Mozart!, they could have been pulling gears and shafts in a factory. Her mother in her best blue dress, smiling and nodding her head to the beat. Emine so superior to this and so relieved. She would never be bored and useless. She had Oğuz with whom she never had to pretend, with whom she was never polite and indulgent. He laughed with her about the Hilton and so much else, not to make fun of her mother—she loved and respected her mother, of course she did—but because he understood. They shared a culture. Cosmopolitan. Careful now: she was not a rootless cosmopolitan—that old slur against Jews. She was a cosmopolitan who loved her roots. She and Oğuz felt very much at home in Paris or Los Angeles, in Zurich or London. But sorry, my love, I am not comfortable squatting to relieve myself in a field or sleeping in a tent with wild beasts.

If I keep this up, not eating, not sleeping, I'll be the one who needs help. Not Oğuz in spite of his crazy notions. Those girls. The bear.

That bear in Istanbul, she remembered. He didn't really dance. He was smiling, or so it seemed, in spite of the strap around his muzzle, and the necklace of beads. The chain looked so delicate, as though it couldn't hold anything weightier than a pocket watch, and like a watch chain it linked onto the man's pocket opposite from where a white handkerchief drooped out of his waistband like a sad old flag. The man hit the drum and waited for the children to give money.

It shouldn't be allowed, her mother said.

But he looks like he's smiling. Oso oroso, she thought.

Those girls laughed and smiled so easily.

A grimace, said her mother.

She would have expected what? Eyes that were dead or filled with pain, fear, shame. The girls seemed—she found no other word—confident. What could she know of their lives? Women got burned alive here, didn't they, when they didn't bring in a big dowry while those girls were valued, born equipped with a trade. The men might hurt them, beat them. Maybe their husbands were violent, too. Maybe making love—no, having sex—with their husbands was just as much a chore as when they were paid. She knew nothing, nothing. If she didn't stop thinking, she would start to cry. Thinking of women in Afghanistan. Women in Pakistan. While she was free and sleepless, fussing over a disagreement with the man who loved her, whom she loved and had chosen.

They used to talk about everything for the sheer pleasure of it, though so much of the time they were in such natural agreement, they didn't need to speak.

She touched his face, lightly, so as not to wake him and whispered to him. "Mi korazon."

All Oğuz wanted was to do something good in this world, a world where some Muslims preached hate and others were hated. It didn't have to be that way.

She thought of an evening in Glendale, California, she and Oğuz were looking for the Cuban restaurant when they smelled the lahmajun. They didn't discuss a change of plans. They simply followed the aroma. Then they didn't have to talk, each knew exactly what the other was feeling as they hesitated in front of the bakery window, staring at the Armenian letters on the glass. The man behind the counter understood perfectly, too. He came to the door and threw it open: Karşılama, sıcak karşılama! offering a warm welcome in Turkish, letting them know that to him they were not perpetrators of genocide but good, decent people, his fellow countrymen far from home.

Rennie

I don't even know what a material witness is. Chained to the concrete floor, stainless steel toilet with no seat, a slot through which meals are pushed—inedible for the most part. It is very cold. So cold my nose bleeds. The dark circles under my eyes are not from lack of sleep but the pressure of my eyeballs against tender skin. I have no audience. If I were a terrorist, I could imagine enduring this for the cause. The only cause I've got is to hold onto my own humanity in spite of. Nelson Mandela did it. For years. But he believed in something. I'm a white American. The only cause I have is myself and I'm not sure that Rennie is enough.

Humanity. Like that's supposed to be a good thing.

He Who Governs the Border

Marty Keller handed over his passport and the agent looked up and spoke in a language that was incomprehensible though all too familiar. It hadn't occurred to him that traveling on a German passport he'd be expected to spreche Deutsch in Turkey. He'd never wanted to learn his mother's mother tongue, the only words he knew were *Komme hier* and *Fuß*—the canine commands she had used to train Baboo. *Sitz, Plotz, Warte.* Of course he did know *Danke*, which is what he said, reaching out to recover his little red Reisepass, now duly stamped.

As the child of a German citizen—in spite of her marriage to his long absent father and her 30 years in the US, he'd acquired dual nationality. She'd insisted on it: *You can never have too many passports. You never know...* But she did know. His mother knew everything, all the time, very clear in black and white, no shades of gray, beyond a shadow of a doubt. He had only to object to one of her pronouncements when she'd cut him off: *Stop being such a nuance!* Then she'd laugh her throaty laugh because it wasn't a malapropism but a joke. Her English was perfect.

Komme hier, mein Liebe—her love, the dog.

When he got to Evergreen State, away from her for the first time, he felt so good he stopped taking his meds. He didn't feel so good now, trying to outrun his doubts.

In Istanbul he chose the wrong taxi, or maybe exactly the right one. Outcomes are always uncertain, how can you know the ultimate effect of a change of plans? This driver simply did not want to take him to the address he'd copied from a *Lonely Planet* guide, thumbing through it in Barnes and Noble. The city outside the window reminded him of New York the one time he'd been there, with his mother, checking out possible colleges. Columbia, NYU (*NYJew*, she'd said). Sidewalks full of people rushing, construction everywhere, the occasional woman in some kind of babushka adding the touch of exoticism that immigrants gave the streets of Manhattan. He never thought of his mother as an immigrant.

The driver spoke to him in German. From Nietzsche, Marty had learned to be cynical, to expect amoral self-interest in those he met. From Zoroaster, he'd learned to seek the best in each man and woman, to trust others the way he himself wanted to be trusted, to judge strangers only as he himself would want to be judged, and so he acquiesced, *Danke, danke*, to a gleaming highrise on a boulevard of identical hotels, on a street without shrubbery or grass or flowers and yet busy with life: teashops and rug merchants and women rushing up to female tourists to tie headscarves on them murmuring compliments, *çok güzel* (as the guidebook had warned), holding hand mirrors up to the startled faces, and then asking for money, vendors of Kurdish music cassettes—weren't those illegal? He walked through the crowd into the lobby. Whatever the hotel lacked in character—unless maybe this very lack was the character of the new century, the 21st—it was clean, air conditioned, and to his surprise, cheap.

He murmured a blessing on the driver: *ushtâ ahmâi ẏahmâi ushtâ kahmâichît.*

The taxi driver walks—or drives—in righteousness. Score one for Zoroaster.

The Consulate of the Islamic Republic of Iran would not have looked out of place in Paris, he thought, without his ever having been there. Mouse-colored stone (not quite gray, not quite brown), pediment windows tall enough to stand in, all behind wrought-iron gates and guarded by two crouching lions on their columns.

The US passport used to be the passport to the world, but when he'd applied for the visa as an American, he was denied.

He was carefully shaved but casually dressed. He'd decided a formal look would work against him. Coming across like a Mormon missionary, he'd never get a visa that way. If he was a German, he needed to look hearty, a footballer, a trekker, a distance cyclist (which was what he did in fact plan to be). He'd lost more than twenty pounds in training but his cheeks were still red and full. German. Under his breath he repeated the phrases his aunt had taught him. Lucky for him (or due to his mother's foresight) his name—Martin Keller, worked in both languages. (And if he did decide to convert? Mardan—though that was maybe presumptuous, meaning *King of men*. Marzban, perhaps, *He who governs the border*.)

"Guten Morgen. Ich möchte ein Visum."

The man behind the desk sighed. "Do you speak English? Parlez-vous français?"

"English," said Marty. "I would like a visa."

"Tourist?"

"I wish to ride a bicycle in your country."

The man took his passport. "Come back tomorrow."

"Tomorrow?"

"Tomorrow. Morgen. À demain.»

A Dual Nature

You can never have too many passports. If the Turkish authorities stopped him, he still had one.

What else did he have? A round-the-world air ticket round a world hurtling toward destruction. And he was part of the problem! Air travel! Carbon footprint! His plan to cross Iran on a bike—that, at least, Brent would approve of, but what did Brent's approval matter to him now? "You're not like some of them," Brent had said to him, "always seeking approval." Of course not. Martin had learned early in life that approval was something he would never have. "People who want to be liked aren't security conscious. They talk," Brent had said.

At Evergreen, Marty read Nietzsche, *Thus Spake Zarathustra*, and learned that after God died, the worst sin was to blaspheme the earth. That led him to Brent Fassen who spoke of saving the earth and for whom God was very much alive. Then his philosophy professor urged him to research the real original Zoroaster of ancient Persia, the prophet Marty soon took to calling Zorro, not, he insisted, out of disrespect but to draw closer, erasing the centuries and continents that stood between them.

His studies left him two-faced, dual-natured. Martin had two Martins inside him—which had nothing to do with the diagnosis of bipolar. Choose! choose! The will to power or The will to righteousness. To become almost godlike, the Übermensch—so there! he did know a German word or two. Or to see the divine not only in himself but equally in all. Consume the earth, or save it? He'd taken a semester's leave from school to join Brent's crusade and Lori had gone with him. When the time came to take action, security meant he had to push her away. But could he act? Could he be a nihilist with high ideals? Amoral while answering to a higher morality? Instead of following Brent's plan, he panicked.

Probably an overreaction. Probably nothing would have happened. It was probably just a test. Unless it wasn't.

Confiding in his mother was out of the question. *Mother, I adore you*, he'd said once, a little boy wanting her attention. He got a hard slap. *Adoration is for God. He is imaginary. I am real.* But when he was desperate to get away, she bought him the ticket, approvingly, his Wanderjahr. If nothing else, she was generous.

First stop, Frankfurt, Aunt Bettina. So different from her sister. Even her voice soft and caressing. When she was his age, she'd camped out in caves in Tunisia. She thought his adventure would be fabulous, she said she'd go with him except she didn't want to cramp his style. Oh, the solitude! as well as the chance to meet local people. It was so much harder to do when you traveled with a companion. She brushed back her long hair and pushed her glasses back up the bridge of her nose and taught him to say *Ich möchte ein Visum*. She took him to eat döner kebab at a Turkish cafe. "Make time," she said, "for Topkapi and the Blue Mosque"—advice no different than you'd find in any guidebook.

He woke up on her couch, heart racing, lips repeating *Ich möchte ein Visum* faster and faster and faster. He wanted to wake her and tell her about Brent, everything. It weighed heavily, both his cowardice and his guilt.

Are we not a part of Nature? Is not Nature amoral? If we are to defend the environment of which we are a living, breathing and at the moment a thoroughly destructive part, how dare we impose human morality on our actions?

He had dared.

In the morning all he said was he wanted to buy a backpack. Here, in Frankfurt, for the German label. And a few shirts, cycling shorts.

She laughed. "Too many Cold War spy novels, Martin. With globalization, what does a label prove? Anything can be manufactured anywhere."

"The care instructions," he said.

"Ah, yes. You're right."

Unlike his mother, his aunt was entirely comfortable admitting she was wrong.

"Are you nervous?" she asked him. "Scared?"

"Yes," he admitted.

At the bank, they changed $500 to German marks and purchased some lira. In Tehran he would change marks to rials. Because of sanctions, his credit card could not be used there.

"You're not a liar," Bettina assured him. "Fooling an unreasonable government doesn't count." She lightly punched his arm. "Iran will not be so dangerous for you as at home."

Had he told her and then forgotten? Impossible. But she knew.

When he returned to the Consulate, passport and visa were waiting, no questions asked, along with a gift of shortbread cookies topped with pistachios. What a shame Zoroastrians were persecuted in Iran. He loved the country already.

Hello, My Friend, Hello

The German doctor who sat beside him on the plane mistook him for Canadian and Marty let him. In Tehran, his luggage came quickly.

Passing through immigrations and customs, changing money, all of it easy, a breeze. Crowds waited to greet the passengers, there to greet everyone but him, but outside the terminal as he began to reassemble his bike, people gathered round to watch. Put the pedals back on. Reinflate the tires. Men nodding their heads and smiling, taxi drivers coming over for a look, women who'd gone out the women's exit rejoining their men, then hanging back just a little as they watched him, cautious in a public place. And he was cautious too, don't stare at them, he warned himself, the way their head coverings draped so gracefully to reveal high pure foreheads, a soft lock of hair, the cowls somehow setting off the women's eyes so that they glowed, remarkably big and deep. And don't look at the men in green.

"Hello, my friend, hello," male voices coming from all directions in a strange mix of hearty and tentative, not one thing, not the other, while the men in green uniforms kept their distance but kept watching. The men who circled round him, close, wore polyester pants in blue and brown and tan. He smelled his own sweat and the men's cologne and the oil as he checked the bicycle chains.

"English?"

"Yes," he said because English is what he spoke.

"The English," said a bearded man. "Always interfering."

A man crouched beside him. "My brother, she live London. And you?"

Another man crouched next to him. "My cousin—Los Angeles. Tehrangeles."

So he might as well tell the truth. "I live north of LA."

"Maybe you know him?" The man blushed, his olive skin ripening like a plum.

Hugs, backslaps, even men kissing him on both cheeks. Welcome welcome welcome. So much for the Great Satan.

He hoisted his pack onto his back, fastened the sleeping bag to the bike. He pedaled off into the smog and car exhaust to the sounds of honking, not in warning but in farewell. If he thought the cards stuck in the spokes would click to let drivers know of his presence, he was wrong. Even he couldn't hear their sound as he biked along, drivers and passengers waving and the enemies of his country cheering and applauding as off he went on his quest.

He followed a motorbike as it threaded between cars. Some he could not identify at all. Others, obsolete model Chevies and Fords, he recognized from old TV shows on cable. Through the smog and the dust, there was the smell of something roasting, burning, the appetizing smell of something charred but filled as he was with inspiration, he had no need of food. There were construction cranes and yellow wedges dividing the road. Drab faceless buildings but faces everywhere on billboards. Everything oversized: bearded turbaned men loomed huge, coming at him in fragments, then a giant toothbrush. The Ayatollah Khomeini, dead now, his stern face. As Marty passed, the Ayatollah winked.

Impossible.

It was too much. There was too much to see until he felt as though his eyes could no longer see anything.

Where did I get the idea I could do this? Why headscarves? People here should wear gas masks. If he'd left the bike in its box, he could have taken a cab to the outskirts of the city. Not now. Was that a mountain in the distance, through the haze? He wished he were back in Frankfurt, eating dinner with his aunt, someone who didn't see his enthusiasm as pathology. He had such nostalgia now for Frankfurt: only a couple of days ago his journey was still thrillingly before him. Stranded on the sidewalk by a traffic circle he drank from his water bottle. "English? English?" he asked.

"Where do you want to go?" asked a woman, black garment, high forehead, big gray eyes. Her little girl held by the hand, already in headscarf, just like in America, he thought, dressed to push her into womanhood too fast.

"Out of the city, please. The highway south."

He was surrounded again. Pedestrians gestured, men rolled their hands like exaggerated courtiers in comedies, a woman offered him pistachios, a woman offered tea—in this heat, hot tea!—and the men were waving down panel trucks and pickups. There was shouting and honking every time someone pulled over and traffic stopped.

The first, the truck bed full with flats of—he couldn't believe it— bottles of Coca-Cola, and no room for him.

The second, hauling trash. Relieved it wasn't going his way.

A white van stopped. *No no no* said his new friends.

And so on till *Yes yes, come come welcome*, he hoisted his bike into the back where two little boys rode along with a stack of tires chained together, a pile of newspapers tied with twine, a broken swivel chair, a tool box, a box spring and a rolled-up rug. One boy whispered to two sparrows in the birdcage he held on his lap though he glanced shyly up at Marty once or twice. The other never lifted his face from his Game Boy. They headed into the pink haze where a yellow glow at the horizon marked the setting sun.

In His Solitude

Thank you, thank you, why the hell hadn't he learned to say *thank you* in Persian? Or Farsi, or whatever it was called instead of learning from the internet a few ancient prayers in an ancient tongue. The father gestured to Marty to get down, pointed first at the sleeping bag and then to a road. Off he went toward what seemed to be a mosque under construction or a shrine. Poor people—judging by their clothes, camped alongside a wall. No, this was not what he wanted. The plan was to sleep out alone under the desert sky. Where in his solitude Nietzsche would assure him he was on the road to becoming the Übermensch, superior to other men and having no need of them. Or by repeating *Good Thought, Good Word, Good Deed*, he would open himself like the real Zoroaster—his own Zorro—to revelation.

Back home everything he read was true as long as he was reading it except for the nights when it was just as clear that everything, everything was a lie.

Back on the highway, his legs pumped him through a landscape even more barren than the bleak scrub of the high desert at home. There were supposed to be mountains somewhere but as far as the horizon all he saw was flat. At least that made cycling easy. But there was nothing. Not a rock, not a tree. No sound but the wind and the clicking of the cards in the spokes. The clicking was getting on his nerves. Nietzsche wrote never give a hand to the weak. Zorro said never withhold grain when people are hungry. Yes no yes no clickety clickety click. He'd made a commitment: secrecy, solidarity. He rode to clear his mind but his mind was still running, Brent saying, *If sabotage is necessary, hypothetically of course, If you were to do it,*

What if?

Marty pedaled. What if someone else said yes? What if he and Lori had stayed together? He should never have let her go. And what had happened to the Iran he'd seen in photos?—the snowcapped mountains, verdant green valleys, the gardens with their fountains and pools? Where were the nightingales? Pomegranates and nightingales. He would lie down here entirely exposed. How would he even relieve his bladder? But then night fell sudden and black and no one could see him.

He woke in pain, lying on broken ground. His piss evaporated as soon as it hit the earth. He mounted his steed. Where had he gotten the idea he had to make this trip by bike?

Day followed day. He had believed he would tolerate the heat. He had biked north through the California desert on the way to Brent's retreat, which was why he'd run away, why he was here, but this desert, this heat—he'd had no idea. And tolerance: a sad and luke-warm concept. Maybe this was what he needed, the sun to purify and scorch his soul. He followed the highway. His back hurt, his knees hurt, his head was pounding. Should he have had the bike custom-ized? He'd been so confident, paying then riding it straight out of REI. Blisters broke and streamed on his hands and his ass. When he stopped in a village seeking cold water, people offered him hot tea. And he needed a shower or a public bath. He was not an adventurer or a world traveler. He was a pilgrim. Not a saint who required this self-mortification. But maybe this was as it should be: Nietzsche said you have to walk to think but surely cycling was better. Cycling he was nothing but hurting flesh. Body only, his mind and soul, too, were gone. In that absence, Universal Thought, a Mind calling to him from beyond his own, would find the space to enter. Wasn't that the point? The wheels went round. The preventive Lomotil he'd swallowed left him constipated, his stomach cramped.

He stopped to check the tires. In this world, he thought, it is entirely normal to go from elation to despair. The sheer joy of being alive, and having been born in America which meant he could do anything, be anything, achieve whatever he set his Übermensch mind to. There was that. There was also reality. Which was enough to make anyone deflate.

The tires were fine and the chains. All systems go. Onward. Trying to travel in the hours before sunrise, stopping before the worst heat of the day. An hour or two after dusk. If there was scenery, who knew? In the dark. Or head bent over the handlebars, what was there to see? Empty space. Sound reaching him as in a dream, distant calls to prayer. His own mind and soul silenced. He was only a body and then, transcending pain, not even that. He was Martin Keller but he didn't know who he was. Whenever he stopped, dehydrated and dizzy, people greeted him, eager to know where he'd come from. When he said Germany, they told him his country made the chemical weapons Iraq had used against them. Men showed him their scars and talked about a war he'd never even heard of. When he said America, they told him the US had supplied those very weapons to Saddam. But whether he claimed to be German or American, after they said what they had to say, they embraced him and invited him home for tea or dinner or for a place to sleep and he was excited and surprised and grateful but in so much pain (though no one had used a weapon against him, the damage was all self-inflicted) all he wanted was to curl up in a ball in some cool dark place alone.

He slept on his stomach to spare his sunburned back and neck and the skin on his arm, seared where bare skin had touched metal. The only part of him that didn't hurt was his penis and that was what had him most worried because it had tingled a while before going entirely numb. If he were alone, he would think of Lori (or better yet, dark luminous Persian eyes) and he'd touch himself for reassurance— or to know the worst.

Sky Burial

You must see Persepolis. You must visit Esfahan where he did go but only to stock up on water and food. People told him about mosques of extraordinary beauty with extraordinary tile work but how could he enter?—all sweated up in shorts. And he wasn't here as a tourist. His destination was Yazd, the city that would show him the heart of Zoroastrian belief. Into the very heart of Zorro. And despite all the hospitality (after that first night on the ground, he never slept under the sky again), and even though the armed men at the checkpoints were so happy to see him they offered most un-Western displays of affection, he wanted out. Nietzsche was winning. Marty was tired of the company of his fellow men, like the old man who wagged a finger at him and said in the darkest of tones "The Rockefellers!", his view of capitalist evil as behind the times as his car. But in his family's home after dinner his grandson played a Chris Rock DVD and Marty was sure no one in the house could understand the half of it, and not because of the English.

In the morning he rode for hours and saw men with their flocks of sheep, not a blade of grass in sight or a dwelling which made him wonder if they were even real.

That night after he bathed off the dust of the road, his host exclaimed, "Your hair is red! Your skin is white!"

Neighbors—men only—came to meet him.

"The CIA," said a man. "Americans must live in fear. They watch you always."

Maybe after this trip they would.

When he asked, some people changed the subject, others assured him Zoroastrians were not persecuted in Iran. "Persecution for the Bahá'i," he was told. "For the Zoroastrian, discrimination only."

In a coffeehouse that served only tea, a concerned father told him Cabbage Patch Kids carried concealed tape recorders.

"Dolls don't spy on people," Marty said. A lie, he realized, there were those nanny cams.

The man said, "They play a message telling children to jump out the window. As if the war didn't destroy one generation, the dolls are meant to kill the next. But the Zionists aren't that clever. Most of us live on the ground floor. Our children can jump out of windows all they want!"

More brown desert. More of the same. Then white earth like salt or chalk and a pool of turquoise water unless it was a hallucination and dust dust dust until he got to Yazd.

A city of rock-hard mud. Bumps and mounds channeling under-ground water. Sparrows taking their dirt baths in the dust. He couldn't remember when he'd last shaved. His beard growing in curly and more red than auburn or chestnut the way Zoroaster looks in the images, same as Jesus. Was it sacrilege to let his hair grow?— like Zoroaster carved in stone, his hair flowing.

In the center of town, a stooped old man disturbed the dust in front of the coffeehouse with a broom made of twigs. Was it sacrilege to complain about the heat? It left Marty stupefied and reeling. But the sun was cosmic fire. The sun, along with the vultures, purifies the Zoroastrian dead. The corpses laid out for Sky Burial at the Tower of Silence, the dakhma. But the only towers he saw stood tall to catch the desert wind. *There,* someone directed him, *at the top of the hill, the dakhma, over there.*

The Tower of Silence wasn't really a tower and it wasn't silent—tourists even here—and it was no longer used. Viewed from below it looked like a furnace or a water storage tank or a big round baseball stadium made of stone. A deep aboveground well. To reach the dakhma, he had to climb. He left his bike on its side in the dirt. From the hillside he turned back to the panorama of brown buildings, brown earth, brown apartments under construction with dark brown holes staring out from eight floors of windows still waiting for glass. Maybe no one would ever move in, he thought, afraid their children might jump. At the top gazing into the dakhma he looked down into a pit of rubble. Reminding him of something. Lightheaded now he sat, took water from his pack. Below, it was just brown and more brown. A transmission tower stood against the horizon and he felt the most profound sadness he had ever known. Not mere depression. This must be the dark night of the soul, something his soul had surely been demanding year after year and, being medicated—damn his mother!—year after year had been denied.

There was a flash of light—inside of him, he thought, not outside, and then the air went cold and black. He was a pulse pulsing in the void. Not a cobweb brushing his face, not even an ant or spider on his leg, there was nothing, nothing to tell him he was not alone. He fell and lay flat on the earth, the blasphemed earth, his face pressed against it and the earth spoke to him. Without words the earth reminded him of rubble and craters and bombs, the high school field trip to the Nevada Test Site, and of the first time he ever saw Brent Fassen. Marty sat in the campus theatre *What to do what to do what to do I have to do something.* Then the retreat because he wanted to learn to do more. Brent's voice determined and serene: *The time is now, the situation urgent. How committed are you? How far would you go?*

Was it up to him now to tell someone? His body shook. He cried. And out of the nothing a hand touched him.

"You are American?" said the voice. "You've seen the Towers."

He still couldn't speak so he gestured toward the dakhma and nodded.

"We are so sorry," said the stranger. "Your Towers are gone."

The rough hand took his and Marty winced, unhealed blisters. The man led him down. Marty retrieved his bike, wheeled it along, and hand in hand they went, like father and son, back to town.

In the coffeehouse, men were gathered around tables, watching. The television mounted high on the wall beamed out images, sent out its light. The sweeper with his homemade broom stood in the doorway, watching, too.

"Look," said his guide. "Muslims and Zoroastrians crying together, with you, our Christian friend. Our American."

A man shouted, "Look! Look what Israel has done!"

Men were crying and praying, hitting their own chests, tearing at their own clothes and Marty couldn't understand until suddenly he did. Again the world vanished. It slipped away, sucked into a sponge that a huge hand covered and squeezed dry. Nothing left but holes. He saw nothing. Heard nothing. There was no sound. The world was empty until something entered, not revelation, only an acrid smell. Just as suddenly sound came back. A rushing wind that said *Do something.*

"The Jews will say we did it," said a man.

The wind said *It it it.*

Someone said, "Please when you go home, tell your country it wasn't Iran."

"Don't let there be a war, Inshallah."

"Let there be justice, Inshallah."

"But Inshallah, no war."

"The Jews are behind it."

His thigh burned as though the Reisepass rested against him in his pocket.

"Israel did it. Let them bomb Israel."

Israel, as responsible for this, he thought as a Cabbage Patch doll. Some people, he thought, will believe anything. And the film—it had to be the trailer for a disaster movie. The men were crying real tears, but what they were watching…It couldn't be real.

Respect the enemy in your friend, said Nietzsche, which meant you do your friend the honor of never trusting him.

Someone asked, "Are you a Christian?"

He'd been one, more or less, when he met Brent Fassen who said, "Christians do NOT deny our role in climate change. Christians see evolution as one more proof of the limitless creativity of God." And Marty had approached and shook his hand and coughed to cover up a nervous laugh. He quoted Nietzsche: *After coming into contact with a religious man I always feel I must wash my hands.*

"Because it made him realize he was dirty," said Brent Fassen.

The world was dirty now with black smoke. Cinders and ash. If there's a battle between good and evil, how do you tell which is which? He felt himself floating, leaving his body behind and then plunging back inside to all the pain. Flesh hurt, soul hurt. I have to do something, he thought.

On the TV, it was playing over and over and over again, recurrence, the eternal return, and now the men watched in silence, mesmerized. Smoke and rubble and dust and death.

If he were a righteous man, he would say, *My friends, I'm a Jew.*

"I'm not a Christian," he said. "I'm a Zoroastrian. Or I want to be."

They watched the planes. Nothing, he understood nothing. The endless loop with its cryptic demand.

An old man followed him outside. "We are very poor here," said the man. "The Parsis in India are our support. If you wish to learn about our Prophet, you must go to Mumbai."

So he was still on the run. Bus to Shiraz. Flight to Doha—if planes were allowed to fly—and from there, India.

"Please," he said, "I want you to have this bicycle."

"I cannot accept it."

"But I want you to."

"You are my guest. I can take nothing from you."

"It is offered freely. As the Prophet said, *Doing good to others is not a duty, it is a joy, for it increases our own health and happiness.* Please."

The old man ran a hand over the frame, gently but firmly, as though touching a prized horse.

Nietzsche was right. The true man acts. The true man goes beyond the foolish strictures of good and evil. So what? Marty made up his mind. He would become Mardan—or Marzban, and he would henceforth walk in righteousness even if Zorro was his own creation and Zoroaster's truth was lie.

File #5:
After the Towers

If I May Recommend, Sir

Horror and disruption in the States, but Marty's flights to Doha and then Mumbai weren't canceled. In the airports, the same awful footage playing on the screens. Passengers talking in hushed tones.

"Sir," said the taxi driver in Mumbai, "may I express sorrow for your country." And then, "Muslims behave like animals."

A righteous man would have said, "*I am a Muslim*," and said it with great dignity, but he did not. He was not a righteous man. He felt sick: he, too, had been convinced—but not quite—to kill. He hadn't really come close, had he? He felt envious: whoever had done this thing had no doubts. They had the certainty that made it possible to act.

The cab crawled through traffic and Marty stared at pale white modern high-rises, new but seeming pocked with decay as though corroded with salt. Though he'd never been to Florida, a post-apocalyptic Miami Beach is what Marty thought. Then the dark Gothic buildings left by the Brits. It felt wrong to be here at a time like this, so far from home. So safe. He didn't like Mumbai or the way it smelled or the way the taxi driver spoke about Muslims or the way he'd clucked when shown the Malabar Hills address. "No, no, gentle sir"—the second time lately a driver had ignored his instructions. "First a guest house for you and shower and you buy clean clothes also, sir."

Marty rolled down the window and breathed exhaust. He rolled it up and stuck to the seat. Sweat rolled down his face. If he hadn't needed a shower before, he did now. He had time to study people, in cars, buses, rickshaws, sitting in tea shops, on foot on the street and on the overpasses. New clothes? Like what? What the hell did people wear?

Men wore their shirts outside their pants but it seemed however they chose to dress, they were unmistakably Indian. Women, that was another matter. Sure, some had headscarves, even veils, saris, pajama pants and smocks, but the ones in Western clothes? Jeans, short skirts, little summer dresses. After Iran, it was unsettling in a good way to see faces and so much skin. They could be young women in Los Angeles. Or at Evergreen.

Women are classless, he thought. Or else easy to corrupt. They belong to no nation. They have the knack of becoming what they want to be. Maybe centuries of marrying up had done this to the female chromosome. Their aspirations transform them.

His mother—she had that kind of power. Brent was the first man he'd ever known who seemed at first to have it too. But with Brent you did start to see he was playing a role. And what does that say about me? Marty thought. Imagining I could simply turn into a Zoroastrian Parsi.

"A hotel," he said from the backseat. "Not a guest house. I am not a backpacker."

"If I may recommend, sir. Also an umbrella."

To Wear the Kusti

You will have dry clothes. You will have Scotch whiskey.

Chacha Kohiyar smiling. Smooth skin the color of walnut, an Adams apple the size of a walnut jiggling in his throat.

"I didn't know you were allowed alcohol," Marty said.

"Only excess is forbidden." His voice gentle and high-pitched. "Ascetism, this too, is excess."

"Malabar Hills," Marty said. "Wasn't that in *Passage to India*?"

"Marabar," said Chacha Kohiyar. "Made-up place. To your health."

Marty drank and the world began to spin. Well, it always spins, but ordinarily a person doesn't feel it, and he could feel his muscles twitch and twitch a message SOS, SOS no no no and he was going to disgrace himself as a guest.

"I.V. better," said a voice and "Glucose. Electrolytes."

When he opened his eyes, "Am I in a hospital?"

Chacha Kohiyar sat by the bed shaking his head. "No. Better here. You cycled across desert for reason other than survival necessity. This was not good decision."

"It was mental survival," Marty said. "Spiritual survival."

The doctor returned and the bags and poles disappeared and the port from the vein in his arm.

"Now you must get strength," the doctor said. "You will sleep, and eat."

No one said anything about What Had Happened and what would probably happen when the US responded. Marty figured you don't bring bad news to a sick bed.

He woke again, in silk pajamas not his own and when he went to the window, sometimes there was nothing to be seen, the monsoon rains like a thick gray drape, and once late at night the sky cleared and he could see the other buildings, lighted narrow needles that looked more like Worlds Fair landmarks than luxury apartments. Hard to believe there were enough people in this city—in any city—to afford them. Chacha's residence took up the entire 24th floor. Geometric, everything rectangular and flat. Flat screen TV. Low couches. Low tables. Big chairs but no armchairs. Days when the sky was clear, he could see the lush plantings so far below they might as well have been Astroturf. He caught himself scanning the sky for planes. Thinking of Brent Fassen. What had made the man so compelling? Compared to al-Qaeda, he was nothing but a two-bit huckster.

Chacha Kohiyar sat in the living room playing with the remote control.

"The world would become more Western if the West would leave us alone," he said.

"And I want to become Eastern," Marty said. "I've come to you to ask. To visit the Fire Temple. To wear the kusti."

"Never, my son."

Marty's heart stopped at the word, but which one? and the man's brown face wasn't stern but mild with affection.

"You can follow the teachings. The teachings are good, but no one can become a Zoroastrian. You are born, or you are not."

"Chacha," he said, "I am sincere."

"No matter how sincere, you cannot suddenly be what you are not."

He thought of friends at Evergreen suddenly Gypsy, suddenly Native American, claiming legacies they'd learned of in dreams.

"You are fine the way you are," said Chacha. "Be truthful. Be clean in body and mind. Ride the bicycle to conserve fossil fuel. Run to feel the glory of your body, but no marathon."

"I *am* excessive, Chacha. My brain chemistry. Bipolar."

"When you are too full of energy, a warm perfumed bath."

He was exhausted. Neither manic nor despondent. The driver retrieved his backpack from the hotel. He was corrupt. He slept in a feather bed. He was a vegetarian but ate the lamb he was served. "For strength!" Chacha Kohiyar spent the day at business but told Marty to stay indoors. "Monsoon! Too much rain for desert boy!" and it was in vain he tried to describe rainy Olympia, Washington. Visitors showed up at all hours to meet the strange American. Honored guest. Prisoner. To offer condolences but to say nothing more about It. Which was a relief. He could think about it but didn't have to talk about it. One man wagged his finger and said, "Chacha have plans for you!" They showed off the views, invisible through the gray drapes of rain: Arabian Sea this window; this side Back Bay.

Maybe being a young person, a student, was as fluid as being a woman. Classless. You might be headed up or down, who could say? and so here he was, guest of the wealthiest person he'd ever known to whom he was an utter stranger.

He drank tea instead of whiskey. The maid brought pomegranate juice. The world in crisis, he lay around indolent, spoiled, remembering. Cleanliness next to godliness. His aunt said his mother was once so German-clean you could eat off her floors. Then she shed the encumbrance of his father and fell in love with dogs, he grew up amid the dog hair and everything dirty tracked in on the paws and everything the damn animal rolled around in and brought into the house on its fur. Cleanliness, said his mother, is next to

loneliness. She said his immune system would benefit from expo-
sure to microbes.

His mother was excessive. Lori was never satisfied. Whatever
he did was never enough. Brent pushed him to prove himself, to do
things no decent human being would do.

"I take meds," Marty said. "Sometimes I feel ashamed. That if I
just had willpower, I wouldn't need them."

"That sounds to me," said Chacha, "like excess of pride. Not every
priest would agree with me. I've done many things in my life that I
regret. I try, as some of your compatriots would say, to make amends.
But listen, my son, if a medicine helps to achieve balance, abstinence
is an insult to the body and mind. If you need this for moderation, it
is then intended for you."

Every philosophy he'd studied, every person he'd ever known, had
wanted him to be different, better. How was it possible he'd come to
find this, a religion that found him acceptable but would not accept
him?

"My son, you wish to honor Ahura Mazda."

Chacha, Marty thought, meant *uncle,* but this uncle who was not
his uncle called him *son.*

"Without being Parsi, you can do us a great service."

"It would be a privilege."

"You have enthusiasm for the faith while those born to it, in your
country, they become very American."

"I'm sure not all—"

"My resources are great," said Chacha. "We had to leave Uganda
but still there are opportunities in Africa. Many many things. Here in

Mumbai, shipping, steel. But I am not putting all eggs in same pail. Investments in United States also. US dollar. That is security, no? In California, you will go see my lawyer, also the manager for real estate."

"Whatever I can do for you," said Marty. "And your people."

"I try to work with community in California," Chacha said, "but they are not taking initiative. I believe if someone else is building the Tower, they will use. Better than rotting in ground, no? You are from desert," said Chacha. "Best place for Tower, and place with not much population, you understand. So you will acquire property and build dakhma."

When I die, thought Marty, maybe there will be special dispensation. I can't be a Parsi in life but if I build the Tower, surely they will let me end there, exposed to sun and wind, scavenger birds. A bright white light burned and cleansed him and his voice trembled, "Yes."

Maria Knew It First

The sound that came out of her was so terrible no one interrupted to ask why she was watching the news on her computer instead of working. Rennie knew she checked the baseball box scores every morning, but this was not that.

That morning, 9/11, California, west coast, by the time Maria cried out and they knew what had happened, it was all over.

Carsky called his parents in New York—they were OK—and then they all sat in Carsky's office because they didn't want to be alone. They sat silent because there was nothing to say and because no one knew what else to do except for Dr. Tang who also had family in the city and was still trying to reach them. When someone answered at last, he spoke in Chinese and the others didn't know what he said or heard, but saw the look of relief on his face.

Then they stood and gathered in front of Carsky's screen where they could, together, watch again and again what you already know. Until Carsky couldn't take it anymore and told them all to sit.

"America has been attacked," he said. "I have no doubts that this country will soon be at war." He paused. "Here at the Institute, we come from many countries. There may be many points of view and so I am making a policy that we shall all refrain from any discussion of politics and war and peace and terrorism and justice. We have work to do here and we have to do it in cooperation so I am asking for your cooperation. What happened and what is still to occur—off-limits."

Then, of course, he went on to talk about it.

"I'm addressing *all* of you. I know Dr. Tang won't understand a word," he said, "but Emine, you see I'm not singling out Muslims."

"I'm a Jew," she said.

So am I, he thought, what else could I be? But Emine? This surprised him.

"A Turkish Jew," she said. "Not that it should make any difference."

He looked at his hands. "It doesn't. Look, I don't know what we're going to do. We've been playing fast and loose with security levels. What value are any of you if you don't have access to...whatever. Whatever it is you need. But I'm afraid that business as usual...it may end up being treason now. Or something we're not prepared for."

"So," said Maria. "You terminate our contracts?" By which she meant, our visas.

"I don't know."

"My work," said Emine, "is to save lives."

"Oh, come on," he said.

"If I wanted to provide secrets to Iran, I'd be working there, not here," she said.

"What happens with us?" said Maria.

"That's the least of it," said Emine. "Unless someone does something to stop the Administration, they'll be dropping bombs on Afghanistan any day now."

"The sooner the better," said Carsky.

"Bombs don't discriminate," she said. "Civilians. Women and—"

"Smart bombs," he said.

"Americans and bombs are never as smart as they think they are," said Maria.

"Get over it," Carsky said. "Afghanistan is fucked. The women are fucked. The children are fucked. Whether we bomb them back to the Stone Age—which is where they are anyway—or not, they are fucked either way. It makes no fucking difference." He sighed. "No one knows how it's going to shake out. Go home—all of you—till we've got the new world we're stuck with figured out."

"I'm an American," said Petey Koh.

"Oh, yes," said Carsky, vaguely.

The five sat and looked at him. Rennie wondered if she was imagining the tears forming in his eyes.

"Emine, Maria," he said, "take some vacation time."

"Your country's been attacked and you want us to go to Disneyland." Maria stood. So did Emine. So did Petey Koh. They left the room and Rennie followed. Dr. Tang waited to be told what to do and Carson Yampolsky, of course, could not tell him.

The Stone Age

When hundreds of small black birds trembling the surface of the water look like swarming vermin, you know you've got a jaundiced point of view. In the past 24 hours, Emine has decided that cynicism is easier to live with than horror. Yes, there's evil in the world, human beings are destructive, deluded shits, so get used to it. Now the very molecules of the air seemed jittery and diseased. She understood it was her choice to see the world that way and it occurred to her that whenever you make a choice, you reassure yourself that you have power.

She drove north, Maria Castillo beside her. She had wanted to spend a few days in Los Angeles where she used to go every weekend to join Oğuz. Civilization. Museums. Classical music. Good food. Rennie objected: "What if LA's the next target?"

So instead: Transmission lines on rust-colored hills. Dusty tamarisk. The wind. Rennie in the backseat. And the mountains—so-called, black, barren. As bare as the mountains of Iran—best not to mention she'd ever been there—but dwarfed, mere hills. "California mountains," Emine said. "Like they've fallen into sinkholes. Like they've had the midsection removed. Geologic liposuction."

Rennie reminded her of the grandeur of Mt. Whitney.

"Whitney, schmitney," said Emine.

She wore a headscarf folded in a triangle, edged with embroidered scallops and tied beneath her chin, the kind of babushka a Turkish peasant woman would wear but to Rennie, Emine, in her scarf and big dark glasses, looked more like a 1950's movie star.

Rennie squirmed in the backseat trying to see her own face in the rearview. If Emine was Hollywood glamour, Rennie feared she herself looked like a clown, all that white sunscreen smeared over her fair Irish skin. Her Dodgers cap bounced along atop her nervous right knee. It's why Carsky had sent her home, too. She was useless, her mind stunned, her hands shaking too much for lab work. She was grateful that Emine and Maria had invited her to join them. Grateful, yes, and given the terrible events, she wanted to be a high-minded person and not succumb to an emotion as ignoble as jealousy, but still, she couldn't help but notice what she noticed.

Do you put on your seatbelt before turning on the ignition, or do you turn on the ignition before fastening your belt? Emine had always done seatbelt first. Maria Castillo turned on the ignition. Rennie had brought this to Emine's attention. "Seems a bit reckless," she said. "She gonna need to make a fast getaway?" Emine didn't hesitate. "Maybe she's rational, parsimonious with her energy. No point fastening the belt till you know the car will start." That morning, it had hit Rennie hard when Emine in the driver's seat turned the key before belting herself in.

Now they were on the road. Outside the window, Joshua trees, symbol of the high desert. There were none in Desert Haven, pulled up, burned by the developer who went bankrupt and shot himself, leaving a boulevard of dying royal palms and still thriving rows of Russian olive and poplar and live oak.

"I've always gone south before," Emine said.

Maria had wanted to use the days off to go snake collecting. She needed specimens for her project—mapping DNA from venom glands. Emine and Rennie weren't enthusiastic about encountering rattlers. Instead they'd agreed to a road trip ending up at Mono Lake where Emine could see the calcium-carbonate formations and Maria could scoop some interesting bacteria from the muck.

"What do you hear from Oğuz?" Maria asked.

"Nothing," said Emine. "It worries me, if he's keeping his plans from me." It was crazy, she thought. Just when she might lose her visa and have to return to Turkey, her husband would be gone. And where? Please, not to Peshawar. "I hope he goes someplace the US doesn't bomb."

"I hope we don't bomb anyone," Rennie said. "But can we talk about something else?"

So she was excluded when they talked: about the thorny-headed worm's immunosuppressant effect on its host. Could that lead to a better way to prevent transplant rejection? Treat autoimmune diseases? Allergies? They talked about the necessary balance between circumventing the body's defenses and breaking them down to the point of deadly vulnerability.

Maria put on her Panama hat. She took it off. She adjusted the windshield visor to block the sun. No way to know what she was thinking. She focused on work. She focused on being practical and bright, a bit homesick, but that was normal. Emine sensed a darkness inside her but didn't know how to approach or help. Rennie sensed it, too, and didn't want to.

There was more to Maria than met the eye. More to me, too, Rennie thought. She knew how she came across, projecting as best she could what she thought of as the 3 H's: healthy, happy, helpful. Let people see her as some sort of plump and rosy milkmaid. Contented as a cow.

How did she end up living what she could hardly call a life, watching her lizard on the wall, sometimes taking stock and full of self-pity and melodrama crying out (to herself) *Empty hands! Nothing but empty hands!* Not that she'd ever wanted the conventional things. But what did she want? Too bad she wasn't an underachiever which would at least suggest greatness that might still be tapped.

It wasn't like Emine and Maria had such great lives either. At least they had purpose.

So do terrorists, Rennie thought, while listening to talk about the release of serotonin and changes in DNA. Prednisolon was already on the market, alleviating some effects of radiation. Maria mentioned side effects—euphoria, which would be a plus in marketing (or in repeat customers), others more problematic. Emine was in touch with the South African team that had found a Firmicute, whatever that was, living off radiation in a mine miles beneath the earth. They might as well be talking Spanish or Turkish for all Rennie could tell. "We'd get further looking at *Deinococcus radiodurans*,"—this, according to Maria.

Firmicute, radiodurans. They could be talking in code. Rennie repeated the words silently to herself, excluded but appreciative. Words she didn't understand were things of beauty. It was like the pleasure she got watching deaf people's hands move as they signed.

"Radiation doesn't harm it," said Maria. "It repairs itself. It repairs its own DNA."

Rennie could envision where this could lead: she was in the backseat listening to genius: two women who might someday modify the bacteria's DNA to live aboveground and be adapted to breathing oxygen in critical locations where it could decompose radioactive waste. These women—Nobel Prize caliber for sure.

"But can it resist the heavy metals and the other contaminants?" said Emine.

"That's why I'd have to manipulate the genes"—unlikely though it was she'd ever have the chance.

The sun rose higher and Rennie squirmed out of her windbreaker, Emine and Maria shed their denim jackets. Outside, an unexpected rain had brushed the brown trees with a green that looked more like mold than foliage.

Did every trailer and shack along the route always fly the flag? People must have owned them all along, how could they buy one so fast?

"How about," Rennie said, "modifying human genes. Making us resistant to radiation?" It was as though they didn't hear her. As though she hadn't even spoken.

Maria switched on the radio, jumped around the dial through static till a man's voice boomed ...*back to the Stone Age! Put 'em down like mad dogs.*

"Turn it off," said Emine.

It Was a Normal Reaction

That's why Emine didn't want to hear it. Round them up, torture them, kill them. Make them suffer. It's what she'd thought when she was fourteen, though *felt* would express it better, such an overwhelming surge of fear and hate, it overtook her without conscious thought. She hadn't been in the synagogue, her family never went, but her brain generated its own scenes, flashes of light, explosion, bodies blown to bits, washes of blood, the terrorists with machine guns and hand grenades who slaughtered Jews before blowing themselves up in Neve Şalom, the great synagogue of Istanbul.

Why don't we do something? If we killed and killed maybe the world would change back, maybe she'd be sure again that when she walked, her feet would touch ground, that the earth would be there, secure, to hold her up. Now the only certainty was this fear and rage, more solid and real than the world itself.

It was an attack not only on Turkish Jews, but on Turkey itself, on everything she loved about her homeland. These outsiders—Islamic Jihad from Iran, the evil dogs from Syria, the Palestinians we've made welcome here—they hate us. They hate our secular freedoms. Round them up. Kill them all. Attack their nests in Iran and Libya. To protect us. To have revenge for all those bodies.

There were arrests. So what? Prosecution. Diplomats expelled.

Her parents said the way to fight back was by strengthening ties with Europe—the rest of Europe—for Turkey to be a European country. During school vacations she went to London to improve her English, to Switzerland to learn French. While her country with its dangerous borders handled things quietly and she was powerless and it enraged her that her country's power had such limits.

Thank God we couldn't act on our rage is what she thinks now. Thank God, and as the Muslims say, Mashallah.

White Wings Behind a Black Spire

East of the highway, a black wall ran in a straight line north. "But that's not manmade," said Emine. She took the next exit and then a graded dirt road.

"It's black basalt," she said. They stood in a field where black lumps lay scattered about on the dry grass and parched earth, like the petrified defecation of dinosaurs. "Volcanic in origin. Let's head for the wall."

There were tall rocks with vertical scoring as though they'd been clawed. Stones topped by cairns put there by nature or by someone's hand. There were stones that looked to be still bubbling and rocks with edges sharp as flints.

"See that?" Emine pointed toward a red mound to the north. "We'll use that to orient ourselves."

"Some kind of mining slag?" Rennie asked.

"Volcanic cinder cone."

Rocks were pitted and porous, or spotted orange, split and cleaved. Emine took photos. Misshapen with circular penetrations. The sun beat down. They crossed a field littered with shiny flakes of obsidian and stepped over flat rocks to a place that brought dinosaurs again to mind, smooth, polished stones laid out resembling reconstructed skeletons, vertebrae here, pelvic girdle, black and petrified bones.

Rennie lagged behind watching Emine and Maria, agile and trim and united like sisters, while her windbreaker billowed around her.

Maria was most herself when walking, Emine when looking, and me, Rennie thought. When am I myself? When listening.

At the edge of a cliff they looked down into a canyon of rococo curves and carved walls, a maze of inky stone. A lizard scurried into a crevice.

"Look!" Emine stood too frozen in wonder to raise a hand to point. Instead the others had to follow her gaze and just catch a glimpse of white wings before they disappeared. "An owl. In daylight," said Emine.

"But the wings were white," said Rennie. "What is it? Albino?"

The bird appeared again, rising up from behind a boulder. It perched there, regarding them.

"It doesn't have red eyes, and there's some brown edging," said Maria. "Leucistic barred owl would be my guess."

"How on earth do you know that?" said Rennie.

Maria laughed. "Heaven is lying in a hammock with a field guide and a Corona with lime."

"It's beautiful," said Emine.

The owl flew off and they lost it but kept gazing after it until they saw the white wings again, rising behind a black spire.

A gust of wind took Maria's hat and sent it blowing like tumbleweed. They chased after it, slowed down over broken rock, running when they could, losing it from sight from time to time, blinded by the sun.

"There!" The Panama hat waited for them, snagged on razor wire.

Before they could catch up, there was a helicopter overhead and an All-Terrain Vehicle moving toward them. A man got out, armed, in desert camouflage.

"Halt!" He ordered them to show ID.

"What for?" said Rennie. "We're not on your side. I mean, if you're US military or something, of course we're on your side. But we're on this side of the fence, we—"

Maria got stopped a lot. She had hers ready.

"I'm opening up my backpack to get it for you," Emine said, slowly, calmly. To Rennie she said, "Of course everyone is on edge. Just cooperate."

The man's eyes were hidden behind dark glasses but Rennie could feel them shift slowly from one woman to the next till settling on Emine.

"And your camera," he said.

They watched him and he watched them as he passed their licenses and papers and camera to the driver in the vehicle. They heard the crackle of a two-way radio.

They waited. "This is ridiculous," said Rennie. She adjusted her bra strap.

This is just the start, thought Emine.

"Those damn military vehicles," said Maria. "They pack down the soil so the tortoises can't burrow."

When the sentry returned, he held Emine's camera in front of her, set to display a digital image. "Who is this?"

"My husband."

He handed the camera back. "You'll note I did not delete anything."

"We can go now?" Rennie asked.

"Not yet. What are you doing here?"

"I'm a geologist," Emine said.

"We were chasing my hat," said Maria. She still hadn't dared reach for it.

He disentangled it himself, ran a finger under the band and inside and along the slit left by the razor edge, then handed it to her through the fence.

The Altruism of HIV

The next time Emine turned off the highway she saw metamorphosed volcanic rock, granite, and K-spar phenocrysts. The three of them burst out in cheers and then fell silent, the landscape so powerful and strange it overloaded the eyes. Stone arches and giant rocks and boulders piled and melted one on the other, acre after acre of mystery. It was all different from the fairy spires of Cappadocia, the karst terraces of Pamukkale, thought Emine, but every bit as unearthly (if the earth can be unearthly) and magical. Once they caught their breath, they couldn't restrain themselves: wow wow wow. They sounded to Emine like the yipping of small excited dogs.

They sat carefully on the rocks, Maria checking first for snakes, and they ate, Maria's jicama salad and Emine's baba ghanoush and Rennie's cold fried chicken.

Road trips are amazing, Rennie thought. They'd been gone only hours and she felt as though she'd traveled to another world, been gone for days.

And later they stood in the sun and fierce wind on the high desert plain at Manzanar.

Rennie remembered: "I brought Petey Koh here. I was playing Welcome Wagon when he first arrived. He couldn't wait to leave."

Let's get out of here, he'd said. *You Americans can't tell Korean from Japanese. I'll end up in a camp.*

Rennie had laughed. *We don't do that anymore,* she'd said. Now she wasn't so sure.

"What's going to happen to us?" asked Emine.

They stood quiet in front of the camp cemetery. There were probably even more, other, bones somewhere deep beneath this soil, Rennie thought. I don't even know what their tribes were called. We have no memory of them, their names.

"Look!" said Maria.

A desert tortoise moved slowly over the dirt.

"Don't touch it. You'll scare it. It will urinate from fear and then die of dehydration."

Back at the parking lot, they sat in the car for a while, quiet, except for the crunch as they ate raw almonds, carrot sticks. When they drove off, Emine and Maria talked about plasmids and ribotypes, beta and delta subdivisions, and hot springs in Australia. Data from Paralana (Down Under) interested Emine because of the springs she used to visit in Turkey.

"I've got to share this with Rezarta Grazhdani," she said. "In Kosovo. Working on effects of depleted uranium."

"Better not," said Rennie.

"Let's take a look at *Shewanella*," said Maria. "It moves its own proteins to bond with metal oxides. Instead of directly breathing oxygen."

"The stuff would still be toxic."

"Do viruses love each other?" Rennie asked. "I'm thinking of the altruism of HIV. The strongest individuals protect the weak. The strong ones pass their own DNA into ours. And then feed proteins to those who cannot." Was there a lesson here? she wondered. The virus we want to destroy because it kills us is magnanimous to its own kind. "The least and hungriest are fed by the most fortunate, no questions asked, no applications to submit, no demeaning interviews. All for one and one for all."

"Not soluble," Maria continued, to Emine.

"That was amazing about the tortoise," Rennie interrupted.

"If it's true," Maria said. "We tell this to people so they'll leave them alone." She picked up her conversation with Emine: "It won't leach into the water table," and Emine answered, "Worth doing then."

The Endless Loop

They got a room in Lee Vining, just south of Mono Lake. Emine tried
to check email at the motel computer. Access denied.

"He's already cut me off," she said. "We've done nothing and we're
suspects."

"It's a public computer," said Rennie. "Maybe that's why. Maybe it
has nothing to do with—"

They ate red meat and drank a lot at dinner.

"I don't understand this country," said Emine. It was a place where
Oğuz learned how to do pediatric cardiac surgery—heart transplants
and robotics to work on a baby's tiny valves—but the infant and
maternal mortality rates were the highest in the developed world.
Her poor husband, who only wanted to be an ordinary family doctor
and had studied the most sophisticated techniques imaginable just to
accompany her to California, a place where tuberculosis should have
been entirely eradicated but was epidemic in resistant strains in the
gulag of mass incarceration, the detention centers, the prisons, and
the jails. Poisoned water, poisoned air, a public health catastrophe.

"We're in mourning," said Rennie. "We're in shock."

Yes, Emine thought. And we're not in Turkey. Nothing restrains
US power. "Terrible things are going to happen," she said.

Maria and Emine shared the queen-sized bed. For Rennie, the motel
manager rolled in the trundle bed they usually provided for a child
but before sleep, the three of them huddled together on the bed as
they stared at the TV. Emine in a Lakers jersey, Maria in flannel pajamas, Rennie in an oversize Flowstone Drapery T-shirt she had begged

from Carsky. They watched as long as they could bear it, the endless loop of towers and smoke and ash and oh my god people jumping. Everything can change in an instant and then that instant goes on and on, repeating, till everything else is driven out of mind, and it kept running over and over even after Maria shut off the television.

"Will there be a war?" Rennie asked.

"Of course," said Emine.

Maria said, "When have you ever known America not to go to war?"

"Where will you—would you—go?" Rennie didn't know whether she asked out of concern or in retaliation. "If you lose your visa."

"I don't know," said Emine. "It will feel wrong to go back to Istanbul if Oğuz isn't there."

"I don't know," said Maria. "The one place I want to be is where I can't go. Home."

There was a cold mist over Mono Lake and its tufa towers. The formations stood around aimlessly, too small and low to inspire the awe suggested by photographs. But when Emine framed the scene in the camera viewfinder, she shuddered. It was always with her—with all of them—what had happened. What she was looking at shifted to become twisted bits of structural steel, coated with ash, blurred by smoke.

Maria stepped in barefoot with a garden spade undeterred by the swirls of alkali flies over the water—*Ephydra hians*, she said. She handed off a filled and capped test tube and then another to Emine who asked "Where to now?"

"We still want to go to the Borax mine."

"We do?" said Emine.

"I thought you were interested."

"Not particularly," she said. "Not now."

"The Bristlecone Pine Forest?" said Rennie. Ancient trees there, she explained. Some of them 5,000 years old.

"That only matters to you," Emine said, "because your country is so young."

"What have you got against my country all of a sudden?"

"Nothing wrong with being young," said Emine. "Not in America."

Stars and Stripes

They drove through what might or might not have been a ghost town. Every wooden building and every shed had windows broken out or boarded up, but every property flew the Stars and Stripes. Either people still lived in the derelict buildings or some über-patriot had dressed up even the abandoned structures.

"Rennie," said Emine, and it was her usual soft voice, not the sharp tones that had Rennie on alert. "I didn't mean to offend. I do love this country, but I love my own country, and it's a Muslim country, and I'm scared. What happened is horrible. It's unimaginable except that someone did imagine it and made it happen and not because They hate your freedoms."

"You don't sound scared," said Rennie. "You sound pissed off."

"Why do you say that?" said Maria. "I mean why do people say that? Pissed *on* makes sense. You say Fuck *off*. But you don't say you're fucked off when you're pissed off. And what's urine got to do with it?"

"What do you call that part of speech?" Emine asked Rennie.

"Adverb?'"

"But these are unnecessary adverbs. Extra. It's the hardest thing in English to get right."

Rennie spoke no foreign languages but was fascinated by people who did so she should have enjoyed this conversation. Instead she once again felt left out.

"Why do you hang up when you put the phone down?" said Maria.

"Why do they say *Shut up*."

So now we are *they*, Rennie thought.

"Come *on*."

"Carry *on*. Get it *on*."

"Call *on* is not the opposite of call *off*."

"Blow it *up*," Maria said. "Or blow it *down*."

"What the hell!" Emine pulled over onto the dirt shoulder, tears pouring down her face. Her eyelids turned red, then swelled enough to shut closed her eyes.

"You must be allergic to something."

"This never happened before."

"You've always driven to LA," Rennie said. "Now you're behind the Creosote Curtain."

"Creosote?" said Maria. "Desert flats with creosote. That's where you find *Crotalus scutulatus*."

They got out of the car to change places. Rennie got behind the steering wheel and Maria got in the backseat without having to be told it was no time to look for snakes.

"You know, you were right about viruses," she said to Rennie.

So you were listening to me after all, Rennie thought.

"Bacteria too," said Maria. "They stick together. Share resistant genes with their neighbors."

The wind blew over a desert landscape that even desert lovers couldn't love. Flat and brown, not even a Joshua tree, just the low skeletal scrub, the creosote chaparral.

Maria made a cold compress of Emine's headscarf and melted ice water from the cooler. Emine reclined her seat, the cloth over her eyes.

Here and there they passed a truck repair yard, a lone trailer, a shack. The only color was the rust on a corrugated metal roof. There was laundry drying fast, flapping in the wind so you could see that people lived here but you couldn't see why.

"Though you know," said Maria, "if you had irrigation and cattle and you could survey your property on horseback, it wouldn't be bad here."

"You've seen too many cowboy movies," said Rennie. She thought it would still be awful.

"How far are we from home?" Emine asked.

"Let's get you indoors faster than that," Rennie said. "The Visitor Center at the mine."

Once on Rio Tinto property, the speed limit was 37.5 mph.

"Translated from kilometers," said Maria when Rennie laughed. "The company is based in London. I could tell you things they've done in Latin America and it's no joke."

Emine was interested after all. She sat up to look: "Crushers, tanks, thickeners," she said. "Cooling chambers, slurry filters, dryers, conveyors." Then across the railroad tracks and up a graded dirt hill.

"The hell with slurry filters," said Maria. "There's a bathroom."

She was first to claim a stall while Rennie studied the chart near the towel dispenser: eight colored stripes, from clear to brown, mostly shades of yellow. You compared your urine to the color to tell if you were dehydrated.

After Rennie emptied her bladder, she looked in the bowl, then opened the door without flushing. "I can't tell." She would never have asked Emine to look at her pee, but she asked Maria. "Am I dehydrated? Maria?"

"Oh, piss off," said Maria. Then relented and looked. "You're fine." She tapped the chart. "There was a vegetarian restaurant I used to go to in Monterrey. They had illustrations and instructions for breast self-exams hanging on the stall door."

"And guys wonder why we take so long in there," Rennie said.

"Hello? Are you all right in there?" The voice from outside the door was female, not male. "Can I help you? Hello?" Berenice, the docent, herded them out of the restroom and into the Visitor Center, a woman with colors as muted as the desert. Gray sweater, gray slacks, gray hair, gray eyes. "Welcome to the largest open pit mine in California and the largest borate mine in the world." Her left eye twitched as if in sympathy with Emine who would have wanted none and said, "The largest reserve and the largest mine is in Turkey."

"Well, I'm sure Turkey has some, too," said Berenice. "Boron is used in detergents, ceramics, glass, fiberglass, fertilizers."

"And to regulate rates of fission in nuclear reactors," Emine said. "It's a neutron absorber so it can slow or even stop reactions in the event of a disaster."

"Where did you say you are from?" asked Berenice.

"Desert Haven," said Emine. "It's also used for body armor. And what are you doing about slope failure?" Berenice took a step back, so Emine added, "I don't mean you personally. I mean the mine must have slope monitoring techniques. You've got two fracture systems here—the West Jenifer and the Portal fault zones." No reply from

Berenice whose right hand clutched at her left wrist. "Is it possible to speak with one of your engineers?"

It wasn't, but Berenice assured them that the short film in the screening room would explain everything.

It didn't, though it did describe the mine accurately as "one of the two largest in the world" without acknowledging the US was #2.

"USA. Number One!" Emine muttered.

In the car, all across the barren high desert, they chanted "USA. Number One!" Being pissed off is not the same as being a terrorist, Rennie thought.

Snakes and Psychos

In civilized society, like New York or LA, it's reasonable to wonder how seemingly mismatched couples got together. In small towns and rural places, you make do, which had been Carson Yampolsky's excuse from the first night he slept with Tara. A minimum wage cafeteria worker in a nursing home for godsakes who "loved" her job because she also volunteered giving manicures to drooling, demented women who couldn't tell one color nail polish from another. Now she was in the backseat of her stepbrother's van, giggling, then shouting *Kill the motherfuckin' camel fuckers,* making the dog growl as Carsky stood guard outside the storage unit on the outskirts of Mojave, watching Tara's brothers carry out crates of ammunition plus all those weapons he couldn't name.

Stepbrothers, he corrected himself. It was important to remember Tara didn't share their blood. She lived with them along with a steady stream of visitors—assorted (or sordid) desperadoes in his view—at the "family place," a collection of prefab buildings on a dirt road in the chaparral between Desert Haven and California City. Most of the time, Carsky was able to convince himself the *stepbrothers* were amusing in the way of a Tarantino film, making him laugh at something so sick it should scare you. Tonight, he was just scared.

Kyle did most of the heavy lifting; Casey, as usual, gave the orders.

They'd laughed at him. Carsky's version of standing guard was, well, just standing there, shifting from foot to foot. The dog—a pit bull, for fuck's safe, named Terror, no less—had to stay in the van with Tara. She could control the monster; he couldn't.

"We're gonna need it, we're gonna need it," Kyle muttered as he toted and loaded. When he was nervous, if he happened to latch onto a thought, or something resembling one, he tended to repeat it.

Sleeping with Tara so often, Carsky'd had to acknowledge her as his girlfriend and that meant acknowledging her family and they were a mess: prison, heroin, meth—which meant a recurrent temptation for him. They seethed with hatred against anyone who wasn't white and Christian while at the same time treating him not as a Jewboy, but as a prince he liked to think, though, he acknowledged, like a mascot was more like it. He amused them; they amused him. As did their racist contempt for Mexicans which had not stood in the way of their late father marrying a third time—for business reasons if not love—into la Eme, the Mexican mafia.

Clouds caused the quarter moon to appear and disappear. The brothers relied on the van's headlights which showed them to Carsky as shadows and silhouettes as they moved around inside the unit. As they neared and crossed the beam, he'd for a moment see them clearly before the light dissolved them in front of his eyes.

Hurry up, he thought. He was a New Yorker. Wasn't it enough he had learned late in life to drive? Though he couldn't drive the van or use a clutch, and what did he know (or want to know) from guns? Or rattlesnakes. He'd be the first to admit he was more afraid of snakes than Muslim psychopaths.

His teeth chattered. Before he'd transplanted himself to Southern California, he'd given away all his winter clothes and even after a couple of years here in the high desert with its morning freeze and frigid winters he refused to acknowledge he'd been wrong. If it weren't so fucking cold in the wind, he thought, this could be exciting.

He recovered his sense of adventure once they were back in the van, the heater running. "How did you accumulate so much firepower?"

"It's Benny's," said Casey. "Benny Alatorre."

Kyle added, "We're gonna need it."

"We're delivering it to him?"

"It's for us," said Casey. "Can't count on a Messican to be on our side."

"It's Benny's? Benny Alatorre? It's Benny's?" My God, thought Carsky, I'm so freaked out I sound like Kyle.

"But my storage unit," Casey said. "Stashed it with me when he got sent up to Corcoran."

"When does he get out?" said Carsky. He repeated the name in his head over and over *BennyBennyBenny* hoping he could make the name become mere nonsense syllables and he could pretend it wasn't Benny of la Eme whose cache they had just looted.

With this kind of company, he thought, I'll end up dead. Why didn't you stick with your own kind? Because there's no one like me between here and LA. He needed a career move. He'd start sending out feelers and resumés right away. It wouldn't have to be LA or New York. Any city would be better: Boston, Chicago, Pittsburgh, St. Louis, good God, even Omaha. Stick with your own kind. That had a familiar ring to it. Yes, West Side Story. And Ma-REE-ah.

Who at least was educated and civilized. And Emine. He'd call them on Monday. Apologize and acknowledge he had overreacted. I don't know what I was thinking. Please come back.

The Crossing

The train runs to the Pakistan border post only twice a week so Oğuz checked into a hotel in Amritsar. He showered—the first time since Emine's visit. He slept. After two more months in the field, he wanted to sleep and sleep and catch up on more sleep but the cool air after the desert had him energized. He paid a boy to bring Mediker Anti-Lice Treatment to his room and a new shalwar kameez and he sent his clothes, lice and flea-ridden, to be destroyed. He showered and washed his hair again and then shaved his scalp bald. Embarrassed to think he might have left lice in the sheets, he soaked the bed linens and also the Dodgers baseball cap Emine had brought him—the one article of clothing he wasn't willing to lose—in kerosene. He laid it all out on the balcony to dry. Still another day to kill. He visited the local hospital where he was shocked at first to learn that many patients were treated "outside." Like Africa, he thought, people lying on the ground, dying under the sky, waiting for someone to see them. He walked around the building seeking this horrific sight until he realized "outside" merely meant out-patient. He shared shop talk with the doctors. They bragged about the fertility hospital in nearby Jalandhar a short drive on the GT road. Would he like to see it?

No. Emine, I'm sorry, he thought. He had ruined their brief vacation together with his stupid idea. He wished he could turn back time, to start again from the moment he spotted her in New Delhi, one point of stillness in the airport chaos, Emine seeking him without turning her head. With her peripheral vision, he used to tease, short as she was, she could have been a great basketball player. She had no interest in the game, but in California, she assured him, she slept in the Lakers jersey he'd given her. With him, she wore nothing to bed at all. His wife. I'm sorry.

He emailed her from the hotel lobby. *En route to Peshawar!* and read a message from Ahmet: *Al-hamdulillah! Praise God, brother! You will stay with me, of course. No need to pay hotel.*

What time was it in California? He was too tired to figure it, but whatever the hour, Emine was awake and at the computer, too: *Give my love to Ahmet. I hope you've given up on that other plan. Travel safe, mi korazon.*

The skies opened with sheets of gray rain when he reached the border crossing. He assumed there were soldiers facing off across the line but everything was a blur except for the porters directly in front of him who carried merchandise on their heads, covered with oilcloth tarps.

In Pakistan, the sun came out when it was almost time for it to set. The wide avenues left him with a sense of unease. He was sure they'd been designed not as a convenience for traffic, but to allow the passage of military tanks. Design what you will, good luck with your tanks in all this: jammed, noisy with cars, trucks, the jingle buses painted with bright intricate designs and hung with as much dangling junk (except for the air fresheners he figured they could really use) as Christmas trees, as gaudy and bright as a circumcision procession but without the little boy enthroned, not knowing what was soon to befall him.

He chose an auto-rickshaw rather than a cab. "Namak Mandi, please"—where Ahmet wished to meet for dinner. To his relief, the driver knew—or said he knew—exactly where to go. If they would be able to move at all through the motorbikes, bicycles, pedestrians, donkeys, horses, carts, porters, Army jeeps, a striking number of Mercedes Benzes. Not a woman to be seen except for the faces that showed off bright smiles and glossy hair on billboards and the posters visible in market stalls and inside shops.

The three-wheeled cart with open sides and overhead canopy made him ache for Emine, remembering afternoons at her parents' summer place on Büyük Ada. He should have known bringing her to Delhi would be a mistake. They should have met in Istanbul or on the big island. No cars there, just horse-drawn carts that looked so much like this cart—except for the horse. They would take the ferry over, on the upper deck enjoying the breeze off the sea except when they traveled with her parents in the stifling inner cabin. They considered fresh air dangerous. Drafts. Except at sundown, when Jewish families sat outside their houses and visited and talked—something that had always charmed him, compared to his family, preferring to gather with friends behind the walls of home. He missed his wife who, like him, laughed and loved fresh air. On the island, they would climb into a waiting cart and sing to each other about the surrey with the fringe on top. He missed her and he missed how clean everything was at home, the tarps hanging under the horses' backsides so their droppings never hit the ground. We Turks are too much in love with our baths, he thought. Here, you have to be like a sparrow, cleaning your wings in the dust.

Here in Peshawar there were henna-dyed donkeys, men sitting in doorways cradling AK-47s in their laps like house pets. Bright banners hanging over the streets made it seem a happy place. The men sat cross-legged, as Emine did even on chairs, even in restaurants. She was short and said she was too uncomfortable when her feet didn't reach the ground. Kerida, he thought. The men all wore white. A bad choice, he thought, with the constant red dust. White cotton couldn't stay clean. To look at their clothes, you would think cloth could rust. The smell of burning fat, of mutton on the grill turned his stomach now, meat cooking in every eatery open to the street. And there was his brother in white shalmar kameez and a turban, worn Afghan-style, the loose end of white fabric flowing down past his shoulder.

Oğuz stumbled out. They embraced and Ahmet turned the base-ball cap around on Oğuz's head. I don't think he's trying to give me a hiphop look, Oğuz thought. Maybe it's the bill sticking out in front. Is it that clear I don't prostrate myself in prayer, head against the ground?

Ahmet had gained weight. Everything about him spoke of health and ease except for his hands, red and cracked, probably from constant disinfecting. He slapped Oğuz on the shoulder. "What has happened to you? Here is our table. Tonight you will eat!"

"The city looks more like Ankara than Istanbul," he said.

"You think?"

"Well, that street where you took us to eat dinner one night, the second-story restaurants with lights strung on the balconies."

"I don't remember."

Not much of a conversation but the mere fact of speaking Turkish again left him giddy. With Emine, there had been too much tension to feel this. He recalled the exhilaration of learning to speak English, the moment in which almost without preparation he went from a halting stutter to fluency, the sheer pleasure of the words. But this, this pleasure, was more profound. He hadn't realized how pent up he was, so many words and thoughts trapped not just in his mouth but his mind, his heart, waiting for the immense relief of being unloosed in his mother tongue.

He drank green tea and stared at the plate in front of him, piled high with bread and meat. Lots of meat.

"What? Have you become a Hindu vegetarian!?" said Ahmet.

"My digestion," said Oğuz.

Ahmet ate. A bit of grease glistened in his beard. "Nasreen is very glad you've come to see me," he said.

She'd rather be the one to see you, thought Oğuz. The family had been thrilled when Ahmet chose Nasreen. They'd feared their first son would stay single forever. For years Ahmet had been involved with an American woman but she was divorced and he wouldn't commit to someone who had been married before. Maybe, thought Oğuz, he had always been too righteous. If the family had been less concerned, they might not have been so welcoming to Nasreen, the young Iranian refugee from Sardasht, place of mountains and fir trees, birthplace of Zoroaster, site of the Iraqi chemical weapon attack. Some Turks looked down on refugees, especially Kurds. Luckily, from Nasreen's name no one could tell. When her eyesight failed, Ahmet hoped a PKP would help—"Penetrating Keratoplasty," he joked, "not to be confused with PKK," the Kurdish terrorist group. He took her to Canada to the specialists. PKP, then a transplant. All failed. Now he had left his blind wife behind.

While my wife sees clearly, Oğuz thought. He wanted to confide about the troubled week with Emine but it wasn't the sort of conversation he'd ever had with his brother. In recent years, their talk had been more like arguments. The beaches that were closed to Turks so that European tourists could sunbathe nude without offending (or corrupting) the locals; the bathhouses that restricted entry to Turks on days reserved for co-ed encounters and gay retreats. We are selling our morals, our birthright, according to Ahmet. And you think Islam is the solution for hypocrisy? The Turkish newspapers that printed photos of bare-breasted Scandinavians on the front page to accompany stories about tourism. Oğuz argued that either the papers shouldn't print these photos at all or Turkish woman should be as free. They'd been raised in such a puritanical culture. Oğuz only began to feel free in bed when he learned endearments in Jewish Spanish, to whisper into Emine's perfumed hair, into her ear, *kerida, mi amor, mi korazon*. At least in the West, he argued, they aren't hypocrites. Ahmet had the last word: Hypocrites about everything except for sex, said Ahmet.

Oğuz chewed a bit of flat bread. The meat remained untouched, grease congealed. But he poured a bit of powdered sumac on his palm and licked it, the taste of home, and his heart sank when he discovered that after months of fiery Indian food, the spice had no flavor. All the noise of the city seemed to be swallowed for a moment along with the light. Then lights began to twinkle and braziers glowed and fires and sound swelled again, horns honking and radios, and there was noise as stores began to roll down their metal doors and there was a red sky somewhere to the north.

Not the Turban Type

Ahmet, the pilgrim, had a driver and a Jeep with Arabic lettering that Oğuz couldn't read painted on the doors. Their grandfather had wanted them to learn Arabic beyond the verses they had to memorize from the Koran. "All educated people speak it," he'd said. And they'd argued back that educated people speak English.

His brother's apartment was near the military cantonment in a building guarded by armed security. Ahmet was on the fourth floor and the elevator didn't work.

"Intentionally disabled," said Ahmet. "We lose power from time to time. People got trapped."

Ahmet had a couch where Oğuz would sleep, a camp bed in the other room for himself. The furnishings were sparse but included a computer.

"Internet?" It meant he could email Emine each night he was here. "Who pays for all this?"

"The charity."

"Saudi money?" asked Oğuz. It occurred to him he wasn't here to compete with his brother, but to reassure himself about the religious path Ahmet had chosen.

"Does it matter?" said Ahmet. He sat back and lit up a cigarette.

"It's the 21st century," said Oğuz. "Doctors don't smoke."

"This one does," said his brother.

A red glow flamed to the west where above the bright colors black smoke billowed and furled.

"We're in a warzone," Oğuz said, "aren't we?"

"Afghanistan, just over there," Ahmet said, and gestured to the baseball cap Oğuz had left on the coffee table. "You need to replace that." He rose and opened a cabinet. "You're not the turban type." Lined up on a shelf, a full range of headgear. Kufis, pre-wrapped turban cloth, embroidered Sindhi caps, caps made of lambskin, a knit cap made of wool with a pompom on top.

"Your disguises?"

"Folklore," said Ahmet. "I think for you..." He tossed over a flat-topped velvet kufi with mirrorwork.

Visible now, on the shelf behind it, a handgun.

The electricity failed. Until Ahmet lit the oil lamps there was only his cigarette, glowing in the dark.

"In this city," said Ahmet, "you really can't be too prepared." He shut the cabinet and laughed. "At least you have proper trousers. We wouldn't want someone to kidnap you for a pair of jeans."

No electricity. No internet. No chance to write to Emine.

"Oh, brother, brother, what are we doing here?"

"What do you mean? I'm treating patients and training a couple of community health workers. Naila is terrific. Ali less so."

"You in Pakistan," said Oğuz. "And me? I'm traveling around India with peripatetic tribals. Gypsies—while I don't have any real idea how the Roma survive back home. The Khānābādōsh have tents and animals. Back home, Gypsies have homes made of cardboard, don't they? They have nothing. The police pick up their kids, torture them. Look how far we've traveled for zakat. There is misery in Istanbul, and I've never even entered their neighborhoods."

"You can't," said Ahmet. "It's dangerous." Which made them both laugh.

The lights came back on, trembled, and were extinguished again.

The morning call to prayer interrupted breakfast. Ahmet rolled out his prayer rug and went through the motions, something Oğuz had once dismissed as fine for rural people and old men. He used to be embarrassed by his grandfather shuffling in, wearing his slippers with their pushed-down heels, unrolling the rug five times a day, then with his forehead pressed against the ground.

"Muslim yoga," said Ahmet.

They left for the refugee camps. Here in the cantonment area, there were more Army tanks and Jeeps, and more Mercedes Benzes than henna-dyed donkeys.

"War makes good business," said Ahmet. This morning Oğuz was relieved to see he wore a kufi instead of the turban. It would have been unsanitary for a doctor, that flow of cloth dangling.

There were men in military uniforms, men in Western suits and men who looked just as busy and important in their kurtas or shalwar kameez. No women.

"The refugee situation was simpler years ago, during the Soviet occupation," Ahmet said. Now there were Afghans who fled the Russians but didn't return and people who fled the Taliban, and Taliban fighters who fled the US invasion, and people who cared nothing for politics but fled to save their skins. "You don't know who you're talking to and no one trusts anyone." There was the Pakistani military, their intelligence services. Americans all over the place. Military advisors, CIA. Of course, Ahmet said, for him none of that mattered: as a doctor, he treated people who needed him, no questions asked.

"That's as it should be," Oğuz said, "but the way the world is now—"

"More important than ever," his brother said.

At the North End of the Refugee Camp

Women crowded around a truck where water was being dispensed into plastic buckets. Outside a tent, more women, some in blue burqas, some with simple shawls over their heads, held their children, waiting their turn for vaccinations. Naila, in a white smock, white dupatta over her head, stood outside the trailer that served as Ahmet's clinic.

The door opened from the inside. A small man with a skullcap and a mole over his left eyebrow grinned at them.

"Salaam, hakim."

"He has a key?" Oğuz asked in Turkish.

"He shouldn't," said Ahmet.

The space was small and scarcely equipped. A Quonset hut would have been luxury compared to this, but the trailer did have a water supply. There were drums of sanitizing agents but also, Oğuz noted, drums of benzalkonium chloride and bleach standing next to each other, much too close. Mix them and they would explode.

"We don't mix them," said Ahmet.

"If they leak? That'll release chlorine gas."

"My health workers are well informed of the danger." Ahmet smiled, wagged his finger and made the gesture of mixing. "Nah! Khatarr! There. That warning is about the only Pashto I know."

What if it's even more dangerous, thought Oğuz, to let people know the stuff is dangerous?

"The mullahs used to call Pashto the language of hell," said Ahmet. He added, "Naila speaks Dari."

Naila removed her scarf and hung it on a hook, her beautiful hair now on display. If this was allowed, it was a good sign. Not only Ahmet but also Ali was not as pious as he seemed.

Naila got to work mixing sanitizer. With the single window closed, the ceiling fan only spread the fumes. Oğuz coughed and watched the fly strips dangle from the fan blades, round and round like that video cat circling in the air.

Naila washed down the table while the men cleaned their hands and Oğuz studied the posters on the wall. Enlarged photos of the human eye. Blood vessels running vertically inside the upper eyelid: normal. Swollen follicles indicating trachomatous inflammation. He heard the snap of latex gloves pulled on, the crinkle of paper being torn and laid over the table, voices: people waiting their turn outside the door. In the next photo, the swelling so thick, the blood vessels entirely disappeared. Antibiotics might still work but once the eyelashes rub against the eyeball scarring the cornea, without surgery the patient goes blind. In Nasreen's case, it hadn't been trachoma but war.

From outside: voices, dogs barking, trucks honking—day and night the honking never stopped, sirens.

"Ready?" Ahmet said.

Oğuz watched as Naila and Ali laid out grapes on a tray, then forceps and blades. "The grapes?"

"I'll work on the patient. They'll follow my movements with the instruments till it's second nature. Their hands won't shake when it's someone's eye. You can let him in."

The first patient was an old man whose moans spiked up again and again into sharp cries of pain.

"We saw him the other day," said Ahmet. "Eyelids turned in, margin pulled to the eye. His eyelashes pierce like hot needles all the time."

The generator rattled like an old air conditioner. The refrigerator hummed. Naila prepared the Lidocaine.

"She's used to giving shots," said Ahmet. "I can let her do it."

"Shúker," said the man. "Shúker, hakim bey."

Which had to be Pashto for *thank you*. In Turkish, *Teşekkür ederim*, with only stuffy schoolteachers using that long form. *Tashakor* in Dari which is related to Persian which is also called Farsi. And probably all derived from the Arabic: *shukran*. Did that mean it was the Arabs who taught us courtesy? Here were the traces. Language roots. Oğuz thought if he could just squint his hearing, he would understand.

Ahmet everted the left eyelid. He was the one who'd taught Oğuz so many years ago to turn his eyelids inside out to scare their sisters. He handed Oğuz the loupe and through it he could see the white band of scar tissue instead of pink, the thin trails of blood vessels that the girls had found so creepy even though an inner lid that looks that way is healthy. For this man, some corneal damage was already done, a curled-in lash still scraping away, but "We can save at least some vision in this eye," said Ahmet.

Above them, the fly strips rustled.

The cornea of the right eye showed an opaque patch over the

pupil. This eye would not regain sight without a transplant and there'd be none here. Nasreen's eye had rejected the transplant she'd been given.

Ahmet pierced the left lid. The skin swelled and he pressed till blood and fluid pooled out. The trainees stabbed at their grapes. Ahmet scrubbed the area and tied. He swabbed. He sliced a curve and carved a channel, splitting the lid, holding it apart with the forceps, anterior, posterior, and Oğuz watched as fruit squished, we'll have jam before the procedure is done, he thought. Naila started on another grape and, imitating Ahmet, sutured back a flap of peel. Ali muttered. Ahmet painted the wound red, like lipstick on a mouth. Ali bent his head closer and giggled and in an instant, Oğuz saw it too, the opening edged by lashes, the fringe of hair, the lips of the wound becoming a vagina before their eyes, and he wondered if Ali had ever seen a real one.

The old man startled, only the smallest bit of dark iris peeking out from the lips like a parrot's tongue. Naila calmed the patient with soothing tones and Ahmet let her do the suturing to close the repaired lid.

He praised her, and to Oğuz, "She's sewn up other body parts. I trust her."

He opened the door for the next patient, a woman young as Nasreen.

At the time of the attack, Nasreen's eyes had burned, but then seemed OK. It was her mother who died, respiratory apparatus all seared to hell, beyond hope in spite of the tube they pushed down her throat. Ten years later, in Ankara, Nasreen's vision began to fail. Delayed-onset mustard gas keratitis, the lesions, the deterioration, damage to the ocular surface epithelium and the cornea.

How could I ever have distrusted him, thought Oğuz. He truly practices zakat. He did not abandon his wife. He got her the best surgery. He took her to Canada. He tried to get her into clinical trials. He did everything a human could do. How can I criticize his faith? Here he is, restoring sight to others and Inshallah, though he expects nothing in return, maybe Allah will look with compassion on Nasreen and let her eyes look again on the beauty of the world He created.

"Train me to do this," he said.

Oğuz washed his hands and snapped on gloves.

Naila prepared the Lidocaine.

Ali popped dissected grapes into his mouth, one at a time, and gulped them whole.

A Very Bad Idea

"Emine agrees with you," Oğuz told his brother. "She is very much opposed."

"It means dealing with poachers," said Ahmet. "Illegal and very dangerous."

That made Oğuz laugh. "A bhalu-wallah, dangerous! When you can buy anything here: raw opium, weapons—I don't even know what you call most of them. Flame-throwers? Rocket-propelled grenades?" It was all right out in the open, the tribals and the turbaned Afghans checking out AK-47's in the marketplace, as casual as buying a sack of potatoes. While all he wanted was a bear.

Ahmet shrugged. "Your elder brother advises you to go home."

In the morning Oğuz wandered through the Kharkhani Bazaar. *Bhalu-wallah?* It was hard to make himself understood, the language, and the roar of planes overhead, Pakistani air force? US planes over Afghanistan here at the borderlands? He was carrying altogether too much cash to be in a place like this and his skin began to tingle with danger. He didn't know enough of anything, not the names of weapons or what forces were fighting and what for, he just kept repeating *bhalu-wallah, khānābādōsh.*

"You buy?"

He'd expected they would bring the cub to him. Instead he was walking a narrow mountain path accompanied by a fierce young man carrying one of those weapons he couldn't name. His consciousness blinked on and off, alive with risk and fear.

For the first time in months, the air was a pleasure to breathe and his legs hummed with joy. Speaking, thinking, walking, fearing—maybe this was the purpose of life, to put into functional use all of our innate capacities. And when you have a further purpose—so much the better.

His guide stopped. Now that they weren't moving, Oğuz felt the cold. The woven wool cap would have served him better, he thought, then the velvet kufi his brother had chosen for him. He was uneasy standing still, the mirrors on his head could signal him as target. The guide pointed and the sun broke for a moment between the clouds and below them Oğuz saw an encampment in the valley. The guide nodded. That's where they were going.

As Though Boundaries Don't Exist

It was Paradise. Not the walled garden of angels and houris. It was the Shangri-La dreamed by the Brits and the Yanks. It was the Garden of Eden. It was the place of peace where the lion lies down with the lamb.

The woman beautiful as a Madonna never looked up but cradled the bear cub as it fed from a bottle, its paws wrapped in total trust around her arm. Her lips moved. Surely a lullaby. Another cub nursed at the teat of a complacent nanny goat and two others wrestled in play and then stood on hindlegs together, dancing like the dogs he'd seen in a traveling exhibit of pre-Columbian art.

The afternoon drizzle began. Oğuz found himself in the supply tent. Hoisted up on ropes where the bears couldn't reach there were sacks of powdered milk labeled Deseret Dairy, USAID, Australia Gold Cow. It had to be refugee relief, and the box of Micronutrient-Fortified Biscuit. A woman was adding some honey to a bottle and shaking the mixture. She smiled and handed it to him. She wrapped his arm in a discarded sack and then he was sitting on an unrolled carpet mat, a bear cub wriggling and looking up at him and then settling down to feed.

He had left behind the world of Peshawar's inhabitants, the Pashtuns and Hindkowans, the Tajiks and Hazaras, Uzbeks, Persians, Punjabis, Chitralis, the Gypsies who made him feel guilty about how ignorant he was of the Roma back home. They spoke Pashto and Dari and Hindko, Urdu, Hazaragi and Baluchi and Khowar and Saraiki. There were Sunnis and Twelver Shi'as and Ismailis and Alevis. And what of it? Why couldn't Kurds speak Kurdish? Why could Turkey only be Turkey if everyone agreed to speak nothing but Turkish? He cuddled the bear and could feel its heart beating against him. The exhilaration of language gave way to wordless wonder. The little animal made sounds that had to be contentment. Without knowing how to express it, he'd known this truth: nothing is exotic in the essential continuum of life.

We are all part of it, he thought, me and Emine and the children we will have.

His intentions had been pure, maybe tainted just a bit with fraternal rivalry. But now he found his act of charity, zakat, had turned into adventure. And adventure was sheer pleasure. And soon he would return home and he and Emine would have children and they'd go back to being responsible and careful and the only adventures on the horizon would belong to their children, and his stories about travels in India and Pakistan would encourage them to be daring and open to experience. This was how he could justify his self-indulgence, not as charity but his attempt to be a role model for sons and daughters as yet unborn. Emine, he thought, I'm coming home. He would have a baby boy or girl in his arms soon, a tiny human being, and someday he would tell the child how he had held a bear cub and spoken to it *Benim bebeğim, küçükayı, Benim küçük bebeğim.* Sweet thing, he said, I'm going to take you to Baba. The cub looked upon him not as an alien being but as a loving parent. Tranquilized, drugged, the baby would sleep and Oğuz had to believe a little money would cause the eyes at border inspection to close just enough to let them pass. The bear cub trusted him because the power of love crosses all boundaries and we must live from this day on, he thought, as though boundaries don't exist, as though there are none.

It's All About the Dollars

The bhalu-wallah came for him and led him to the next camp and presented him with a creature almost twice the baby's size. A trained bear still whimpering. Its front claws cut out, its canines pulled. The man beat the animal with a staff, kicked it, then tied it to a stake using the rope that ran through its nose. He gestured to Oğuz to feed the creature. Biscuits. Grapes. Oğuz had not been present when the creature was abused and tortured. Now the bear had to learn some human beings would be its friends. The animal hesitated, panting, hungry but suspicious. Hungry too, thought Oğuz, for the affection it had once received before this cruel, inhuman man had taken it away. The bear approached and took a biscuit from Oğuz's palm, chewed with its back molars. All around the holes in its nose the skin and flesh were angry and red and in places swollen white and dripping with pus. Without the antibiotics Oğuz carried, he was sure the young bear would die. How many died here in training? He didn't know what was happening to him, this tenderness he'd never felt for animals before, and his pain and rage at what had been done. He wished he could buy them all.

He took out the package in which he carried the money.

The bhalu-wallah didn't even count it. Oğuz couldn't understand at first what he was saying, other than that he was angry. The man threw a 1000-rupee note to the ground and stepped on it. "Dollars! Amrikaayi!"

He shook his head. "No dollars. I have Pakistan rupees. India rupees."

An empty sack of milk powder over his head made him sneeze. His hands were tied behind him. He urged his face forward, trying to wipe his nose clean but only disturbed more powder. Someone pushed him.

When the sack came off, Americans. "You speak English," he said happily before they threw him to the ground. Shouts of *Al Qaeda! Terrorist!* "I'm a doctor," he said. "Like al-Zawahiri," someone answered. They kicked him with their boots. By then he had a black hood over his head so he saw nothing. Emine, he murmured like a prayer, kerida, mi amor, the words of love he'd learned from her, Emine, mi amor, mi korazon.

Rennie

Ms. Rubin in high school told us to memorize poetry so we'd have something to sustain us if They came for us. I didn't listen. I'd write my own, or my confession, or my evidence, or whatever They want, but no one gives me paper or pen. Instead, I'm reduced to thinking!

File #6:
Outlaw Science

Simple Things Can Be Easily Misconstrued

Dawit Tesfaye smiled, which is what he always did to put strangers at ease. He thought McMillan was a potential investor, they came through Manatech sometimes, usually better dressed, and though they sometimes spoke to him, an inconsequential question or two, this visitor said nothing, only looked at him a long time while listening to Dr. Avakian. Soon after they walked away, Tesfaye was called to the office. The man was seated behind Dr. Avakian's desk. "Close the door," he said, and once they were left alone, he showed a badge. "Have a seat. J.T. McMillan. FBI."

Dawit's teeth started to chatter. They always used to when he was nervous. That had stopped after 9/11. He and Gladys had already known the evil human beings were capable of and with the child-like Americans around them so overwhelmed with the knowledge, he took it upon himself to project an image of strength. After the attacks he began to stand a little straighter. His voice was clear. He wanted to protect everyone but it came across wrong, as though he'd discovered pride because of the terrorist acts.

Take a deep breath, he told himself. It was probably about Special Registration which would be a problem, yes, but he did have an explanation. He was an American citizen, had been naturalized as a boy so he didn't think the new rules applied to him, and anyway, he wasn't sure which group he fell into: born in Eritrea, or maybe Ethiopia, in Sudan, in Somalia. He'd been born, he'd believed for years in what was now Eritrea, but it hadn't been a country then, and later he learned he'd been born in a refugee camp and there were so many stories, so many lies, he wasn't sure over which border, if any, or where. Somewhere in the Horn of Africa. Had his mother fled across the border with him already in her belly? Or was his tortured murdered father not his father at all? She was raped in the camp. His father could have been one of those. His father could be anyone. Eritrean, Ethiopian, Somali, Arab. If she was raped in the camp, it was almost certainly more than once, by more than one. What was printed on his documents most likely wasn't true, and this agent probably knew it.

"Did I pronounce your name correctly?"

Dawit nodded. However anyone pronounced it, he always agreed. All that new confidence gone. Why couldn't he have been David Levy? If the Levys had formally adopted him, given him their name, none of this would be happening but they'd insisted he retain his own culture. Bacteria have cultures, he'd thought at the time, but had been too timid and possibly grateful to say it aloud.

The first round of registrations had been the Iranian men. Hundreds detained and locked up without cause, unable to contact their families. When the second round started, Maher from the mailroom, with whom he'd never spoken before, asked "Are you registering? Do you know if I have to?" "Where are you from?" "Palestine." Far be it from me, Dawit thought, to tell the man his country isn't a country. But neither, possibly, was his own.

"Masters in Biochemistry," said McMillan, "course work in bacteriology, experienced in flow cytometry."

He nodded. Could they possibly believe he would use biological weapons against his own people, because that's what Americans were, his own.

"And the work you're doing here?"

"Cell biologist," he said.

"And the project?"

"That's, uh, proprietary information. I signed an NDO."

McMillan smiled. That was apparently the right answer.

"And I was appointed supervisor of lab safety protocols."

"What about biosecurity?"

"I'm not aware of..." Did this mean he had not been trusted? "I know about Asilomar, of course, but..."

"The languages you speak?" said McMillan.

"English."

"And?"

"I studied Spanish. I wouldn't call myself proficient."

"And?"

"I picked up a little French. Vacations. Conferences."

"And?"

Obvious what the man wanted. "My mother tongue," he said, "or more precisely, my *mother's* tongue, was Tigrinya."

"Don't they speak Arabic in Eritrea?"

"Many people do," he said. He wanted to say I'm not an Arab, and not all Arabs are terrorists. "We came to the US when I was very young. Then my mother...died." She had killed herself. He had found her. He hardly remembered or didn't want to. He was 18 before the only mother he knew—Natalie Levy—told him: his birth mother had already suffered so much. In Los Angeles, she was assaulted but not in the end raped. The man expressed disgust at her circumcision, beat her, and left her. Found bleeding in the street, jaw broken, she was taken to the police and to a counselor. *That's how we know what happened. It broke her spirit. It broke her mind,* said his mom. *When she killed herself, it wasn't that she didn't love you.*

"I don't remember the language at all."

This time it was the wrong answer. McMillan pressed his lips together.

Dawit told himself, I've never given cause for complaint. He was OK as long as he could look at what he was doing instead of being looked at. Now in the spotlight, he concentrated on the man's face.

"Well," said McMillan, "we'd hoped to find not just a scientist but a linguist." Then he said, "Would you like to serve your country?"

Questions of Dual Use

A month later, he concluded going to work for the FBI had been the mistake of his life. Dawit had given up his research—his dream of accomplishing something that would save lives—to save even more from imminent danger, but now, after training sessions in Los Angeles and Washington, DC on recombinant DNA and genetically engineered pathogens, he sat around doing nothing.

Didn't he wish to prove his loyalty? He wasn't sure what the word meant. It was just by chance that a person was born in Kabul or born in New York, just luck that he had been brought to Los Angeles, luck that turned bad for his mother. Didn't he want to serve his country? And he thought, not his country, but its people. Its poor, frightened, unprepared people.

If the Bureau really did need him, the problem was that no one had figured out what to do with him.

"I'm a biochemist. I'm not going to carry a gun."

He had no background in forensics, he was useless at crime scenes and in the lab. He sat around in the bullpen waiting for a field agent to consult with him. Was this all his fault, that he wasn't sufficiently motivated to find a role for himself? Which made him not all that different from the other men—and two women—in the office. In spite of all the urgency, people put in their hours and did their jobs, unwilling to be seen as obsessed. Finally, the special agent-in-charge agreed to schedule some time for him to offer a presentation.

"Can we teleconference with other field offices?" It turned out they lacked the technological capacity.

Five agents showed up, four men, one woman.

"You're all familiar with Biowatch, monitoring the air in major cities and at sensitive sites to give early warning of a biological or chemical attack. I'm on board now to assist in prevention—not only the prevention of an imminent attack, but preventing our enemies from gaining access to the research and technology they could use to hurt us."

For decades, he explained, the US mostly depended on scientists to monitor themselves and to cooperate by withholding from publication any research that could be classified. "We've relied on export control regulations. The point is, we also have to prevent the export of classified ideas and research—intangibles—just like the tangibles." He was no good at this at all. He read from his notes. "We used to focus on research specifically with relation to weapons systems. Today, bombs and rockets are a small part of our concern. Instead of hardware engineering, we're concerned with bioengineering, genetic manipulations that could either on their own create bioweapons or suggest techniques that could be adapted to do so. I'm talking about dual use—technology you can use for peaceful purposes or for war." He chose not to share his wife's words According to Gladys, the FBI was dual use: *They can protect us, or oppress us.* "We have foreign scientists and graduate students in our universities and labs and research institutions," he said. "What do we really know about these individuals as they gain knowledge and specialized training?" There was an even greater concern—one that no one really worried about before. "Wherever you live, there are sheds, garages, backyards, closets, any one of which may be a laboratory holding seeds of destruction. It's DIY science. Do-It-Yourself. They call themselves Citizen Scientists. I call it Outlaw Biology. Outlaw Chemistry. These people can obtain sophisticated equipment over the internet and operate without any controls." He put down his index cards, removed his glasses, caught himself cleaning the lenses with his tie. Much too obvious that he was nervous. "No proper training or safety standards, making them an immediate danger to their neighbors," he said. "And we don't know who they are, or what their intentions are. Worried about someone cooking meth next door? Maybe, but maybe they're making bioweapons." Certainly he'd made the threat clear. Certainly he would find a purpose. "Certainly we encourage our kids to create ever more elaborate projects and experiments for science fairs and competitions." These days, it was hard to find a middle school student who hadn't already extracted DNA from strawberries. "So we're in a situation where I can be of help, as a scientist familiar with lab procedures and government restrictions. If your investigations take you into these areas, please call on me."

Everyone said thank you. Then he went back to his desk and waited till it was time to leave.

An African Birthright

Driving home after dark, winding up Beverly Glen. The early nightfall, he thought, is how Angelenos know it's winter. And the rain. When the skies opened, so did his heart, to both joy and dread. The emotion that ran through his body—he liked to believe it was a remnant of memory, something African that had survived childhood amnesia. He'd come from a parched land that welcomed rain as a blessing till it turned, as it always did, to disaster: flood and waterborne disease.

He went over what he'd said. What he should have said. He clutched the steering wheel. Dawit didn't like to drive.

Bike riders were supposedly the good guys but he wished they'd stay off the roads, especially in bad weather, especially at night. On the narrow roads over the hills to the Valley, they pedaled away in black clothes and without lights. Or what about the arrogance of the cyclists who rode together three or four abreast holding up everyone behind them. Tonight, coming toward him, a cyclist with a flashing light in front, his safety warning was a strobe. Dawit had to stop though there was no safe place to pull over and sit. He set his hazard lights flashing until his eyesight stabilized again and he could see.

The next morning, Daniel Chen approached him and asked for help and no one was surprised. Everyone knows about Asians and science.

"So where are you from?" Chen asked.

"The Valley," he managed to say. "Encino." He hated talking about it: The classes in kids kung fu he had to take in case he was ever bullied at school. He wasn't. Worse, the dinners in Little Ethiopia where he was expected to honor his heritage by eating without utensils, scooping up food with his right hand. He never told them how it made him feel dirty and even now for special occasions that's where they take him.

They tried so damn hard.

When he had what they referred to as his little problem, *It couldn't hurt*, his mother said when the healer knocked on their door. The woman burned sage and anointed him with oil. "They call me a shaman though I myself would not presume." She beat a drum and chanted and shook some rattles over his head. He felt warmth. Maybe she had built a fire? He was sweating and things broke from his skin, growing, in his mind's eye he saw the horns, spiky, growing out of his body, and at the end of each spike, an eye.

"It's natural for Africans to believe in magic." She did presume to know *that*. Like her, he was an American. He'd grown up to be a scientist. "It's in your blood, in your genes, your soul," she said. "The ancestors speak to you. And through you."

Then they came through him, their dark heads popping out from his body, like cats with their little pink tongues, bright pink tissue of their open mouths. They spoke rapidly in languages he didn't understand. Not only Tigrinya because Natalie had told him how clever Africans were, they spoke several languages, all of them, unlike Americans who were ignorant. The heads were conjured up with unblinking eyes, and then the eyelashes flashed and the African heads blinked harder and harder until they created a great wind and the wind blinded him with dust and in the whirlwind he recognized his dead mother's voice.

"Why didn't you adopt me?" he asked his Natalie-mother.

"You don't look like a David Levy, do you?" she said. "Dawit's a beautiful name, like the chirping of a bird."

"Whoopi Goldberg," he said.

"Not her real name," said Natalie. "She took it to be funny. And you are not a joke."

Chirp, chirp, in a classroom of American boys. Not a joke?

She assured him he wouldn't age out, he would always have a home with them and, aside from some charitable bequests, he was the sole beneficiary of their wills. "We're your Mom and Dad."

His parents never fought though once, after Gladys and her mother moved in, he heard his Dad raise his voice behind a closed door: "Does a person have to be African to get any attention from you?"

His father made sure to tell him that after 9/11 he'd gone to each halal meat market in the Valley to say "You people have been good neighbors" which was obviously a better response than what was being said by most Americans around the country but still Dawit cringed to hear "you people."

Glad's mother on racism: "You can hardly blame them, the Americans. They haven't had time. Their country is so young."

He heard Americans touting one new idea or product after another: *It will change your life!* but he didn't want his life to ever change. Who would want to leave the Levy home? The magnolia trees in blossom, dropping their grenades, the Jacaranda Walk, the bougainvillea on the walls, Ramiro, the jardinero, who sang rancheras as he worked and still used a rake both for fallen leaves and to maintain the Zen garden where Natalie meditated by the pond and Ramiro sometimes talked to the carp in his pretend Japanese. How on earth did it happen that a boy like Dawit Tesfaye was able to live like this? There were roses, a cactus and succulent garden, and to mark the autumn even here, trees that changed color: the brilliant red of the sweet gum, the yellow poplar leaves. So perfect that Barry Greenburg, visiting, said, with a sweep of the arm, "None of this is real." So what was real? He and Glad on the tennis court, neither trying to defeat the other. The challenge was to see how long they could keep the volley going while his father shouted at them, "That's not the way to play!"

He bought her a silk scarf, black and gold and flaming red.

"My daughter isn't cut," said her mother. "I wouldn't allow it." She stared at him, her eyes small in her fat face. "I never expect she will marry African man."

"I'm an American," he said.

She said, "Naturalized."

Now, living more modestly, he didn't want anything to change. He had just what he wanted. He didn't need a circle of friends. He had Gladys.

The Levys' own heritage was lost somewhere in Europe and they seemed unperturbed by the loss or were satisfied with broad strokes, some respect for a world of Eastern European Jewry that no longer existed. They had no need of specifics, not the names of great-grandparents or the cities or towns in which they lived and died, though he suspected there was an unspoken or even unconscious emptiness, a disconnection, or a sense of guilt that made them so concerned with preserving his, Dawit's, so-called culture. (Eritreans had gone to war, they had killed and died to have their own nation. It had to count for something.)

The Horn. Horned Moses with the tablets. The ram's horn. The dust glowing across the Horn of Africa. His childhood before the US came to him in flashes that might have been memory or dream or elaborations of news stories he'd seen about other refugees, other camps. A baby in its mother's arms under an African sky. All those beautiful friendly animals. It was a memory all right, it was the *Lion King*. And does he really remember this? Women cutting themselves and collecting blood in plastic basins, not some African ritual, but to feed their children the way herdsmen tapped blood from their cattle back when people still had cattle to herd. His people herded goats, not cattle, he thinks. Which doesn't matter. Only this: Had his mother given him her own blood to drink? He pictures his face smeared with blood and tears, which can't be right, if he were inside his own body, he wouldn't be able to see his face, it's not as though they had mirrors. They had nothing. Dust, fear. Cactus poking out of rocks same as in the canyons of Southern California. The nutri-biscuits so hard and dry his teeth fell out in his mouth, but they were only baby teeth, it didn't matter, and that must have been where the memory came from, from the hole in his gums, the metal taste in his mouth of blood. His mother wiping his face with the fabric edge of her head wrap. Rain falling at night and in the morning, green over the earth like mold on bread, gone by the morrow. The dry air carried whimpers, screams, pounding footfalls of racing camels and women calling out as they gathered their children, truck engines, cries, his own cry of alarm at the vaccination needle. And somewhere in his memory a drumming sound, a slapping sound, hundreds of women slapping their breasts to encourage milk the way he believes an addict tries to find life in an overused vein. You could see the veins lining the dark empty breasts. In America, with Gladys, picnicking in the Alabama Hills at Lone Pine, they even picked up the map and dutifully visited every site used as a location for Hollywood films they'd never seen, the parched earth and granite domes and rock arches made him shiver nonetheless with something recognized though not remembered. The memories were fantasy. Had to be. Most likely, he had lived it without seeing anything. His eyes were infected. It was only because a foreign doctor visited the camp that he didn't go blind. Till the temporary blindness and the healer. He was sure his sight would have come back on its own without her. He was, after all, a scientist.

How Does It Feel to Be *They*?

"That's what you are now," said Chen. "The infamous *They*. Inspiring paranoia in the Left."

Dawit had agreed to work with the FBI, but only if he would never have to carry a gun. He thought, I want to get through my life on earth without hurting anyone.

Chen was always talkative when working with someone new, a way to avoid talking about himself, something he found as uncomfortable as Dawit did. "And libertarians. They're paranoid too. *They* are watching you. *They* will entrap you. *They* are part of the almighty evil Big Brother surveillance state."

"I thought the terrorists were the *They*."

"*They* will always be the hostile force without a name or a face," Chen said. "But *we* have to see individuals. When you—we—investigate or interrogate, it's always an individual human being. We go in knowing as much as it's possible to know and then we elicit bits and pieces. It's a mosaic, Tesfaye."

Dawit Tesfaye preferred being called Dawit, pronounced Dah-Wheat. In the US, people always seemed to pronounce the W like a V, to make it sound like David. In high school he'd been Davy; in college, Dave.

Chen preferred to go by his last name. Given his slight stature, too many people over the years had persisted in calling him "Danny Boy," a nickname that would only work, he believed, if you were Filipino. He was Chinese, sort of, born in Singapore when it was still part of Malaysia. Cantonese-speaking, if you consider that means understanding most of what your mother used to say to you as a little boy before the family began to communicate primarily and then exclusively in English.

What a Mutt and Jeff pair. Chen, short, slight—he looked like the scientist. Dawit was, at least, imposing in size but if he didn't actually have an identifiable accent, there was something in his speech that hinted at foreign birth. If they hadn't carried badges and ID, whoever would have taken them for FBI? They did wear suits and ties. In some ways the Bureau hadn't changed since the days of J. Edgar Hoover, though with agents like Dawit and Chen—and Dawit was actually a specialist, not an agent—the FBI had become an exemplary model of diversity.

"Now they—we—talk about a failure to connect the dots," said Chen. "That's not how I look at it. The dots just give you an outline.

We need the whole picture. A mosaic. You don't see at first how things relate. Nothing comes to you in chronological order. But discard nothing. Better yet, instead of a mosaic, think jigsaw puzzle. Look at the big picture, as much of it as you've got. Your eyes scan the board. You pick up the new bit of intelligence and you ask, Is this part of the design? And if so, you have to ask where does it fit? Or what I prefer to do, I start putting it together by looking at the piece that looks out of place. That doesn't fit."

I've always been that piece, thought Dawit. "I thought we'd be going to places like JPL," he said.

"Federally funded. Background checks and a security survey. We know what they're doing there. We pay for it."

"So we're *We*, not *They*."

"Good to know which side we're on," Chen said. He hoped the *We* would stay small, manageable. That the FBI would stay independent, not get stuck inside the new bureaucracy they were dreaming up in DC, Homeland Security now in the works.

They drove to Granada Hills to check out the delivery of an online order of arsenic, charged to the credit card registered to a felon. Who turned out to be the current boyfriend of the mother of a high school academic decathlon champ—an Asian kid, of course. "I'm growing Mono Lake bacteria," said the kid, "to show it can swap out phosphorus for arsenic. Awesome!"

"So," said Chen after they left. "We check out every smart geek in Southern California?"

"Just Los Angeles and Kern Counties."

Chen said, "Even before 9/11, we had our hands full. The environmental movement, for one thing. Saboteurs in trees—sitting in them or booby trapping them, attacks on research facilities, smart alecks trying to disrupt the sale of public lands—"

"Animal rights," said Dawit.

"College kids blowing up gas guzzlers on car lots."

"We don't go to JPL," Dawit said, "but we'll do real science when we visit the legitimate labs." They would have to look at technology with dual use that could be used for good or for evil. Since Bush, he'd noticed, even scientists were comfortable talking about evil. "If you can clean up the site of a nuclear accident—a very good thing to do—are you more likely to use a nuclear weapon, trusting in your own ability to remediate? If you have the antidote, might you use a bioweapon?"

Of course, Dawit thought, it was costing the US millions, maybe billions, just to do the studies. Remediation itself? Billions more. Even if Iran stole the so-called secrets, how could a country like Iran afford to do what the US couldn't?"

"Of course they can't," said Chen. "But people are dangerous when they think they can."

"Or when they think they know what they're doing," said Dawit. It was still outlaw science that worried him most. Toxins available by mail order. Seemingly legitimate research institutions like DHI providing material and technical support to sci-fi nerds and antisocial weirdos.

"Forget anthrax," said Chen. "Maybe they're making Frankenstein."

Just a Friendly Interview

Desert Haven Institute. DHI. DEE-Hi. In January, they interviewed the Chairman and CEO, JB Singh.

After he sold his startup, Singh told them readily, he left Silicon Valley and moved to LA with more money than he knew what to do with. He still didn't have power. "When you're this rich, it's easy to do evil," he said. "Making a positive contribution—on your own terms— to humanity, that's hard. There are always gatekeepers in the way."

His grandfather had left the Punjab before WWI. A poor man who never thought about power, just about sending money home to his young wife and three babies, his family barred from immigration while he worked for a pittance in the Central Valley fields. Living just long enough to see US immigration laws change so that in the days before he died, he was able to bring one son, his son's second wife, and his 4-year-old grandson JB to America.

"This nonsense didn't exist in the fields," Singh told Dawit. "The workers got along. Now to the Hindus, we Sikhs are assassins. To the Christians, we are Muslim terrorists. Of course to my family, I'm an apostate. I converted to Catholicism, in name only, to please my Irish wife. You see, I'm a scientist. I have no truck with superstition. With that famous manger where the Baby Jesus gets his face licked by the sacred cow."

"The Desert Haven Institute," Dawit prompted.

Because of gatekeepers, Singh explained. Investors who only see results in terms of balance sheets. Government funds under this nincompoop Bush taken away if you look at stem cells or climate change or environmental remediation or any earth science that conflicts with Biblical myth.

"I wanted to make movies," said Singh. "A movie that I myself would want to see. That I would want my children to see and everyone's children. A work of art. So I started a production company and what happens? The agents send me crap. The same crap you see on the big screen every day—if you bother to go—or on your home entertainment system if that's your preference, but who would choose to watch this crap? Do you understand that what we experience actually changes the organization of our brains? Even when it's vicarious experience. The rush and pleasure people get from watching violence along with the terror we experience. We live in a worldwide culture that is creating human monsters."

"I think you are, in spite of your protest, a deeply religious man," said Dawit.

"These days, I think about wearing a turban, in defiance of the bigots. You can't just ask for scripts. You get overwhelmed. Thousands of submissions, hundreds of thousands. If you try to read them yourself. So I, too, resorted to gatekeepers. And ended up with an army of underlings trying to guess at my taste or applying their own woefully inadequate judgment."

"Why not write your own screenplay?"

"Oh, I would if I had the time. Carson Yampolsky understood. His background in the music business, trying to get his bands past the gatekeepers. The movie business. The music business. It's too venal, too corrupt. Carson came to me with his idea, a way to finance his band. Yes, a spiritual ensemble of men and women. They had a gong blessed by the Dalai Lama. Why not sell financial interests in Flowstone Drapery? Provide the seed capital for them to record, distribute, tour and reach the public. Investors would own shares and receive a percentage of profits. I knew it wouldn't work, but I wanted to help, so I gave them $50,000 and never saw a penny of it back. But that's how the idea was born. Why not sell shares in scientific research? Benefit humanity and realize a profit. We created DHI as an investment opportunity. I provided the initial injection of capital. I recruited other investors."

"You'll give us names?"

"Of course. As for day-to-day operations, the area is remote. We had trouble holding onto administrators till he gave up on the music business. Till we hired Carson."

"You knew he had a drug problem."

"I knew it would be advantageous to him to remove himself from his environment."

The First Visit to DHI

Shortly after the Singh interview, they met the research staff, shook hands with Carson Yampolsky. A fish out of water, Dawit thought. Then Chen used the script he'd memorized as the words were not the sort he would ever use: "I make no bones about it, ladies and gentlemen, we're all at risk of the leak of classified information and I'm not at liberty to tell you what." No lab data was to be taken home, nothing hand-carried ever again off the premises.

Now the fish out of water was all shook up. Carsky, baby, now you've got Law Enforcement Homeland Security all sticking their beaks into a place that till recently no one knew about and no one cared about. He was the Director, sure, but it's not like he handled classified information himself. And if the foreigners did? That was Rennie's fault. She was supposed to monitor all that. They were scientists and he wasn't and what was he supposed to do now the FBI was sniffing around the science? I mean scientists talk to each other. They communicate. They share. International collaboration is the norm—or was, and so no surprise they took a rather expansive view of what was allowed. Petty minds devise petty restrictions so—though he'll have to check with Rennie on that—at the Institute, he thought, we probably ignored them. But now we've got the New Normal.

Rennie Mulcahy turned over the list of private clients, the DIY files. Almost too cooperative, too eager to do so, Dawit thought. She's showing off, thought Chen, bragging how it was her idea.

When they returned a second time and asked to see Emine Albaz, she was somewhere she should not have been allowed to be.

Motives, Motivations, Reasons

"We have some questions," said Chen.

"Ah yes," said Isabeau Huisman. "Inquiring minds. Did I leave South Africa because of apartheid or because I knew it was coming to an end? No, I do not consider myself an exile. Yes, I have lived in Southern California for the last 30 years, but here I represent the interests of my country. I promote good will and investment. I help Americans—and visiting Chinese—explore financial opportunity."

"We're more interested in your own investment," said Chen. "DHI."

"Oh that," she said. "A favor for my dear friend JB Singh. He encouraged me to leave that Yankee rat of a second husband so when he asked for capital, it seemed only right that part of the settlement should go to support his project. Don't judge my financial acumen on that. When I advise clients, I'm hardheaded, profit first. For JB, I was sentimental."

Not Yet a Suspect

"A majority shareholder at DHI," said Chen, "turns out to also be the chair of the annual Anti-Semitism Week at one of our public universities."

"Such a thing exists?" said Dawit.

"The first entry that comes up if you google his name. After the Brooklyn artist and the basketball player since I don't think we're looking at either of them."

"It is my pleasure to have FBI in my office," said Asem al-Masri when they met on campus. "There is much I have wondered. For example, is it true 300 or more active serial killers are free in this country on any day?"

You'd think a man with the same name as the al-Qaeda terrorist would avoid speaking with such—what word would you use? *gusto?* about killing.

"Al-Masri simply means The Egyptian," he said. "Many from different nations of origin all have Egypt in their history."

The problem with these Arabs, they all have several names, on top of that thousands of them have the same name, not to mention the same name that gets transliterated half a dozen different ways into English.

"I had the most interesting conversation once with a forensic psychiatrist," al-Masri said. "Apparently many people who commit terrible acts do so in a very logical manner. For example, a man who bit off his wife's ear because he believed that even people who hate their own looks, who are very critical—weight, shape, skin—they rely on their ears to look normal."

Is he daring us, playing with us? wondered Dawit. Surely he knew how many of his co-religionists had been arrested in sweeps. Sure, most of the cases couldn't be proved. They ended up convicted on minor immigration violations. So the ACLU howled, but most Americans love that kind of move. It's legendary, how we took down Al Capone. If you want someone off the street and can't make serious charges stick, go with what you've got, even if it's an arrest for spitting on the sidewalk. Most of the time this made good sense to Dawit, but now, with al-Masri calmly teasing, he felt an uneasy kinship with the suspect. Who was not yet a suspect, he reminded himself.

"My father left his family home and olive groves in Palestine to study in Cairo. The disaster fell upon us. My grandparents and uncles remained but my father was not allowed by Israel to return. We became al-Masri. It was my good fortune to emigrate to the United States.

"So yes," he said, "I organize an annual event on the past, present, and future of Palestine. Impossible to address this subject if one avoids mentioning Israel, is it not so? But that is not the same as being anti-Semitic. Surely you see this.

"Or disloyal. Consider my research, how to use sugars from bacteria and from algae to make plastics. No need of petroleum products. I am working to make my adopted country, which is also yours, independent of Middle East oil.

"As for DHI, I review research proposals. Sometimes I recommend persons who might wish to invest."

"We'll need their names," said Chen.

"I think your manner of profiling misses the point," said al-Masri. "Let me tell you a story. When I was in college, during one break when I could not afford to fly home, an American student invited me to visit his family. At mealtimes, no water or other beverage was taken. I thought this must be their religion, or perhaps a tradition of their ethnic group. Then I learned it was their practice because of a health food newsletter. They believe that swallowing solid food and swallowing liquid each employs different mechanisms and it is very dangerous to change back and forth from one to the other. And so, no drinking with meals."

And the point of this? thought Chen.

"You see, I came to understand, in the United States, it is the media alone that determines tribal loyalties. You belong if you watch this TV, listen to this radio, read this newspaper or newsletter or magazine. Father and son, brother and brother belong to different tribes if they visit different places on the World Wide Web."

"Have you visited al-Qaeda websites or watched al-Qaeda videos online?"

"Ah, a trick question," he said. "I'm sure you have monitored my computer. You know I have. And I will tell you why. I am worried. Your security forces don't speak Arabic."

"Some do," said Dawit.

"Thoroughly inadequate," said al-Masri. "I must protect myself and my family."

"Would you protect only your family," said Chen, "or will you share the information with us?"

Al-Masri smiled without showing his teeth. "Until the circumstance arrives," he said, "one can't predict whether one's actions will be heroic, or dastardly."

They Had the Linguist on the Secure Line

Millicent Ann Reverdy spoke English with a Deep South drawl. She didn't speak Turkish at all, another Bureau screw-up. Once they finally had access to Oğuz's emails, Chen needed someone to translate them. "Hebrew and Farsi," she said. "That's my calling." And she wasn't ready to terminate the call. "I revere the Jews, the Chosen People. And Persian Jews seem to me the closest we can get to antiquity. We live in a corrupt age, Mr. Chen. You have to go back in time. Consider the Irish. The Irish people are wonderful, not like Irish Americans. The Italian people. The ancient Hebrews and Israelites. Dear me, not at all like the Israelis in LA. And," she said, "Persians are *not* Arabs."

"Neither are Turks," he muttered and hung up but not before she said, "Have a blessed day."

Life-Forms Other Than Human

Caitlin Virshaw, DHI client (or would you say customer) opened her door. Chinese, thought Dawit. Japanese—rather, Japanese American, thought Chen, correctly.

Virshaw was obviously Asian in spite of her name and long blond hair. She wore it in a pony tail and just to confuse matters more, her roots weren't dark. Instead the tail's tip was black as though dipped in ink.

"You're not zoned for residential," Chen said wondering why a person who lived in Los Angeles would choose to live in a warehouse district where the streets were dirty and blocked with delivery trucks and you didn't see a single tree.

"It's my workspace," said Caitlin Virshaw. Even blocking the door with her body, she knew they could see the bed. "So maybe I take a nap from time to time. Access the unconscious."

Outside, the beep beep beep of a delivery truck backing up and then the usual clatter and clang and voices shouting in Spanish and she stood, hands on hips. The sleeves had been cut off her smock—or torn off, given how ragged the edges. They could see her tattooed biceps, none of the usual designs but rather each arm with the diagram of a chemical compound.

"Ms. Virshaw, we're not here to hassle you about zoning," Dawit said. The tattoo on her left arm—Clostridium botulinum Type A—was another matter. "We need to talk to you about your work."

She rose up just a bit on her toes when she spoke to him. "Since when does the FBI send art critics?"

"Ms. Virshaw," Dawit tried again. "My background isn't in law enforcement. It's in science. That's my interest in your work, and your collaboration with the Desert Haven Institute. The intersection of science and art."

"Science is an art," she said. "Art is a science. Both move forward through experimentation."

"Replicable experiments," said Dawit.

"Both fields, you need precision in your skills but ultimately both fields depend on what's in your mind. Your vision."

The words sounded rehearsed. Maybe she was quoting from her Artist's Statement prepared for an upcoming gallery show. An earlier Virshaw quote had caught Chen's eye when they prepared for the visit: *It is in my nature to be inward and reclusive...I find I relate best to life-forms other than human.*

"We're interested in the bacterial samples you sent to DHI," he said.

"My latest series. I want to look at the most despised and

misunderstood life-form—though there are misanthropes who would say it's human beings, not bacteria, that fit the bill. I thought I might find beauty and order even in a colony of bacteria, but I was ready to accept the truth of whatever I might find."

"Can we see?" said Chen.

"I know what you people did in Buffalo," she said.

"Buffalo," said Chen. "That was very wrong. Very unfortunate." The artist in jail, his wife dead, all his savings gone to legal bills and the charges against him, at least according to Dawit, entirely bogus. "We're trying to learn from that mistake. We need people like you to talk to us, to explain what you're doing. We just don't get it." Like most modern art, he thought. "And until we do, much as I hate to say it, it's only too likely we'll screw up again."

"It's my job to prevent that," Dawit said.

He tried to do the job right but it wasn't easy. People said *Tell us what's permitted and what isn't and we'll abide by the rules*, and he had to answer *Tell me exactly what you're doing and then I'll tell you whether or not you're breaking the law* and they would say, *And what if we're breaking it only because we didn't know it was illegal?* and Chen would say, *Then it's up to the courts to decide* and then you couldn't get another word out of them. You could hardly blame them. *I heard we're allowed to have closed beakers but not open ones*, said the mother of a precocious child who, if they hadn't confiscated his lab, could have won the Westinghouse Science Fair.

"Just last month," Dawit told Caitlin Virshaw, "I managed to abort a raid. On a chocolate lab. I convinced the agent-in-charge it wasn't a facility but a dog." This wasn't true but it had worked in the past to lighten the mood and build rapport.

She stared up at him. Her bottom lip bulged as she ran her tongue inside her mouth as though she expected to find a pressure point that would trigger the right decision.

"OK," she said. "Come in."

The canvasses were huge, the size, Chen thought, for a living room wall in a McMansion. Flowers emerging from fireworks, loops and chains holding fast to capsules. But the one that both Chen and Dawit approached, then stepped back from, checked out from different angles, showed what looked like a view of the ocean floor, tubes and corals and a barrel cactus, all caught somehow in embedded lengths of barbed wire. Everything a green color they'd never seen in life but with a glow that came from nowhere and everywhere, its source uncertain.

"That's lactic acid from cottage cheese," she said. "A good bacteria. I blow up the image, then add the other elements."

"It's nice," said Chen. But then he looked with evident distaste at a canvas covered with what looked like maggots and discarded cockroach egg casings.

"I call it Dirty Lucre," she said. "The bacteria off the surface of a one-hundred-dollar bill. For real. I didn't doctor it."

If she'd intended to distract them, she succeeded only for awhile.

Dawit was already at her worktable, examining the agar plates.

"Nutrient," she said, "to culture the colonies. I lay biotech membrane over the surface."

"You can buy that online?"

"Anyone can. The strips go to Dee-Hi and they send me the imagery from the electron microscope scan."

"But you have to fix the strips here, no?" Dawit said. "Formaldehyde?"

"Yes, sir. And I use safety equipment. Respirator, gloves, safety goggles. Ventilation fans. Believe me, I don't intend to get sick," she said. "I don't have health insurance."

"But why?" he said.

"I can't afford it."

"Not the insurance. Why bacteria?"

"There's good bacteria and bad bacteria. Like I said, bacteria get stereotyped—dirty, harmful."

Like what we do to people, Dawit thought.

"There's bacteria that do us harm," she said, "some do us good. We couldn't survive without them. Others live in harmony with us without any effect one way or the other. I'm sure you already know that."

Dawit peered down at her. Again she rose up on her toes. He couldn't tell if this was to challenge and confront him or to meet him. "You must understand our concern. The tattoo on your left arm."

"Did you look at my right arm, too?" she said "The antidote."

A person who has the antidote isn't afraid to spread the toxin, he thought. "You ordered botulism toxin online," he said.

"Shipped directly to Dee-Hi. It was never on the premises. I'm still waiting for the scans," she said. "The piece will be about acknowledging danger and seeking remedy. Asserting that remedies do exist."

Chen had joined them. He held her laptop. "We'll have to take this."

"When do I get it back?" she said.

"We'll let you know."

"I guess it doesn't apply anymore," she said. "The old view that there's a remedy for every wrong. These days, when an innocent person is wronged by the law itself, there is no remedy. But that's the point of Art—or my art, at least—to dream what doesn't exist so that more practical people can bring what we dream into being."

"And you dream death and destruction?" said Chen.

"Those are my nightmares, not my dreams."

Not Our Purview

The laptop went into the trunk next to the carton holding hundreds of anti-bacterial hand sanitizer sprays. They were supposed to hand them out as though they were party favors, the label reading TODAY'S FBI: IT'S FOR YOU. He also ignored the case holding the handheld biochemical analyzer. The only time Dawit had ever opened the case was to look at the unit and battery and decide the damn thing was useless. The manufacturer had made the keypad so small it couldn't be used by anyone with the big gloved fingers that went with a bio-hazard suit. The Bureau got the sets cheap and Dawit figured if toxins were present enough to register, you'd know it just by dying.

Chen pulled the driver's seat up closer. His turn to drive. "What do you think?"

"About her or the art?"

"Those tattoos. Interesting what people choose to display." He was thinking about Edgar, his arms all scratched up, and his unaccount-able attachment to his cats. But he never mentioned Edgar to Dawit. "Filthy lucre," he said. "Anti-capitalist?"

"That's not our purview," Dawit said. "Anyway, that piece will hardly bring down the System. Who uses paper money anymore?" Well, OK, he thought, ATM's dispense twenties. But large denomina-tions? Hundred dollar bills?

"It's not really Art, is it?" said Chen. "The designs come from Nature. She didn't create them."

"What are you saying? Nature? God?"

"If you believe in God."

"So God put the music in Beethoven's head."

"Whatever," said Chen. "Some of it was pretty but she didn't make the designs. She just exploited them."

"That's a question, isn't it? Like is photography an art. Are you an artist when you notice and control the context and the presentation?"

They got stuck behind a delivery truck. Chen leaned on the horn, drowning out Dawit's words.

Chen Liked the Desert

Long term, the hot wind might damage skin but short term, it sucked the occasional pimple clean. Every trip to the Mojave meant a clear complexion. And breathing desert air was bracingly harsh and hot, like drawing on a cigarette. Chen hadn't had a smoke in years. Dawit did not like the desert. His eyelids swelled, his eyes burned. Allergies always attacked him behind the Creosote Curtain.

Tumbleweed blew across the cracked asphalt outside the Middle School. They stepped out of the car to see five locals armed with rifles and shotguns while sheriff's deputies kept their hands on holstered guns and faced them.

The school had been evacuated, ten kids transported to the hospital with vomiting, dizziness, blurred vision, and pain. At least it wasn't an active shooter, Chen thought.

"Where is he?" said Dawit. The wind carried his words off. Blew more tumbleweed, looked like a ball of barbed wire. He spoke again, shouting.

The deputy shouted back, "You're the FBI?"

Chen would never get used to the tone of surprise, would always resent it. Dawit always wanted to correct them. I'm *from* the FBI. Being seen as the embodiment of the Bureau, it was as though his own identity was punctured, left to drain away.

The deputy jerked his head toward the patrol car, to the suspect handcuffed in the back. "Cafeteria worker. Named Benjamin Voss." The windows were rolled up. You wouldn't leave a dog in the car in this heat, Dawit thought.

They're protecting him from the parents, thought Chen.

"Get him out of the car and get him some water," Dawit said.

They took the man out of the car. He was still wearing a hairnet and food handler gloves, his eyes were glazed and a little wild with what could have been drugs or mental illness or, Dawit believed, dehydration. "We'll interview him inside the building—"

"We don't have hazmat suits," said the deputy.

"—after I go in with the monitor to be sure it's safe."

"You don't need that," said the suspect. "I told them."

He was a young white male with a stud beneath his lower lip and a ring in his right ear and a wristwatch on his left wrist with a cartoon of a dog on the watch face.

Dawit took the monitor from the trunk and went inside, faking it. He considered it useless. When he returned, Voss was still breathing heavily, still dazed.

"Water. Didn't anyone give him water?"

"He put pesticide on the cornflakes," said the deputy.

"Come on," said Dawit. "Let's get you into the A/C and to a water fountain."

"He's the science guy." Chen placated the deputy. Then both of them followed Dawit and the suspect inside.

Voss shivered, lifted his cuffed hands to wipe at his forehead, the cold sweat.

"Poisoned yourself, too, I see," said the deputy.

Voss bent over the fountain and let water splash his face before he began to drink in gulps. He doubled over. "Bathroom," he said.

"Take the cuffs off him," said Dawit.

The deputy didn't move. It was common knowledge, thought Chen. If you're going to commit a crime, stay out of Kern. Do it on the other side of the county line.

"You're armed. Your men already patted him down. Station someone outside the window if you want to."

"Move," said Chen.

The Cafeteria Was the Crime Scene

Dawit chose a table by the wall. "OK, you want to tell me what happened?"

"I already told them," Voss said. "I didn't put the pesticides in. I was taking the pesticides out." More than half the kids in the Middle School qualified for the free breakfast program. Every morning, they received an individual box of cornflakes, a container of milk, and a piece of fruit. "Just because they're poor doesn't mean they should be poisoned." He carefully opened the boxes, mixed in crumbled clay and resealed the boxes. "Mojave calcium bentonite. I dug it up myself but people pay good money for it. Made from volcanic ash, all the impurities burned away. It's supercharged with powerful benefit." The doctored boxes went on the serving trays. "They've been eating clay for almost two weeks. But no one noticed till today. If the kids got sick, it's all in their heads."

He's almost certainly right about that, thought Dawit.

"I grew up on a farm," Voss said. "But I never knew till my high school teacher told us—the animal feed? It's mixed with clay. The clay coats the aflatoxins so they pass right through the cow or pig without causing harm. People deserve as much protection."

A little bit of knowledge, thought Dawit. "The corn for human consumption meets higher standards. It's not an issue."

"So they say," said Voss. "Corn is sprayed. There's pesticide residue, other foreign substances. No one cares about these kids."

Chen stepped up behind him. "Product tampering is a federal crime."

"I didn't cross state lines! No interstate commerce!"

"And this high school teacher?" Chen said.

"Had nothing to do with it. I acted alone."

"And you didn't mean to hurt anyone, but the kids did get sick," Dawit said. And some of their parents are out there with weapons, he thought. If Voss was lucky, he'd get off with a fine and probation, but at the moment, his best move was to say *thank you* as he was taken into federal custody and away from the crowd waiting outside.

"Her name," said Chen.

"She had nothing to do with it," said Voss. Then: "Mrs. Horne. Deborah Horne."

"She teaches here?"

"Used to. She, she's not herself."

"Meaning?"

"Her son got sick. She kind of got crazy."

"Any idea where we can find her?"

"Look, man. I don't know. I heard some other guy from school bought some land. Kind of helping her out. She has a cabin there with her son."

"This other guy have a name?"

"Her son?"

"No, the property owner."

"Martin Keller."

There Was Another file

"DHI again?" Dawit suggested. "I've heard those names. Maybe we should pay them a call."

"Maybe we should, but we can't," said Chen. "Keller's flagged because we've got a CI on him. It's Sackertac."

"It's a what?"

"Sacramento Regional Terrorism Threat Assessment Center. I think with Portland office liaison."

"And what does that mean?"

"It means he's theirs. We can't get involved."

A Long and Winding Road

"Esposito," said Chen. "He's probably Neapolitan. It's the last name they used to give abandoned children, exposed to the elements and left to die."

"In other words, he's a bastard."

"Not him. His antecedents," said Chen.

"Actually, he's a cardiac surgeon and so's my father. I should take the lead here," said Dawit.

"So you're the FBI," said Dr. Esposito, "and Shel Levy's son." He dabbed at his nose with a handkerchief. A cloth handkerchief. Was this an environmental statement? Dawit wondered. Esposito used the hand sanitizer and said, "I know your father, by reputation. And now I have a consult waiting so, if you please, without preamble, please inform me what you wish of me."

"You provide funding to the Desert Haven Institute," Chen said.

"And this is a problem?"

"Potential problem," said Dawit, "wherever there is biological experimentation."

"You might not appreciate it," said Chen, "being Italian..."

Oh boy, thought Dawit, here comes the discrimination complaint.

"...because you say *sicurezza*," said Chen. "A single word for two concepts. For you, safety and security are the same thing."

"You speak Italian?"

"Junior year in Firenze. You're from the South," said Chen.

"And now you specialize in organized crime? The so-called Mafia?"

"I started out in Art History."

"We specialize in security. Biosecurity," said Dawit. "For us, we understand that procedures may be done *safely* to prevent accidents, but are the materials *secure*? Secure, that is, from intentional—"

"I speak English and I am very familiar with security," the doctor said. "My home was firebombed by the Animal Liberation Front. I have required a high level of security ever since. And this is my interest in the Institute. Two interests, actually. We have always used valves from cows and pigs to replace the leaky valve in humans. This was the cause of the incident, or so I believe."

"And it was definitely ALF and not Muslims," Chen said.

"So it's true you seek to blame Islam for—"

"If you knew how many terrorist threats and attempts we find out about every day," Dawit began.

"I do have some sense of how many people are killed in this country on a daily basis by handguns and assault weapons," said the doctor, "killings that have nothing to do with Islam. Which, by the way, allows for the transplant of pig's valve to save a Muslim's life if a Muslim physician sees the necessity. Strangely enough, it's the secular Jews who *don't* follow kosher rules who tend to have allergic reactions. Regardless, for many reasons, growing replacement parts from a patient's own cells would be ideal, and for that I enlisted the help of the Institute."

"You provided specific funding to the Castillo Lab."

"For a project that went nowhere. I don't know what became of her work on the thorny-headed worm. I was intrigued by the possibility—the expression of serotonin in the paratenic host. There could be a way to isolate the immunosuppressant effect. We need ways to minimize the chance of organ rejection."

"And how were you recruited—?"

"*Recruited* is a strange word to use. JB Singh sent out notices and press releases and took out ads in journals. I wonder how you were recruited, starting out in Art History."

"It's a long and winding road," said Chen.

"I hope we're done as I have a candidate for surgery waiting. But perhaps you would satisfy my curiosity, too. Is it true—you would know—if whenever there's a serial killer, the FBI gets calls from hundreds of women convinced their ex-husband or ex-boyfriend fits the profile? While the women actually married to serial killers never guess? You would know, statistically, how the number of serial killers operating in the US compares to the number on TV. But it's true, isn't it, that the actual number keeps increasing."

"You know Professor al-Masri?" said Chen.

"No. Why?"

"You both put money into DHI. You seem to have the same concerns."

Dawit said, "Did he tell you about our visit?"

Esposito ignored the question. "A person has to wonder. Maybe it's like carrying a water bottle everywhere or paying for clothing with advertising names and logos on it. Can it be that no one would have thought of it and then all of a sudden almost everyone is doing it. It's part of the culture. Maybe serial killers would never have gotten the idea if it hadn't been presented to them. I doubt you'd accept a claim of entrapment, but then you deny it even when your agents buy explosives and teach people how to use them. Isn't that what you do? Don't you? Please give my regards to your father."

"You think there's anything between Esposito and al-Masri?"

"A person has to wonder," said Chen.

"What I'm wondering," said Dawit, "Art History."

"I had to get practical about employment," said Chen. "Singh's name keeps coming up. Puppet master?"

"Take a closer look at him?"

"He's a citizen, right?"

"You didn't seem to know much about art when we interviewed that painter," said Dawit.

"She's not history. Yet," said Chen. "I read too many mysteries as a kid. I thought I'd get to recover stolen art, track down forgers. What about you?"

"I thought I'd get to save lives," Dawit said.

"Isn't that what you were doing at the biotech place?"

"Long-term research. But with terrorism, weapons of mass destruction, I thought the need here was urgent."

"Ever regret that bright idea?"

"Someday we're going to regret what we've done," Dawit said.

"And what we didn't do," said Chen.

Dawit said, "At least some of it."

"At least some of us," Chen said.

Rennie

I curl up on the floor, like an animal, scratching. The sores on my ankle from the chain. The cold chapped skin. My nose bleeds I am so cold and dry.

Where is he? The interrogator who would establish rapport. Who would gently draw me out. Who would be stern and demanding when I fall short. He would hang on my every word. He would see me.

File #7:

Evasions

The first time they asked for EE-mine

If they hadn't used her last name and said it right, Rennie wouldn't have known who they were talking about.

"EH-min-eh," she said. "She's up at Hanford."

"Hanford," Dawit repeated, not because he didn't know what Hanford was but because if the Turk was there, someone had screwed up.

"She's working to ascertain whether the proposed remediation efforts would leak radioactive contaminants into the Columbia River," said Rennie. Rather self-importantly, he thought. "She studies surface water and groundwater connections, hydraulic connectivity, the advection and diffusion of the transport processes."

Yes, Turkey was an ally, but not an ally you could trust and these days you couldn't trust even those and EH-min-eh, the Turk, shouldn't have been allowed anywhere near the place.

"We would like to talk to her," said Dawit. He was frustrated. Chen wasn't. For the time being, Rennie would be a better source. You don't go directly to the target. And don't start at the top. Yampolsky might be useful at some point. His drug problem could be used against him. But as a general rule, if you want gossip, go to the person who always has the dirt. The secretary, the office manager. At the Desert Haven Institute, you want to go to Rennie Mulcahy.

"Sure, you want to know anything about this place, ask me," she said. "The revenue stream? All my idea. I figured we could utilize our equipment to serve independent researchers. It's not like I'm happy about it, doing all this crap. Tox screens on corpses. Paternity tests. Those are the worst—exploiting people's suspicions for results that aren't even admissible in court. Then this vigilante group wants to send us soil samples to test for chemicals found around marijuana plantations and meth labs. If we report back it's positive, who knows what they'll do."

"That's our concern," Chen said. "You run a mail order lab. How do you know who you are working for?"

"We try to be careful. But if we took on the expense of background checks of every client, that would eat up our profit," she said, "which is the only reason to do it in the first place."

"But there are issues here of national security," Chen said. "Ethical concerns."

"We're being forced to operate like a business. Everyone says you have to follow the business model. So it's a business decision. When has business ever been ethical?"

"But the incalculable harm—"

"Tell me about it," Rennie said. "The Bush family fortune was made through trading with the enemy. Which is what Halliburton does right now."

"Where do you get these ideas?"

"The internet," she admitted. "But it's true, isn't it? And what do you want with Emine?"

They hesitated. Then Dawit said, "It's about Oggus."

"August? I'll check her calendar for August."

"Oggus," said the agent. "Oggus. Her husband."

"It's Oğuz," said Rennie Mulcahy. "Ohz, rhymes with rose. Is he OK?"

We've got Oggus. August. Ohz.

He's what we call an out-of-place Muslim. I mean what's he doing there? We know your objections: What is the CIA doing there? The US military? What are the Western NGO's doing there? They're not out of place. He is.

And where was Emine Albaz?

Once More She Gave Them the Slip

Yampolsky had assured them Emine Albaz was available and at her desk, but by the time they drove up to Desert Haven, she'd been unexpectedly called to a meeting on the Shoshone Reservation outside Vegas. Or so said Rennie Mulcahy. Wasted trip.

Maybe not.

"Can I speak to you privately? Confidentially?" There was no place where they were likely to remain uninterrupted for long but Petey Koh led Dawit to the break room. "You're a scientist," Koh said. "But you chose instead to serve your country. That's what I want to do."

"We should bring Chen in."

"You're the one I want to talk to," Koh said. "Am I on some kind of list? For working here."

"Why would you think—?"

"I mean, look how many times the FBI has been here."

"Of course, lists exist. But you'll help us?"

"I'll help my country. At least it's what I want to do." Koh went on and on about cyber warfare, the new frontier. Cyber security. Disrupting networks, hacking into sensitive storage, protecting our own defense and secrets against attack. "I applied to the NSA. I thought everything was moving forward. Then nothing. No one will even tell me they don't want me. So that's why I'm asking. Am I on some kind of list? And if I am, how do I get off of it?"

"I wouldn't know," said Dawit. "But you appreciate, these days, the agencies have to be very cautious."

"I'm an American. Born in Queens, New York, and I'm just trying to be of service."

"And why are we having this conversation privately?"

"I hardly want my colleagues here to know I'm planning to leave." Even if, he thought, someone here has done something. "Guilt by association," he said. "It's not right."

"So which of your associates," said Dawit, "is guilty?"

Maria, Koh thought. She was hiding from someone, something.

"I can try to help you," Dawit said. His teeth threatened to chatter and he made an effort to keep his jaw still. "But we need some help here. We're interested in traffic routed through Uzbekistan."

"That's interesting," said Koh. It meant the FBI had better cyber resources than he'd expected. What did that mean about Maria's safety? And he wanted her safe. She was going to save the tiger. "Uzbekistan," he said. "Is that near Turkey? I'll see what I can find out," he lied.

Emine Albaz, En Route to the Navajo Nation

They miss her again, because months earlier, Pueblo people had come to the Institute, men in suits except for the elder with a blanket around his shoulders. They wanted the latest information on remediation because of the tailings and contamination and Los Alamos fallout. The unpublished studies were raw data, but rather than tell them they wouldn't understand, Emine explained it was all unfinished, but in case she was unable to complete the studies, they might be in a position to carry it forward. Here. She gave them her data, copied onto a spare thumb drive.

She was en route to New Mexico now because the Navajo also needed information more than 20 years after the Church Rock uranium disaster. She hadn't been able to get and analyze samples but she could give them the documents, what was already known, who was responsible, who had blocked the investigation. She thought of that woman, Alula, who grew up here, and her brain tumor and her uranium chunk. The woman wrote letters; Emine didn't respond.

From the moment she'd stepped off the plane, Emine had the oddest sensation of returning home. The landscape was nothing like the world she'd grown up in, but the land had the same ancient hum, she could feel the earth breathing beneath her feet. She thought of her friend Maria feeling God.

The place captured her. Sun and wind, yes, but this was desert light, not Mediterranean light. She closed her eyes and let the wind touch her everywhere. Oh, the things we do when our mothers aren't there to see. Fear of *aire*. She'd thought it was a Jewish superstition but Maria's mother had the same fear. *Aire!* If you go outdoors after a meal, the draft will hit you and leave you with a crooked mouth!

Her mother, who gave Oğuz such condescending respect. The Ottomans restricted education to the nationalities. The native Turks, the Anatolians were kept in ignorance. Why? There's no accounting for the things that Empires do. *And such good people. And look, within a few generations how smart, how successful they've become!*

A weekend in Pamukkale...her mother wouldn't swim. She seated herself with sunbonnet and dark glasses where she could watch her daughter in the thermal pool, but Emine let her mother fade entirely from view. The hot water hypnotized her. The earth had subsided or the hot springs had overcome the surface of the earth and submerged a civilization. The water rose up over columns and broken statues and bathed them and Emine's body. She drifted, carried back through time, back even before the 15th century when they left Spain and boarded the ship the Sultan sent to carry the Spanish Jews to his welcoming realm, further back to when the Greeks worshipped and left the images of their gods and goddesses, back to a world submerged like Atlantis but not quite vanished. Rediscovered. In the thermal pools it was as though the gods still gave off an energy that expressed itself as heat. Their divinity entered through her pores. She was becoming non-flesh, pure spirit, ancient, merged with mystery, and she had no mother then. The sun went down. She saw flames on the water and then she moved through the dark and through the past. Suddenly, bright lights flash. Loud music, *I Will Survive*, and they come—where did they come from?—five, ten, maybe more, in bikinis, screaming and splashing, one of them topless, Germans? Swedes? It didn't matter who they were. The gods were dead.

And so that's what it was, in New Mexico, the same sense of mystery that could be so easily shattered. This vibration under her soles, she feared wasn't soul, but rather the radiation from the uranium fields she had come to track. The so-called greater good, contamination of barren reservation land in the name of national security. Toxic beauty.

Lately she saw the dark side of everything. When she picked up the rental car, they made her mark up a sketch of the vehicle to note any existing damage. She thought at once of how they mark up an outline of a body when a casualty is brought into the ER.

Adobe here for building, not stone. Mesas, not fairy spires. But look, there, sunflowers against a terracotta wall, there would be whole fields of them on the plains of Anatolia and women at work, their backsides in patterned trousers lifting in the air like flowers, too. They should plant whole fields of them here, sunflowers, sucking up the poison, making the soil clean.

And the rocks. Black and red. Slabs and sculpted. She always loved rock.

Pamukkale, where her life course was set at age eight. Rock formations like snow, like cream, and yet solid enough to hold you safe on the earth. Emine frozen with wonder, static ecstatic, the electric shock that both startles and paralyzes, the *coup de foudre*. Sedimentation, water turning itself to stone by casting out its own constituent part. Building up something beautiful out of what was always inside.

The blinding white terraces, travertine frozen in place like glaciers, icebergs, step by step. the pool of thermal waters flowing out toward the cliffs and the horizon as though flowing on forever, an optical illusion of the infinite.

The rock, invisible, dissolved in the water. The water painting the landscape with rock, the blinding white stone, and contaminants spreading through the karst aquifer.

Things come into solid being to deny their insubstantiability—and vice versa.

The souvenir statue of the goddess that melted when she tried to wash it clean of dirt not knowing it was made of salt.

In the car, the temperature gauge showed the red zone. She shut off the A/C. Opened the windows to the hot wind. The needle moved higher. She turned on the heat to draw it off the engine. What do you expect? Midsummer in the desert. The beautiful desert. Toxic.

Her feet burned but the car kept going.

She followed the road automatically. Sometimes her mind froze. Even the red sandstone cliffs, the broken black malpais didn't register. The mesas distant on the horizon. Sunflowers and herds of sheep and wide-haunched women. Her thoughts shattered to pieces and flew in all directions. *Kerido, kerido*, thoughts of her husband and thoughts that went further back to childhood. Her concentration was a stripped gear, it slipped, it didn't catch. She traveled, letting her thoughts go where they would during the journey, trusting she'd regain focus when she arrived.

Emine remembered the Pueblo elder.

She remembered intercalated gray limestones and marl. $Ca\text{-}SO_4\text{-}HCO_3$ type and meteoric in origin, brown conglomerates, sandstones, claystones.

Oğuz had told her about a bear, and she remembered.

The man with the tambourine. *Bam bam* and the bear would stand.

"It shouldn't be allowed," her mother said.

"But he looks like he's smiling."

"A grimace," said her mother.

Where She Went

Once more, she evades them and both Yampolsky and Mulcahy deny knowing her whereabouts.

Chen says, "She's in the wind?"

And Yampolsky: "You guys actually say that? Not just on TV?"

She drove to Los Angeles to the Turkish Consulate, certain her own people would help.

So Erdoğan's wife wears a headscarf. So do almost all the women in the countryside and that doesn't make them fanatics. Anyway, her name, too, is Emine, that is something they share. And he wasn't that bad a mayor, she's not worried. It's not like he's acting like a strong man, a dictator. At least not yet. For a moment, thinking just stops. She doesn't want to think ahead. But look, the Saudis come to Istanbul for drink and for sex, everyone knows that. It's unlikely Turks will follow their hard line. We have flaws but we are not hypocrites. We see corruption from all sides, both West and East, and Turkey of course has always been the bridge and our only defense is our Turkishness, we will not imitate, we will not submit. She has to rely on that.

"My husband has disappeared in Pakistan," she said.

It was months since she'd heard from Oğuz and yes, he didn't often have access to the internet, but she was worried. His brother Ahmet had looked for him, and nothing. Now he no longer felt safe in Peshawar. He was going home.

The man nodded his head but didn't even take notes.

She took another day off and drove to the Turkish Consulate in San Francisco.

The woman there was at least sympathetic and attentive. She said she'd make inquiries but keep in mind, the world has changed. Everyone's energy was focused on terrorism. The visit left her more worried than ever.

Third trip: Oğuz was in trouble and where she'd gone wrong was thinking the consular offices could help. They were people who processed forms, who stood behind counters. Wasted effort. She should have gone to the Turkish Embassy at the very start.

This would be a short trip. She'd park at the airport. No need to bother Rennie for a ride.

She made coffee to take in a travel mug for the drive to LAX.

Even after the wait to get through security, she had hours to sit at the gate with her laptop, still hoping for a personal connection, checking email for responses from all the family and friends she'd written to. *Do you know Osman Faruk Logoglu?* hoping someone could vouch for her to the ambassador.

Nothing.

She logged off. As usual, the Americans around her were hypnotized by the TV monitor but there was something different, she thought, about their attention. When she looked up at CNN, in a loop of yesterday's news, Colin Powell was repeating over and over that Saddam Hussein had and would use weapons of mass destruction. There were some silly little charts.

They're going to start another war, she thought.

And she knew her trip would now be pointless. The embassy staff would be in meetings at the highest level. Everything secret. The air base at Incirlik would be a staging area. The US would be asking—demanding—freedom in Turkish air space. I could be the ambassador's sister and he still wouldn't see me, she thought, and she couldn't blame him. Concern himself with one Turkish doctor who'd gone missing? When hundreds of thousands of people were going to die. And for what? Iraq had nothing to do with 9/11. Didn't people know that?

She watched the screen. There was something so trustworthy, reliable about that man's face and his measured tone of voice.

Her trip would be futile but she would go anyway. And she would fly back to California the same night, a late flight, and she would retrieve the car, drive up through the Antelope Valley, the high winds blowing tumbleweed in her way just like in the movies, and above her, a black sky thick with stars.

Someday she'd be able to tell her husband she had never given up and he would tell her he'd known she was doing everything possible for him. He would tell her he'd never felt alone.

Yampolsky Let Them Have the Conference Room

Tuesday, April 1 (April Fools Day), 2003

They sat and Yampolsky went out and then brought Dr. Emine Albaz to them. Finally. Dawit found himself leaning toward her.

It wasn't her soft voice. He could hear her well enough. But her warmth—the warmth that radiated from her body in the air-conditioned room—drew him. He braced his hands on the table, pushed to make himself sit straight, back against the padded executive chair.

"It's routine," he assured her. "But you understand, a foreign national seeking access to two restricted sites."

"One restricted site," she said. "My work for Lawrence Livermore was theoretical and done from here."

No, he thought. You would have access in cyberspace. And he realized there was something about her, so graceful it was easy to overlook the strength that reminded him of Gladys.

"And anyway," she said, "I'm not equipped, intellectually, to do it without Dr. Tang."

Chen had already had the technicians hack into Dr. Tang's hard drive. Tang had a visionary—or crazy—idea for nuclear waste disposal: blast it right into the center of the sun. "It's his project," she said. "I don't know how practical it would be."

"An expensive proposition," Dawit said.

"Though, who knows?" she said. "Whatever the cost, we might not have a choice in the end. Think of it," she said. "The waste keeps accumulating. Always a danger, while in the sun it might be incinerated harmlessly." Tang, she explained, needed to model the sort of extreme conditions and temperature that don't exist on earth, "equal to what's going on inside a nuclear blast or a star."

"So," he said, "that was your interest in the National Ignition Facility."

"Yes, though it's still under construction at Lawrence Livermore, we were already in contact. Their goal is to keep the stockpile of nuclear weapons safe. We saw other uses. I was assisting Dr. Tang in designing a platform for the investigation of radiation hydrodynamics."

As though we'd let foreign nationals design such a program, Dawit thought. "Extraordinary conceptual work," he said. He meant it.

"Given the restrictions, he's given up on it. We both have."

He liked her, or at least that was the impression he was supposed to give, building rapport. We are just two people having an interesting conversation. This is what Chen had told him to think when conducting an interview. Even terrorists like to talk about themselves. Stroke their egos. Let them brag. Show interest in their expertise. Don't let on the real reason for the interview: the money wired to India; her travels; her husband's travels; emails to her office and home computers from Peshawar.

"I understand your sister-in-law is Iranian," said Chen. "And you rather pointedly contradicted the DOE findings."

"The Western Shoshone Reservation?" she said. "I didn't contradict. I just wanted to do an independent assessment."

"You know the bunker busters are intended to protect the world against Iran's nuclear program."

"Nasreen, by the way, is in *exile*," she said. "I was protecting Americans. The ground there in Nevada is contaminated from old nuclear tests. People on the reservation worry any new blasts will release massive amounts of radioactivity."

"The DOE—" said Chen.

"Yes, tried to warn me off. They told me the assessment was already done. No risk through the water table to people. But they wouldn't share the data and I won't know there's no risk till I've done the work."

"You've received radioactive materials," Dawit said.

"Do you mean the mushrooms?" she said.

"The radioactive mushrooms."

"We got an inquiry," she said, "from a woman who couldn't afford to hire us but she more or less decided we would do the work anyway.

It's true that mushrooms can draw heavy metals from contaminated soil but then what do you do with the toxic mushrooms? She wanted us to create and send her genetically modified bacteria designed to break down the radioactive waste."

Exactly the sort of work he himself should have been doing. Though in his hands it would have been entirely benign. In others? Some people would use a bioweapon if they also had the antidote.

"But we didn't do it," she said. "I passed her letter on to Maria—Dr. Castillo. She did a post-doc in microbiology before she came to DHI. But we agreed, the woman didn't seem stable. We decided not to get involved."

"She shipped you the materials."

"That's what I mean. We said no. But one day, the container was delivered. All properly packaged as biohazard. And it turns out the mushrooms she sent weren't even radioactive." Emine looked down at her hands, closed her eyes, looked up again at Dawit and away.

"I think you have something else to tell me," he said.

"I—we—we're all still in shock. About the attack."

"And?"

"We could use your help," she said. "You mentioned Livermore. I can't seem to get through—"

"You're not going to get clearance."

"That's not it. I can't get anyone to listen. Dr. Castillo and I are both concerned about the Biowatch program. We don't see how the sampler kits they're using can detect lethal pathogens. They're almost designed to show false positives."

"But sometimes they'll detect—"

"When you have one false alarm after another and the assays are so unreliable, it's only natural for people to stop paying attention."

"Why are you so concerned with national security policy?" he asked.

"I live here. I have friends here. And even if I didn't, terrorism threatens everyone," she said. "And contamination. The other place I've been blocked. The Santa Susana Field Laboratory."

"I grew up not far from there."

Her smile was instant. "Then maybe you will help."

She told him what he already knew, about the former nuclear-energy and rocket-testing facility where, in 1959, a nuclear reactor had a partial meltdown that only recently came to public notice. On top of that, perchlorate was simply dumped out on the ground or burned as waste. "The site is surrounded by residential communities. People who built there, moved there, had no idea." Now they were recording high rates of cancer. They were worried about drinking water. "It really should be a Superfund site," she said.

Of course he knew the Bush administration was determined to keep the EPA away. National security.

"Community members came to me but I can't seem to gain traction. Does the FBI have any influence on this?" she asked. "Isn't it a crime?" She touched his arm. "No study. No remediation."

She didn't seem to realize she was under investigation. Unless she was doing what Gladys once told him she'd learned to do: when faced with a man in what felt like a threatening situation, she would put on a trusting face and ask for his help, trying to push that button that switched off the male impulse to violence and turned on the impulse to protect.

"The seeps, the ponds. There's experimentation going on at other sites using algae—*Closterium moniliferum*, to sequester radioactive materials. That's just one approach."

She couldn't possibly be oblivious to their suspicions, but she kept talking. "From what I can gather without actually being there," Emine said, "the site is built on sedimentary rock that was deposited 65-85 million years ago. There's shale, with low porosity. The sandstone acts more like a sponge, soaking up chemicals, holding onto the contaminants. I want to drill and extract some continuous core samples, find where the fractures are. To understand contaminant transport and fate, I suggest using temperature profiling, gamma probes and pulses of energy. TV probes outfitted with magnetometers to figure out which fractures in the rock are moving water. How much, and in what direction."

And she told Dawit about Pamukkale. "In my country." The World Heritage Site now with contaminants spreading through the karst aquifer. Thermal springs disappearing. Drying up.

"I became a hydrogeologist because I wanted to help preserve it."

So she, too, was trying to build rapport.

"Why are the most beautiful places the most endangered?" she asked. "Have you been there?"

"Pamukkale?"

"No. The Field Station. You said you grew up near there. I couldn't enter the site, but Mr. Tesfaye, all around, there are the sandstone cliffs. Wildflowers and oaks and willows. So much beauty."

She began to draft a sketch. Vats and vessels. A prefilter to remove sediment. Then a series of vessels. "Here, first," she said, "aluminum silicate and dissolved oxygen. You have to precipitate and filter out any metals in the water so they don't clog up the works. But there's others—iron, manganese, and zinc—here we have tiny plastic beads with a reactive surface." She kept drawing. What was there about her that was so familiar? The word "assiduous" came to mind. She seemed entirely caught up in what she was doing but her voice betrayed no enthusiasm, her hand moved steadily, there was a serenity about her. He thought of a cat, conscientious in the litter box. "The water moves through trays and we turn some of the contaminants to vapor. The water and contaminated air then pass through activated carbon. The clean air is released, but the water is treated with peroxide to start the breakdown of larger contaminants. UV light agitates them more until they break up into safe compounds. You could drink it now," she said. "Why not go ahead and do this?"

"Pure enough to drink," he said.

"Actually, too pure," she said.

He wondered if she were too pure. Open without being forward. And her calm. Talking to her interrogator as she would to anyone. It was either simplicity or painstakingly developed control.

"The water that goes back into the environment? We'd add calcium and other minerals. Elements that the wildlife in the canyon will need to survive."

"Do you think it's possible for a person to be too pure?" he asked. "The purity of the fanatic."

She laughed. "Fanatics aren't pure," she said. "I think they shout very loud so they won't hear the inner voice."

And she, who spoke so softly. Was she trying to mislead?

Chen interrupted. "Do you know many fanatics?"

"They are out there, many of them, don't you think?" she said.

She spoke so softly.

He hesitated. Should he show his hand?

"Peshawar," said Chen and the word hit her like a spark.

"My husband was there," she said. The serenity was gone. She was trembling. "He's not an American citizen so I understand he is not your concern. But please. I have not heard from him in months. I've made inquiries and...nothing." She closed her eyes a moment. It wasn't clear to Chen whether this was out of emotion or whether she was deciding how much to tell him. "I know something is going on. The last time I flew, I was stopped at LAX, held in a little room for hours."

That would have been DHS, not us, thought Chen. They knew we were looking for her and they didn't call us.

"No one told me why," said Emine. "My visa is good. I've done nothing wrong but they held me. It must mean something. It must mean we were being watched, so surely someone knows where my husband is now." Her cool fingers touched the back of Chen's hand. "Now I no longer know where to turn. So I will take this chance to ask you. Mr. Tesfaye, Mr. Chen. My husband has disappeared in a very dangerous place." And if she did speak faster than before, her voice was still musical and low. "Please. Can you help me?"

Rennie

Two of them come in. I lie face down on the floor. They remove the chain. "For good behavior," they say. The chain is permanent in the floor so they move me—without even shackling my ankles!—to another cell, still here underground, still no window, no natural light. Still a mattress without a sheet. Still a stainless-steel toilet. But no chain and once a week, the shower, cold, and a new jumpsuit. At least I think so. I have no calendar and after a while I stop counting days.

For whole moments, it's so quiet I slap my stomach to hear a drum.

I listen to my pulse. It's still too quiet. Hello hello hello. Then the silence comes to a violent end. The doors slamming. Other people's chains against cement. Sometimes voices shouting Heil Hitler! probably prisoners but who can say, it might be guards.

But I can move around the entire space now. I can move into the corner. I back into the space, into its outspread wings and two walls press against me, arms to hold me.

File #8:

Business Plans

Red Tape, Red Flags

People were marching all over the world, all that post-9/11 solidarity gone. Millions of people stood up to challenge the US. Bombing Afghanistan was awful enough. For some reason, the American administration was hellbent on destroying Iraq. So what? Lara Figurski wasn't going to Baghdad. She was headed for LA. America? Everyone may protest, but they all still want to be there, she thought.

At LAX, the immigration agent smiled at her and asked, "Aspiring actress?"

"Director," Lara told him, firm but polite.

He winked and said, "Too bad."

So is true, no? she thought. In America, you are automatic beauty if blonde.

She handed him the printout of her HIV test. Negative.

"We don't need that," he said.

That should have been the first warning. But she thought oh, so difficult to get visa information accurate in Ukraine. The red tape, the inefficiency. For this reason she had come to LA. The education was good enough in Kyiv, but after all the training it was impossible to get anything done.

Her bags went through Customs no problem though the man in uniform questioned her again. "Student visa?"

"AFI. American Film Institute."

Then she was outside and met, as promised, the man holding up the sign: Lara Figurski.

"I'm Boro."

He didn't help with her bags, but the driver got out of the car and loaded them into the trunk. She sat in the backseat. It didn't seem strange that Boro sat beside her. A matter of status. Boro must be more important than he looked.

He spoke to her in Russian. She wanted to practice her English, she would need it now, but he was just, she was sure, being helpful. He was taking her to where she would live.

"Student dormitory? Hostel?"

"Better idea," he said. "House with others who work in film."

When she was very very young, when searchlights made arcs across the sky, she would imagine it was Hollywood calling to her. The light would turn to a staircase in the night and she would climb it all the way to sunny California. Now where were the lights of Holly-wood? Here only headlights, taillights, endless.

"When do I register?"

"When you...what?"

"For classes. AFI."

He patted her hand. "Pay tuition first."

She said. "I have scholarship. Fund for woman directors. In Ukraine, they tell me—"

He made a tsking sound. "Miss Figurski, no. Was internship. All arranged by me. You work for film, then enroll."

That couldn't be right. She had a student visa.

"Ah, yes, of course," he said. "Women director workshop start in May. Five months, you work in film industry."

She was not allowed to work.

"Work-study," he said. Then "No worries. Boro take care," he said, and though she knew, should have known, this was a bad idea, she gave him her passport when he asked.

Like Bobby De Niro

```
EXT. CHERNOBYL NUCLEAR FACILITY, 1986
WIDE ANGLE POV OF MASSIVE INSTALLATION
Flat grey sky.

ZOOM IN, smoke rising.
The CAMERA is running backward, shaky, till
it stops, freezes, and EXPLOSION!
O.S. sounds: EQUIPMENT CLANKING, HEAVY SHOES
RUNNING. SHOUTS in RUSSIAN. A man's BREATHING.

                OFFICIAL (O.S.)
     Into the decontamination chamber! Quickly!

CAMERA pans FACES of CONFUSED, FRIGHTENED MEN.

                OFFICIAL (O.S.)
     What are you waiting for? Take your clothes off!

ZOOM IN, MAN #1 unzipping, dropping PANTS,
BOXERS. ERECT PENIS.
DOLLY INTO:
INT. TILED SHOWER ROOM
WIDE ANGLE POV, three men, NAKED, AROUSED.
MAN #1 looks UP. HIS POV, WATER pours from
```

SHOWER HEAD.

                    OFFICIAL (O.S.)
                    (chuckling)
                Don't drop the soap!

CAMERA PULLS BACK and NATASHA, NAKED, ENTERS
SHOWER.
NATASHA's POV: The ERECT PENISES.
O.S. SOUND of HEAVY BREATHING from all.

                        NATASHA
            If we're all going to die tomorrow...!
                    (pointing to MAN #1)
                You first!

SOFT FADE TO:
INT. BEDROOM
MAN #1 POV: NATASHA's BREASTS. NATASHA's MOUND.

ZOOM IN on SEX ACT (genital penetration):
NATASHA and MAN #1

SMASH CUT TO: 20 YEARS LATER. NADIA

Lara awakened to the bump of dollies, the loud voices. The smell of coffee.

She showered and dressed quickly. What had been the living room was now a sound stage. Cameras and cable and lights. The short man with goatee was telling the crew, "Later. We'll use the Anheuser-Busch brewery as backdrop. Industrial enough, right? And maybe some stock footage." He turned to her, looked her up and down, and introduced himself. "Robert Rupple. I'm the director. My close friends call me Bobby, like Bobby De Niro," and that should have been the third warning. Even Lara knew De Niro's friends did not call him Bobby.

Robert Rupple handed her the script.

242

"Format is very amateur," she said. "And missed opportunity. Scene of group sex."

"Check out the sci-fi angle. Nadia is born and looks just like her mother Natasha except: she glows. When she's horny, she glows."

"Chernobyl was tragedy," said Lara. "Was warning."

"Yeah, well this is business," he said.

"Show biz," she said.

"Business. Period. What I'm doing, this is something new in adult entertainment. We already know the demographics. Most consumers of porn live in Texas, the South, the Bible Belt. Conservative Americans. Adult films excite them more than other people because they really do think dirty movies are dirty. But I'm the first to make movies that speak directly to their values and their belief-system. The hook here is that radiation is not only safe, it's absolutely beneficial. Nadia's a mutant, see? and she's got this power. Every part of her body triggers orgasm."

Lara didn't know the word.

"And everyone she makes love to—male or female—becomes infected with the same power. Far out, no? I even have some lines about how global warming is a hoax. So. Show me your certificate, get your clothes off, and let's get to work."

"I am not actress," said Lara. "I am director."

"Sure, sure," he said.

"Simulate," she said. "Very easy with special effects."

"Hey, people need to know it's real," he said.

"Why?" she said.

"Explicit sex scenes...what's your problem? You see it in art houses, film festivals. *Faces of Women*. You know it?"

"*Visages de femmes*, Désiré Ecaré, Ivory Coast, 1985."

He smiled. "You do know your stuff. Hand-held camera, right? And you can't tell me that sex scene in the river was simulated."

"What I tell you," she said, "I am film student. AFI."

"Hey, come on," he said. "It's no biggie what I'm asking you. Doing adult film, it's not like being a prostitute."

"Of course not. Prostitute work for rubles."

"I rent this location by the day and I rent you from Boro by the day." He grabbed her arm but spoke softly. "Tell you what, do the role and you can give me notes. Maybe we get you an assistant director credit."

"Let me go."

"You don't have a choice here."

She took off her clothes. She lay frozen, hardly breathing, beneath a heavy man and kept her eyes squeezed shut, as he jammed It inside her.

"The look on your face, goddammit. Cut!"

The man pulled It out of her. It was still big and hard and prodded and bounced against her leg.

"What the fuck's the matter with you? Sex is good. It's life-affirming. My films combat misogyny." Bobby paced the room. "In my film, Nadia loves men. She loves sex. This is a goddamn feminist film! Every guy watching this, no matter how pathetic he may be, feels she would accept him and be turned on by him. Totally. If he's poor. If he's fat. If he's disabled. Ugly. Smells bad. No matter. Nadia would love him. And you! You're looking cold, aloof, remote, superior. Yeah, some men want that kind of woman but at the same time, she fills them with rage because they know she looks on them with contempt. They know damn well they can't have her. Don't you ever get wet?" he said. "Don't you masturbate?"

"I am woman!" she said, "not man!"

"Don't you understand the concept here?

"Bobby," she said, "I understand money shot."

"I'll bet," he said.

"Is like Alfred Hitchcock."

"Yeah?"

"Interview with Truffaut. My English not so good," she apologized and tried to explain how Hitchcock talked about the scene in *Psycho*, the car sinking down in the water. Audiences, he said, want to see the car sink. Not because they identify with the killer or want him to get away with what he's done but because we all have an inner drive to see an act-in-progress completed. "This is why only money shot is satisfaction."

"Wow. You do understand," Bobby said.

But he didn't. Couldn't. Americans were so different. Lara didn't even have the words. A doctor or nurse could tell you scientific or medical names of body parts. To the ordinary person? Sexual parts are It. And sex? Doing It. Selling It. Unless you use the very crude and degrading and violent words Ukrainian people learned from the Russians.

Some people must feel pleasure. Must! How Soviet the formulation! Must, as though it's a duty! If they do, they never speak of it. So when It is something one's body or one's hunger or one's pimp forces you to do, the deadness and disgust you feel—for all you know to the contrary—it feels normal. In Ukraine, if she had sold It, she would not have understood why men bothered to buy. Some fever that compelled them. Something they do almost against their will and then suffer over.

In Kyiv, she'd gone several times with internationals. Not for money, for a bit of something extra. Some high life. Dinner in a restaurant. An excursion with foreign businessman. And then, if they want It, why not? That's not hooky-hooky. What's the harm? "Is just body."

"You compartmentalize," said Bobby.

"This means?"

"It means you separate—body here, soul there. You still have your soul."

She said, "You believe in soul?"

"I believe in making films that are sex positive."

She thought, Positive is AIDS, and she started to cry.

"Forget her face," said Bobby Rupple. "Let's go for the money shot."

The dollies moved the cameras in. It happened fast.

A Woman Who Wanted Kyle

I'm not a sex addict, thought Carsky as he walked home. I'm a prisoner of my needs. How am I supposed to function without Tara?

His second bedroom was for guests from LA. He invited them, they never came, but in the master bedroom, he consoled himself, he and Tara sure did.

"Came a lot," he sang to her. He had to explain the joke: *Camelot*. And then explain that in New York, everyone, regardless of race, color, creed or sexual orientation, grows up on show tunes. It was the sort of statement that amused Tara and her brothers and made them love him. Or at least refrain from hurting him.

But even confidence that he was not about to suffer physical pain wasn't enough to make Kyle's shitcan of a car parked in the street and Kyle himself sitting on the porch—the patch of bare concrete under the awning where Carsky had never placed a chair or laid a welcome mat—a welcome sight. He held his grocery bag to his chest and hoped Kyle hadn't noticed the slight hesitation hitch in his step.

"Kyle," he said. "Tara's not here."

"But she's on her way, right? I'll wait."

He was going to have to open the door and let Kyle in if he didn't want to stand outside till the ice cream melted and the frozen foods thawed.

Inside, Kyle regarded what was supposed to be Carsky's dinner. "You gonna nuke it?" and to Carsky it sounded less like Dr. Strangelove and more like a foreigner showing off his acquisition of American slang. "You want real Chinese food? The two of you take a ride up to Tehachapi with me."

"Your sister and I have plans," he said. More an exaggeration than a lie. They planned to go out and do something. They just hadn't talked about what.

"Come on," said Kyle. "I want you to meet Yoli. My girl."

Carsky tried to get his head around this. "You have a daughter?"

"My girl*friend*."

That was even harder to believe. A woman who actually wanted Kyle? Everything about him spoke of bad luck. His right arm was half the length of the left, just a little kid when Casey broke it and being tight inside a cast for too long, it never grew the way it should. Casey treated his kid brother like an idiot and Carsky was still trying to decide whether this was an under- or overestimate. Kyle looked better, as he did this day, with his head shaved because when the hair grew out, in certain light, it took on an olive-green tinge. Instead of an earring, he had an asterisk—he called it a star—tattooed on his right ear, and on his short arm, a seahorse. Why a seahorse? Carsky had asked him once, and Kyle narrowed his eyes and grinned.

Food safely stowed in the freezer, Carsky tossed a bag of chips onto the kitchen table. "Beer?"

"Naw. Got something else." Kyle rolled a joint.

Carsky joined him in smoking it. He did not, after all, consider marijuana a drug.

Now Kyle carried the joint daintily to the counter and turned on the radio. He was in his usual camo, the fool, and today instead of cowboy boots he was wearing those running shoes the kids liked, the kind where lights flashed on and off with every step. Carsky hadn't known such things came in adult sizes. Kyle. Twinkle Toes. The country station was on a nostalgia kick. Kyle's lips moved while Lefty Frizzell asked *How far down can I go?* Oh, man, that's the question.

The song ended and the DJ spun *Teddy Bears' Picnic* and referred to the worldwide protests against war as the Terrorists' Picnic. At least the son-of-a-bitch acknowledged that millions of people were marching.

"Yoli," he said. Funny name, maybe a foreigner looking for a green card. As though there weren't already too many foreigners in his life. "So where's she from?"

"Dana Point," said Kyle.

Should've been a surprise, but Carsky knew damn well that two things erase any distinctions of social class: drug addiction, and living in a place like Desert Haven.

Tara showed up. "Separate vehicles," said Kyle. He used his jumper cables to start Carsky's Range Rover. They would need the extra space, he said, and Carsky chose not to ask what for.

Night Yard

In Tehachapi, they pulled up to a fake Old West façade, took the angled parking in front of the board plank sidewalk. It's Disneyland everywhere, Carsky thought, sneering at the sidewalk and the hitching post. Wong's, he thought.

Yolanda Hill was already there, leaning against a panel truck decorated with cartoon cats and dogs. Short black hair, obvious dye job, Carsky thought. Very red lipstick. Vampire chic. She stretched, unbuttoned her long-sleeved cotton blouse and tossed it inside before hugging Kyle and biting his neck. Carsky didn't know which was more notable, the long brown nipples protruding from her white tank top or the wrist-to-shoulder tattoos. Ink like that didn't come cheap. She looked like the girls he used to (briefly) get involved with, the ones who would say things like *I'm not an addict, I'm just trying to lose weight.*

Kyle did the introductions. Not in the very unDisney front room with the Formica tables and shrine to Buddha, the empty aquarium that inspired Carsky to ask, "Did the fish die, or were they on the menu?", but through the archway to the saloon the Wongs had acquired when the original owners went bust.

Even now in the middle of the day, the room was dark, the bar long and lit to highlight the row of specialty tequilas, the trophy heads on the walls only dimly visible in the gloom. There was a small bandstand, cabaret tables sporting white tablecloths and candles in ruby red glass holders and, along the walls, red Naugahyde booths, one of which they claimed before the waiter appeared.

"This is where we met," said Kyle. "At the bar." Karaoke on Fridays, honky-tonk band on Saturdays, and as it was Sunday, they'd be spared entertainment as the Elvis impersonators wouldn't arrive till 7:00 and with any luck, Carsky thought, they'd be gone by then.

"I wanted you here," said Kyle, "to introduce you. Yoli's leaving this great metropolis and moving in with me."

Carsky wondered where Kyle had picked up the word *metropolis*.

The waitress, looked Filipina, brought the menus, teapot, the fried noodles, the little dishes of sauce.

"So I figured you could help. Her truck, my car, the Rover. She doesn't have a lot of stuff to move."

Yoli blew air from her nostrils. "Metropolis. It's a shithole."

Sure, if you're rich and from Dana Point, thought Carsky. Wait till you see Desert Haven.

Tara had one hand on his thigh, the other busy moving fried chow mein noodles from bowl, to hot mustard, to duck sauce, to mouth, and repeat. Tara wore bras with padding she didn't need in order to avoid "embarrassment in the A/C," a degree of modesty that almost charmed him, being so out of character. She liked her jeans cut so they didn't rub her crotch but fit snugly behind, like a hand grabbing my ass, she said less modestly. Yoli's bra—she was wearing one, the straps showed—avoided nothing.

Kyle opened her handbag—looked like an expensive one—and Yoli went to work. Put in the diamond stud earrings, the silver feather ear cuff. The ruby centered underneath her lower lip, something that looked unfortunately like a pimple, not a jewel. Yoli sighed and made little sounds of frustration when she couldn't get the ring into her bellybutton until Kyle helped her find the hole.

"Such a hassle. Prison visits are worse than the airport," Yoli said. "The clothes you have to wear." Rings went on every finger, some sort of stretchy bracelets and bangles up and down her arms. Jesus, and Tara sitting there with her ponytail held back with a scrunchy. "Now I feel dressed."

After all the pretension of Los Angeles with Hunan, Sichuan, Mandarin, dim sum, Shanghainese, Hainan, what-the-fuck fusion Chinese, it was refreshing to be served a plate of soggy things that didn't even merit the designation of American-Cantonese, heavy on the onion and celery, even though he expected it would taste like shit. This was Tehachapi, and it was part of Carsky's education, Tara's family never failing to broaden his horizons as to what was all too lamentably possible.

"I only moved up here to be close to Daddy," Yoli said. And went on to tell more than he wanted to know, though he loved every detail. Mr. Hill was doing a bid in state prison for drug possession and distribution. "I'd have to get up so early in the morning to get here for visits." Anyway, the Dana Point mansion along with Daddy's cars and his boat had been subject to property forfeiture. "The only reason I have the truck is he put it in my name and they never proved a thing." Yoli's Mercedes Benz Sprinter van, the Mobile Groom Room. "The trafficking, that was bullshit," she said. "He used the house for porn shoots, which is entirely legal." The drugs were just to keep the cast happy. The ecstasy for professional use. But he had the cars, the boat, the connections. One thing led to another. The famous slippery slope. "At least it didn't go federal."

"What's wrong with federal?" said Carsky. "Country club prisons."

"Mandatory minimums," said Yoli.

All those rings, Carsky thought, drawing attention to her fingers. Why? The nails bitten to the quick, cuticles torn. "Warden here isn't bad," she said. "Sometimes they let them have Night Yard, outside after dark to look at the stars." What was she putting across? Poor little rich girl. He knew the type, you'd find her holed up in some scuzzy hotel room with the bad boy of the month. And when the shit hits the fan, no one blames her. I know you, he thought, the thin veneer of toughness not quite covering the vulnerability and hurt which hid the raging sense of entitlement. Not that any of it was fake. She really was self-destructive and vulnerable. She really had been hurt growing up in a house used for porn shoots. Shit. What if he'd scored one of her father's films? Too weird. He wasn't going to find out. And she really was a bitch. She could put her hand right on your heart and squeeze.

The Groom Room. Didn't that prove what an amateur her father was? Her Daddy had the notion that you had a few dogs and cats in the transport vehicle, it would confuse the German shepherds sniffing out drugs.

"He never got around to trying it," Yoli said. She rolled her eyes. "Off-road tires. I mean for a desert landing strip, OK. But to shampoo a dog?"

"Maybe ranch animals?" said Kyle.

"So you inherited the dogs?" said Tara.

"Two large mix breeds. Mutts. Big ones."

"Truck must be a gas guzzler," said Carsky. "How much it cost to drive it up from O.C.?"

"Money will not be a problem," said Kyle. "We've got plans."

"Pet grooming?" said Tara.

"No way," Yoli said. "I hate dogs."

"I told her Casey would take 'em. But we left them for animal services," said Kyle.

Yoli said, "I kept the cat."

"You don't have to walk a cat," said Kyle.

The waiter cleared their plates and Mr. Wong himself came to the table, holding a tray of fortune cookies in one hand, poultry shears in the other. He nodded to Yoli and grinned.

"You already got me," she said.

"You blonde then."

He turned to Tara, raised his eyebrows.

"He collects hair," said Yoli.

What's with the fetish pervert? Carsky placed his hand, hard, on Tara's shoulder. "No," and she didn't react at all, not a word, not a pout, typical passive Tara.

"Cut under," said Wong. "Won't show. Free drink."

Yoli stepped away from the table with Wong, then returned with a big drink garnished with maraschino cherry and paper umbrella.

"I didn't know people still did that," Carsky said.

They crumbled their fortune cookies. "Your fortune is in another cookie," Carsky read aloud. No one else shared. They watched Yoli drink.

"So what's the big plan?" Tara asked.

"Yoli's getting me an audition."

"My friend Bobby's just getting started," said Yoli. "Not as professional as Daddy. Van Nuys is not exactly Dana Point, but you have to start somewhere. There's always need for talent."

Kyle rubbed his short arm. "Not all of me is undersized," he said. "Six-inch diameter."

"Your arm?" Then Carsky got it. "Six inches. I think you mean circumference."

"No. I think I mean diameter. You don't believe? Wanna see?"

"No thank you."

"It's true! It's true!" said Yoli.

Morons. "Are you registered to vote?" said Carsky. He felt on the verge of understanding how Bush got elected. He himself was too smart to vote. He said, "I still think you mean circumference."

It Was Yoli's Idea

She really didn't mind, no biggie. I mean except for the occasional project thrown his way by his brother, Kyle wasn't working. Daddy's assets were frozen. They were going to need quite a spot of cash for a down payment if they were going to buy.

"Some place nice," he agreed. "Maybe not Dana Point. But how about Bakersfield?"

A home of her own. For now, they were living next to Casey's place in a shack—what else could you call it? That was getting old fast. They needed money. So: a mattress in the back of the Groom Room, ice chest with beer and, duh, ice, a shelf with plastic cups and airline-type little liquor bottles, radio if they wanted music, boxes of condoms, Kyle driving around Desert Haven, Boron, Mojave, trolling for clientele. Someday it would make a good story. Maybe she'd even write a book.

She thought about it sometimes, the book, the publicity tour, while she lay on her stomach at home—i.e., in the shack—when Kyle wasn't there. The cat would climb on her back and start treading. Kneading. Those urgent paws, pressing, pushing. The cat purring and breathing hard. Insistent. Pressing harder.

He walked in on them once. What the fuck! he repeated. Scat! The cat ran.

"It does nothing for me," she assured him. In front of Kyle, the cat was always "it" or "the cat." Only in private did she call it Stephen, the name of the first boy she'd loved. "It's same as with the clients," she said. "They need it. Me? I just wait for them to finish."

He loomed above her, scowling, not at her, she thought, but the strain of thinking. "You pretend the customers are cats?" he asked.

The client would get in the van. Security panel behind the front seat was there from before when it protected the driver from the dogs. Now they hung a black curtain, too, for privacy. It bothered her that Kyle could hear the sounds she made but at least that meant he'd also hear a call for help. Sometimes they pulled over to the side of the road or into a parking lot. Some men wanted the dome light on. Some liked it off. Some liked the feel of the vehicle in motion, really open it up on the highway. She liked that too, the road vibrations, the feeling she might be going somewhere. None of it was that bad as long as she stayed high. Well, Dr. Tang was bad at first. He'd become a regular and that was awkward, picking him up at the Institute, the place of business of someone she knew socially. But Tang was sweet. He missed his wife and son. She knew all about it. They were held hostage to be sure he went back. The only question in her mind, was China holding them so as not to lose a scientist, or was the US denying them visas to be sure he wouldn't stay once he'd been used? Governments were all the same. Land of the free. Right, she thought. Tell it to my father. Tell it to the judge. The problem was when Kyle braked hard.

"When I'm with the clients," she lied, "I don't think anything. It's a job. Does anyone love their job?"

Sore point. "You don't know what it's like," he'd told her, "all the people watching and the bright lights and cameras and shit. I thought it would be like, this is work? Fucking for money, but..."

"Tell me about it," she said. Poor Kyle. Wannabe porn star who couldn't get it up. Who thought he was specially photogenic 'cause he wasn't what he called circumferenced.

The cat jumped back on the bed and she stroked it slowly from the top of its head, down its soft back, up to the tip of its tail. Truth was, she loved knowing she could give furry little Stephen so much pleasure. She really loved the cat.

"How old are you, babe?"

"Twenty-three," said Yoli.

"Ready for early retirement?"

All they had to do, Kyle told her, was get the broke-down horse trailer Casey left by the storage shed and tow it off-road. Fix it up. "Bobby's got a girl as useless as I was. I can have her if I give him a cut. She'd live in the trailer and work the van. "I pick a place where you can't see the highway. There's no windows in the Groom Room, right? So when I pick her up and drive her back, I don't go direct. Drive around in circles to confuse her." No violence necessary. No security needed. Her—eventually their, once Bobby offered him more girls—departure would be discouraged by the fact she would have no idea where she was except for being surrounded by miles of desert, coyotes, and rattlesnakes.

"You figure this out yourself?" she asked.

"Hey, it's just a start. Once the cheddar starts coming in, I get more girls from Bobby, and maybe buy a nice Airstream or two. They can work right there. How does this sound? Mojave Mustang?"

"You'd need hookups," she said.

"No, it's the clients need hookups."

"For water," she said. "Sewage."

"Help me figure a budget," said Kyle. "Have to pay Bobby something 'cause he's still paying Boro. It's gonna take gas to drive around, and food to feed them. And I guess soap and shampoo and shit."

"How you gonna convince her to come out here?"

"That's what the gun is for," he said.

What he hadn't figured was that with early retirement, Yoli had nothing to do all day and all night in a place like Desert Haven. Not to mention her Daddy got transferred to RJ Donovan, down by San Diego. A metropolis even if the warden didn't allow Night Yard.

She left behind her brass bed and half their savings. She took Kyle's car.

A week after Lara arrived, Yoli was gone.

File #9:

Your Contract Will Not Be Renewed

He Used to Have Great Ideas

Our own Rennie Mulcahy is hard at work preparing the annual report and financial statement for 2002, but here we are, a few months into 2003, and I want to share with you, even if belatedly, a brief summary of what's been accomplished here at DHI in the last exciting 12 months of research and development—and what remains to be done.

No kidding about the lifespan of your typical small business. By that metric, DHI had beat the odds and no blame could be laid at the doorstep, so to speak, of Carson Yampolsky. And what about 9/11? That hurt in so many ways. The psychic wounds, for godsake, and the economic crash, and the political repercussions. Emine Albaz—no security clearance, no more funding from DOE. Maria's funding had always been iffy. He'd only taken her on as a favor to someone who owed a favor to someone, etc., you get the idea.

Here he was, Carson Y., brave entrepreneur, looking for investors and working the phones like this was some boiler room operation. Tang was going. Petey Koh had given notice, too, so on top of all this shit, he sat shuffling CV's from people who wanted to be hired and who might be fucking geniuses but when it came to the practical realities of keeping a startup afloat they were fucking clueless.

The annual report? Anything he could say would be bullshit.

Better to say nothing. JB Singh kept phoning. Other investors, too. Rennie screened their calls and made sure Carsky was never available. He'd already let Emine go. Her DOE contracts all canceled so how was he supposed to keep her on? While Maria and Petey Koh sat there playing video games.

"This isn't an arcade," said Carsky.

"We aren't fucking around," said Petey Koh. "We're folding proteins and ray-tracing seismic ray path. And cloning tigers."

Why couldn't his staff have sex with inappropriate human beings like he did? Instead, they got smitten: Emine with rocks, Maria with snakes, Rennie? who knew what, Petey Koh with a Siberian tiger. He'd given Maria a bit of fluff from the Exotic Feline place. You can get DNA from hair. The latest thing: Frozen zoos. Cultured IPS cells that could be induced into forming sperm and egg cells.

"We're a long long way from being able to clone," said Maria.

"Right," Carsky said. "That's my point. You're supposed to be coming up with new pharmaceuticals."

"I could give you a new drug tomorrow—"

"Yes?" He was suddenly hopeful.

"Hypothetically, Director. We'd still have to interest Big Pharma and the clinical trials would take years."

"You have to think long term," said Petey Koh. "Not quarterly reports."

"Annual," said Carsky.

No wonder research was migrating same as manufacturing jobs.

No wonder Dr. Tang was muttering about returning to China, especially since the seismologists at Caltech and his collaborators at the Jet Propulsion Lab found out they were barred from communicating—much less collaborating—with him. It turned out running a research institute was much like managing a band. They were underfinanced, over-extended, over-scrutinized by petty critics, ignored by the people who counted, seriously in danger of shutting down.

"The tigers can't go into the report. You people have to grow up." He sounded like his father. *You're not a teenager anymore. There's a reason it's called playing music, not working music.* "It's great to love what you do, but you need to get serious."

Why is that? he wondered.

What a bunch of ficken freaks they'd been, his first band, the Fick-Qs, a bunch of NYU graduates and dropouts. He was ingenious when it came to making money. Carson Yampolsky could always find an angle, some unconventional way of getting ahead. Why couldn't he figure a way ahead for DHI? Once upon a time, he was quick to improvise. Like when they left New York. Stefan bought a used van and almost on a whim they headed for California where the Fick-Qs promptly went LA on him. Rechristened themselves Blackwelder after a street in Culver City. Their guitars still served up feedback but now it was laid over a background of LA street sounds, the thwack of helicopters—news and traffic and police, curses and shouts in a dozen different languages, some invented. Then there was their marketing concept: Blackwelder played one-night stands in abandoned storefronts. There were a lot of free or low-cost venues in those days, before all the urban renewal, community reinvestment, Hollywood renaissance, whatever they call gentrification these days, made success a prerequisite to success.

They publicized their gigs through mysterious xeroxed invitations and soon had people lined up hours in advance hoping to get in. Through old friends and former classmates, Carsky got them mentioned in the New York *Times*, for godsake, and *GQ*. They got booked at Madame Wong's, the Starwood Cafe, but still, no record company executives came to call. They never made money, but they were *known*, with entrée to any nightspot in town and groupies and hangers-on always there to offer drugs.

He used to be a fine one for great ideas.

They hired Eva, a mediocre vocalist who would sew her lips together with coarse black thread if the audience didn't cheer and demand an encore. For their big break, Whisky A Go Go, Carsky joined the bouncer checking IDs so he could memorize the name of a babe. Later, to the background thwack of a ghetto-bird, he turned the searchlight on the audience and Richie spoke into the mike. *Gloria Kim! We have you surrounded. Come out and get down on the ground with your hands on your head.* Rat a tat tat from the drum. She went home with Carson that night and then, from the sadistic to the sublime, she asked if he could help out her friends. Flowstone Drapery.

The Drapes came from Eugene, Oregon and lived together in a clothing-optional house in Topanga. A singer with a high pure voice reminiscent of the young Joan Baez. A flute. Bolivian sampoña. Claves. Singing bowls from Nepal. Chimes. And a huge gong supposedly blessed by the Dalai Lama. They could have played trance music at raves but instead Carsky booked them into street fairs and festivals of world and sacred music and city and county-sponsored cultural events and fell in love so unexpectedly with their sound. He helped Leo of the Tibetan gong go solo—spiritual retreats and yoga studios.

And Leo introduced him to the joys of opium. Coke and ecstasy and most of all meth had shot him full of energy, the hyperactivity he had confused with his personality. Through sweet opium smoke he became acquainted with another Carson Yampolsky, quiet, meditative, one who was himself a gong. Touch him and he vibrated. Sound the gong and he shattered, not like glass, but gently like a piece of sugar candy.

He was still adept with a mission statement and a business plan though now he couldn't even fake an annual report. Back when he sold shared in the Drapes, investors listened to him. He listened to Leo.

Leo told him that Paiste, the company that made the gong, had started out fabricating military drums and cymbals. And now, they brought to the world these instruments promoting mindfulness and peace. Paiste, Carson thought. Proof that transformation was possible.

He quit drugs. He went to grad school, nonprofit administration and public policy. He changed his life. But now he wondered if he'd changed anything for the better.

They needed work, any work. Had he been too quick to dismiss projects, too abrupt with Rennie?

"Do we get involved?" Rennie had asked. "Do we report this? To where?"

Three times now she'd received hair samples from Mardan Keller and forwarded the results, as requested to Deborah Horne. Each time, the Gas Chromatography/Mass Spectrometry analysis showed heavy metals: arsenic, lead, mercury, cadmium, chromium. The arsenic you might find in agricultural workers. So she tested, too, for pesticides. Sure enough: N-diethyltoluamine and diazinon and probably others.

"Is this a public health emergency?" she asked. She'd heard nothing back from either of them, Keller or Horne. "Are we supposed to do something?"

"How should I know?" said Carsky.

Then there'd been those confounding conflicts of interest. "I don't know if this is a good idea," Carsky told Rennie back in October when she came to him about the vigilantes with their soil samples. They were looking for telltale chemicals they could take to the sheriff for probable cause. He had to give her some cockamamie doubletalk about professional ethics. He couldn't very well be more specific, like, for instance, bringing up the matter of meth production by Tara's kin. As much as he'd changed, he still had needs. Wherever he went, weakness dragged him down.

And *kin?* Well yes, OK, and he'd developed a taste for country music, too. He liked the puns and wordplay. *Trailer-trash Cole Porter*, he called it. When he managed Blackwelder, it's not like they had anything even resembling a lyric. And before that, back in New York, when they were still the Fick-Qs, at the hardcore matinees back home at CB's, if they shrieked anything more than *You Suck! You Suck!* it just got lost in the feedback. Now he thought Leann Rimes nailed his life with Tara: *the right kind of wrong.* Country-fried Gershwin. Once upon a time he'd made a name for himself being wrong. He'd stood out, standing in the back on the Bowery, the Bowery, at 315, dressed in suit and horn rims, narrow tie, not a single tattoo or piercing. Completely out of place. Just shtick. Now it was his life. And now there was nothing so therapeutic as a maudlin country song to get him to laugh at himself when what he really wanted was a good wallow in self-pity.

Rennie had shrugged. She was such a *secretary*. Where do the girls learn this shit? She stood there, talking about vigilantes while holding a pumpkin in her arms. What office etiquette manual teaches them that an office must have seasonal decor? Happy Halloween: extreme seasonality.

This was exactly the life he'd tried his best to avoid.

Rennie wasn't as dumb as she looked. He'd overheard her:

"Let's face it. We don't have the capacity to do any of the work you all say you're doing."

"Discoveries happen in unexpected places," Maria said.

"Not in a rinky-dink place like this."

"Rinky-dink," repeated Maria.

"Mickey Mouse. Inconsequential, pathetic, bullshit," said Rennie.

"Well, we're a startup," said Petey Koh. "We're just beginning."

"Beginning of the end," said Rennie.

Yes, it was crunch time. "The least you can do," Carsky said. "Try to maintain the clients we've already got, and are losing. Visit Deborah Horne."

Where Vultures Roost

Mid-March and mornings in the desert are still brutally cold. At least that meant fewer flies. Deborah Horne didn't mind the bodies. It was the flies that still got to her, and worse, when there were maggots, but there are no limits to what you'll do for your child. She put on the yellow gloves and picked up the squirrel and laid it in the bed of the truck. "Warn't for the flies, you'd make good eatin' for *me*," she said. That was not her natural speech. She was—had been—a high school teacher. And a great job she'd made of it, too. One top student arrested for tampering with cafeteria food. Another—Marty…hard to understand what had happened to him. And as a mother…with her son, Tommy, dying in the cabin—no sirree, not on my watch!—sick, not dying! Mornings when she made the rounds, she hated to leave him.

Roadkill jackpot. A coyote. Add that to the squirrel and the rabbit and that'll last them. This one was partly decomposed. Excellent, she thought, but even with the gloves she didn't want to touch it. She maneuvered the shovel under its weight—heavier than she expected—and beetles scurried from the carcass as she lifted it and let it slide off onto a piece of corrugated cardboard in the truck bed.

The hunter-gatherer returns in triumph.

How can a person live this way? It's better than dying.

The vultures hobbled around, happy to see her. With their naked heads and necks they looked like penises with beaks. Or maybe she only thought so because it was so long since she'd seen a real one. The only man in her life for several years now was her dying—no, he was not—her living son. And when she cleaned him she tried not to look. The bird she called Lloyd—they didn't all have names, just her favorites—Lloyd followed her around tame as a dog. He came up and obediently opened his beak. She took a couple of little perforated metal balls from her suit jacket pocket, each ball filled with cotton. There. In a few hours, the balls would pass through. She'd wait and collect them. Squeeze the gastric juice from the cotton. Tommy's idea.

She tossed the coyote parts out to the ground and then the rabbit and squirrel. The naked heads went diving, beaks through the frosted pelts and into the soft meat. Mardan had wanted her to keep the birds penned, but he'd lost interest now and as long as they were fed, they didn't go far. She'd let Trinity Wireless put a cell phone tower in the back pasture, not so much for the money as to give the birds a place to roost. They liked it fine.

Then the new one. She hadn't named him (or her, hard to tell) because he/she/it didn't like her. She ran up behind it, grabbed the wings and crossed them behind the bird's back. Gotcha! She lifted the heavy body and the frightened vulture let loose a stream of birdshit over the yellow gloves.

The cotton balls hadn't come up yet but she couldn't wait.

"I'm home," she called to Tommy from the kitchen. The blender was in the fridge, ready to go. Yogurt, banana (including the peel), a sprinkling of wheat germ. Her clean hand placed it on the counter, plugged it in. With a spatula she cleaned off the glove, into the mix. Two years of feeding this to her only son and the idea of it still got her sick, but it probably just tasted like banana yogurt and she—all she tried to do was what he told her, he was her child.

"I'm cold," he said. He was shivering under the blankets. Space heater glowing red. She sat on the bed beside him. A narrow single bed but these days there was plenty of room for them both, and more.

"I had a good morning," she said. "Come on, sit up." She helped him and then spooned some yogurt into his mouth. "Finish this," she said, "and then, tell you what, we'll have a smoke." The other thing she hated was the way she automatically spoke to him as though he were a child.

It's Against the Law to Keep a Vulture as a Pet

Rennie wondered why, not to mention why anyone would want to, but she figured the law wouldn't exist, would it? unless at some point someone was keeping tame vultures and someone else decided the prohibition was necessary.

You couldn't miss the birds. Maria, who was not afraid of rattlesnakes, let out a little frightened cry when one of them came hopping, swaying, flapping. It flew right at her, then landed with a thump atop a junked car.

"Don't worry," Rennie reassured her. "They don't attack," though how the hell did she know? She didn't. She knocked, then opened the door because no one said not to. The stench stopped her in her tracks: stale sweat and scorched dust on the coils of the heater, something like sour milk, the smell of shit and something sweet, like mildew in an old book, something that Rennie remembered from the way the blood in your nose and throat taste when you're a kid in bed with a fever. Her body blocked the doorway so at first only she could see the woman, at first not sure Deborah *was* a woman, dressed as she was in the clothes a male hobo would wear—a suit jacket sizes too big, a crushed-in black fedora. She perched on the side of a narrow bed, stroking the forehead of a skeletal being.

"What the hell do you want?" Deborah said.

"I'm sorry," said Rennie.

"You must be Deborah Horne," Maria said. "We're from Desert Haven."

"Not interested," said the woman.

"Just checking. Checking up," said Maria. "We did some analysis for you. Was it satisfactory?"

"It takes two of you to ask in person? That's intimidation," said Deborah Horne. She cut her eyes at Maria who was inspecting what looked like blood in a set of tubes in a rack. A row of buckets on the floor.

"This is Dr. Castillo," Rennie said.

"So what?" said the woman. "We've had enough of doctors."

The skeleton in the bed cleared his throat, or tried to. He stuck out his hand, yellow except where it was purple. "Thanks for coming," he whispered. He withdrew his hand before anyone could shake it.

"The skin tears," said the woman.

"I'm Thomas Horne, but you probably already know that," he said. They didn't. "And my mother, Deborah."

"We were running tox screens on hair samples," said Maria. "For Mardan Keller."

"We caretake for him," said Deborah, "or used to." She laughed and the skeleton in the bed coughed. "Your Mardan," she said. "One of these middle-class boys who lives in poverty by choice and spends money like there's no tomorrow. When he was still Marty, he was a student of mine. High school science. Then one day, years later, I mean, he shows up in white robes and a white cap."

"Tell them what it said," rasped her son.

"*Zoroastrians Kick Ass.* He's tall and milk white himself except for freckles and his curly red hair. With a hairnet over his beard. So is that traditional? I asked him. No, it's his idea of personal fashion but it's sad really, he tells us, to see Parsi men in business suits. You know how it is, converts can be more zealous than those born into a faith."

"What was he planning?" said Rennie.

"An attack?" Deborah laughed. "He got money from some million-aire over in India to create a Tower here. So Parsis in America could go back to traditional practice. They're not supposed to bury their dead. They're supposed to expose their corpses to vultures and the sun."

"The vultures," said Maria. "And that cell phone tower."

"No, no, no. He built a stone tower out back but never used it. Your analyses showed American corpses are so full of lead and mercury and pharmaceuticals, it's not safe for the birds to feed on them. So he dropped the whole thing. Now Mardan says some corpses need lead-lined coffins."

Maria laughed. "American corpses, like vampires. You can continue taking lives even after death."

"Well, we happen to disagree with Mardan," Deborah said, "and we're glad to have the vultures. Tommy was in med school."

"Preparing for a career in research," he rasped.

"Then heroin happened," said his mother.

From their blackened teeth, Rennie had thought meth. And the smell all around the place, like cat pee, though she saw no cats, and a whiff of rotten egg.

"Yeah," Tommy said, "them ivy drugs wraps up all 'round you and holds on tight."

"Don't be fooled when we talk that way. We're just fooling," said Deborah.

"HIV-AIDS," said the son.

"It's a scientific fact," said Deborah, "that a vulture can eat rotting meat because its gastric juice can kill just about anything. And because it steps in, well, all kinds of nasty stuff, its shit kills off any bacteria on its legs."

"AIDS is a virus," Rennie said. She knew that much.

"Digestive systems kill viruses, too. Virus in, vulture droppings out, and the droppings have no trace of the virus at all. Besides which," Deborah said, "he has not had a single opportunistic infection—from *bacteria*—since we started."

"That's very good," Maria said carefully. "I don't know when you last saw a doctor, but you know, treatment has made great advances. One pill a day can keep an AIDS patient healthy."

"We're not looking to support Big Pharma," Deborah said.

"Thomas," said Maria, "you don't have to live this way." Or die this way, she thought.

Deborah said, "We're after a cure."

"Then you can still use some lab services," Rennie said. "Some consults, some—"

"We don't need you," Deborah said. "We can order what we want from the internet, and we don't need the fancy stuff. An eyedropper's just as good as a $200 digital pipette. You've got your PCR cycler. All we need are these buckets and a meat thermometer."

"What do you need a cycler for? I mean, the buckets? That's blood, isn't it?" said Maria.

"Tommy's blood."

"Bravo," said Maria. "But it can be dangerous. Let us work with you. Safety protocols—"

"Who created Silicon Valley?" said Deborah. "Universities and think tanks or geeks tinkering in their garages?"

"But this isn't about bytes and chips," Maria said. "You're talking about life."

"Yes, my son's life," Deborah said. "Whether you and your kind like it or not, molecular medicine is going to come out of kitchen labs and bathroom labs. Without the interference of the so-called experts of the scientific community. We don't need you nosing around. Marden doesn't need you anymore and neither do we."

For Maria, The Day Gets Worse

"That was the most awful thing I've ever seen," said Maria.

Then the Director told her to get rid of the snakes.

"The venom's about our only money-maker now," she argued. He wouldn't listen. "Without the snakes, there's no point in my being here." He didn't care. "You're getting rid of me." She didn't blame him. She blamed Rennie.

Of course, it was true that Maria had been going cross-eyed, spending her days growing yeast cells and transferring them carefully with a toothpick from Petri dish to growth medium. Forcing herself to keep going. Believing she could make a decent start with shotgun sequences for microsatellite marker development. Bored to death. She had her thermal cycler to amplify PCRs and build her clone library of DNA fragments and the electrophoresis chamber to map and sequence. Toothpick from petri dish to agar plate. Toothpick from petri dish.... This was what she'd asked for and it was hell. Hours, days, weeks, in the lab. She looked forward to the morning task of cleaning snake feces in the hot room. Moving the rattlers to the feeding box for the weekly rat, pushing them into their hide boxes and protecting her hand with a plastic shield. She couldn't trust anyone else near the rattlers. Then for hours: Toothpick from petri dish. She complained. Of course, she complained. Repetitive, mind so numbed it could shatter. Without her feet walking the earth, Maria was beyond the reach of God.

But she never asked, suggested, hinted that Rennie go to the high school science fair and find tall, polite, unhappy Jared. She didn't ask Rennie to arrange for Petey Koh to pick the kid up from the

Mormon trailer park and drive him over to DHI to be her assistant over Spring Break.

"I understand about precision," he'd said. "I'm very precise."

"The work can be tedious," she warned him.

"Not as tedious as school."

He was diligent, and with this tall, sad boy by her side, Maria couldn't help but think of Alex, back in Mexico, poor child. No idea if he was dead or alive. This boy, too, seemed eager to learn.

One afternoon she walked him over to the hot room. They didn't go in, but Jared looked through the window set in the heavy locked door. He was so tall, he had to stoop to see five glass cages. Four looked empty, the snakes camouflaged or hiding.

"Four species of rattlers," she said. "That's what we're working on. And a harmless king snake for training."

"Cool!" he said.

And the next day, she decided to take him inside.

"Before we go in, you need to be serious about how serious this is."

"I'm always serious," he said.

Poor kid, she thought. "These snakes could kill you," she said. "When you're working with venomous snakes, you need as much focus and concentration as when you're colony picking." She didn't ordinarily allow anyone in there with her, she explained. It was important to have open space, no surprises, no extra legs or shadows, no place for a snake to hide in case one got loose—because you can never be 100% sure. "At any time, something can go wrong with a rattler. I'm telling you this now because I'm not going to do a lot of talking once I unlock."

She pointed at the chart, inside on the wall. "That's vital information, what to do in case of snakebite. The nearest hospital, the kind of anti-venom, what to do while waiting for transport."

She let him into the hot room, just a gesture of thanks for his days of painstaking work.

The thanks she got was that he unlocked the door while she was giving a talk in San Diego. Of course, a snake escaped. And Rennie—sometimes the girl did come through—evacuated the building and went back to grab the snake hook and Rubbermaid and trap the runaway behind Dr. Tang's heat-producing computer monitor.

"Get rid of them," said the Director.

"It was the Red Diamond," she assured him. "They don't strike."

"No more Jared. No more snakes. Today."

Maybe she'd known all along that eventually she would have to kill them. Cut out the venom gland for sampling. What was the organ-specific distribution of genes? As long as her project had been the overall map, she was free to be the snake girl spending part of every day caring for her rattlers. She went home for her machete.

Not Even in the Name of Science

She couldn't do it.

"You're going home," she told the snakes. She would release them. The king snake she let go in the empty field behind the Institute. *Crotalus ruber* amid the Joshua trees and chaparral. *Crotalus stephensi* was her excuse to wander through Red Rock Canyon away from the campsites hoping no one would see her. The rattlers would return to their native habitats. Her compassion for them would get her out of the building, out in the field, away from the Director.

"Que Dios te cuide," said the atheist to the rattlesnake.

In those words, her mother had commended her to God's care when she left home. Her mother, dead soon after of pneumonia. You're not supposed to die from pneumonia.

Maria tipped the bin and kept it between her body and her *Crotalus cerastes cerastes*. Leave no trace. Does that mean you're not supposed to return a venomous creature to the wild? It swished away. She'd chosen a bare place amid the chaparral. It left its sidewinder trace in the sand.

For the last rattler, she headed to Los Padres National Forest—part of the natural range of the Southern Pacific rattlesnake. She was very sorry to see this one go. Her snake had turned out to be a mixed breed with a good genetic share of Mojave rattler. Which had made the usually calm herp more aggressive. Which would have been an interesting variation to investigate—*Crotalus oreganus helleri* mixed with *Crotalus scutulatus*.

She found a dirt Forest Service road that ran past a shed that didn't look to be in use. Probably budget cuts. She took the snake, left the car and found the trail. At a distance, the mountains were brown, but here there was shade among the drought-resistant Coast Live Oaks. Last year's fallen leaves, curled and dry, made noise underfoot. She walked, rustle and crunch, the Rubbermaid in her arms, machete slapping her thigh, snake hook sticking out of her backpack like an antenna.

When the trail forked, she went left to climb out of the grove and into a hot open place where she set her snake free. He slithered, coiled, then disappeared into a cleft in the rock. She could have left it at that and turned around. But there was that smell. Maria went back to the trees and walked toward it.

She came up upon tadpoles, dozens of them, maybe a hundred, dead and dying. It wasn't for lack of water. The bodies lay, floated, writhed in a stream, poisoned by chemical or fertilizer run-off. She thought, I know what this is. And yes, there it was, the black plastic tubing, like a harmless, endless pilot black snake. The PVC line would run to a marijuana plantation and the people she was running from. She thought, They are everywhere.

What They Stand for

Driving home to the home that was not her home, she knew her time at DHI was over—or would be as soon as she figured out her next move. She thought, What is going to become of me? And her answer: You will be a snake.

Didn't they stand for renewal and healing? Of course they did, but that was legend and symbolism imposed by man. It had nothing to do with the snakes. The way their smooth scales fit together, not really separate, not a true mosaic but mosaic-looking, perfect and discrete, yet all of a piece. They were perfect as they were, not needing any of the appendages other creatures found indispensable, at least till they lost them. She tells herself nothing, no one, is indispensable. Snakes coiled and slithered, their tongues flicked. It amazed her to spend time with creatures whose way of apprehending the world was so far from her own. And the rattlers. Hated by humans, she would say, because the rattlesnake was fair-minded. We're the most violent of creatures while the rattler never seeks to hurt without first giving warning. So many explanations she had offered over the years without believing her own words. When she went to collect rattlesnakes, no one ever wanted to accompany her. She was free to go to the sierra alone. So many rationalizations and justifications to keep people from judging her.

What was there in the end to be ashamed of? Being around snakes made her happy. And now she had none.

A Charity from Mojave Came for her Furniture

Emine couldn't remember another time in her life when she had been so aimless. Had it meant anything? All the work. Now it was unfinished but done. Her visa would not be renewed. In the bank, after more than four years at DHI, she had $4,002.13 in savings. They control you through your visa. You get paid much less than an American, but she hadn't been there for the money. And of course, she had spent a lot—wire transfers to Oğuz and—though Oğuz and Ahmet didn't know it—before Ahmet went home, to Nasreen. Now she asked for a cashier's check for $2,000 made out to herself, put aside to be sure she'd have more than enough for a flight home. She wanted the rest in cash. Good grief, the small-town bank. "I've never closed an account before," the teller said. "I'm not sure how," and the vice president was out and the other necessary officer at lunch and it took three days to get the cash.

She would travel until the money ran out. This was her last chance, she thought, as it seemed likely she would not be allowed back in the United States. She would come back to Desert Haven to see Maria and Rennie one more time. To say goodbye.

Two thousand dollars. Figure even cheap motels have to be 30, 40 dollars a night or more. Gas, food. It would all be gone in a month. What if she only rented a room every other night, to shower, sleep in a bed? She made a bedroll, sheets, blankets, and comforter wrapped in her shower curtain to keep it waterproof.

She headed back to New Mexico to bed down on the living, breathing earth. Where she awoke to a weight pressing on her. She stirred so slowly, her movement didn't startle the creature, a small—though weighty—mammal with bright eyes and brown fur. Its nose twitched. It touched her face with a paw, then slid off her body and away and Emine felt in some way blessed, but you don't push your luck. After that night, when she didn't pay for a motel room, she slept in the car.

The car. At some point she'd have to sell it, or find a charity, or abandon it.

No One There

In the motel, while she waited for her laptop to boot up, she pitied herself enough to allow a moment of hope. *This time* there would be a message from Oğuz. *This time* she'd know everything was all right. Everything would be explained.

Not tonight.

She moved on. North of the Navajo lands she crossed into Utah. The map showed a "primitive area." That would be rugged, solitary. She thought of Maria. That's where I'll go. The road was a single dirt lane, switchbacks along a cliff and she froze, unable to force herself to go on. There was no one behind her, no one to be impatient, no one to honk. No one to see if she went over the side. Who would find her?

Who would know? She wanted to go back to the highway, but with no room to turn the car around, she had no choice. I can't, she thought. But I have to. One deep breath, another. She drove.

There was a flat expanse of red dirt at Grand Gulch. Emine looked down into a giant amphitheater. Steps made for the legs of giants, sentinel rocks like torches, and down there, the slickrock bowl. Alone and reckless. Hair blowing in her eyes. Her body still trembling and vibrating from hours in the car. Stretching her leg down, thrown off-balance by her backpack, stumbling and righting herself with a hand on hot stone. Even with dark glasses, to look up at the sky was to be blinded. If she fell and was hurt, there was no one to help her. But she thought again of Maria, who was frightened only of people and what they can do.

It was all slickrock here, buffed to a shine, the gleaming red surface spilling in all directions. Not a person, a bird, an insect, a lizard, a snake. (Oh, Maria!) Arches and bridges.

In the distance, she saw vegetation and thought *water*. She walked on and found a small pond, more like a bright green puddle, just enough to support some desert grasses and one leafless bush. She drank from the bottle she carried till it was empty and then refilled it from the pond. Not to drink. This water should be tested, a beautiful bright maybe radioactive green.

The earth here did not breathe but she lay down anyway, burned her arms on sun-scorched stone, smooth as hot ice.

She thought to see herself mirrored in the polished surface but there was nothing. White glare, her face annihilated by the sun.

If It Were Up to Gladys Tesfaye

They would not leave LA. If Dawit saw the move to Sacramento as a promotion, she saw it as a threat. Maybe he would turn it down. After all, he hadn't even told his partner, Chen. If it were up to her, Dawit would go back to being a scientist. He would cut all ties with the FBI.

But it wasn't up to her, just like she couldn't ignore the Pledge of Allegiance when it came blaring over the PA at the start of the school day. Not that she wasn't loyal to her adopted country, but half the kids in her class and their families could be deported at any minute. Why on earth should they pledge to the flag of the country that wouldn't accept them? And now, some of the places they came from were being bombed. But the children insisted, standing straight, right hands over their hearts. They wanted to—believed they did—belong.

How could she leave them?

And leave them to the next folly: No Child Left Behind. Gladys took one look at the script and tossed it in the bottom drawer. For Heaven's sake, it even told her when to stand, when to sit, when to make eye contact with the children. She would just keep doing what she did, starting every class passing out lengths of colored string. She played the djembe drum while the kids chose partners and held the string taut around their hands, then looping and pinching the places where the string formed x's, played cat's cradle while anyone who wanted to tapped along with their feet as she drummed. She had no idea why or how it worked, but it did. The movement of their fingers made something happen in their brains, not to mention the adjustment in their attitudes. Gladys knew she could get away with breaking the rules because her students excelled.

That afternoon, Shila caught her in the parking lot.

"Uh oh."

"What's wrong?"

"I'm afraid you are going to add to your collection."

A tiny black kitten lay curled on the hood of her Civic. It lifted its little head as she approached. She murmured to it, a triangular little face, two big ears. Sitting up now, its little arms stuck out like wings. "You look more like a bat than a cat," Gladys said.

In the car, on the way home, the little bat-cat flew from front seat to back, launched himself into her lap, scrambled over the steering wheel, interfered with her feet on the brakes and gas, No sweetheart, no, you'll cause an accident, and please retract your claws, darling, when you land on my flesh, oh! The pickup truck in front of her slammed on the brakes. So did she. Up ahead, a big dog lay dead in the road. Tan, and the size of a St. Bernard. Hit like her poor tomcat Kodak. No, no, kitten, see what can happen. The other cats were used to roaming outdoors, she didn't have the heart to deprive them, but you, my little bat-cat, you will be an always-indoors always-safe and happy kitten, she said as a man got out of the pickup, walked over to the dead dog and kicked it. The dog bounced up in the air, much too light to be a creature of flesh and blood, landed on the sidewalk, a big stuffed toy, while the kitten, calm now, found a perch on top of Gladys's head, claws clinging to her hair, caught up behind in a twist, and stayed there, purring the rest of the way home.

Cat Number Five. Dawit, when he returned from Sacramento, would understand.

There was a reason they'd bought the little house in Sherman Oaks instead of renting. What landlord would have allowed it? Of course, they knew from the start they would adopt a cat. Dawit grew up with one. At the shelter, she'd burst into tears at the double rows of cages, all those cats looking into her face, please, please, reaching their paws out between the bars. She'd wanted to save them all. She started with just one. The three-legged male, his gray face boxed with white stripes, pushed his face towards her and when she leaned closer, he pressed his nose to hers, as though he understood she was the one who needed comforting. His face was an African mask. His coat had made her think of Africa, too, coarse and flat as goatskin. She had to adopt him. Who else would have? Handicapped and not in the least soft and furry. Kodak. Because Dawit looked at the three legs and, ever the scientist, called him a tripod. Which made her think of cameras and film and therefore Kodak though, according to Dawit, Kodak—the company—was behind the times and missing the digital boat. Kodak the cat was a love. The way he'd place both front paws on her shoulders and balance there while nuzzling her face and neck, purring away. Kissing her mouth.

He must have lost that leg being hit by a car. Kodak patrolled the sidewalk and herded back to safety any cat that ventured into the street.

They lived on a side street but it still had traffic—the shopping center with Gelson's and drug store and multiplex cinema just across the way. And when Kodak brought home the longhaired calico, how could they refuse to keep her? Kodak and Sugar Girl touching noses, grooming each other. Gladys felt such love to see them show such love.

Then that tawny little lion of a cat—Simba, what else?—came to the back door. Well, she had lured him, sort of. Watched him prowling around until she began to leave a bowl of food on the back steps. If she forgot, he'd be at the back door crying. Simba ate the food she left him but wouldn't let her near. If she walked out into the yard to pick lemons off the tree, he ran. But in time, he began to venture inside if she left the door open—though he'd dart out or under the furniture if she approached. Left alone, he'd make himself comfortable on Dawit's favorite chair, hissing and swatting if the others came near. Sugar Girl didn't like to fight, but she'd stretch out to full length against the wall, claws outstretched, deterrence.

Tiger met her one day when she'd pulled into the driveway and stepped out of the car. This cat had a beautiful voice, wonderful stripes, and a ringed tail that stood straight up except for the tip bent towards her in greeting. Tiger rubbed herself against Gladys's legs so she didn't object when cat Number 4 followed her in. But Tiger turned out to be an aggressive—almost scary—cat, hissing, spitting, clawing, sparks flying from her eyes, in love with people but not other cats. Whenever Tiger's mean spirit took over, Sugar Girl would leap to the top of the bookcase to escape while Gladys's lion fought her tiger, poor three-legged Kodak in the midst of it all.

Now when she parked, the cats came running at the sound of the car. They were so excited, so happy to see her. Like her students. She unlocked the door, the kitten clinging to her, purring against her heart.

She opened cans, filled their bowls. They never fought while they were being fed, not even when Kodak hung around to gobble down anything another cat left over.

"Simba, meet Mercy," she said. Short for *Murciélago*. Bat. Being a teacher in Los Angeles, she'd been teaching herself Spanish. "Kodak, Sugar Girl. You too, Tiger, you little monster. This is a baby. You don't attack a little kitten, OK?" So Tiger went instead for Simba while Gladys introduced the kitten to the litter box.

Mercy took a flying leap and landed beside Kodak, reached out with a paw and a nose to touch the big male. Kodak swatted the kitten away. Mercy tried again and again received a swat. But later, Gladys sat on the couch with a microwave dinner, television on though she was not really watching the news. Her phone was in her pocket, turned to vibrate. When Dawit's call came, she wanted to feel it. Kodak did his thing: his paws on her shoulders, nuzzling and kissing. "Why aren't you nicer to the baby?" she asked. "Don't you know that you're his role model?"—words that turned out to be even more true than she'd known. As soon as Kodak tumbled away and off to the water dish, Mercy was beside her, the little copycat, paws against her shoulders, purring as he nuzzled her face and neck, his little mouth against her lips, just like Kodak.

Male role models. She and Shila had grown up without fathers and it hadn't harmed them at all. Maybe it was different for boys, the way at school they constantly told her about the children in her class who were "at risk." She didn't want to go to Sacramento. She didn't want to leave them.

The phone sent a buzz through her body. Then Dawit's voice in one ear, the kitten's tongue in the other. She gasped and the kitten flew away.

Dawit sounded cheerful but she wasn't convinced. Nothing about this career change had gone as expected. The kitten landed on the bookshelf and began pulling books down to the floor. Gladys saw *The Life of Pi* land with a crash. I feel the same way, she sent a psychic message to Mercy—treating animals as symbols instead of as animals!—while Dawit assured her parts of Sacramento were quite lovely.

You'll be a liaison with Sackertac, they'd told him.

SACRTTAC - Sacramento Regional Terrorism Threat Assessment Center.

But he hadn't made up his mind. Gladys held onto hope.

The Bureau had flown him up and an agent drove him around the neighborhood in the pouring rain. Just blocks from the office, the man pointed out a mosque and Islamic elementary school— "Maybe Gladys can work here"—and a leafy suburb of homes clearly beyond the financial capability of a GS-9. "Houses start at half a million here in Mohamed Oaks Estates," the agent said. "Muslim Americans and immigrants with a lot of money. It would be interesting to know what they're up to. Where their charitable contributions go." Dawit said nothing. "What you people call *zakat*," said the agent. "We can help with the down payment and mortgage if you choose to live here." Dawit didn't say that if he wanted to live in Mohamed Oaks, he had a trust fund.

The windshield wipers slid and slapped.

He thought, I'm a scientist, not a spy. Besides, he thought, I'm not a Muslim.

"What do you think we should do with the house?" he asked Gladys. "We might want to come back."

Why can't we just stay? she thought. Why do we have to leave?

Yes, her kids would move up to the next grade, but she'd still be able to greet them every morning, to see them in the halls and let them know how much she cared, would always care.

If they had to go to Sacramento, one day, of course, they would return to LA. Of course, they could buy something new, but they might not be able to find another backyard with lemon and grapefruit trees, and a bathroom paneled all in beautiful wood, and the built-in cabinets, all the workmanship of another era. She knew how proud he was of this little place, that they had been able to buy it on their own, no help from Natalie and Shel. It was too small for children.

She did well with kids. She believed her students loved her. Only recently she'd dared to ask, "Do you think we are healthy enough—psychologically—to adopt?"

"Well, in the end we are African," he said. "An African isn't human without a family."

Scarred inside, she couldn't conceive or give birth naturally. They didn't consider reproductive technology but, "We could do what my parents did," Dawit said. "See how it works with a foster child."

Gladys liked that idea but still they had done nothing. Like Dawit, she had spent her early years in a refugee camp. Unlike Dawit, she remembered everything and chose not to speak of it. Her mother hadn't cut her, but men in the camp did, with a broken bottle. That was only one of the things they did to her when she was just a child, again and again. While her mother still—Dawit had learned the American way of referring to this attitude—her mother was in denial. After so much suffering followed by survival, Dawit's mother-in-law had to believe she could control events. She who had been cowed and ostracized and spat upon embraced America where one could brazenly be shameless. Glad's mother was in charge of her own and her daughter's destiny. Anything that went wrong was something that simply had never happened.

But it had happened. Dawit couldn't bring himself to enter her where she was scarred. They held each other at night. He caressed her with hands and lips and tongue, seeking anywhere on her body where she might feel pleasure. Sometimes when he had his mouth on sensitive skin, Glad made a sound like a merry teakettle just coming to a boil and he hoped this meant she was feeling the ecstasy women were meant to feel.

They were Americans and therefore they considered therapy.

"What if one of us begins to want, you know, and the other doesn't?" Gladys had asked.

He came instantly when she touched him. He would never be able to satisfy her the ordinary way. "Are you happy like this?" he asked.

"Oh, yes. What about you?"

"I'm happier than I thought possible."

All his longing for her brought him to bursting. He was pollen.

For now, she had the cats.

Mercy, back again, scrambled up to reach her lap, treating her leg like a tree trunk, digging in his claws. She suppressed a cry. Even over the phone, Dawit mustn't hear it. He couldn't handle her pain.

"Will you be home tonight?" she asked.

"I had hoped so. No, not till tomorrow." Turn down the reassignment, she urged him silently. You don't have to do this. "We may have to buy up here," he said. "Same problem. Finding a rental that will allow four cats."

"Five," she said.

Gladys Used to Undress Behind a Closed Door in the Dark

Now, in the bathroom, the door left open so the cats wouldn't cry and paw and throw themselves against the barrier, she examined the marks Mercy had left on her legs. She sang aloud. *Oh my darlin', oh my darlin'.* They had learned to sing *Clementine* all those years ago in the camp. And here, see all the traceries of cat scratches around the old keloid scars on her thighs. Mercy jumped to grab the end of her bra strap and swung. Oh, you make me laugh. Scars on her stomach, too. At school, in the locker room before and after gym, the other girls laughed at her modesty. It was Bettina Albanese who saw it once. *What happened to you? Appendectomy,* she lied. *Did you do it yourself?* In the camp, they sang *Clementine* with church harmonies, the sound so glorious that Gladys would see golden balls shimmering before her, waves and zigzags of brilliant green. Moments of beauty she'd had to forget while her mother was still alive. We were never there. It never happened. Simba wound around her, tail brushing between her legs. Lines in white, some pink, some purplish. The cats were just playing, they forgot to retract their claws. She loved them and they loved her and meant no harm.

"A little bit of kitty S&M," she'd joked once to Shila, never to Dawit. Shila laughed. "Kitty porn."

Gladys lay in bed, under the sheet, holding her breath till with a thump, thump, another thump, the cats began landing beside her, such a comfort with Dawit gone. The kitten explored her up and down, sniffing and licking, till he settled with his paws wrapped in her hair, Kodak nestled in her arms, Sugar Baby stretched out along her back, Tiger and Simba at her feet. In bed, all fighting and hissing and growling ceased. They understood that if they wanted a warm human to lie with at night, they had to come to a peaceful allocation of space. They had to share. She liked to think someday human beings would learn to do the same.

Pennies from Heaven

Brent Fassen was once more unhoused. The FBI had cut him loose. He kept promising actionable intelligence. He gave them a conspiracy but he'd screwed up the tape and the only evidence was his word. He'd failed to deliver Martin Keller, the one he assured them was ready to act. So now Brent Fassen was back on the college circuit and still talked the talk but there was no point instigating trouble if the FBI wasn't picking up his tab. Instead of money, he was showered with girls, that certain sort of girl who looked on an affair with a professor as her rite of passage. Her right. And these days when a professor could be fired, sued, or even jailed, that certain sort of girl had to make do with fascinating older campus visitors, men just passing through, e.g., Brent.

"Janice." He nudged her. He wanted to wake her, but not cruelly. "Janice, you have to go."

He'd spotted her in the bar where the admirers took him after his talk. He sat drinking, trapped amid the clutch—in the clutches—of undergraduates all agog. She sat alone, regarding him shyly—or slyly—over the cover of his freshly autographed book.

"Join us," he said.

"No, it's Joanie," she said, doing as he suggested.

She thought he'd called her Janice. Perfect. That's what he would call her. A private joke is a form of intimacy. Even better when accompanied by embarrassment.

Without the blunder, he thought, there can be no forgiveness. Without forgiveness, no redemption.

"Penny." He shook her again, harder.

A penny falling all the way from heaven. Think of the impact. It would kill you.

He wanted her gone. He wanted to sleep. Her breathing disturbed him. These college gigs meant a hotel room, a bed, a shower. The rest of the time he was living in his vehicle again. The Fascist truck. Not a tactical decision at all. A home.

It was always the same, waiting them out. It got later and later and the girls and boys would leave at last, one by one, two by two, until one bright penny remained. And fuck it, he wasn't young anymore. If he were going to fuck, he wanted to fuck after dinner, or in the morning, or in the lovely late afternoon, not at two in the fucking AM.

She wasn't dead. Just dead to the world. Or faking, biding her time so he'd have to take her to breakfast in the morning.

"Joanie," he said. "JoAnne. Joelle. Jody. Get up. You got what you came for."

Your grownup experience. Sex with Someone Important. She rolled over and sighed. He left her in the bed. I wonder where Marty is now, he thought. Probably back at Evergreen, content to live a life without purpose. Meaningless. He went out to the Fascist truck to sleep.

File #10:

Packing It In

Dr. Tang Looked Like He Hadn't Slept

"You'll miss your Russian whore," said Carsky. Only the man's imminent departure made such a remark possible.

"No whore," said Dr. Tang. "And Ukraine." You wouldn't exactly call Tang a Good Samaritan. He didn't say a word about Lara till he was heading back to China and would no longer need her services. "You help," he said.

Yeah. Like help her, like how? "Sure, sure," said Carsky. Tang would never know one way or the other. And sex work was a job like any other, wasn't it? Sex workers tried to form unions. They wanted to be covered by Social Security, protected by OSHA. They lobbied legislatures and City Hall. You have to respect the dignity of all work. I mean any work at all takes a toll on your body and/or your soul. We're all selling something, right? For women it's a choice—it's what Yoli chose, right? and women—even if they're screwed up like Yoli—have the right to choose. So maybe it's not a great choice but maybe it's her choice. When he wrote music for those films, it's not like it was something he wanted to do, but no one forced him. Right? And OK, he's got a conflict of interest. Again. We're talking about Kyle here. Tara's stepbrother. And more to the point, Casey's brother. Not someone you want to cross.

Carsky never considered himself lonely, not as long as he had sex. But now he wished he had someone to talk to. He couldn't take this to Tara. Talking to Rennie would open up a can of worms.

Which had already been opened. Nothing got past her.

"We should call the police," she said. "Or those FBI guys."

"No police," said Carsky. "Maybe she doesn't want to be saved," though he knew Kyle and so he knew better.

"I don't see why—"

"Lots of reasons," said Maria. "Leave it up to *her*. Police don't get involved unless *she* wants."

Emine would have been sensible. If Emine were around, everything would have been straightforward and easier.

"It's the van, isn't it?" said Maria. "Out front every day. With the dogs and cats on it?"

So many times they'd seen Tang hitch his bicycle to the back of the Groom Room and climb in.

"So we follow the van," Rennie said. One look at Carsky's face and she corrected herself. "*I* follow the van."

You Must Plan for Future

Kyle kept the gun on her when he opened the back of the trailer. The loading ramp was missing so she stepped out onto cinder blocks and collected what he'd brought her—takeout crap from McDonald's, demijohns of water to clean herself up with. He kept the gun pointed at her when she emptied the slop bucket, heated water on the camping stove, undressed, got in the washtub. This routine was, Lara thought, more humiliating than having to fuck the men.

There was something wrong with the men. What sort of person uses another's body and it's just a transaction? How is that human? How is this called pleasure? And their transaction was never with her. It was with the stupid boy who drove the van and took the cash. They used her, all the time acting like she wasn't there. Most of the time, she wasn't. She separated herself from her body and then they could do whatever they wanted. Until she learned how, it didn't matter that she said, *I do not do this because I want to.* They didn't hear. *I am a prisoner.* They didn't care. She wasn't even a thing to them. A thing you are careful with, it shouldn't break. When they did to her what they did, they erased her. Which made her wonder, Who are they fucking if it isn't me?

Fucking the men was at least something to do. At least there was a mattress. In the trailer, hardly room to stretch out on the floor. Compared to the trailer, she thought a Russian prison cell would be deluxe. In the trailer, she didn't let her mind go away. She was afraid if it left, it would never come back. Was it possible to be both in despair and bored out of your mind? It was. What to do? Pacing in the confined space—if you could call it that, moving back and forward, running in place, turning in tight circles till she was dizzy enough to fall. On the floor, arms wrapped around herself, rocking her body where everything ached. Always holding onto her self.

When this ends, she thought—because it had to end. This cannot be the rest of my life, she thought. This is silly boy, not big gangster. I will escape and I will still be Lara Figurski. I will still be me.

Look, she thought. I am free to make a choice. She could keep out the cold, leave the plastic sheets and over there, the horse blanket tacked over the slit windows. Or she could take the blanket down to let in fresh air and the light. Take it down, tack it up. Her decision. The blanket still smelled of horses. Sometimes the smell was a comfort. Sometimes so strong, horse sweat and her own body, the slop bucket, the smell of the men. It sickened, choked her. The windows so narrow, she tried—but couldn't—squeeze through. And out there, desert as far as she could see. Where would she run to? And the stupid boy wasn't all that stupid. He had taken her shoes.

All day, she thought, I am only walking. A cramped circle, over and over—what was that? A poem she once read? The son-of-a-bitch left her bottles of vodka which she didn't drink and stacks of magazines she didn't read, written on behalf of advertisers for women who were morons. *Variety*, she asked for, *Hollywood Reporter*. Can I keep radio here? He looked at her like she was, well, what for the time being she was. The Chinese guy slipped her scientific offprints which she didn't understand—too much math—but he also slipped her a pencil. She used the flipside of the paper to work on a screenplay. Chinese mobster falls for Russian pole dancer. No, if we're talking Hollywood, better Russian mobster and Chinese pole dancer. Concentrate. Write your script. But how can a human being do this to another human being? How can a person treat another this way? What she looked like now, how she smelled…How was it possible, what sort of man could it be who would pay good US dollars to have her? It didn't help to wonder, to have these thoughts. Plan for your future, she told herself, and you will have one. Think of anything except where you are now. How about casting? Liev Schreiber or Tim Roth for the Russian, better yet, if you can, De Niro. Lucy Liu for the dancer? Lea Salonga? Alexandra Chun? Maybe didn't matter. If you had male box office, enough that woman look good.

The Chinese guy liked to talk but even with him, she understood he was merely using her to practice his English. He could make mistakes in front of a whore and not be ashamed.

"You are scientist!" She wanted him to tell her more.

"You are Russian spy!" he said.

"No." She made it very clear to him who she was.

Whatever happens to me, she thought, whatever I must do, you cannot take away from me who I am.

I have never been helpless, she thought, not a day in my life. And this guy, yeah, he has gun, but he is not Boro. This guy, he's upizdysh, sukin sin, also a fool. So one morning, when he opened the door, she threw the contents of the bucket at him. He hollered, his clothing and best of all his face spattered. Her vomit, her urine, her shit. She ran for the truck and should have known. No keys in the ignition.

"I could kill you," he said. "I should kill you." He had the gun. He locked her back inside. "Don't think this means a day off."

She watched from a narrow window as he stripped, wiped his face with his boxers, tossed the filthy clothes on the ground. He got in the truck naked except for those silly shoes that flashed those lights on and off, off and on.

No one Gave Rennie Credit

If they only realized, she was good at everything. Who knew she had the perfect instincts for a P.I.? Some might suspect she'd had training in tradecraft.

She drove to Mojave at sundown and trolled the truck stops and motels looking for the Groom Room. What if she was wrong and he drove all the way to Tehachapi? No, Kyle was lazy. Besides which, men in Tehachapi would have more options. Kyle had a specific market to exploit, she thought. She settled on a small independent service station on the highway. It looked discreet—not a truck plaza with floodlights and activity. A truck was parked in the back and there was room for more. She pulled over, her car shielded from view behind the wall of the wash station.

On TV, cops on a stakeout drink coffee and eat junk food and scatter the wrappers on the floor. But she brought a small container of hummus, pita chips, baby carrots. She drank nothing. Couldn't take the chance of needing to pee and missing Kyle. She got lucky. The van appeared and a man emerged from the service office and handed over what had to be money before Kyle slid the side door open. She clocked it—ten minutes—then kept her headlights off and followed the Groom Room along Route 58 and watched Kyle pull up briefly to the lobby entrance of each motel. Two more customers. How did they know? Word of mouth? Desk clerks? Of course she'd seen a phone number on the side of the truck along with the slogan, *Got Tail?* Could they be more obvious? What if someone called about their dog? Not likely, she thought. Who for 60 miles around here would ever pay to have their dog shampooed?

California City. More customers. Then onto the highway. She stopped by the side of the road when Kyle drove off the pavement and onto the desert. Her car couldn't manage off-road. She went a short distance past the spot, turned around and parked facing the other direction.

Just like on TV, waiting in the dark was a bore, and she didn't even have a partner for the exchange of sardonic repartee, till lights appeared, illuminating the sand and dust kicked up by the tires, then everything disappeared for moments before the headlights lit the night again. There must have been dips in the terrain, flat though it seemed to be, and the place where the woman was stashed had to be deep in the desert. How the hell would she find her? This wasn't going to work. She started the engine even though she knew the sound would carry. It was time to get away before Kyle reached the road and spotted her there waiting.

If she couldn't find where he kept her, she would have to grab her out of the Groom Room. With Emine gone, Rennie had no choice but to work with Maria.

He stops at a red light, we pull up next to him, open the side door. Yeah, and he comes out with a gun. Drug him with animal tranquilizer? They don't work fast enough—assuming I could get any. At the red light, we spike a tire. Then what? He gets towed. How do we know he won't stay with the van? Should we try it? They started to get silly. Threaten him with a rattlesnake. Block the intersection with a herd of sheep.

Carsky said, "Kyle'll be out-of-town all day Saturday. Maybe all weekend."

That would give them time to drive around the high desert. Rennie at least had a general location. Maybe it would be enough time to find her.

"It's a white supremacist shindig," Carsky said. "And then they're heading to some kind of paramilitary training."

"You going with?" said Rennie.

"I declined the invitation."

"You better go. You need an alibi in case we find her. He comes back and she's gone."

"We'll need 4-wheel drive," said Maria.

"A vehicle," said Rennie, "that can handle the terrain."

"Like your Range Rover," said Maria.

"I feel like I've been carjacked," said Carsky as he handed over the keys.

Patriot Days

They traveled all along the Kern River, staying north, where it's unincorporated and fully loaded open carry is legal. "I don't get concealed carry," said Kyle. "Why bother to pack if you're not gonna show it."

Carsky had phoned him. I changed my mind, he said, and Kyle picked him up in the Groom Room. Thank God he was too dumb to notice the Range Rover was missing.

Men in DayGlo orange vests directed traffic to designated Patriot Days parking: motorbikes left, cars right, trucks and vans pull straight ahead. American flags and huge posters: USA #1. Kyle nudged Carsky and jerked his head at the lineup of blue PortaPotties. "How do I get one of those?" They spotted Casey's van surrounded by Hummers and pulled up as close as they could get. Three men stood talking to Casey and running their fingers through their beards. They wore Stars and Stripes bandanas around their foreheads, but small Confederate flags stuck up from the Hummers. And why would anyone wear a heavy black belted jacket and boots in this heat, Carsky thought. Red swastika armbands. The men slapped Casey on the back and made fun of the Groom Room which, Carsky thought, was a helluva lot better than their noticing him or Kyle's flashing shoes which in a crowd like this would have to draw the wrong kind of attention.

Big men on motorcycles buzzed around them while a small DayGlo woman pointed away to the bike parking but it was clear she couldn't direct anyone anywhere. Her weak smile said she was just offering helpful information.

Men were shouting, about taking the war to the enemy here at home. Someone handed him a flyer. There in bold print, the word JEW. He tensed, scared, kept his head down and tried to read. The words blurred and danced. Jews and Arabs both Semites, treacherous, vermin. If the federal government won't clear them out, it's up to us.

The brothers unloaded the weapons from the back of Casey's van—Benny's weapons, Carsky remembered only too well—and loaded them into the back of one of the Hummers.

After which, things got almost normal. Like any street fair, the smell of sausage and peppers (but no Mexican food) and spilled beer, sunscreen. The milling crowds, mothers pushing strollers, fathers with babies strapped to their chests, two bandstands, an afternoon in the park, only difference being the rifles, shotguns, handguns on display, swastika armbands, camo, paper targets featuring men in turbans, all for sale at the booths. The banners, White Pride, Pride of the 'Dale, Save the White Nation, American Patriots, Resist (well, you could see that at any demonstration), men marching along the river bank and past the pump jacks, some working, some rusted stiff. It was mostly undeveloped oil company land.

"So why'd you change your mind?" asked Casey.

"Resistance Records is here. Professional interest," said Carsky though he was most definitely not interested in racist rock, heavy metal bash, and dulcet Aryan maidens. OK, interested, yes, but not enough to risk getting anywhere near them. "So if America's taken over," he said, "which you prefer? Mexicans, Muslims, or Chinese?"

"Ain't gonna happen," said Casey. "The Jews won't let go."

Good, you need Jews, Carsky thought.

There was an incident up ahead. Someone shouting through a megaphone about the First Amendment.

"I thought it was the Second they all love," said Carsky.

"See if they need help."

Carsky reluctantly followed Casey. Security guards were trying to confiscate a large poster, a birthday card to Hitler that people had lined up to sign. A woman in a suit was talking in the I'm-a-reasonable-person-but-you've-got-me-aggravated tones of white women in Republican attack ads.

The oil company had gladly given permission for a Patriots Picnic on the land, she said. These days, oil companies were looked at as the enemy in spite of employing millions of American workers and running our cars and heating our homes. This generous support of the picnic was meant to be good PR. A birthday party for Hitler was not the kind of publicity the company was expecting in return for its community engagement.

"She's honest at least," said Carsky.

"I should have stayed home," said Kyle. "Like Tara."

"She's not home," said Carsky. "She's *at* the Home. Weekend shift."

"You don't really want to be here," said Kyle. "Let's go."

"Home?" Where Rennie was no doubt doing something reckless. "Already?" said Carsky.

Rescue Mission

Maria was behind the wheel. Rennie claimed she could do absolutely anything but she couldn't drive stick. Maria, on the other hand, had navigated over trackless terrain more rugged than this. Of course, she had also kicked up rocks and destroyed the undercarriage on more vehicles than one. But those were old Jeeps heading up narrow mountain trails. The high desert was bumpy but flat and Carsky's Range Rover was a fucking pretentious sturdy piece of work. Though they'd needed jumper cables to recharge the battery. The fucking pretentious Director never drove.

They took it slow off-road only because so much dust was flying, they could have been looking directly at the brothel and not known it.

Rennie said, "We're going to need a carwash before he sees it again."

"What are we looking for anyway?" Maria asked. "A trailer? A house? A shack?"

Rennie didn't answer. They heard the sickening sound—sounded bad but really wasn't—of tumbleweed stuck in the undercarriage.

"Yeah, yeah," said Maria. "We'll know it when we see it." If we see it. She stopped the truck and Rennie got out, climbed under and pulled away the dry vegetation.

Then she stood and looked around.

"We've got all day," said Rennie.

Maria joined her, carrying her compass and water and snake hook just in case. In the back seat they left what implements they owned: a machete, an ax, a hammer, a tire iron.

When they saw the tire tracks, on foot through the chaparral, they followed them.

No barbed wire. No security system. No guard. No dogs.

Maria said, "This is—what was that word? Rinky dink."

Three deadbolts on the outside of the loading door. And the woman banging on the metal siding for help. Who would've thought it could be so easy?

The stench hit them when they opened the door. Lara stumbled on the cinderblock step as she rushed out. She stood there, crying.

"It's all right now," said Rennie. "You're going to be all right." She wanted to hug this woman but figured too many people had touched her without her consent. "What are we waiting for? Let's get out of here."

"Wait!" said Lara. She ran back into the trailer. Rennie watched her pouring vodka on the mattress, the magazines, the floor. She asked, "You have match?"

Maria lit one.

In the Range Rover, Lara said, "Thank you. Thank you. Thank you," and "No police."

Most Small Businesses

"Home?" said Kyle. "Hell, no. I'd rather get trashed. Trashed."

In the Groom Room, they crossed the river, skipped the malls and headed downtown. "That's the place." Carsky saw the cat outlined in neon from a block away. Inside, they had the establishment to themselves, the truckers and bikers and drillers at the shindig, the black and Latino residents of Bakersfield and the reasonable whites thinking it a good day to stay indoors.

"Game?" Kyle twitched his head toward the pool table.

"I don't know how," said Carsky. He checked out the jukebox. Unplugged. He asked the bartender for a beer. "Whatever's on tap."

"What kinda shot you want with that?"

Carsky asked for bourbon which he hated, but it seemed right even though, in his humble opinion, it tasted like kerosene.

"She was into my tat," Kyle said. "My tat. Said with seahorses, it's the male gets pregnant. That's bullshit, don't you think? But don't mention it to Casey, OK? You know the kind of girl she was?" he said. "Yoli'd try just about any drug you name, but couldn't stand a needle. Shoulda seen when I took her for a flu shot. She has to close her eyes and hold onto this stuffed animal they gave her all the time I'm stroking her hair."

"Yeah," said Carsky. "She came across pretty tough but underneath—"

"I'm as tough as Casey is," said Kyle. "He's so macho, gotta prove it too, the man needs to whack off at their fucken boot camp. Not for me. But," he said, "I was weak for that woman. She left me the business," he said.

Right. You were driving around in it when she split, thought Carsky.

"I'll say that for her," said Kyle. "You know she painted those long pink tongues on the dog and the cat? Talented, you think? I get the Groom Room. She took the fucking cat."

"You wanted the cat?"

"She loved that cat. Big fluffy calico thing with a black patch under the nose. Hitler mustache. She loved that damn animal more'n me. All this Hitler stuff today," he said. "Reminds me of Yoli. Gets me morose."

"Me, too," said Carsky.

"I'm down anyway. I'm down these days, Carsky, my man. I thought I was building something," said Kyle. "But you have no idea, no concept, man. Gas, food, booze, aggravation. After Bobby gets his cut, what's left for me? For me! And I'm the one on the job every night. When do I get a night off? When do I get to have fun?"

Carsky said, "You know most small businesses fail within the year."

"Well, fuck me," said Kyle. "I can see why."

Rennie Has a Plan

Lara had been scared and humiliated and bored. Now that she was safe, sort of, bored was exactly what she wanted to be. Empty. There were books here, a computer, any publications she asked for, friendly women willing to talk or just listen and she just wanted to sleep. To let water pound over her in the shower, to soak in the tub. To stay blank.

The one named Maria said she could get a U-visa if she testified.

"No police," she said. Boro might still be involved which meant her family back home could get hurt.

She knew she needed to be tested, and Maria said it could be done in the lab, confidentially, and that sounded good, but she wasn't ready to face the results. So instead she slept.

Maria said, "I remember what it was like. I was in shock, too, didn't want to get out of bed, but I had to run."

"You don't know what I feel," said Lara. "What I *don't* feel."

Rennie, the American, talked about her like she wasn't there: "We should call someone. She needs help."

"You don't get it," said Maria. "You're an American."

"And this is America," said Rennie.

"Yeh yeh no no," said Lara.

"You need a reason to get up in the morning," said Maria. "You need work." No, she didn't mean *that* work.

I am their captive now, thought Lara.

Rennie lurked outside the bathroom door. She kept hoping to hear Lara singing in the shower. Then she'd know the woman was going to be OK. In the meantime, as usual, Rennie thought, she was the one who'd have to come up with a plan. She figured prostitutes— even though Lara wasn't really one—were used to dealing with the ugliness of the body and the psychological disturbances that can afflict. After what she'd been through, Lara surely had the requisite experience for taking care of a demented elder.

"Listen," she said. "My mother's in a care facility and I want to bring her home." Do I really want to? she thought. But the condo felt so empty. No dinners with Emine, and even the lizard, *her* lizard, had somehow got out. Gone. "I go to work," she said, "and my mother can't be alone. Stay here and hide as long as you like. Till you figure out what you want, you've got free room and board and internet. I'll pay you something too." All she'd have to do was keep Mrs. Mulcahy clean and dressed—or at least in adult diapers.

"And Netflix?" said Lara, something Rennie had never heard of but which she agreed to at once.

"Mom, this is Lara."

"Larva!" said Mrs. Mulcahy.

"Lara!" said Rennie. "Lara!"

"Larva!"

"Yeh, yeh, sure, sure," Lara said. "Call me Larva."

Maria Needed a Visa for Somewhere Else

"Don't you know anyone in Europe?" Rennie asked.

They were drinking wine at the kitchen table while Lara played a pattycake game with Rennie's mother who sat, naked except for an adult diaper, on the living room sofa. Mrs. Mulcahy no longer used a wheelchair. The Home had required it: strapping her in had helped the staff keep her clothes on. Now in her own home, as long as she didn't venture outdoors, why shouldn't she dress or undress as she pleased?

"I did that conference in Frankfurt," said Maria. "But I didn't really connect with anyone." Frankfurt was clean and safe and everything as it should be. "There's something to be said for order," she said. "But it's not home." Europe wasn't the place for her. It had made her long for heat and exuberant disorder.

"My home," said Lara. "Kyiv. Kyiv is clean place. But Odessa? Gangsters."

"Bugsy Siegel used to send me chocolates," said Mrs. Mulcahy.

"Believe me, I know gangsters," said Maria. "Dr. Sergio and the Institute saved me."

"*You* rescued me," said Lara.

"Obviously Mexico has problems," said Maria. "But damn! you gringos are so passive. This war—"

"Against terrorists," said Lara. "Like Chechen animals."

"We'd be blocking highways," said Maria, "setting up encampments in front of government buildings, calling general strikes." California, at least, was turning Latino though in Desert Haven you wouldn't notice. She thought how much she loved her people. Even the simplest people in Mexico, no matter how limited their horizons, they always wondered about what was beyond. They knew how much they didn't know and pushed, always, against those limits. While gringos, she thought, either denied their ignorance or seemed proud of it. But she didn't say any of this. She said, only, "I wish I were home."

"So go," said Lara.

"I'm between a rock," Maria said. "If I can't go to Mexico, at least Latin America."

"I can call Rory," said Rennie.

"Last time I looked, Texas was still part of the United States, like it or not."

"He's well-connected," Rennie said. "He knows everyone in Brazil."

"It's a big country."

"I mean everyone in research."

"Will you do that for me?" said Maria. "Ask him to talk to someone high up on the food ladder."

Rennie said, "If he'll even take my call."

Rennie Had No Idea

Not a day or night passed that Rorion didn't want to phone her. Rennie was like a big warm loaf of bread. Not that he wanted to slice her, take a bite. Rorion still just wanted to hold her, feel that warmth. She'd made him want to do things he'd never wanted before.

Now he was left with no one, and afraid to pick up the phone and call. Other women had tried to seduce him. Rennie succeeded. She learned so quickly. Never approach him from in front. If he could see a woman coming toward him, his cells would shriek, he'd back away. It was automatic, it was instinct, it was out of his control—words that made him think of his grandmother and the automatic spirit writing she believed would bring her word of his mother. Rennie knew to come up behind him and hold him close, his back cushioned against her breasts. Rainbows danced along his spine and dissolved into sighs, then hardened into the hunger that made it possible to fuck—to use her word—face to face. Her language could be alarming.

"Looks like I lucked out!" she'd said once. "A 40-year-old man who's never been in a relationship!" Something he'd been ashamed of. "No baggage!" she said.

Now he had Rennie-baggage. And there was—had always been—plenty more.

When he squeezed her, he was flooded with the aroma of Anadama bread, delicious, the kind they served at Harvard, soft, break it open to the molasses smell of fragrant wood as it's sawn.

At work in the lab, he always needed to touch her.

He couldn't believe she had refused to go with him.

Too much loss.

So he got the recipe and baked his own bread. The astrophysicist with his fingers gummy with dough. Kneading it, stretching it, watching it rise, the stuff of life.

There's more to me, always has been, than my particular, peculiar brain.

How could you make an American understand? Being a Communist in Brazil wasn't as sinister and extraordinary as in the USA. It was entirely normal for a university student. No one thought it strange, in fact, it was so predictable it was equally natural for the generals to declare war on the universities, for students—like his mother—to be killed. Presumably. She was disappeared before his first birthday. And good Communist that she was, or believed herself to be—marriage was a bourgeois impediment. She never named his father. So he was raised by his grandmother who professed allegiance not to Karl Marx but to Allan Kardec and spiritism, to seances and ouija boards, always calling on Helena, Helena, her lost daughter. She was every bit as superstitious as the umbandistas but heaven forbid there could be any suggestion of Africa, she followed the teachings of a dead Frenchman who claimed to be a dead Druid, never never deigning to respect the traditional rites of the poor and the black.

And Rennie thought he had no baggage.

At Rennie's Condo

Lara borrowed Maria's camcorder and taped cinema verité-style footage of an old woman who, at least on tape, was usually appropriately clothed. One segment began with Mrs. Mulcahy making figure eights with her arms and humming and talking about the million dollars she kept in a coffee can. Her fingernails were painted in a rainbow of colors. Tara's work. An offscreen voice says, "More loud please." Then, in closeup, there's too much makeup caked in her wrinkles. Her smile is timeless and mindless. The camera pulls back to show the teddy bear held to her chest. "When I was a child," she says, "the city was still countryside. We had orange and grapefruit trees. The neighbors had horses and chickens and that awful rooster, waking everyone up." Her eyes dart and her breath comes out in frightened puffs. "Maybe that was my mother?" The offscreen voice assures her, *Yes, yes, calm, Mrs. M. You are good, very good. You are telling us of childhood?* "My name was Rosemary Stiegmuller and I had a wonderful childhood." Her tongue peeks out from between painted lips. "And that's what's happening here. A skirmishing for every little ball." She clears her throat, over and over and over again and no more words come.

The tape played back on the VCR much to Mrs. Mulcahy's delight: "I'm resuming my career thanks to Larva. About time, don't you think?"

In the evenings, when Rennie came home from DHI, Maria would ask "Have you heard from Rorion?" and then ignore Rennie for the rest of the evening. As though it's my fault, Rennie thought, he hasn't called.

Emine was gone and Lara was Maria's new best friend with Rennie pushed to the margins again, in her own home, left to care for her mother which was supposed to be Lara's job.

She coaxed her mother into eating soft food while Maria and Lara worked at the computer, rarely speaking because Lara had learned form-Z in the German version—"for special effects"— and had no idea how to explain the 3D modeling capabilities in English beyond saying, "Like apple pie. Is easy." Mrs. Mulcahy, on the other hand, never shut up. Talking, muttering, humming, singing, making sounds of either pleasure or distaste as she ate. Shapes and forms and spirals danced across the screen and Maria would start saying *sí sí sí sí sí* so rapidly it sounded more like a snake or a stutter than enlightenment and then Lara would move aside, Maria would sit and start inputting what? data? and more designs that meant nothing to Rennie as she appeared at Maria's elbow with a plate of sandwiches.

Sometimes Maria stayed late, she and Lara talking. Rennie hadn't understood the conversations Maria had with Emine, all beta and delta subdivisions, those firmicutes, plasmids and ribotypes and now this was just as bad.

"You know Potemkin Stairs? Sure, you know, must know from Eisenstein great film."

"You mean Odessa Steps?" said Maria.

Rennie tucked her mother into bed. "Sweet dreams, Mom."

"Underwater," said her mother. "I sleep underwater. I used to be a mermaid. In the deep blue sea."

"Sure. Now is escalator," said Lara. "Go from harbor to boulevard. Is broken, and the money to fix—stolen! Typical Odessa."

"You call them Potemkin Stairs?"

"Pot'omkins'ki Skhody"

"I've always wondered...the Czarist soldiers keep marching down the steps but they don't ever step on the fallen bodies. Was that to show how precise and orderly they were in their killing? The opposite of the panicked crowd? Or did Eisenstein just not have any special effects or stuntmen? Was it impossible to shoot trampling without actually trampling people?"

"Odessa Steps is not true. Never happen. What I want to know—the scene in *Untouchables*. Railroad station shootout. This is homage, no? Same sequence, baby in carriage going down steps. But De Palma baby is not killed."

Maria laughed. "American movies are the bloodiest, most violent in the world. The most guns, too, but the American audience will not tolerate a dead baby."

From the bedroom, Rennie's mother shouted, "Answer the door!"

When Maria left, Lara sat at the computer and checked out dating sites.

"I find American husband," she told Rennie. "American man always want Russian bride."

"I thought you were Ukrainian," Rennie said.

"Nobody know Ukraine. On date site, Lara is Russian, name Irina."

Rorion Calls Back

What with him being Latin, Rennie assumed she couldn't just come out and ask him for help without some friendly chitchat first. Wazzup? How are you? What have you been doing? etc.

"People are so friendly here," he said. "I get on a bus and every stranger says *Howdy* and I'm expected to say *Howdy* back. White people here are strange. You drive around the back roads, you're expected to lift your hand off the steering wheel and wave at everyone. I'm told it's not a greeting, it's to show you don't have a gun. But the purpose of your call?"

Sometimes she forgot Rorion wasn't normal. Latin or not, with him you were expected to get to the point. She explained about Maria.

"Hmmm. Let me think who I know up the food ladder."

Rennie had always said *food chain*. Now she thought maybe she was the one who kept getting it wrong.

Mothers Day

Magaly brought flowers. Red roses.

"No!" said Lara.

"Is OK. I take thorns." She presented the bouquet to Mrs. Mulcahy who closed her eyes and breathed in the perfume, then lifted out a single flower and held it to the nose of her teddy bear.

Lara captured it on the camcorder.

Magaly squeezed the old woman's shoulder, then kissed her cheek. "Happy Mother's Day, mi amor."

"You watch," said Lara. She inserted a tape into the VCR. "See what we make," she said, and there was Mrs. Mulcahy, fully clothed, looking straight into the camera.

"Rennie, daughter. I love you." She went on talking but her words were lost as Magaly applauded and Rennie began to cry. Maria held her as she sobbed and so, when the phone rang, it was Lara who answered. She talked for a long time before saying, "Maria, is for you."

"Yes, yes! Thank you! Rennie, can you get me something to write on? It's Rory."

"He's at the door!" said Mrs. Mulcahy.

"He's got something for me," said Maria. "A research station in Recife. And *Crotalus durissus cascavella*."

"Good, very good," said Lara. "You write down, then give me phone."

"Whore-ee-o and whore," said Lara. "Is fate." Rennie stared at her. "He need wife. And in Austin, is film community. So, you drive me Los Angeles, Greyhound bus."

"But you can't," Rennie said. She didn't know what she felt or what she ought to feel. "What am I supposed to do with my mother? You have no passport."

"On bus, I sleep. Then wake and oh no! I say passport is stolen."

"He's a good man," Rennie said.

"Go," said Magaly. "Go now. I stay tonight with Mom."

To Lara, Rennie said, "Don't hurt him."

I am hoping, Lara thought. And she thought hope is a poison. Growing up in the East, you are cynical to the bone, you trust no one. Then, when you are ready to give up, someone offers you an opportunity too good to be true, and you take it.

"You know my sad, stupid story," she said. "I am one of many. But I am Lara Figurski. I am different."

Just Another Gringo Party

Natalie Levy had never been happy about Dawit's work for the FBI. Of course, she never expressed anything except support. But she was pleased when he said he was leaving, until he added he was accepting a transfer up to Sacramento. Getting in deeper. But what can you do? She and Shel threw him a farewell party where, of course, being the sensitive hostess, she tried to make the most out-of-place guest feel welcome.

"Edgar," said Natalie Levy. "I don't suppose you were named for—"

"J. Edgar Hoover," said Edgar. "Most certainly not."

It was just another gringo party, he thought, where people talk and don't dance.

Natalie was good at this, keeping up the friendly chat while her mind was a thousand miles away in Texas, where Khadija, who called herself Kandi, sat on Death Row. She pushed the dip in Edgar's direction and glanced over to the poolside patio where Gladys had left Daniel Chen and Shila.

Poor Gladys. Poor Shila. Obviously unaware of what was clear to Natalie. Chen already had a match: Edgar, this very out Latino. As short as Chen, but stocky where Chen was slight. Both of them with buzz cut heads. They should have let their hair grow, she thought, it would be black as a raven's wing. Or wear it sticking up in spikes the way Ramiro's cousin did. Porcupine hair.

"You're also with the Bureau?" she said.

He laughed. What a great mouth of teeth. "ER nurse."

These days nothing worked out as expected. Her own son working for the FBI and now this farewell barbecue before he moved away up to Sacramento with Gladys, more daughter than daughter-in-law. "They grew up almost like brother and sister," she said to Edgar who wasn't listening, distracted it seemed by Desi who was grooming herself now by his feet.

"Gladys used to be afraid of cats," Natalie said. "I suppose they just move too fast. They appear out of nowhere so suddenly. But the first time she had a soft warm kitten purring in her lap, the look on her face, Edgar. Sheer surprise and delight."

The cat was gorgeous. That beautiful face, green eyes set off by that long black hair that shaded into a russet color and seemed to trick the eye, it had to be alchemy that burnished the fur gold in the sun without it ever ceasing to be black. Edgar couldn't take his eyes off him—or her. People said you could always tell a person's orientation by whether his eyes followed a woman passing by or a man. And me, Edgar thought, what does it mean that my eyes are drawn instantly to the cat?

Complicated People

Dr. Levy—Shel—had already lit the coals. Now he was mixing mojitos under the ramada and listening to Eli, one of Dawit's former colleagues from Manatech.

"Genomic medicine is going to put you out of business," Eli said. "Repair heart defects without surgery. Spot predispositions early and keep people healthy."

"Um hmm," said Shel.

Eli wore fashionable sunglasses, the lenses a bright cobalt blue, but topped off as he was with a floppy white fisherman's cap, he looked goofy as a character in a cartoon. "This country pays way too much for poor health outcomes. How many patients die after a so-called successful surgery?" Eli grinned as though the thought of people dying pleased him. "*You* want people to be sick," Eli said. "That's where the money comes from—heads in beds."

Shel controlled his hand: just bruise the mint leaf, don't smash it.

"We'll keep people healthy at home," Eli said. "A nurse for treatment, a mathematician for quantitative cognitive support." Shel noted the torn fingernails. If this guy actually did his own lab work, he'd snag the latex every time gloves came on or off. "Hospice workers will visit toward the end."

"So people will still actually die," said Shel.

Gladys joined them, held up three fingers to her father-in-law and waited while he arranged mint leaves and lime wedges on the glasses. If she didn't say a word, maybe Eli wouldn't notice her, wouldn't follow her.

Eli picked at his cuticles and peered up at Shel. "Less than a decade and you're obsolete."

The day you go into congestive heart failure—not that I wish it on you, Shel thought, you'll forget about molecular medicine. You'll be lucky to get in to see me.

Eli was single but clearly not the match Gladys had wanted for Shila. Dr. Levy set the three glasses on a tray and she carried it away. With any luck, Eli had mistaken her for the maid.

"Thirty-two percent of cancer patients get the wrong diagnosis and wrong treatment from you experts."

"I'm not an oncologist," Shel said mildly. And he hadn't gotten rich—not this rich—off people's suffering. Family money, too, and investments, none of Eli's business.

"Gene therapy and stem cells. We'll be able to correct any flaw."

"Including personality?" said Shel.

"I believe it's biologically based," Eli said.

This was Dawit's friend, Dawit's party. And where the hell was his son anyway? The boy had always kept his thoughts to himself. All you can do is give love, Shel thought. He couldn't possibly begin to understand what so much trauma in early life had done to the child.

"Yes, people like us can only be Americans," Shila said to Chen. "Otherwise we are too complicated." She was born in Uganda, her African mother a servant in the home of a Parsi businessman. Seduction, rape, who knows? Her mother was pregnant when the Asian community was expelled and her father had to leave for his homeland. "But what country will that be?" He'd been born in territory that, since Partition, was Pakistan. After Partition, his family emigrated to Africa. Now he had to leave, but as a religious minority, he chose to go to India. "I never met him," said Shila. He never acknowledged paternity but some years on, he became their benefactor. "He arranged our immigration here with visas for investment and business. He put a chain of laundromats in my mother's name."

"Better than a motel," said Chen.

"Yes, in some godforsaken place," said Shila. "I can't even imagine."

The laundromats had been a good choice. Her mother practically lived at the one nearest their apartment. She talked to people, helped fold sheets fresh from the dryer. The warmth and the smell, she loved it.

Gladys brought the drinks.

"Thank you. What a treat," said Chen.

A polite man, she thought. If he'd been straight, he would have been perfect.

Making conversation with Natalie, Edgar was also being polite. Foolish, wasn't it? how happy he'd been when Chen decided to bring him along. Out together in public in a place that wasn't gay. Maybe it was just because Dawit was leaving, it no longer mattered what he knew or didn't know.

Natalie had apparently asked a question and he had missed it. He'd lost sight of the cat. "What's the cat's name?" he asked.

"Desi," she said.

"I have two. Rubén and Darío." And he'd rather be home with them right now. Chen, of course, claimed to hate cats, that was why they'd never live together. More likely he feared a more formal relationship would lead to a background check. Edgar had dropped out of medical school back in El Salvador to join the FMLN. Only as a medic, only to save lives, he assured Chen. In this country, he had a thing for men in law enforcement. Cops, deputies, agents. Chen saw it as making amends. To Edgar it was just the mystery of sexual desire, powerful enough to trump politics. "No peace officer gonna die on my watch," he liked to say because the English language amused him, this Orwellian use of the word *peace.*

Dawit lay in the hammock tied between two coast oaks, his knees bent to accommodate his long legs. His mother's cat stretched out beside him and purred as he stroked her. Since Gladys had been bringing cats home, Dawit didn't feel quite right without one. Before the cats came, Gladys had slept as she'd done as a child, on her back with the sheet pulled over her face so that if bad guys broke in, they'd be scared off by the sight of a corpse. Desi lifted her head, alert, when a squirrel moved the leaves above them, but preferred Dawit's company to the chase. She snuggled against him. As always, he caught himself listening for a car coming up the long drive, uncertain who it was that he expected. It was all so familiar and so strange. He could hear the chatter, his parents, his guests. When he was growing up, there were always kids here, swimming, or on the tennis courts. They came for the facilities, he thought, not for me, but surely that wasn't true, many of them came from homes with pools, game rooms, screening rooms. These days, Chen was probably the closest thing he had to a friend, and now he was leaving Chen behind.

He'd been lying in this hammock for twenty years. He and Gladys spending most Sundays with the folks. Till now.

"Do you run the business?" Chen asked Shila.

"I sold it," she said, "I teach fourth grade, like Gladys. In fact, I'm responsible for the only business loss we ever took. My Colombian boyfriend"—ex-boyfriend actually, but she wanted Chen to see she had no designs on him—"he suggested we start a mobile service like they have in Bogotá. Delivering a washer and dryer right to someone's apartment or house so they can do the laundry without leaving home. The concept didn't translate to America."

"Didn't travel," he said.

"No, it was not very mobile."

Gladys joined them. "Never trust a man with your money." She didn't believe that but her timing was perfect because at that moment, Eli intruded and tried to sell them on some investment opportunity in biotech.

Shila took a cue from Gladys and ignored him.

Secrets

If they're not talking about me now, they will talk once they're on the way home, thought Dawit. Even Shila, who knew something of his background, had never been to the house—the estate, he thought, had never seen how he grew up. Eli would tell everyone back at the lab, that is, if anyone listened to Eli. Chen and Edgar. Now I know

Chen's secret and he knows mine. Lying here, he thought, not joining in just makes it worse.

"The FBI would prefer gay agents to be out," said Edgar. "That removes any opportunity for blackmail. But he's Chinese and he's scared. You know, let a thousand flowers bloom and when they lift up their heads, lop 'em off."

She somehow doubted Chen knew much about the Chinese Cultural Revolution. But Edgar did. The lover of an FBI agent, an unlikely leftist. As unlikely as her son joining the FBI. As unlikely as the life she'd married into, up at the end of the long drive lined with centuries-old oaks. Here, the magnolias in bloom dropped their grenades. She had swept the Jacaranda Walk early that morning and then again shortly before people started to arrive so no one would slip on fallen blossoms. Natalie believed in doing things for herself and somehow she had ended up with a staff. She never used the word *servant*. She was glad Connie had the day off, and Ramiro along with the cousin who worked with him, the young man certainly undocumented, at least she hoped so, she wanted to give a chance to someone who would find chances hard to come by. Closed borders kill people. Like Amalia Torres, strangled to death. She could never remember Ramiro's cousin's name. Maybe she should have been inclusive, invited them all to the barbecue as guests. "I'm sorry. I'm a bit distracted," she said to Edgar.

"Death penalty appeal?"

She searched his face. "Yes, a particularly terrible one. This Saudi woman—girl, really? She came to the US with her family as a child." With the obvious result: they were strict; she was American. "She ran away from home, ended up on the streets in Hollywood." A thirteen-year-old girl busted for soliciting needs help, not punishment, Natalie thought. "In and out of Juvie and foster homes. After the prostitution busts, her family wouldn't take her back." Then came the more serious bust, prostitution and drugs, at age nineteen. Adult. "It landed her in deportation proceedings. She's terrified. She's going to be shipped back to Riyadh with documents showing she's a prostitute and addict. They'll behead her, or stone her to death."

"You're representing a case in a Saudi court?" Edgar asked.

"No. It gets worse. In the immigration detention center, it's overcrowded. They had all these women sleeping on plastic under the cafeteria tables. She stripped one night and used the legs of her jumpsuit to strangle the woman sleeping next to her. She figured the death penalty in the United States would be more humane."

Edgar had been kind to listen, but now he was speechless.

Sometimes I hate this country, Natalie thought. Khadija was a killer but she was also a very screwed-up teen. And our immigration policy shared responsibility. Khadija should never have been in deportation proceedings. Amalia Torres should never have been taken from her children, who are orphans now. And my son, Natalie thought, is working for the government I can't trust.

"How did we get here?" she'd once asked Shel.

"We bought before the real estate boom," he said, a good man who didn't understand.

Someone at the FBI must have known—there was a background check, but Chen had no idea that Dawit grew up this way. So, almost as a parting gift, each one of them had been willing to reveal a truth.

The grounds! The house itself wasn't large. He did a walkthrough when he went inside to use the bathroom. Living room with African carvings on display. Dining room he suspected was rarely used. The art on the walls was contemporary and large. The kind of thing that woman, Virshaw, would do. Though these couldn't be hers. What a weird conflict that would have been. For some reason, he found himself thinking of Norman Rockwell, the image of the children in a classroom, the little boy reaching forward to dunk the girl's pigtails in the inkwell. Of course, Virshaw had brought that to mind, the inky ends of her ponytail. Large eat-in kitchen with the de rigueur island, copper-bottomed pans, two different kinds of ovens in the wall. Steps leading down to a sunroom at the back of the house. He hadn't even reached Dawit's old bedroom when Eli walked in and caught him snooping.

"Looking for the bathroom?" Chen said, and pointed. "That way."

Engaged in the Struggle

Dawit knew he would have to join the guests but just the sight of Eli coming out of the house made something tremble inside him. Resentment is not part of my makeup, he believed, and so whatever this emotion was, he couldn't name it. He hadn't known that leaving Manatech would be so hard. The Human Genome project wasn't even 100% complete, but Eli was already identifying mutations that predisposed a woman to breast cancer, building on work Dawit had started.

Change happened so fast these days. Dawit was left behind. At DHI, he didn't even recognize all the equipment while those years at Manatech, he'd had access to the best. And then those visits to amateurs, people who had their own cryogenics tanks and G-Boxes in their garages. Now at the FBI, his computer didn't even have internet access. No email capability except for interoffice. No Google. And he couldn't take files home to his own computer thanks to all the security rules. Now he didn't even have anyone on his own level to talk to. Today, he had the chance. Unfortunately the chance was Eli and so he wasn't going to take it.

He used to have so much enthusiasm for his work. Now he spied on people who under other circumstances would have been colleagues, trying to convince himself they posed a threat. If they were benign, his days and his skills were wasted. And what would become of Rennie Mulcahy? *She's a glorified secretary*, he wrote in the report. *They always want you to think they know more than the boss.* But someone somewhere made the decision and it was out of his hands. If this was what his country wanted of him, it's what he would do. This trait was indeed part of his makeup: gratitude. To Shel and Natalie. And America.

"You should be proud of your son," said Eli.

"I am," Shel said.

"He understood his limitations as a scientist. To do science, you need a single-minded focus. Hard to do if you're not single."

As you are, thought Shel, and not because of science.

Yet he couldn't quite say Eli was wrong. Dawit and Gladys. Of course he approved. Of course he did, though the relationship sometimes seemed to him extreme. And now, more alarming still, Dawit talked about evil, about there being real evil in the world. At least, thought Shel, he's not enlisting, not going to fight. Of course he wouldn't. That would mean leaving Gladys behind. The woman who seemed to answer all his emotional needs but had robbed the boy of his edge.

"Sufficient scale," said Eli, picking up where he'd left off. "Platform integration."

Shel prepared two glasses. "Eli, my friend, would you mind bringing these to my wife and the young man?"

The bougainvillea on the walls. The roses, the cactus and succulent garden. It often crossed Natalie's mind that in Africa, this could only be the home of an oppressor. Eli approached and handed them drinks.

Eli, the only one from Manatech who'd come to say goodbye. She knew if Dawit had moved on to a position with higher pay, more opportunity, they wouldn't have dropped him. But this. It wasn't that they were radicals—at least she didn't think so—and it wasn't that they'd now dismissed him as a loser. She was sure they were bitter, they believed he sat in judgment over them just because his choice was different from theirs.

She knew how it happened. After she married Shel, she of course needed to work—that was in her character, but she no longer needed to earn. She left the firm and took on pro bono death penalty appeals and then not a single one of the attorneys she'd considered her friends remained in her life. Of course they did work long hours. But she would not excuse the people who had dropped her son. Not a one of Dawit's colleagues could have been as dismayed as she was. FBI!

You have to let go. She could have stopped the Bureau from taking Dawit, but she'd kept quiet. That first family portrait, the flash of the camera dazzling his eyes. Dawit, blind. The doctors had acknowledged his history of trachoma, but all cured they said. The blindness had to be psychosomatic. If people knew, who would ever hire him? Certainly not now, the era of Homeland Security. Back then, months had passed and the darkness lifted and he could see again and what had happened was nobody's business.

When Dawit explained to her about dual purpose, she should have warned him he, too, was at risk: People think they are serving humanity and then their talents are enlisted to do harm.

"With your background," she said to Edgar, taking a chance, "it must be difficult, being with an agent of the US government."

"What your government does in other countries is terrible," he said, "But it's not like that here."

"Or so we'd like to believe," she said.

Shel took out the steaks and the aroma made everyone turn in his direction as soon as he placed them on the grill along with corn still unhusked. He circulated at last, only to ask "Rare? Medium? Well done?"

"Thanks, sweetheart," said Natalie. "Medium rare." He leaned in toward her for a kiss on the cheek.

To Edgar, he said, "We may have crossed paths without actually meeting. The ER."

"I don't know," Edgar said. "It's more gunshots than heart attacks where I work." A slight exaggeration. "But you got Edgar on the job and you're in uniform, you not gonna die. Not on my watch," he said.

"Edgar, Edgar," she said when Shel moved on. "Hoover, I mean. He was the most famous man in America for a while. Everyone knew his face. But my grandmother," she said. "Two agents came to the door and one of them shows her his badge. It's signed by the Director, of course, and she's so flustered she's thinks that's who she's talking to, *Come in, Mr. Hoover. Yes, Mr. Hoover, No, Mr. Hoover.*"

"Your grandmother engaged in the struggle?" he asked.

His choice of words, she thought, revealed what had been left unspoken.

"Marxism wasn't her ideology," Natalie said. "She used to say it was her mother tongue."

"The days," he said, "when a Jew who was merely a socialist was considered rightwing."

How did he know so much? And it hadn't been quite that way in Natalie's family back in the Bronx. From what she understood, whenever a neighbor spoke of the Bolshevik Revolution and the coming Workers Paradise, her great-grandmother replied, *Nothing good ever came out of Russia except black bread.* If one of her children happened to be present, she might remember to add, *And your father.*

"At home," Natalie said, "broken English met broken Yiddish. People talked about the cost of food, where to maybe find a job, never about dreams or ideas. In the Marxist study groups she got access to a language."

"I think I know what you mean," he said.

"In El Salvador—?" she said.

"I was a medic. I never carried a gun." More truthful to say he hardly ever fired one.

Part of the Picture

"Yes," said Gladys. "Come. I'll show you where."

Chen had asked, surprised, "You grew up here, too?"

Strange, Gladys thought, how men could spend eight hours a day together and tell each other nothing. They headed off across the lawn to the guest house, Gladys, Shila, Eli, and Chen. They stopped for

Edgar. Chen took him by the hand. On they went, past the half-court with the basketball hoop.

"I'll bet Dawit was a ringer," said Chen.

"Not at all," said Gladys. "With his height, it wasn't a challenge." She had been the one, so single-minded, shooting from the foul line, hours at a time, till every shot went in, and then that wasn't good enough, the words in her mind repeating *nothing but net*. "Edgar, I hear you love cats," she said, and went on to describe her own.

Natalie watched the group go, a perfect vision of the new America. She felt such love and a little self-centered regret: she had just missed being part of this picture.

The way she'd heard the story so many times, dancing was forbidden in the Kaplan household, along with premarital sex and drinking gin. It was as though, Natalie always thought, those immigrants learned about the Puritans in citizenship class and thought that was the way to be American. But when the Communist Party sponsored interracial dances—*How can we know the will of the masses unless we fraternize?*—her grandmother Shirley felt she had to go. *Lenin was moved to tears by music! Dancing is healthy exercise, filling a legitimate physical need!*

Shirley and three of her friends remained wallflowers, rigid and fearful. Four Jewish girls with so many voices in their heads, the Party telling them white chauvinism could not be tolerated, their parents insisting that they make something of themselves—but not a spectacle! Joe Simpson, a white comrade, came for them and he took one girl and after they danced one dance he returned her to the wall and asked the next girl. He took them in order, down the line.

He made it clear this was duty, nothing personal or even pleasant about it. Natalie's grandmother was next, and then she saw a way out: a Negro man on crutches who stood alone, leaning against the wall, just far enough inside the room to leave free passage through the double doors. She ran to his side.

"I don't dance," she said, "but I would love to talk."

Two picnic tables pushed together. Napkins blowing away and the tablecloth fluttering in the breeze.

"Gladys, there's salad in the kitchen. Would you mind?"

I could have been biracial, Natalie thought. Part of the future instead of the past.

Shel served the steaks. There was not a vegetarian in sight.

Edgar made kissy sounds and held out the back of his hand for the cat to sniff. Desi ignored him.

Natalie was thinking of the new client on Death Row in Georgia. She had a plane to catch in the morning. A black man. She thought of her grandmother and the man at the dance. They became friends. Who knows how serious it was? But Shirley's parents got worried. There was a cousin in Los Angeles. They put their daughter on the train to Chicago, to connect there for LA. What was it people used to say? I'm not a racist, but it wouldn't be fair to the children. What would have become of her mother? If she'd been mixed, if they'd stayed in New York, maybe she would have married a Puerto Rican. The family would have gone on mixing and mixing. She herself, she would have had a wonderful life somehow and somewhere, but probably not here.

"Did she name names?" Edgar asked. "Your grandmother."

"I don't know," said Natalie, but maybe...Joe Simpson.

Eli's long arms seemed to be everywhere, reaching for salt, butter, ketchup. Still talking though his mouth was full.

Shila and Gladys sat side by side, laughing, and Natalie watched them. It seemed all her life she had always watched girls, not so much thinking of the daughter she'd never had, but studying other women for cues on how to be one. No, she thought not how to be a woman, but the kind of woman I don't despise.

Desi wound around the chairs, the sweet cat that had earned her respect. My role model, she liked to say. Poor thing was too arthritic now to jump up to the seat of her favorite chair. When Natalie lifted her, the cat jumped right down and eventually found a chair with rungs that she could get up by herself. I hope I can age with as much dignity, thought Natalie. When her circumstances change, Desi gives up what she must and finds a new way to live without relying on anyone but herself.

For now, Natalie gave up nothing. Could any other place be as beautiful as this? Here she was, eating steak with her African son.

Benny from la Eme

"I'm really fucked," said Kyle. "I don't know how, but that bitch escaped and I still owe Boro."

He doesn't know I'm involved, thought Carsky.

"And Benny's home."

That meant from prison, thought Carsky.

"He wants his stuff back," said Kyle.

"So give it back."

"Can't," said Kyle. "Can't." He waited for Carsky to ask why not.

Carsky said nothing. Which wasn't right. Carsky had been there when they raided Benny's storage unit. If Kyle was scared shitless, Carsky should be too. "Everything's in Bakersfield. Everything."

"So go get it," said Carsky. "It all belongs to Benny. And if Benny wants it, you have got to give it back."

"Can't," said Kyle. "Casey turned it over to the Patriots. You remember them, from that picnic?"

"Unforgettable," said Carsky. So I'm fucked, too, he thought.

"No way will they give up their weapons," Kyle said.

"*His* weapons."

"No way—to a Messican."

Carsky said nothing.

"They let Casey keep a couple automatics. For self-defense," said Kyle and then fought down tremors and panic at the thought that he would have to defend himself. Against the Mexican Mafia. "I called Yoli. Thought I could move down to San Diego, to San Diego. Till it blows over."

"That sounds like a good idea," said Carsky.

"She said no." She already had a new guy living with her. If he told that to Casey, all he'd hear was *Loser, loser*. Carsky was different—a good listener, but fucking useless.

I'm in over my head, thought Carsky. I'm in over my head.

Remember them? Jesus. And what did they plan to do next? Kill more Muslims? Jews? Cops? Kill Coptic Christians? Questions, questions, while there was no question about what la Eme would do or who Benny's peeps would choose to kill.

As soon as Kyle was gone, Carson Yampolsky headed for DHI. He locked all the Institute doors. What was the point? Rennie pulled her rescue act and was staying home with her mother and that woman. Petey Koh gave a couple of weeks notice before moving to Seattle—Microsoft—with his wife. Maria stopped coming in after he made her get rid of the snakes. Emine was "in the wind". Everyone was gone—except Tara, the brothers, and now, oh God, Benny. Carsky went home and packed. I'm in over my head. Thank God the Range Rover started. He drove off, leaving behind the furniture, leaving the key under the mat.

Before Dawit Moved North

Chen decided they should do it in the evening and pick Rennie Mulcahy up at home, when and where they expected she would be alone. Instead, when she opened the door, there was an elderly woman, stark naked, doing a hula dance. She smiled at the men and said, "Reach down to the beach and lift the shell."

"Sorry, sorry," Rennie said.

"Why are *you* apologizing?" said Maria. To the men, "What are you doing here? Do you have a warrant? You can see this is not a good time."

"I just lost her caregiver," said Rennie. She guided her mother away. Was there a back door? Chen and Dawit exchanged glances and Chen followed.

"Dr. Castillo," said Dawit. "I'm surprised to see you here."

She touched his arm. "Sit at the computer." She led him to the kitchen table. "See, we can model in 3-D."

We. Meaning Emine?

"You must miss it," Maria said.

She was trying to distract him. And she unnerved him, the skeletal teeth in receding gums and the sunbaked brown skin that gave her the look of a mummy, the way she regarded him squarely with what seemed like defiance but might have been pity.

"Miss what?"

"Research," said Maria. "You used to care about expanding knowledge. I googled you."

From the bedroom came a scream and then a falsetto voice singing in what sounded like Russian.

"What are you learning, Dr. Castillo?" he said.

"This software. Look at this—"

He wondered why Rennie Mulcahy had such sophisticated software at home.

"You want to disrupt retroviral protease?" Maria said. "Specifically, M-PMV. You know what that—?"

"Yes, yes. The enzyme," Dawit said. "You're looking to disrupt the multiplication of HIV."

"Maria, I need help," Rennie called.

In the bedroom, Mrs. Mulcahy was squirming and swinging her arms, only one of which was inside a sleeve.

Maria pushed past Chen and said, "You could lend a hand."

Rennie said, "Come on. You know she won't let a man touch her."

Maria put a teddy bear in Mrs. Mulcahy's arms while Rennie stroked her hair. They calmed her enough to get her to sit on the hospital bed, and then Rennie slowly pulled on a pair of underpants. Her mother released her bladder, without malice, without shame. The only one who blushed was Chen. Maria stripped the bed. Rennie stripped off the panties. Mrs. Mulcahy, somewhat subdued now, let them adjust an adult diaper. Dawit hovered in the doorway as Rennie made the bed with fresh sheets.

"Get the door," said her mother.

They got her to lie down and pulled up the railings around the bed.

"That will usually keep her," said Rennie. "Go to sleep, Mom. Bob Hope won't be here tonight."

"Who is Bob Hope?" asked Dawit.

Chen followed Rennie as she took the dirty linens to the laundry room and started the wash.

"You guys investigating the hate crimes?" she asked.

"The—?"

"The white terrorists who shot the halal butcher and his son in their store," she said. "And the attack on the Sikh gurdwara. The—"

"That's a different task force," he said, wondering if such a task force existed.

"You need a model for molecular replacement," said Maria. Click click, she showed Dawit. "I know I'm going very fast. We already figured this out, I just want you to see it." A ploy, treating him as a colleague. The images and the words: partial threading, crystal structure.

Rennie joined them. "You should start a lab in your garage," she said to Dawit. "It's not hard to do these days."

They wanted him to be a scientist, not an investigator. Did that mean he was getting too close? But his own lab, he thought. Then nothing he created could be patented by a corporation for profit. His discovery would not be owned. His employer couldn't call it proprietary information. If he made a breakthrough, he'd assign the patent to humanity. He'd give it away, open source, where anyone could build on it. And then, he thought, he'd be investigated too.

"It's really Dr. Albaz we'd like to talk to," said Chen.

"She's not here," Rennie said.

"We can see that."

"Will someone please answer the door!" came a shout from the bedroom.

Rennie shook her head. "I thought she'd sleep."

"What we need to know—" said Dawit.

"Here's the core of the protein. Tuck the loop here. You're going to need backbone rearrangement. Now here you see the monomer surface—"

"Makes more sense to me than vulture vomit," said Rennie.

"Emine Albaz," Chen prompted.

"The Director told her to take all her vacation time," Rennie said. "I don't know where she went."

Dawit said, "My work was on BRCA1 and BRCA2."

"Estrogen receptor reporter genes," said Maria.

She didn't use the words *breast cancer*. A way perhaps of distancing herself from that possibility, he thought. It was a choice, he thought, to live without fear, and he thought again of his wife, how women's bodies were so fragile and women so strong.

"You handle all the travel arrangements," said Chen.

"Not the personal—"

"Answer the door!"

"I'll get it, Mom," said Rennie, and stayed where she sat.

"We want to predict," said Dawit, "from the genetic profile who actually benefits from chemo and/or radiation." NDO be damned, he wanted to talk. How easily a researcher can be seduced, he thought.

"Of course that's valuable," said Maria. Pat on the head. "But imagine finding a way to repair the mutation. Or design a drug that specifically targets a specific woman's specific disease." Or a bio-weapon, he thought, targeting a specific race or gender or individual high-value target human being. "That's actionable information," she said. Actionable intelligence, he thought. "Make a cut in the cell. Insert what the patient needs."

"Simple," said Rennie because now they were in territory she understood and she had nothing, really nothing more, to say to Chen. "You create the blueprint, then you send it out for actual fabrication of the bioengineered gene."

"And where would I send it out to?"

"To us," said Rennie.

"But you see, this is the problem," said Dawit. "People who haven't been vetted receiving whatever they want—any kind of pathogen, for example—by mail order." Lethal snake venom, he thought, and wondered if it could be aerosolized, and he wondered why they'd been told to pick Mulcahy up, and not Dr. Castillo.

"Oh, please," said Rennie. "I'm talking about designer genes, recombinant DNA." She chattered on. "We need a revenue stream. No more depending on government or being beholden to corporations."

"Even recombinant DNA, it's a risk."

"It's the entrepreneurial small business model," she said. "We've done too much low-fee work for amateurs. We have to up our game."

The singing began again.

Dawit wasn't happy about it, but the decision had been made.

"It would be very helpful to have you come to the office, walk us through some of your procedures."

"Now? At night?"

"We're 24/7 these days," said Chen.

It's her own fault, thought Dawit. Why did she have to act the know-it-all? But he couldn't help feeling bad about her and wondering what would happen to the old lady.

"You don't have to go with them," said Maria. "Rennie, don't go."

"OK, Mom," said Rennie. "I'm checking the door." She laughed and picked up her shoulder bag. Chen assumed she was glad for the excuse to leave Maria stuck with her mother. But the laughter hit Dawit hard. He was sure she was entirely unconcerned, thinking *No problem. This is America.*

Rennie

The slot opens. The tray is pushed in. When I don't eat, sometimes I find a note the next time. This is America. We don't allow hunger strikes here. And I keep the notes so I'll have paper in case I ever come into possession of a pencil or for when the toilet paper runs out and they make me wait before they give me more.

File #11:

To Five Rivers

Restless Winds

Emine didn't like being alone, but in New Mexico she found a certain rapture in loneliness. The chittering of the prairie dogs, the clouds she simply could not describe but tried to in an email to Maria and Rennie. *Sometimes you see white or gray stripes that mimic the mesas on the horizon but mostly clouds aren't a backdrop. They're a living mass that moves toward you in pregnant billows, in startling 3-D. You can't capture it in a flat photograph. I've seen some paintings, though, that almost do.* And, she thought, Petey Koh could probably simulate the effect on the computer.

She wrote them from the motel lobby, the night of the thunderstorm when she simply had to pay for a room. She stood outside beneath the overhang watching fantastic lightning strikes over the desert while the wind lashed her with rain. Back inside, she changed into dry clothes and wrote some more: *I'm in Gallup, near Red Rock Park which is in New Mexico but reminds me so much of Red Rock Canyon on Route 14. Is it possible I'm homesick for a place I never considered home? I miss you both.*

No reply from either one. So out-of-character for Rennie but of course it was entirely true to character for Rennie to be so damn sensitive, her feelings probably hurt by the joint email rather than one sent to her alone. But was that a reason not to answer? Being cut off this way annoyed Emine more than she wished to admit.

Not that I'm such a nice person either, she thought. What about Alula Wright? Arbitrary the way she ignored her. That woman came along and something inside Emine just rebelled, said *Enough!* It occurred to her now she'd felt powerless with life—everything—beyond her control. Every now and then she claimed—she needed to—the only power she had. To say *No.*

Now she would put off as long as she could the return to Istanbul. Where she would have to see her family. And *his*. What would she tell them?

And then? Without Oğuz, without work, what on earth would she do with herself? The steering wheel slid against her palms, through the curve of fingers, smooth as her husband's penis. How crazy it was for them to be apart.

The Grand Canyon was too huge to take in. America, where bigger had to be better. Emine's eyes were drawn instead to the junipers along the canyon rim. She thought of Petey Koh again, wondered if he would stay married to his anti-social wife.

She was married too. Sometimes she felt her heart catch and stop. Oğuz.

As long as she kept moving, no one knew where she was. No one could reach her. His silence meant nothing.

Bryce Canyon. The hoodoos, misshapen red pillars, wind and water-carved, rising up amid the fir trees from the canyon floor. But if the hoodoos of her own country were touched by fairy-folk, something other than human, this landscape was simply inhuman. Instead of Cappadocia's soft colors, the playfulness, the invitation to enter its honeycomb of refuge, here there were jagged walls, splendid in their savagery, red like open wounds. It all took her breath away, canyons and cliffs, on and on, more and more and more till she thinks you can only look at so much sandstone.

Zion National Park. She rode the shuttle. Recorded commentary she could hardly hear over the children shouting, tourists talking. She was getting a headache: the mechanical voice, the rock walls almost too high to take in from the windows, columns and peaks, *the patriarchs, Abraham Isaac Jacob almost hidden behind the Angel Moroni millions of year sand dunes sandstone sedimentation minerals groundwater.*...Is it possible, she thought, I'm getting tired of rocks? The voice tells her: *The person responsible for your safety is you.*

Cows grazing on the lawn in front of the luxury condo development. Lovely pastoral scene, but she doubts the residents appreciate the cowflops.

Fields striped with shadows of clouds.

A sign: *Caution: Open Range.* And she misreads it: *Rage.*

A car tailgating so close behind a truck, it looks like it's being towed.

A bicycle on a rack behind an SUV, the front wheel spinning.

She drives with ease on paved roads where once Native people planted squash and whatever else and found a way to live on this wild terrain. She thinks of the Mormon emigrants, how awed they had to be by these canyons, how brave and full of faith to venture across so hard and dangerous a land. The road vibrates through her body day and night and she thinks with admiration of bus drivers and long-distance truckers.

What has happened to her that a landscape makes her think, first, of people?

She allowed herself to cry. This was ridiculous, being a tourist. She should head back to Desert Haven, one last time, to say goodbye. No need for a motel there. Rennie hadn't bothered to email but surely if Emine showed up she'd be welcomed.

California and the desert scrub sparkles with shards of glass. No hiking here, over mile after mile of broken bottles. Across Death Valley and on to Desert Haven.

The Lights Were Off at the Institute

No one answered the door or the phone and at Rennie's, no one was home. The door to her own place had been left open and dust and sand had blown in and crawling things had made their homes on her floors.

Desert Haven was a ghost town. Not like the one they'd seen during that road trip, Red Mountain with its old mining shafts and wooden buildings, the old-timey general store, the wagon wheels that drew at least a few tourists on the weekends. A hundred years from now, Emine wondered, will anyone drive out of their way to see a faux Spanish-colonial subdivision in foreclosure? Where she had spent four years.

Alula, Emine thought. Why not? Now she sent an email. Yes, she would come.

And if she was headed to the Northwest, there was still work to do.

She tried to phone Don Billingsley at the Hanford site about the remediation plan. Eleven million tons of contaminated radioactive soil dug up from along the Columbia River was just a start and she didn't like what the contractor planned (or didn't plan) next. As far as she could determine, sediment contaminated with cobalt-60, cesium-137, and plutonium-239/240 (exactly the substances poor Alula wanted to get her hands on!) could migrate downward to the water table. While her findings, admittedly, were not definitive, the risk was too great to ignore.

The security code had been changed. No surprise. Her email was blocked so she would have to go in person and track him down. Before the new security protocols came in, she'd done what she always did and copied the files to her laptop so she could work at home. Now she had the update, her own executive summary, the raw data, the maps and charts all on the thumb drive to give him. Before Hanford, Pendleton, the Umatilla Reservation. She'd leave a copy with the tribal council. There were places near the river where the vadose zone was less than a meter in depth, and this beneath the most sensitive, contaminated areas. According to her computer modeling, at times when the river ran high, contaminated groundwater would find channels between the gravel sequence and the more compact Ringold Unit. None of it apparent during previous measurements when the river was at low or normal flow. Billingsley and DOE would have to listen, but if he—they—didn't, the tribe could take it to legal counsel.

Otherwise it would be as bad as 9/11, but in slow motion.

And look, just look at what 9/11 had done to the Americans. They waved flags. They dropped bombs. They tortured. And mass murder--did they really have no idea what they had unleashed in Iraq? While at home, they took periodic blackouts and road closures and gas main explosions and collapsing bridges and homeless people in the streets and disgruntled employees with assault weapons and illiterate teenagers for granted. Everything that Americans considered normal still surprised her.

But it wasn't her business. It wasn't her country and she'd be gone soon.

She Couldn't Keep Wandering

Headed north again, at Lone Pine she turned off the highway and into the Alabama Hills. She'd driven this way by chance that time when the three of them had burst out in cheers and then fell silent, the landscape so powerful and strange it overloaded the eyes. Stone arches and giant rocks and boulders piled and melted one on the other, acre after acre of mystery. Today, her eyes took it in without emotion. I guess you can't ever go back, she thought, though going back was exactly what she had to do. She couldn't keep wandering.

She tried to picture her life, her old life, starting with the old house in Istanbul. The house where she'd spent her first seven years. She could not for the life of her see it in her mind's eye. Did she have a room to herself? What color? Was the floor wooden or tiled or carpeted? She'd spent the last four years debating whether enzymatic degradation or specific binding of pollutants would be more effective, picturing borehole samples, pebble-to-cobble gravel in a sandy matrix, the complex interstratified beds and lenses, the angular basaltic detritus of the Hanford formation, all of this and more instead of her husband, her home, her life.

Back to 395 and north. Past Manzanar. They'd stopped there too to see the museum that documented-while-sanitizing America's shame. She wasn't interested in seeing it again, though one of the few souvenirs she kept of California was the copy of the tag issued to Togo Tanaka, Family No. 3885, an editor of the Japanese-language newspaper in Los Angeles, who was arrested and then shipped off to the internment camp right after Pearl Harbor. She remembered how they had stood in front of the old cemetery and the cold winds came whipping over the desolate terrain, chilling their bones. Of course, Americans weren't Nazis and Manzanar wasn't a death camp, but it occurred to her now that white Americans had no way of knowing that. When their Japanese American neighbors were rounded up and taken away, they had no way of knowing they would not be tortured and slaughtered. They trusted their government without question.

She pulled over to consult the map. OK, she'd have to go through Nevada, then back across the line to Susanville to what looked like a meandering but still major road. Join up with I-5 near Mt. Shasta and onward to Oregon. To Alula.

The visit would give her a weird American story to share with Oğuz. The more stories she gathered, the more she felt sure that she would soon be with him again.

Her eyes blurred with tears. Oğuz, she thought. What have they done to you? What have we done? I'll go to Ankara, she thought. I'll spend all day in the government offices. Ahmet got nowhere but someone will talk to me. I'll wait until someone takes notice. Someone had to help.

Maybe it wasn't her eyes that failed to respond. Maybe it was her heart. If she let herself feel, she wasn't sure she could go on.

May 28, 2003

I, too, was bound for Five Rivers, on a freelance assignment to interview two women who had succeeded where so many fail in making a difference. They got the Forest Service to stop using toxic Agent Orange defoliants—2,4-D and 2,4,5-T—in their community. Now they were working to ban cell phone towers. I thought I could learn from them about organizing and persistence. What can one person do? In a world of war and lies and inequality and injustice I wanted to tell a positive story. I was looking for reasons to hope.

Alula Had Been Dropping Things

The house was lately a minefield of broken glass. A side effect? The beginning of Parkinson's? No, it seemed to be a new form of laziness, that she reached for things without instructing her fingers to close. She had to retrain herself to pay attention. Grip! Grip! Maybe it was the same with the words she had lost. That she kept losing. If her mind would just close around them, if she refrained from speech until the word was securely in her grasp. She could feel it, the edges of its consonants, the smooth soft center of its vowels. From her hand up through her arm until it moved inside her, into her throat and then out with her breath. She hadn't lost them, not at all, they were just a little hard to get to.

Oh, April! and then May, and Alula sat in her garden crying. The turkey buzzards hadn't come to signal spring planting, or maybe they'd come and gone and she hadn't noticed, or had noticed and had forgotten. She'd come to the garden for something, but damned if she knew what. She tried to stand and fell back onto the black tarp over the composted sod. Maybe that's why she'd come? To distribute it? Divot, divot, her mind said divot, but she no longer remembered why. Though she had trouble finding words, the memories were still there, the problem was naming them.

She could still talk to herself and she had no trouble rereading all the words she'd already written in her garden journal.

March 27, tristar everbearing strawberries
April 4, planted snow peas. first yellow tulips.
4/10 first glads. cleaned out woodshed.
April 17, lilac blooming. rhodie—creamy with pink tinge.

It was like speaking a foreign language you used to know. You can't summon up the word but you recognize it as soon as you see it.

Years since she'd seen a blue heron. In the winter, you might hear a cheep from an LBJ—that's as specific in nomenclature as she got for those Little Brown Jobs. Even when her brain worked as it should, there was so much she didn't know, the other birds all flown south, and summer she still sometimes heard the upward trill of the thrush, the Swainson's thrush in the spruce trees or collecting moss for a nest. But where were the buzzards? Will a hawk eat a slug? Slugs she had aplenty, didn't they love the fragrant lilies as soon as they began to come up at February's end.

Bees and hummingbirds gone from the garden too, where they'd spent the summer tasting the poor man's orchids.

November she'd still be picking green beans and tomatoes, those that hadn't gone to rot or to the voles. The dahlias still blooming, only a few years now since she thought to plant decoratives instead of allowing only what she could eat. She wanted flowers now, right now and not on her grave. One load of dead leaves for compost on the garden beds even before the maple and alder shed all their leaves. But now it was spring. She stood again. Took a few steps. Fell again, this time on top of the shears. Probably leaving a bruise but the blades at least were closed. The headaches had started again. The dizzy spells. And she'd come to once or twice on the floor which made her suspect there'd been more seizures which made her suspect that in spite of the WBRT the cancer in her brain was back. Which was worse? The confusion or the fatigue? Was it normal for your neck to sweat when you try to think? If she stayed in bed all day, which is what she felt like doing, Monty wouldn't allow it. Here he was, licking her face, licking away her tears, filling her senses with his lovely dog scent so that she could no longer smell the...lilacs! She'd come to cut some lilacs because Emine was coming at last. After years of what Alula would have called a courtship, if she could remember that word. Letters, phone calls. She even got a laptop (used) and internet access to stay in touch. Then just when she had given up, that email, entirely unexpected: *If your invitation is still open, I expect to be in Oregon in a couple of weeks and would be happy for us to meet.* Alula hadn't answered. She tried but the keyboard was missing the caps on the letters so she couldn't tell one from another. She started the email with what she hoped would be an apology but what did you call these sticks, poles, sticking up like allotropa, cells, she was lost already and why should she tell Emine NOW that she'd been not well at all and her experiments all had failed. I don't need you now, she thought, but why tell her that? I'm still alive, Alula thought, and what a pleasure it would be. Monty the best companion ever, but still. Maybe she wouldn't lose words so easily if she had someone to talk to who answered her in human speech. Something beyond the dragonfly. Dragonflies, damselflies, flitting. They aren't bug bugs. Nothing creepy. Maybe because of their names, or the almost transparent iridescence of their wings or the way this one speaks suddenly in Emine's voice. *Hello, Alula, here I am* and suddenly there she is, Alula herself, in New Mexico, sixteen years old. She knows who she is and where, somewhere in the pit of her abdomen. She sees nothing. Hears nothing. Her five senses find nothing to identify so what she does sense must be her soul. Her own being, very specific, and formless. Heavy, turned to lead.

Maybe Emine could tell her where she'd gone wrong.

Alula thought, I would have warned her, if I were able, to bring a biohazard suit. She struggled to her feet, stooped to retrieve the shears and fell again. The electric thing started happening, the thing she could never quite remember or describe after consciousness returned.

April 20. pulled straw from around strawberries. few signs of new life. glads poking through soil.

April 26. think Russian sage didn't make it. neither did blueberry tulips. sad.

April 30: distribute composted sod. fill divots. plant peas.

May 1, transplant potted tomatoes

She held up three fingers. Wednesday. It didn't really matter to her knowing the day of the week, but she had a feeling that once she stopped caring about measurements of time, her time would be up. And though it was years since she'd been employed, she still counted

Monday as the first day of the week, Sunday wasn't the start. It was the end of her weekend off.

She consulted the garden journal. Last year's entries might tell her what she needed to do next.

May 7 bearded iris
May 10 mowing
May 14: few peas coming up; chicken manure

She had to keep living for a while longer, there was still so much to come. Buy laptop, sticks up, dialup what do you call them, sticks up, things for people want them, not in Five Rivers, no! so why sick? Why me? Cell Towels. No. Must get internewt stay in torch Alrax. Dad use Spell Check. How about Sense check. Making cents. Make change. winter just little brown jobs, what're they called, with wings. Emine.

May 18: onions, carrots, beets, chard

Why was June missing?

That was wrong. That was not the name of the month. It was the name of a girl. Or a bug. So what comes after May? She tried her usual trick, starting with A... names of months...A... Ab...Ac...Ad...

July 29, strung cut up pie tins on fishing line to scare off birds.
July! But what comes before July!

August 2, started picking blueberries. Pulled Italian purple garlic (too soon; should have waited; planted back in December, added bone meal then)

What about the millions of gallons of water discharged by the mines? What about that, Dr. Hydrogeologist!

August 10. Sunny and fine.
August 16. Chipmunk with puffy cheeks, MY cascade berries!

This must have been a bad week: Dr. Elba, reading over my nose and can't make change. Here. Not depressed, but brain is always on my mind.

All she had to do was look at the calendar printed right there in the journal. June. Just a few days from now. Emine was coming and next month was called June.

Nothing's Been Decided

What got to Marty were the lies, the utter shameless hypocrisy of it all. He carried the shame for all those who didn't feel it.

It takes the dead to teach us about life. Those corpses full of poison, that's what tipped the scales of justice. If he killed, he would send a message that could not be ignored. He could get his hands on a few assault weapons. This is America. Easy. But would you use such a weapon? Marty asked himself. No, he thought. Real damage is a bomb.

If I'm going to do it—and he still prefaced his plans with *if*—*If* I'm going to do it, Marty/Mardan told himself, it will be without the blessing of Brent, without having to listen to the narcissistic bloviating of that so-called environmentalist, that TV evangelist clone, that smarmy motivational speaker, that asshole. Even though he was right.

And I'll choose the target. Why Missouri? Why Verfaille? Greedy capitalist. Everyone knew he was a pig. Someone had to strike out, instead, at the complicit institutions. With something that spoke louder than a keyed car.

He wouldn't need fertilizer from Joseph. What for? The simpler the plan, the fewer people involved, the more likely to succeed. *If.*

A plan is not an act. He could figure it out—if he wanted to—on the internet. A thousand match heads. He could get a radio-controlled plane from any toy store. Cash at the register, just pay and go, no story about a nephew's birthday, don't call attention. Buying things doesn't mean it's been decided. Two pressure cookers, two different stores. Nails from the hardware store.

Innocent life? It wasn't that he thought everyone was guilty. It was that we were all dying slowly, breathing poison, eating poison, drinking poison. And if we're not buried in lead-lined caskets, we poison the earth. And what about the lead? How much easier a fast and sudden death. Not for himself, of course. *If* he did it, the plan was a remote detonation.

He started to save his Lincoln pennies, shrapnel with meaning, though he wasn't sure if he meant emancipation or civil war.

His bike wouldn't do. For this, he needed a car. Then he'd go back to OSU. He'd learned more. Decades of lies. Expert opinion for sale, professors testifying that Agent Orange was entirely safe, in spite of deformed children born in Vietnam while right down the road from the university, aerial spraying turned water sources toxic, poison rained down on homes, babies were born without brains, or with spina bifida, women miscarried, kittens were born with four eyes or none at all. And now they defended RoundUp, Monsanto's RoundUp. Weapons of mass destruction.

What makes a man, a respectable man, willing to endorse such horrors? he wondered. To become part of the killing machine. What motivates such people?

As for agro chemicals, he wouldn't touch them even for the attack. If anyone deserved to be blown off the face of the earth, the Ag School was it.

He didn't bother to check the rental car for dents or scratches. He handed back the diagram and smiled. Every day, every hour, every minute that went by, more damage was done. "No damage," he said.

Marty hugged the cliffside in the fog between Mendocino and Ft. Bragg. If he plunged to his death here it would be meaningless. But he stayed on the coast road north to Oregon because of Lori. See her? Yes. No. Yes. As uncertain as his plan. He had an address for her in Florence. He parked and climbed down to the beach. The waves caught his shoes, broke on the high rocks. Maybe they would walk here together. Probably she wouldn't be home.

She answered the bell. Awkward moments as he stood in her doorway. She didn't ask him in. Maybe there was someone—some guy—inside. He wanted to tell her, to explain, but all Lori had ever done was criticize, hold him back. Though maybe that was what he wanted. So yeah, what's new, how are you? She was working for Peace-Health. Part time. So what makes it Peace? he asked. The healing comes through Jesus, she said. Oh, great, he said, you pray over people. No, I'm a sterile processing technician, for the surgical instruments. Oh, you mean they do real medicine? She scowled at him. What do you think? It's a hospital.

He thought, There is no cure.

Unless, maybe, *if* he did it, start to cut and blast away everything gone rotten.

Her words echoed. His head hurt and he felt the urgency again, to be done with it.

Dawit wasn't a Muslim

Since 9/11 he wanted people to think he was, because he was above reproach and that proved they—we—were not all bad. Dawit, the unlikely FBI agent who was not actually an agent but a specialist, stood at the curb at the airport waiting for Jimmy Greene, Portland office, who was already an hour and a half late. No dark glasses here where there was daylight without sunlight, clarity without glare. He'd thought it would follow him everywhere, that terrible sensitivity to light.

He phoned again. *Yeah, yeah,* said the voice. *I told you, I'm on my way.*

"Excuse me," said the woman, an old woman, red and gold scarf, accent. "Do you know, is there some other place to wait?"

"I don't know."

"Almost one hour I am waiting."

"Maybe I'm in the wrong place, too."

He didn't want to be here at all. He'd met the suspect once and liked her. The thought of waiting for her in Five Rivers, intercepting her, taking her into custody made his teeth chatter. In DC they'd been told arresting a terrorism suspect was different. Such people were trained to communicate with their co-conspirators in code.

Hands behind the back so they can't signal with their fingers. Hood over head so they can't blink out Morse or other code. Hold them upright and control their movements. Tonal languages such as Chinese and Swedish might be represented by a terrorist raising and lowering his body, changing height.

"Fifty years ago," the woman said, "I come to America. I work. I care for very sick mother and now she's gone, I travel."

"That's nice," he said.

"To see friends. Fifty years ago, we go each to different place."

"So, your friend ended up in Portland," he said.

"Corvallis," she said, "but my friend she is dead. Her granddaughter come for me. We never met and maybe this is wrong place. You, too," she said. "You are waiting. And you come to America from—?"

A young woman, tall, blonde, interrupted. "Are you Eva? You said you'd be wearing a *green* scarf. I've been here waiting," and they were gone.

"So where're you from?" Greene asked after Dawit slid into the front passenger seat.

"Sacramento."

"I mean before."

"Encino. That's San Fernando Valley. LA."

Like most of the agents Dawit had met, Greene didn't look anything like the agents on TV. Small, weasel-face. So many of the agents were small, like Chen.

"Where," he said daringly, "are *you* from?"

"Bangor, Maine. Born in Bangor, raised in Millinocket, went to see my baby with a rubber in my pocket....ha ha ha. Luckily Bangor and not Portland. Portland, Maine would have confused matters. What sort of name is Tesfaye?"

Of course, that was what the man had meant all along. "Eritrean."

What sort of name was Jimmy for a grown man? Well, there was Jimmy Carter. But Greene's given name was Edward. Dawit's mother would say, Go figure.

Before Jimmy could ask where Eritrea was, "You've heard of Ethiopia."

"Starving babies," said Jimmy. "So you survived god knows what only to end up in"—then, said with a sneer—"California. I'm lucky I got assigned here. You know Paradise? It's not seven thousand virgins or whatever the terrorists believe. It's fly-fishing on the Metolius River."

Dawit thought everyone in the world wanted to be in California. The Golden State.

"What do you do there?" Jimmy asked.

I know he means for self-fulfillment, or what he considers fun, Dawit thought. Instead he offered a rundown of how he usually spent his days. Then: "I've never had to do this before, detain a terrorist."

Jimmy laughed. "My big moment till now? Checking out Brent Fassen."

The name was familiar. "Wait," said Dawit. "Weren't we supposed to leave him alone?"

"He was on the payroll till I got a look at him. At one of his revival meetings in Seattle where he's supposed to be uncovering these radical environmentalists, right? He carries on how all sacred books should be read as metaphor. Like he says, *You don't really believe Jesus had a penis, do you?* Jesus, Mary, and Penis," said Jimmy and laughed again.

Dawit hesitated, then laughed politely though he didn't get the joke.

Dawit couldn't quite believe Emine was what They suspected. Her husband was clearly dangerous according to the Other Agency, but Dawit wasn't sure they were always right. Her brother-in-law certainly looked like trouble. Out-of-place Muslims, both of them. What the hell were those men doing in Peshawar if they weren't up to no good? But Emine, her soft voice and serene brown eyes. She reminded him of Gladys. Glad, who was unhappy about the move to Sacramento. Glad who made him glad. For whom he had Ramiro, years ago, plant a border of gladiolus. Yellow, pink, striped red. Whose mother wasn't pleased: *Remember, you are brother and sister only.*

"Yes, there are indications about her," he said to Jimmy. "But I'm not at all sure." He felt uneasy, too, about Rennie Mulcahy. No one seemed to remember whose idea it had been to take her into custody. No one's idea, no one's mistake. And no one had the authority to correct it.

"Can't wait to be sure," said Jimmy. He said nothing more for what seemed like minutes. Then "Why weren't we able to stop it? This is a failure that...whatever acts of terror we prevent from here on in, it still doesn't change that failure. I don't think I'll ever—"

"Were you in the Portland office then?"

Jimmy nodded.

"Then you didn't miss anything. There was nothing you over-looked." Though maybe there had been. In all that data, too much of it, Dawit thought. We know everything and nothing. We know so much and still get it wrong. "Nothing you could have done," he said.

"You haven't been with the Bureau long enough," said Jimmy. Then he laughed. A forced hearty laugh. "Look, growing up in Bangor? I was a Red Sox fan and Luis Tiant betrayed us at the end of the '78 season. He signed with the Yankees. I couldn't believe it. For weeks after, I kept dreaming that my arm was ripped from my body. It was so vivid, I still think about those dreams. I didn't understand it then, but later, I got it. The fans are the mystical body of the team. When the team is torn, we feel it in our own bodies. The agents are the mystical body of the FBI." He gave Dawit a long hard look. "Every one of us in the Bureau feels the shame."

The Trees Breathe Water

Jimmy took the Powell exit and stopped for drive-through espresso. *Stopped* was the operative word, the only customers in sight and yet they waited and waited and waited, more like gridlock on the freeway than a drive-through until they gave up and moved on. They stopped for gas and waited for the attendant, a man who stood on the island beside one of the pumps and studied the sky. Admittedly, thought Dawit, it was a particularly beautiful sky, a silk scarf, gray mottled white and streaked with blue, light gray revolving and moving almost imperceptibly to dark gray and black streaks and then again to white. It looked so solid and so soft. Like the body of his wife. Gladys, naked, took his breath away, her face and arms darkened from the sun, the lighter brown of her belly and breasts, the almost purple berries of her nipples, the purple shadows of the creases at the joining of her scarred thighs. He would look at her and feel such profound joy, a body healthy and well fed.

"I'll pump," he said. "Not allowed in Oregon," said Jimmy, and so they waited till the silky sky was suddenly so thin you could put your fingers through it. The attendant ambled over. How strange to find dolce far niente in this northern culture. *Attend*—in French it meant *wait*. The attendant did make them wait, standing by the gas pumps like a statue with its chin tilted up to the sky. They waited for him to come to life and pump their gas. If this was Oregon culture, it could explain why Jimmy had been so late.

Dawit went looking for a bathroom. The decal on the door to the convenience store read Oregon Meth Watch. When he returned to the car the attendant was holding Jimmy's credit card, looking at it as if he'd never seen such a thing before.

"Bet they didn't feed you on the plane," Jimmy said. "You must be hungry."

If your digestive juices had nothing to work on, would they begin digesting *you*? His fear as a boy, whenever his stomach growled, it was a wild animal waiting to devour him from the inside out.

The people at the Vietnamese takeout place weren't assimilated Oregonians yet. Jimmy was back in minutes with the food. A handful of strange carrots— orange, yellow, ruby, purple—and a couple of bánh mì. Jimmy scrutinized him as he handed over the sandwich. "Barbecue pork."

"That's OK. I'm not kosher," said Dawit.

"Ha ha ha," said Jimmy.

Dawit was more cautious about the carrots, their color.

"Natural, organic," said Jimmy and Dawit held up a purple carrot asking "What's so natural about this?" and Jimmy said ha ha ha.

The purple circles under Gladys's eyes.

The sandwich tasted sharp, like vinegar, smelled like curry.

Gladys wanted to visit a cosmetic surgeon.

But you are perfect, he said.

People will think you hit me!

Out the window he saw a tree bent over like a weeping willow except its wands, trailing on the ground, were covered with green fur.

"What kind of tree—?" he asked. "Looks like a tree dressed up for Halloween."

"No idea," said Jimmy.

They passed a Feed & Seed store, the top story caved in while it looked like the ground floor was still in business unless the bins and sacks were simply left behind and abandoned along with the building.

There were no people in Oregon. Why were there no people? They were invisible behind the tinted windows of their vehicles. There was no one on the street or in the fields, just the horses, the occasional big dog. Where there was emptiness, there was a vacuum, and vacuums too often sucked at him till the African heads popped out of his skin. He focused on Jimmy beside him, breathing and real. Memories: telling Gladys *you are perfect.* But in America, a person can always do better.

The flat green expanse of the Willamette Valley, the straight rows of the tree farms, the low small cottages placed on the landscape like moveable pieces on a game board, the grapevines in the new vineyards, the sky. An army of poplars stood like statues—the ones that had been unearthed somewhere in China. He thought of Dr. Tang who left the country before anyone could think to stop him.

They were off the highway now, speeding around curves, entering the forest. To the south, the stubbled prickly earth up on the clear-cut ridge.

His world had never been so depopulated. Even growing up, the big house, acres in the hills north of Mulholland, there were always people, the gardener who kept the property green, or what Dawit had considered green until now, it was never, even after rain, as green as this, Kirk the pool guy, Roberta who came to teach him to swim, Connie who came to clean. Gladys and her mother in the Encino guesthouse after they were evicted in Pacoima. Someone to supervise Dawit when his dad kept long hours in surgery and his mom traveled the country visiting someone on Death Row.

Up up up the drive. Moss, he remembered from somewhere, grows on the north side of trees. But here there was moss everywhere. The trees seemed to breathe water. Leaves opening on the maple and the alder, opening thousands of mouths, whispering, the spruce and Douglas fir, branches thick and draped.

At home when guests were expected after dark, they lit the long string of lights, the quarter-mile driveway transformed to a city street at Christmastime. Up to the front door with its brass knocker, the wood carved with round shapes that looked like hooves or paws. The knock knock when the healer came. And her final pronouncement. Not illness, but the ancestors speaking through him.

"This is a jungle," he said.

Greene laughed. "21st-century, my friend. We say rainforest."

And Dawit thought of his wife. Her first year of teaching, she was hired by an expensive private school, shocked by the mother who came to the parent-teacher conference in the tight red T-shirt with the slogan: *You say to-mah-toe, I say Fuck you.*

His birth mother had risked landmines and hunger and thirst and the bullets of her own people to get him across the border before he could be taken away from her. They took the children, she told him, to raise them first in the nurseries and then the Revolutionary Schools to prepare them to fight. In this regard, his Jewish parents raised him as his birth mother would have wanted. Natalie Levy teaching him to recite *Conscientious Objector*, the poem by Edna St. Vincent Millay—hers such a wonderful name, so much more poetic than the names of people who inhabited his world. Like her, he would surely refuse to deliver friends into the hands of Death, but unlike her, he was now sworn to hand over the enemy. His father, the heart surgeon, taught him the difference between hurt and harm: *I hurt people every day to preserve life. What you must avoid at all costs is to do harm.*

Do no harm. In America, it was surely easier to become a millionaire than to do no harm.

They would find Emine Albaz. Their job was to bring her in. He liked her. She'd be questioned and if she'd done nothing wrong, she'd be released.

If they questioned him, with the bright light in his eyes and the unbearable noise, if they wanted him to tell—to tell what? what really did he have to tell?

He felt the push against his skin, popping up like bulbs, the little black woolly heads breaking through from his arms and his legs, from his shoulders and his thighs, teeth chattering. Silence, they warned him. And if they stripped him naked. If they let loose the snarling dogs.

"Before you get out, there's an orange vest in the backseat," said Jimmy. "Bear-hunting season."

A dog came running now, barking, leaping in front of the car.

Above their beards, the trees stared down. Their ancient eyes kept asking but the heads of the ancestors counseled silence.

Something Planted in the Brain

Monty barked a warning and Alula heard a car straining up the hill. Emine! But when she opened her eyes there was a man, sharp pruning shears in his hand. She screamed.

He said "Are you all right? You had a seizure. I'm just moving these things out of the way." The shears, the hoe. She saw the black man, patting Monty, saying "Good dog, good dog," and then to the white man, "Careful, there, you're crushing the glads." He knew what mattered. Whoever they were—all she knew was they were not Emine—they helped her back to the cabin.

The white man brought her a glass of water. He picked up the card she'd written to give Emine.

> Dearest Emine,
> Welcome! Your being here fulfills my wildest
> hopes...

The black man—he obviously loved flowers—picked up and skimmed through her garden journal.

> September 4, 6:00 AM, 48 degrees: high 80 degrees deck shade, sunny
> Yesterday finished deck drip system and turned on. Setting: every other day, six AM, 10 minutes (everything swamped, changed to 2 minutes then 1), will click in on Monday.

Oct 1: drip hoses and soaker hoses

October 2: Mint: be ruthless

October 20: One salmon bounding and bucking its way up the creek!

November 3. Still picking green beans and tomatoes, some rotten, mold, some gone to the voles. Dahlias were still blooming. Planted 40 tulips. Pulled out the nasties. Still not well. Should call doctor.

Vote by mail!

But she can't be sure. There might or might not be two men or maybe more in her cabin. I'm back in the hospital, she thought, because this is what doctors look like when you've been given too much Percoset. Those faces peering at her growing bigger and bigger and then suddenly shrinking pulled away to a distant horizon. The drugs also caused hallucinations. Like the name *Emine, Emine Albaz* swirling in yellow letters from their lips.

November 8: Appointment for December 7. Dad says radiation no more to be feared than typhoid!

December: surgery on the 14th.

March 3. Out of here! Dad still sleeping. Got the ore but couldn't find Geiger counter. ThriftWay for corrugated boxes.

The black one is excited, reading aloud: "Cesium-137...$115; Cobalt-60: $79; Polonium-210: $79; Strontium-90: $79; Thallium-204: $79 Total: $431.00" and he's asking questions. How about answering some? She asks him "How big is a microcurie anyway?" People don't call Marie Curie crazy!

"Emine Albaz." He says her name and that reminds Alula she would have to tell Emine it wasn't just the uranium. There was mercury too, the little silver balls of it rolling. Look, her father sharing his fascination. She never understood the science or the purpose. The click click click. The gyroscope whirling like a toy top in his workshop. On what? A cord? A piece of string? Her mother's clothesline? The mercury like... she couldn't quite remember. Like semen, she thought, when it spilled on her body instead of inside, those gloppy beads of white mercury. Watch what's in your mind in front of these men! The trail, then, of a garden slug, if you could capture it speeded up, the quicksilver shimmer.

She had given up coffee. Drank hot water in a brown mug so she could pretend. Sold her Zuni turquoise. Stopped buying propane and cooked on the woodstove. But then there were Monty's vet bills and only enough money for the cesium and cobalt. On the credit card. She might not be around to pay it off anyway. Maybe none of us. 9-11. Now more than ever.

Dear Dr. Almaz,
December 20, 2001 -
Dear Dr. Albaz,
    October 2001 mushroom festival Yachats -
they say find matsutake mycelium under candy
canes.
    The hummingbirds beat their wings until
your name swells through the vibrations.
    Glomus in blender. through window screen,
then .0007". distilled water. no centrifuge - use
egg beater? ? soak cardboard in hot water. let
mushrooms sleep. agar/spawn/fresh bulk
substrate two or three weeks, mother patch.

"Dr. Albaz," said the white one.

She'd enjoyed writing letters to her and Emine must have enjoyed hearing from her, otherwise it would have been characterized as stalking. Long distance relationships and penpals were really best. Alula wrote to prisoners for a while. They said getting a letter in prison was like Christmas and your birthday rolled into one, but when she realized they might someday get out, she quit. There was a kind of delicious surrender in the acceptance of absence. So much easier than accepting someone's presence. That had always been...well, if one dwelled too much on disappointment, one became disappointed. That was what she would not accept, would not surrender to.

Writing a letter to Emine was like chocolate. "I had to ration it," she said. And the anticipation while she waited! After the WBRT they told her she'd have a couple more months. Instead it had been more than two years, and she thinks it was Emine who kept her alive. There was something to wait for, hoping Emine would answer, hoping she'd come.

If Alula could find the words, this is what she would tell Emine: She was not what the inspirational elements of the medical community call a fighter. She liked to grow things, there was research to accomplish, but she wasn't all that interested in being alive. She would be as she thought a Buddhist would be, seeking only to live and die in harmony with the natural order. She went on tending the garden though she might not live to eat the vegetables or see the flowers come into bloom. It was just too late to change what she did or didn't do. That's what she would tell Emine and she would thank her for coming, she would ask her to adopt Monty. Emine, on her way, like the Angel of Death.

It was entirely possible these men with huge faces weren't real. They were asking questions, questions, questions. They had no idea the words had scampered off to eat her tomatoes and as far as she could tell, no one could stop them.

To the Best of My Knowledge

No one answered the phone. Dr. Singh came to check on his investment. In Carson Yampolsky's abandoned house, he found two men shot execution-style. One with a swastika on his arm, the other with a seahorse tattoo. No sign of Yampolsky.

I can find no trace of him on the internet, no social media presence, nothing after May 2003. Maybe he's out there somewhere using another name or it may be that his cadaver, showing signs of torture, rests somewhere in the desert in an unmarked grave.

*   *   *   *

As of this writing, a man named Oğuz Demir remains a prisoner at the US military base at Guantánamo. The Turkish government has appealed for his release but the American authorities state the detainee in question is not a Turkish citizen but rather a native of Turkmenistan. No hearing has been scheduled.

*   *   *   *

In Brazil, Maria Castillo found if her colleagues spoke Portuguese with a Spanish accent, she could usually understand them. Her research has expanded beyond *Crotalus durissus cascavella* to include *Micrurus corallinus* and the rare and most venomous viper, *Bothrops insularis*. By now I assume she is fluent in Portuguese and I hope she still has ten fingers.

*   *   *   *

The afternoon of May 28, 2003, on Highway 34, a car rigged with explosive devices blew up prematurely when Martin Keller floored the gas on the curve to pass two cars and plowed into a logging truck coming around the bend right at him.

The resulting brush and forest fire burned for days over thousands of acres. What matters more, the incident caused three fatalities, all declared dead at the scene: the truck driver, Keller and, in the third car, Emine Albaz. The FBI would have you believe she was Keller's accomplice, driving what was to have been the getaway vehicle. The driver of a fourth car was airlifted to the Burn Center at Legacy Emanual in critical condition.

The fourth car was mine. The explosion left me as you see me—or prefer not to.

*   *   *   *

I think of the women I never got to interview. I try to remain hopeful.

Since I'm telling the story, I've decided Dawit and Gladys returned to LA and now are parents of a daughter and a son.

Tara? I can't resist the idea that she tells herself, *Tomorrow is another day.*

I want to believe that Lara and Rorion married, that she makes startling short videos with handheld camera in black and white much admired at obscure festivals and by her many friends.

*　　*　　*　　*

What of Rennie?—whose only importance was through association and in her own mind. There's a photograph in her file, a cinderblock wall with a message scrawled in what may be blood:

If I ever get out of here, I want to grow into my life until it fits.

Acknowledgements

This book would not be in your hands (or on your screen) without the talent, vision, and commitment of Marc Estrin and Donna Bister.

Portions of the novel were first published in *Red Earth Review* and, in very different form, in *El Portal* and *RE:AL*.

Thank you to:

Gregory Dubois-Felsmann who planted the seed for this work many years ago;

Carol Gomez, in solidarity;

Mona Linstromberg for friendship and Five Rivers;

Cat Parnell and Max Frazier, for helping me get the word out;

Friends here and around the globe who gave me so much and taught me so much but, given the state of the world today, are likely safer if left unnamed, and

Joseph C. Berland, wherever you are. One night in the mid-80's, I walked into the American Museum of Natural History and heard you lecture about your travels in Pakistan with the peripatetic Qalandar people. When you said you were seeking a woman researcher who could accompany and study the seasonal sex workers, I decided to approach you and volunteer. The moment came, I chickened out and settled for buying your extraordinary book, *No Five Fingers Are Alike*. It took me decades, but I finally made the journey—in imagination— with people inspired by your fieldwork. Their way of life and their remarkable abilities have haunted me for so long.

Fomite

More novels from Fomite...

Joshua Amses—*During This, Our Nadir*
Joshua Amses—*Ghatsr*
Joshua Amses—*Raven or Crow*
Joshua Amses—*The Moment Before an Injury*
Charles Bell—*The Married Land*
Charles Bell—*The Half Gods*
Jaysinh Birjepatel—*Nothing Beside Remains*
Jaysinh Birjepatel—*The Good Muslim of Jackson Heights*
David Brizer—*Victor Rand*
L. M Brown—*Hinterland*
Paula Closson Buck— *Summer on the Cold War Planet*
Dan Chodorkoff—*Loisaida*
Dan Chodorkoff—*Sugaring Down*
David Adams Cleveland—*Time's Betrayal*
Paul Cody— *Sphyxia*
Jaimee Wriston Colbert—*Vanishing Acts*
Roger Coleman—*Skywreck Afternoons*
Stephen Downes—*The Hands of Pianists*
Marc Estrin—*Hyde*
Marc Estrin—*Kafka's Roach*
Marc Estrin—*Speckled Vanities*
Marc Estrin—*The Annotated Nose*
Zdravka Evtimova—*In the Town of Joy and Peace*
Zdravka Evtimova—*Sinfonia Bulgarica*
Zdravka Evtimova—*You Can Smile on Wednesdays*
Daniel Forbes — *Derail This Train Wreck*
 Peter Fortunato—*Carnevale*
Greg Guma—*Dons of Time*
Richard Hawley—*The Three Lives of Jonathan Force*
Lamar Herrin—*Father Figure*
Michael Horner—*Damage Control*
Ron Jacobs—*All the Sinners Saints*
Ron Jacobs—*Short Order Frame Up*
Ron Jacobs—*The Co-conspirator's Tale*
Scott Archer Jones—*And Throw Away the Skins*
Scott Archer Jones—*A Rising Tide of People Swept Away*
Julie Justicz—*Degrees of Difficulty*
Maggie Kast—*A Free Unsullied Land*
Darrell Kastin—*Shadowboxing with Bukowski*
Coleen Kearon—*#triggerwarning*
Coleen Kearon—*Feminist on Fire*
Jan English Leary—*Thicker Than Blood*
Diane Lefer—*Confessions of a Carnivore*

Fomite

Writing a review on social media sites for readers will help the progress of independent publishing. To submit a review, go to the book page on any of the sites and follow the links for reviews. More reviews help books get more attention from readers and other reviewers.

For more information or to order any of our books, visit:
http://www.fomitepress.com/our-books.html

CPSIA information can be obtained
at www.ICGtesting.com
Printed in the USA
LVHW101038140522
718792LV00004B/260

9 781953 236043